"I don't mind bei

Hud's eyes twinkled when he saw Rose. "Especially when I get to escort Cinderella to the ball." He slung an arm around Rose's shoulders and pulled her against his side.

"If I'm Cinderella then I'll have to be home before midnight," Rose told him.

"Honey, the do-si-do stuff ends at ten," Luna told her.

"And"—Hud walked Rose to the truck—"I figure that'll give us time to get some ice cream and still get you home before midnight. If you lose a shoe, I'll be by tomorrow to see if it fits you."

"And if it does?" she asked.

"Then I'll have to carry you off to my mansion on Canyon Creek, where you'll be a princess forever and ever amen," he replied.

"Lord, help my soul." Aunt Luna threw a hand over her heart. "That's the most romantic thing I've heard in years."

Rose felt the heat start at her neck and work its way up to her cheeks. By the time Hud was in the driver's seat, the temperature in the truck had jacked up at least ten degrees—maybe even a few more when she took a second look at him in his ironed jeans, pearl snap shirt the color of his eyes, and his polished black boots. Prince Charming didn't have a thing on Hudson Baker that night!

High Praise for Carolyn Brown

"Carolyn Brown makes the sun shine brighter and the tea taste sweeter. Southern comfort in a book."
—Shelia Roberts, *USA Today* bestselling author

"Carolyn Brown is one of my go-to authors when I want a feel-good story that will make me smile."
—*Fresh Fiction*

"Carolyn Brown writes about everyday things that happen to all of us and she does it with panache, class, empathy, and humor."
—*Night Owl Reviews*

"I highly recommend Carolyn Brown as a go-to author for all things sexy cowboy."
—*Harlequin Junkie*

COWBOY REBEL

"Brown's capable fourth Longhorn Canyon contemporary western romance...suggests that love can make even the baddest of bad boy cowboys want to settle down. Sweet, sexy romance and a strong heroine elevate the story. Fans of romance series filled with small-town charm and a cast of supportive family and friends will appreciate this installment and seek out earlier ones."
—*Publishers Weekly*

COWBOY BRAVE

"Sizzling romance between believable characters is the mainstay of this whimsical novel, which is enhanced by plenty of romantic yearning."

—*Publishers Weekly*

"Over 300 pages of warmth, humor, and sweet romance... Carolyn Brown always manages to write feel-good stories, and this is definitely a... special read."

—*Harlequin Junkie*, Top Pick

COWBOY HONOR

"The slow-simmering romance between Claire and Levi is enhanced by the kind supporting characters and the simple pleasures of ranch life in a story that's sure to please fans of cowboy romances."

—*Publishers Weekly*

"Friendship, family, love, and trust abound in *Cowboy Honor*."

—*Fresh Fiction*

COWBOY BOLD

"Lighthearted banter, heart-tugging emotion, and a good-natured Sooner/Longhorn football rivalry make this a delightful romance and terrific launch for the new series."

—*Library Journal*

Cowboy Courage

Also by Carolyn Brown

The Longhorn Canyon Series

Cowboy Bold
Cowboy Honor
Cowboy Brave
Cowboy Rebel
Christmas with a Cowboy

The Happy, Texas Series

Luckiest Cowboy of All
Long, Tall Cowboy Christmas
Toughest Cowboy in Texas

The Lucky Penny Ranch Series

Wild Cowboy Ways
Hot Cowboy Nights
Merry Cowboy Christmas
Wicked Cowboy Charm

Digital Novellas

Wildflower Ranch

Cowboy Courage

Carolyn Brown

FOREVER

New York   Boston

Cowboy Courage copyright © 2020 by Carolyn Brown
Wildflower Ranch copyright © 2020 by Carolyn Brown

Cover photography by Rob Lang. Cover design by Elizabeth Turner Stokes. Cover copyright © 2020 by Hachette Book Group, Inc.

Forever
Hachette Book Group
1290 Avenue of the Americas, New York, NY 10104
read-forever.com
twitter.com/readforeverpub

First mass market edition: January 2020

Forever is an imprint of Grand Central Publishing. The Forever name and logo are trademarks of Hachette Book Group, Inc.

The publisher is not responsible for websites (or their content) that are not owned by the publisher.

The Hachette Speakers Bureau provides a wide range of authors for speaking events. To find out more, go to www.hachettespeakersbureau.com or call (866) 376-6591.

ISBNs: 978-1-5387-4877-0 (mass market); 978-1-5387-4876-3 (ebook)

Printed in the United States of America

OPM

10 9 8 7 6 5 4 3 2 1

To my dear friend Sandra Pennese,
thank you for everything!

Dear Readers,

All my life I've heard that a person never truly forgets their first love. They may move on and love again, maybe even stronger than they did that first time around, but they never forget that person who truly made their heart do flip-flops for the very first time.

This is the story of Hud Baker and Rose O'Malley, who didn't quite put out the embers that blazed when they were in middle school. Fate, Destiny, or God—maybe all three combined—have thrown them together again halfway across the state of Texas from where they grew up.

Having these characters in my head the whole time I was writing this story was quite an experience. At times I cried with them. At others, I giggled until tears rolled down my cheeks, and sometimes they even got into my dreams to tell me how to write the next chapter. I truly hope y'all enjoy reading their story as much as I did writing it.

As always, I have so many people to thank for helping me take this from an idea to the finished product you see on the shelves today. Let's have a big round of applause for my agent, Erin Niumata, who's been with me for more than twenty years, and for my agency, Folio Literary Management. Let's hear it for Grand Central/Forever for continuing to believe in me, and for my editor, Leah Hultenschmidt, for all her hard work in helping me to grow as a writer. And to my team at Grand Central for all the behind-the-scenes work that goes into copyedits, proofing, publicizing, and making the gorgeous covers for my books.

Now I'd like a standing ovation for my husband, Mr. B, who is always willing to do whatever it takes so I can write one more chapter. And who can be ready in thirty minutes to go on a road trip so I can see the areas that I'm writing about. It takes a special person to live with an author, and he does an amazing job of it. One more thank-you—to all my readers. For your notes, your encouragement, your reviews, your book club selections—I bow to you!

Until next time,
Happy Reading!
Carolyn Brown

Chapter One

Hud Baker felt like a rodeo bull in a lingerie shop. Give him a feed store that smelled like hay or a western-wear place with the heady aroma of leather and he was right at home, but a gift shop that specialized in scented candles and potpourri—definitely not a place for a Texas cowboy.

Several signs on the shelves warned that if he broke something, he would be buying it. He was afraid to turn around for fear he'd knock over more than one candle or cute little crystal angel. No one was there to wait on him, and there were no other customers. The bell on the checkout counter beside the cash register had a sign right beside it that said RING FOR ASSISTANCE.

He took a step forward to ring the bell, stuck his foot in a plastic bowl that had been catching a drip from the ceiling, and stumbled around like a peg-legged pirate. Those little signs about breaking it and buying it flashed through his mind as icy cold water splashed up over the top of his cowboy boot.

"Holy crap! I thought the ceiling had fallen down." A petite woman came out of the back room with a big box in her hands.

She startled Hud so badly that he spun around and started to fall forward. He reached out to grab something to stop his momentum, but he drew his hands back just seconds before he latched on to a glass shelf. If he'd brought down a whole rack of those expensive candles and crystal things with the dried grass in them, he'd have to sell his half of the ranch to pay the bill. Finally, he got control, but his foot was still stuck in the oversize bowl, which now had far less water in it, since so much was in his boot.

"Well, hello, Hudson Baker." She flashed that brilliant smile that he remembered from junior high school. "I wondered if you'd ever get around to coming to see me. I was beginning to think maybe I'd have to call you."

"Hello to you, Cactus Rose." He'd thought he'd never see her again, and now she was right there before him—a gorgeous woman in place of a cute teenager—and he started off with that line? He wanted to pop himself on the forehead with his wet boot.

"Just Rose these days. I dropped the Cactus years ago." She leaned against the counter. "You sure took your own good time about droppin' by the shop. I've been here two weeks."

He didn't tell her that he'd driven by the Rose Garden B&B nearly every day, but he had to build up his courage to come inside. She'd been his first love, his first kiss, and he'd never forgotten her—and now she was back, but he had no idea how long she planned to stay.

He pulled his foot out of the water and set it down on the tile floor. "I was giving you time to get settled before I dropped by. I answer to Hud now, not Hudson."

"Guess we've both done some changin'." Her grin got even bigger.

"I hope so." He wiggled a dark eyebrow. "After all, we aren't in junior high school anymore."

"Thank God," she said.

"And just what does that mean?" he asked.

"For starters, I have learned kiss a little better," she laughed.

"I thought that first one was pretty dang good," he said.

"Oh, really?" One of her eyebrows shot up. "I figured you and Tag would have had lots of practice, as popular as you were."

"Tag might have, but not me. Kissin' you that day was my first one," he admitted. "Sooooo, how long are you in Bowie for?"

"At least until Aunt Molly comes home from her long vacation," she answered.

"Did you ever get married?"

"Well, you never were one to beat around the bush, huh?" She stepped away from the counter, tiptoed, and hugged him. "It's really good to see you again, and no, I'm not married, engaged, or even dating." She took a step back and stared right up into his eyes. "I'll be here another couple of weeks at the least. If I had your phone number I might call you sometime."

"Well now, darlin', I'd love to see you," he drawled.

"If you'll give me your phone, I'll make it easy for you," she said.

He fished it out of his pocket and handed it over to her. She programmed her number into it and gave it back. Then she picked up his hand and wrote the land line number for the inn on his palm. "Now we have no excuse not to call each other, unless you're married, engaged, or dating. I don't trespass on another woman's property."

"No, ma'am. None of the above." He shook his head and wondered if she felt the same sparks he did. "Why didn't you talk like this a couple of weeks ago when I saw you at the Christmas party?"

She turned around and started across the floor without answering. Which in some ways gave him all the answer he needed. "We should get this mess cleaned up," she said.

"Where's a mop? I made this mess. I'll clean it up."

"That's sweet of you." Rose led him into the storeroom. "The mop is in the closet along with more of those cheap plastic bowls."

He found the mop and carried it back out to the shop. "I came to buy my sister a present for her birthday," he told her.

She laid a hand over her heart. "My poor little heart is broken. I thought you came in just to see me."

"You lied to me, Rose O'Malley." He leaned on the mop. "You said you'd changed. I don't see that at all."

She cocked her head to one side, just like she had the first time he'd sat down beside her in the school cafeteria. "What exactly do you mean?"

"That you're still sassy as ever," he answered.

"I'll take that as a compliment," she said. "Now, do you see something you'd like for Emily's birthday?"

She remembered his sister's name—that had to be a good thing, right?

"I haven't had time to look around. I was too busy sticking my foot in a big bowl of water," he joked.

"How about scented candles?" Rose asked.

"She'd probably like that," Hud said.

"Over on the far wall." She motioned, and started that way.

"By the way, where's Tag these days? Did he move to this area with you?"

His twin brother had an aura of dangerous excitement that drew women to him like drunks to a honky-tonk. Hud had lived his whole life in the shadow of Taggart Baker, and that's the main reason why Tag never knew about the teenage crush Hud had had on Rose O'Malley all those years ago.

"He's married now," Hud told her, "and his wife, Nikki, is a nurse at the hospital here in Bowie."

"That surprises me." She took what looked like crystal cupids from one of the boxes. "Not that his wife is a nurse, but that he settled down. That boy was so wild in junior high school I figured that a jealous boyfriend or even husband would've shot him by the time he graduated."

"Nikki tamed him down a lot." His foot was still wet, and with the freezing temperature outside, his toes would probably be frostbitten when he got home, but flirting with Rose was well worth whatever price he had to pay.

Hud had learned a lot from his twin brother—like how to sweet-talk a woman off the dance floor and into bed— but this was *Rose*, the little red-haired girl he'd fallen hard for when he was only fourteen years old. The woman he'd never forgotten, and who would probably be leaving in only two more weeks. He remembered the day he'd first seen her in the hallway at the junior high school. The last bell had rung, and in five minutes they needed to be in homeroom.

"Are you new here?" he'd asked. "I haven't seen you around."

She nodded. "I'm Cactus Rose O'Malley."

"Eighth grade?" he guessed.

Another nod.

He'd motioned with his hand. "Follow me. We go to homeroom first thing in the morning. I'll show you where it is."

A whiff of her perfume as she walked past him brought him from the past to the present, and he had to fight the urge to follow her as she made her way behind the counter and perched on a stool. "So what have you been doing since you left Texas?"

"We moved to Louisiana, way down deep in the bayou country," she said.

"Did you go to public school there?" he asked.

She shook her head. "Mama had always homeschooled me until we came to Texas. Mama had to fight my daddy to let me attend public school. It had always been her dream to go, and she wanted me to have the experience, even if it was for only a year or two."

* * *

Rose's thoughts went back to the days when she and Hud were in the same classes at the Tulia Junior High School out in the panhandle of Texas. That first day of school she'd gone with Hud to homeroom, and that's when she'd met Tag. He and Hud weren't identical twins, and they looked like brothers, but their personalities were as different as day and night. Tag reminded her of a couple of the boys in Kentucky who flirted with any girl next to them. From that first day she could see that the other schoolgirls were ga-ga over Tag, but she was more drawn to Hud with his sweet smile and pretty green eyes.

"So you've been in Louisiana all these years?" Hud propped the mop at the end of the counter.

"No, we were only there for a little while. The next year we went to Florida." She hopped off the counter and re-arranged a shelf of crystal cupids. Then she took a step back to look at her work. One minute, she'd been looking right at Hud's green eyes and thinking about how sweet he'd been in junior high school—always saving her a place on the bus, or a chair right beside his in the cafeteria at lunch, and walking with her every morning from her locker to homeroom. She wasn't paying a bit of attention where she stepped when she stepped backward and her foot slipped on a puddle of water. Everything moved in slow motion. He reached out to grab her. Her knees buckled and she went down butt first into the bowl that was still half full of water.

Rose giggled and then guffawed. Tears rolled down her cheeks as she tried to wiggle her way out of the green plastic bowl. The mop hit the floor with a bang, and Hud's arms were still outstretched. He took a couple of steps forward and extended his hands. "I tried to catch you. Are you hurt?"

She put her hands in his and let him pull her up. The bowl actually made a popping sound when she unstuck it from her butt. "No, I'm not hurt"—she continued to giggle even though water dripped from her rear end onto the floor—"it's not funny, but it kinda is. Thank you for the hand. I would have looked pretty funny wearing that bowl like a turtle shell on my rear end for the rest of the day. Might have a bruise or two, and my dignity is shattered, but other than that, I'm fine."

His big, calloused hands were still wrapped around hers even though she was standing on her own two feet. "I guess we both need to watch where we're steppin'."

"Yep." She grinned. "On the positive side, though, the bowl is empty now. I've got to go upstairs and change into dry clothes. Be back in a minute. Feel free to look around for a present for your sister while I'm gone."

When she was in her bedroom, she kicked her shoes off and then peeled out of her skinny jeans and underpants. She couldn't go back downstairs smelling like funky water, so she adjusted the water in her shower. Thank goodness her hair hadn't gotten wet, or she'd have taken longer than five minutes to get cleaned up. She dried off, slung on a new set of clothing, and was back downstairs in under ten minutes. Hud was looking up at the ceiling, which was now sending down a faster drip than it had been earlier in the day.

"Have you picked out something?" she asked.

"Not yet," he answered. "Is your bedroom right above this shop?"

"Yep." She followed his eyes to the thin stream of water. "Did you run water while you were up there?"

"I took a quick shower to get that smell off me," she answered.

"You've got a busted pipe in the wall or in the floor," he said.

"Oh, sweet lord! I thought it was just a leak because of all the rain, and would go away when the sun came out. I'll have to call Aunt Molly and see who she uses for a plumber." Her eyes went from the ceiling to the bowl and back again.

"I'll look at it if you want me to," he offered.

"Not only do you have sexy eyes, you can do plumbing? You're every woman's dream!"

He chuckled. "I'll be right back. Let me just get some tools from my truck."

She watched from the window in the door as he made his way from the porch to his truck. The Baker swagger was still there—that's one thing that he and Tag had in common—and it still gave her heart a little extra beat like it did when she met Hud in the hallway on her first day of school. He left the truck door open while he put on a different pair of boots, and then closed it, picked up a toolbox, and carried it back to the B&B. She watched him every step of the way and opened the door for him when he got close.

He set the toolbox on the floor and removed his coat. Once he'd hung it and his cowboy hat on a rack right inside the door, he raised an eyebrow in a question. "Lead the way, and I'll follow."

"Does that mean I get to lead you on?" she said over her shoulder as she started up the stairs.

"Sure thing, darlin'." He grinned. "I'll let you lead me anywhere you want."

"Why, Hud Baker," she laughed. "You have changed, whether you want to admit it or not. You'd have never said that in junior high school."

"You'd have never offered such a thing when we were that young," he shot back.

"I was still a little bit afraid of my daddy then," she said, turning left at the top of the stairs.

"And you're not now?" he asked.

"Not so much as I was then." She showed him into one of the six bedrooms that Aunt Molly rented out at her B&B. Rose was glad that the place was closed to guests for the weeks Aunt Molly was traveling with her friends. All Rose had to do was oversee the gift shop.

She entered her room and quickly scanned it. Thank goodness there weren't any panties or bras scattered about. Between growing up in a commune where women were expected to keep a spotless home and strict army regulations about barracks, Rose automatically kept her space neat, and her bed was made with crisp hospital corners.

The tall, broad-shouldered cowboy seemed to fill the tiny bathroom. He opened the doors under the vanity and pulled up a board. Rose peered over his shoulder—close enough that she caught a whiff of his shaving lotion. It was something woodsy, with just a hint of musk. She inhaled deeply and hoped he didn't notice her practically smelling him.

Hud pointed to a rusted-out hole in the old pipe. "There's the problem. I can have it fixed in five minutes. I have to run back out to my truck and get what I need to splice in a piece."

Rose backed out of the bathroom and sat down on the edge of her bed. "Were you a plumber? How do you know this stuff?"

"Tag and I bought a small ranch over east of Sunset. The house on the place is pretty old, and we've had to do some repairs. A few weeks ago I had to fix a problem like this." He shrugged. "I watched a tutorial on YouTube. Be right back."

"Hmmm," Rose muttered. In the army everyone had a job. Rose served as a translator for several languages. Other folks did maintenance work, and still others mechanical or technical. Few people could step in and do someone else's job or would even be willing to watch a tutorial on how to fix something. That Hud—the rich, handsome kid from Tulia—could do plumbing just blew her away.

Something glittered in her peripheral vision and drew her attention to the dresser across the room. With a smile on her face, she stood up and went to a small jewelry box with a heart on the top. She'd left it open the last time she got something out of it, and now a little cowboy boot charm hanging on a necklace was dangling over the side. When Aunt Molly had given the necklace to Rose, she'd had to keep it hidden away. Teenage girls in the commune didn't wear jewelry. That was considered frivolous.

Rose held one up to her ear and remembered the first time she'd worn them—on a girls' night out with several of her newfound army friends.

Her great-aunt Molly had come into this very room the night before she and her parents left Texas on their way to Louisiana, and given her the necklace. She'd kissed Rose on the forehead and told her, "You come back to see me someday, darlin' girl, and I'll find a cowboy for you."

Could Hud be her cowboy? Rose shook her head at the crazy thought. She had only a few more weeks in Texas before going to Kentucky to spend some time with her folks on the commune. By then, it would be time to figure out whether she would reenlist or start hunting for a civilian job.

When Hud came back to the bedroom, he held up a piece of white pipe. "This should fix the problem just fine."

He went right back into the bathroom and dropped down on his knees, giving her a full view of the way his Wranglers hugged his butt and thighs. Suddenly, it was entirely too hot in the room.

He sat down on the floor. "This will fix it, but I noticed a water mark on the ceiling in the foyer, so if you want, I could come back in a day or two and we'll check the plumbing in the other bedrooms."

Thank you, sweet Jesus, Rose thought. *Now he's got a reason to come back.*

"Molly really needs to have all the pipes replaced if she's going to stay in business," he said.

Rose didn't want to talk about plumbing issues. She wanted to go back to the place where they were flirting. That was a helluva lot more fun.

The phone rang and she reached over to the landline beside her bed. "Good morning. Rose Garden Bed-and-Breakfast. Can I help you?"

"Yes, this is Linda O'Cleary. I have reservations there for Friday night. I'm just calling to tell you that we'll be a little late getting there. It's our fiftieth anniversary, and the kids are taking us to dinner before we drive over to Bowie for the night."

Rose's heart raced, and her hands shook. Aunt Molly had told her that the place was closed for the month. She didn't mind guests, but holy crap on a cracker, she couldn't boil water without setting the house on fire, so what was she going to do about breakfast?

"I'm sorry, but—"

"The reservation might be under Ralph O'Cleary, if you're looking for it," Linda said. "He made the first call. We're so excited to get to stay in room four. That's where we stayed on our honeymoon."

Rose couldn't turn them away after she heard that. "I'll have that room all ready for you." She threw herself back on the bed and groaned.

"You okay in there?" Hud asked.

"I'm fine, but I've got a problem," she moaned.

"Well, darlin', if I can help..." He let the sentence hang.

"Can you cook?" she asked.

"I make a good grilled steak, a pretty fine omelet, and a mean peanut butter and jelly sandwich," he answered as he finished up the plumbing job.

"Want to come over here about eight o'clock on Saturday morning and help me—" She then jumped out of the bed and did a stomp dance. "Dammit, Chester! You scared the hell out of me."

Hud flipped around to see what was going on. "Are you all right? And who's Chester?"

Rose pointed to a huge gray and white cat that ignored all the noise and settled down on the pillows to take a nap. "That is Aunt Molly's cat, and he just cold nosed my cheek."

Hud chuckled as he gathered up his tools. "What was that about helping you?"

"I can't cook and—" She went on to explain that Aunt Molly had evidently forgotten to cancel a reservation. "So you make a fine omelet?"

"I do, and I'll be glad to help you out. Last time I stayed at a bed-and-breakfast, they served little omelets, muffins, and a bowl of fresh fruit. You could buy the muffins and heat them in the oven, cut up some fruit, and I'll make the omelets and toast. Think that would work?"

"Perfectly well," she sighed. "You've saved me twice in one day. Can I buy you lunch to repay you?"

"No, but you can let me buy you lunch." He grinned.

"That doesn't hardly seem fair, but I am hungry," she said. "Where are we going?"

"Your choice," he said as he pulled on his work boots. "We've got Italian, Mexican, burgers, Chinese, and pizza."

"Italian sounds great," she said.

"My truck is parked behind your car, so we might as well go in it." He picked up his toolbox in one hand and his good boots in the other. "No need in taking two vehicles. The restaurant is only a few blocks from here."

She didn't care if it was ten miles from Bowie and located out in the middle of a cow pasture, or if they rode there in a truck, a car, or a horse and buggy. She was just excited that they'd have some time together, and she'd have someone to talk to. She'd had very few customers in the gift shop each day, but Aunt Molly said January was always a slow month. Christmas was over, and it was a little too early for Valentine's. Rose had forgotten how much she loved being around people until the past two weeks, when about all she'd had to talk to was Chester.

You might not like him once you get to know him. He's not a kid anymore. That pesky voice in her head—the one that she never did like—reminded her.

He had helped her up out of the bucket of water. He had done what he could to fix the water leak. He had invited her to eat with him.

What's not to like? she thought.

Chapter Two

Hud slung his toolbox over into the back of the truck, and then opened the door for Rose. Dammit! She could have at least fallen on the wet grass and fallen right into his arms, but oh, no, she could only be a klutz when there was a bucket of nasty water behind her.

Just as he'd said, it was only a short distance to the restaurant. She felt like a queen when he opened the truck door for her again. He held out his hand to help her out of her seat. She put hers in it, slid out of the truck, and wondered if everyone in the parking lot could feel the hot vibes that she did. When he held the door of the restaurant for her, she was met with the aroma of garlic, tomatoes, and all those flavors she'd come to love when she was stationed in Rome for a year.

"I love food," Rose said as she followed the waiter to a booth. "And Italian is right at the top of my favorite five."

"The other four?" Hud helped her remove her jacket.

"Oh, they change daily, maybe hourly, depending on how hungry I am." She smiled. "But Italian is always, always on the list. What about you, Hud? What's your favorite?"

"Probably my granny's fried chicken," he said.

"My mama made wonderful fried chicken." Rose slid into her side of the booth.

"I never did get to meet your parents," he said.

"Consider yourself lucky." She managed a weak smile.

"How's that?"

"You would probably like my mama, but my dad, not so much. He's controlling, and his opinion is the only one that matters," she answered.

"I've known folks like that," he said.

"Knowin' them and livin' with them are two different things." She picked up the menu. "It's been a while since I've seen a menu in English."

"Oh?" Hud raised an eyebrow. "So you speak Italian?"

"Among others," she said. "I've been in the military ever since I graduated from high school."

Hud cocked his head to one side and grinned. "So you know lots of languages, then? What do you speak in Kentucky?"

"Redneck," she laughed.

"Do your languages stay with you or do you forget it all when you come back home and speak English and Redneck?" Hud asked.

The waitress appeared at her elbow and handed both of them a menu. "While you're deciding, could I get you something to drink?"

"Do you have Coors?" Rose asked.

"Tap, can, or longneck bottle?" the waitress asked.

"Longneck," Rose answered.

"Your usual?" She turned and smiled at Hud.

"Yes, thank you, Kylie," Hud said. "Coors on tap, and I'll have my usual lasagna, too."

"I want the taster's delight." Rose handed the menu back to Kylie. "In addition to being a little on the clumsy side at times, I never can make up my mind when it comes to food, so I love it when they offer a choice that has a sampling of several different things."

"Sounds like you've had a pretty interesting life," Hud said.

She shook her head. "I always wanted to travel, to see what was outside the commune. I got a little more than two years, but it was just a taste of what I really wanted," she answered. "Daddy said that a woman's place was to be a wife and mother, and he hated the time we were away from the commune. You should've seen his face when I hitched a ride to town and joined the army on my eighteenth birthday."

She didn't even have to close her eyes to see the hard look on her daddy's face when she told him what she'd done. First of all he screamed at her for leaving the commune without his permission, and then he followed that up by saying that she'd join the military over his dead body.

The twinkle in her mother's eye and the very slight smile on her face let Rose know that she disagreed with every word, and later she'd come into Rose's bedroom to tell her that she was proud of her. "You are living the dream I didn't have the courage to do." Her mom had hugged her tightly.

"It's hard to picture you in the army. How did you ever learn to take orders? I remember you being pretty independent," Hud said.

"It's been my life for the past ten years." She shrugged. "I'm on a six-week leave, and after that I'll make up my mind whether I want to reenlist for another hitch."

"Do you want to be in the military? Is that where your heart is?" he asked.

"Right now I'm not sure I can trust my heart," she answered.

"Why's that?"

"It's complicated. Let's just leave it at that for now," she replied.

"How much more time until you have to make up your mind?" Hud asked.

"A little less than a month. Sometime around Valentine's Day is when I need to let them know," she replied.

"Have you heard from Molly?" Hud asked.

"She and her friends are in France for a week, then Spain this week, and London next week. I'm a little bit mad at her. All those years I was stationed abroad, and I couldn't sweet-talk her into coming to spend time with me."

Kylie brought their food and set it in front of them. "Enjoy, and if you need anything, just holler."

"Thank you," Hud said and turned his attention back to Rose. "So where did they station you first?"

"London," she answered.

"Did your dad forgive you when you came home for a visit?" Hud asked between bites.

"Nope," she answered. "Every time I got back to the States, I'd go spend a day or two with Mama, and put up with Daddy still giving me the silent treatment, and then I'd come to Bowie and stay with Aunt Molly the rest of the time."

"If you don't reenlist, where are you going to settle down?" he asked.

She shrugged. "Who knows? Probably wherever I can find a job, and my only skill is knowing languages. Not much call for that in north Texas."

When they finished their meal and he'd paid the bill, he

drove her back to the Rose Garden. She was so busy look-ing at everything that she didn't see the woman on the porch until he pointed.

"Looks like you've got a guest," he said.

The woman had purple hair. Part of it had been braided into small ropes complete with multicolored beads and hung over her shoulders to her waist. The back half was pulled up in a ponytail with a pink and orange paisley scarf tied around it. Rose might not have been shocked to see a teenager with hair like that, but this woman was at least eighty and had plenty of wrinkles to prove it.

Hud parked the truck, and the woman stood up and waved. That was the first time Rose noticed the suitcase that her floral, flowing skirt had covered when she was sitting down.

"Think we should call the police?" Hud whispered.

"Is that you, Cactus Rose?" the old woman yelled out. "Molly told me you might be coming to visit. Come on up here and let me in the house. I'm tired. That last ride I hitched was with a truck driver, and riding in his vehicle damn near broke my back."

Rose waved. "Is that you, Aunt Luna?" She could hardly believe that her great-aunt Molly's only living sister was right there in front of her.

"In the flesh, darlin'," she hollered across the yard.

Rose whipped her phone out of her hip pocket and hit the speed dial for her great-aunt. Thank God, Molly answered on the first ring.

"Aunt Molly, Aunt Luna is on the front porch," Rose said.

"Good God Almighty!" Molly said. "Does she have her hair dyed some gawd-awful color?"

"Yep," Rose said.

Molly sighed. "Give her a room. She never stays more than a week. She and Wilbur have a big fight about every five years, and she comes to my place for a week until they both cool off."

"Wilbur?" Rose asked.

"That's her common-law husband. They've been together for years. He knows where to call when he gets tired of being a jackass. Soon as he calls she'll get on a bus and go back to Alabama."

"I'd forgotten about her bein' part of the family," Rose said.

"Honey, she don't even keep in touch except to come see me when Wilbur makes her mad. Bye now," Molly said and ended the call.

"You know that woman, then?" Hud asked.

"She's my great-aunt who hardly ever comes around," Rose said.

Luna had started down the sidewalk leading up to the porch. The wind blew her billowing skirt away from her tall, lanky frame. A red sweatshirt with an image of Rudolph on the front showed beneath a long, black trench coat that billowed out to the sides.

Hud got out of the truck and rushed around to open the door for Rose. She opened her mouth to tell him to take her to the nearest recruiting office, but Luna was coming full force by then with her arms outstretched for a hug. There was nothing to do but get out and hug the woman.

Aunt Luna went right past her and grabbed Hud in a bear hug. "I haven't seen Cactus Rose since she was just a little girl. I named her. Her mama, Echo, couldn't decide on a name. I told her that I'd always wanted a child, and since I couldn't have one, I should get to name the first one in the new generation."

"I dropped the Cactus part years ago. I just go by Rose now," Rose told her.

"Too bad. It's such a beautiful name," Luna said. "I hope you're not like your daddy. Never did like that man. He reminded me of Wilbur, and there's times when I could shoot that sumbitch. Now come give me a hug and help get me settled into my room."

"It was real nice to meet you, Miz Luna"—Hud tipped his hat toward her—"but you ladies need to get in out of the cold. Can I help with your baggage before I get going?"

"Naw, honey, we can get that suitcase." Luna looped her arm in Rose's. "Besides, us girls has got some catchin' up to do."

Rose glanced over her shoulder to see Hud practically jogging back to his truck. There went any possibility of Hud coming back around again. The old gal might be harmless, but she looked like she ate roadkill for breakfast. Rose hoped the sumbitch Wilbur decided to come take her home—wherever the hell that was—before a whole week ended.

Chapter Three

Aunt Luna hit the door talking and parked her big suitcase in the middle of the foyer. "I usually take that bedroom when I'm here." She pointed to the room right across from the gift shop. "I quit doin' them stairs when I got to be eighty. I guess Molly is gone on one of her vacations?"

Rose nodded. "Yes, ma'am."

"Well, darlin', I'm glad to help out wherever I can while I'm here. I can make a mean breakfast"—Luna headed for the kitchen—"but I ain't worth my salt when it comes to any other meal." She opened the refrigerator door and rolled her blue eyes. "We need to go to the grocery store." She sighed. "Looks like I'll be havin' cold pizza and beer for my dinner."

"It could be cold pizza and warm beer," Rose told her.

Luna giggled. "I knew when you was a baby that you'd have a sense of humor. You had that certain sparkle in your eyes that said you was going to be a real corker."

"So you can really cook breakfast?" Rose changed the subject.

"I can make biscuits that will melt in your mouth and sausage gravy that will make you slap your granny." Luna put two slices of pizza on a paper towel, stuck them in the microwave, and turned it on. "And, honey, my hummingbird pancakes even make Molly sit up and take notice. She always lets me cook breakfast for the guests when I'm here."

Thank you, Jesus! Rose thought, then wanted to kick herself. Now Hud would have no reason to come to the B&B on Saturday morning.

The microwave timer dinged and Luna removed the pizza, carried it to the table, and sat down. "You can get me and you both a beer, and we'll talk about that cowboy. You sleepin' with him?"

Rose sputtered and stuttered. "No, ma'am, I am not!"

"Too bad." Luna clucked like an old hen gathering in her baby chicks. "We'll damn sure have to work on that while I'm here. He looks like he'd be right fine in the sheets. If I hadn't jumped over the broom with Wilbur all them years ago, I might just test out the waters for you." She pointed toward the refrigerator. "Now where's them beers? Maybe you just need to get a buzz on before you seduce him. That always helped me with Wilbur before we got out the broom."

Rose took two longneck bottles of Coors out of the fridge, twisted the tops off, and set them both on the table. "Broom? What's this about a broom?"

Luna took a long sip. "Me and Wilbur and your Granny Dee, none of us believed in none of that guv'ment crap about havin' to buy a marriage license and get a preacher to marry us. But we wanted a ceremony, so we had one like they had in old days. We got a brand-new broom, tied us some ribbons on it, said some vows, and jumped over it.

Then after it was over, we had a new broom to sweep the house with."

"That's not legal." Rose tipped up her beer and took a drink.

"It damn sure is," Luna argued. "And Wilbur best remember that when that woman down at the grocery store bats her eyes at him." She patted her hip. "Me and Madam Derringer can take that sumbitch right out of commission if he ain't faithful."

"You've got a gun?" Rose gasped.

"Don't go nowhere without Madam." Luna patted her hip again. "Wouldn't be safe to hitch a ride all the way from Alabama to Bowie without some protection."

Before Rose could get in a word of protest, Luna continued: "This pizza is great." She polished off her second piece, turned up the beer to get the last drop, and then burped loud enough to rattle the walls. "We'll have to remember to order it again while I'm here. Wilbur don't like pizza, so we don't get it often. I miss that old sumbitch, but he shouldn't have been flirtin' with that floozy down at the grocery store. He knows I'm jealous."

It can't be too soon, Rose thought. *If I had his phone number, I'd call him and offer to send him a plane ticket.*

* * *

Hud had just finished unloading bags of feed and stacking them in the barn on the Canyon Creek ranch when he remembered that he still hadn't bought a present for his sister's birthday. His family was having a get-together the next evening, and he knew better than to show up without a gift. Fortunately, it was a couple of hours before the shop at the Rose Garden closed. After taking a quick shower, he pulled on a pair of worn jeans, a T-shirt from a Blake Shelton concert, and his work boots.

He hopped in his truck and made it into town in record time. He pulled into a parking space right beside Rose's bright red vehicle, picked up his cowboy hat from the passenger seat and settled it on his head, and then headed inside. The little bell above the door into the shop rang, but the place seemed to be empty.

"Hello?" he called out.

No answer.

He was more than a little disappointed that Rose wasn't behind the counter. Looking to kill a little time, he picked up several candles to sniff but couldn't decide which one to buy, so he moved on down to a collection of small crystal vases. In the spring when the roses Justin had planted for her were blooming, she might like a pretty vase to put them in.

"No." He shook his head and went back to the candles. "Emily loves putting flowers in quart jars. She's just not a crystal person."

He started to reach for a couple of vanilla-scented candles, heard footsteps out in the foyer, and turned too quickly. The whole glass display wobbled slightly. He grabbed the shelf and steadied it, heaved a sigh of relief that he hadn't broken anything, and turned to face the door just as Rose entered the shop.

"You came back?" She sounded surprised.

"I forgot to buy Emily a present," he stammered. "She likes candles so I thought..."

"That's is a lovely idea. I'll be glad to put it in a gift bag, and get it all ready to give to her," Rose said.

"Is your aunt still here? Is she staying a while?" he asked.

Rose was ringing up his purchases when a loud siren went off right outside. He fished his phone from his hip pocket and hit a speed-dial number, listened for a minute, and said, "I'll have to come back tomorrow morning. I'm a volunteer fireman and we've got a house ablaze between here and Sunset."

She nodded. "I'll put them under the counter for you."

"Thanks," he said over his shoulder as he rushed outside.

He drove ninety miles an hour to the site of the fire and wondered the whole time if every time he walked into Rose's shop there would be a disaster. When he reached the site of the fire, he braked so hard that he left black streaks on the pavement. Smoke poured out of the windows of the old two-story house, and the blaze was already licking the dead grass around the place. The other volunteer firemen had just gotten the hoses hooked to the red fire hydrant on the corner.

"Anyone in there?" Hud yelled as he ran toward the truck.

"Don't think so," one of the other firemen answered. "It's an old abandoned place. Hasn't been lived in since I was a kid."

As Hud looked over to the burning house, he saw movement in one of the second-floor windows. Was it a person or just the flames playing tricks on him?

He saw movement again. Yup, that was definitely a hand. A human hand and it was waving frantically from an upstairs window.

He pointed toward the place and hollered over his shoulder, "I think I saw someone in there. I'm going in to see."

Hud knew it was a risk going into the house without his gear. But he was way ahead of any of the other men, and the fire was spreading too fast. He grabbed his handkerchief and held it to his mouth, ducking low as he made his way through the back door. Adrenaline rushed through his veins as he took the stairs two at a time. All the smoke made it near impossible to see. The sound of sobbing steered him toward the left, and as he rounded a corner, he found a woman in a heap with her body wrapped around a baby. She had one hand plastered to the window, and when she saw him, she handed him the baby.

"Save my daughter," she begged.

He threw the woman over his shoulder, tucked the baby under his arm, and ran down the stairs and across the yard like he was sprinting for the goal line at a football game.

An ambulance came rearing up to the house with the sirens blaring. Hud didn't even slow down until he made it to the vehicle. The woman was shaking like a leaf in a windstorm and weeping uncontrollably, along with the now-screaming baby, as he handed her off to the EMT.

"I'm going with them," Hud said as he helped get them into the ambulance.

"You'll have to follow us," the EMT said. "There's not enough room in here for you."

"Then I'll see you at the ER." Hud sprinted to his truck and pulled out before the ambulance left. He could see the flashing lights in his rearview all the way to Bowie, and prayed that the poor baby wouldn't be dead when he got there. Poor little thing didn't have the lung capacity that an adult had. That it was screaming and crying was a good sign, but that didn't mean its lungs weren't damaged.

The hospital was a fifteen-minute drive, but he and the ambulance made it in ten. Hud snagged a parking place not far from the emergency room door and was right there when the EMTs rolled the mother and baby through the doors. The mother had an oxygen mask on. The baby was still sobbing uncontrollably.

He followed them right back into a cubicle. The EMT

holding the baby handed her off to Hud, while he and the other guy got the woman onto a bed. A nurse came in and checked vitals, and by the time the doctor arrived, the mother's eyes were fluttering open.

"Where am I? Where's my baby? Is she all right?" She tugged at the oxygen mask and tried to sit up but fell back on the bed in a heap. "I thought if I could get to the roof, we'd be all right, but I couldn't find the attic door."

"Right here, ma'am." Hud stepped forward with the child in his arms. "She appears to be fine, but the doctor is going to have to—" Before he could go on, the doctor pushed the curtain back.

"Baby first. Lay her right here." He motioned toward a small examination table in the corner.

The baby continued to cry and had started to reach for her mother.

"I'm so sorry, sweetheart, but this is necessary," Hud whispered.

"What happened?" the doctor said as he put the stethoscope on the baby's chest.

The EMT filled him in on what had happened. "From what the lady says, she got confused and was trying to find a way to get to the roof. The downstairs was in flames."

"She was lying on the floor and wrapped around the baby, trying to protect her," Hud added.

"Fire and smoke would cause panic." The doctor nodded. "This baby looks to be fine. She probably needs a bath to get all these smoky-smelling clothes off her, but I think she can go home. Just keep an eye on her for a day or two." He picked up the little girl, handed her back to Hud, and turned around to check the mother.

"Please don't keep me in here." The woman coughed so hard that she threw up. The EMT was quick enough to grab a bag, and when she'd finished, he helped lay her back down.

When she was settled again, the doctor told her: "You're not going anywhere until tomorrow. Daddy will be fine with the baby for a night or two."

"I don't have insurance or a job," the woman moaned. "I can't stay."

"Yes, you can. I'll send in Robin. She can help you fill out paperwork to pay the bill, but you will stay at least one night." The doctor left no room for argument.

Hud opened his mouth to say that he wasn't the baby's father and that he'd never seen the woman before, but then he snapped it shut. The child had stopped crying and was looking right into his eyes, as if she was telling him that she was being quiet now—and so should he.

"Get a room ready for"—he looked at her chart—"for Dixie. She'll be here overnight. And get discharge papers ready for Sally," the doctor said and then disappeared behind the curtain.

"Yes, sir." The nurse followed him.

Both EMTs left right behind them.

"What am I going to do?" Dixie said. Tears mixed with smoke rolled down her cheeks, leaving long black streaks. "Please don't put her in foster care. I'll never get her back."

"Can you tell me what happened?"

Dixie wiped her face, smearing the streaks into what looked like war paint. "We were just borrowing the house for the night, to get in out of the cold. We planned to be gone tomorrow. We didn't set that fire, I promise. There was a mattress on the floor in one of the upstairs bedrooms, so we were sleeping on it. I woke up coughing and when I ran to the stairs, I saw flames, so I started hunting for an attic door to get to the roof. I couldn't find it and I panicked. I heard sirens." She coughed again, but she didn't throw up. "I put my hand on the window, hopin' someone would see that we were in there. Then you came. I don't know you, but please help me."

"I can keep your baby overnight for you, or I can call someone to come get her for you," Hud said. "Or I can call Social Services to help you out."

A fresh batch of tears began to roll down Dixie's face. "Please don't call Social Services. They'll take Sally from me, since we don't have somewhere to live."

"Hey, I hear you're the hero today." Hud's sister-in-law, Nikki, pushed back the curtain. "Your brother is supposed to be the risk taker, not you. And what's this beautiful baby's name?" She reached over and touched the child's forehead.

"Sally," Dixie answered. "You know this man?"

"He's my brother-in-law, and he saved your life," Nikki said.

"She doesn't want me to call Social Services," Hud whispered.

"Then she better call a family member," Nikki said.

"I can call my mama down in Sweetwater," Dixie said between coughing fits.

Hud handed her his cell phone and she made the call. "Mama, I got as far as Bowie, but me and the baby were in a house that caught on fire. Can you come get me?"

Hud couldn't hear what was said on the other end, but it had to be bad news because her face fell, and even more tears left streaks down her dirty face. She didn't say anything else but handed the phone back to him.

"Is she coming?" he asked.

Dixie shook her head.

"I've got a sister who would help you out," Hud said. "I can take Sally there."

"Thank you," she muttered. "Just please don't let them put her in the system. I won't never get her out if you do."

"Emily will be glad to help," Nikki said.

"I know she will," Hud said.

"Okay then." Nikki grinned. "I'll holler at you when I get off work to see if you need anything."

"Her diaper bag..." Dixie started.

"I've got some formula samples and diapers from the maternity ward that I can share with him." Nikki patted Dixie's arm. "You just get well."

Thank you, she mouthed.

"We're taking Dixie to her room now. I suggest you take the baby home and get her cleaned up and fed." A nurse's aide had popped into the cubicle. "You can come back tonight to see her."

With the baby in his arms, he followed Nikki down a hallway to the nursery. She pulled a tote bag out from under a cabinet and handed it to him. "This is what we give new mothers when they leave the hospital. It'll do until you can get to the store to buy what you need, and will give you an idea of what to buy."

"Thanks." He bent and kissed Nikki on the forehead.

"Drive carefully," Nikki warned. "I'd give you a car seat but we're fresh out."

Obeying Nikki's advice about not driving fast wasn't difficult. Driving with one hand while trying to keep a squirming baby in his arms was a whole new experience for Hud. Thank goodness it wasn't but a mile or two to the Rose Garden B&B, where he planned to pick up the candles he'd bought, and then take Sally on out to the ranch. He heaved a long sigh of relief when he parked in front of the place. He'd gotten this far, and he'd only be a minute or two in the B&B. He grabbed the tote bag, slung it over his shoulder, and held Sally as close to his body as he could to keep her warm.

Aunt Luna met them at the door with Rose right behind her.

"What on earth?" Rose asked.

"Is that a baby?" Luna tiptoed so she could get a closer look.

"Holy crap on a cracker!" Luna said. "What happened? You and that child both smell like you walked through hell."

Rose reached for the child, and Hud handed her over. Immediately, Sally began to chew on her hands. "She's hungry. I hope there's a bottle in that bag on your shoulder."

"Nikki gave it to me at the hospital." He gave it to Luna. "Her mama is Dixie and she's homeless and..." He went on to tell them the rest of what had happened.

"Poor darlin's," Luna crooned. "Ain't no need in takin' her any farther. Me and Rose can help out. First thing we're goin' to do is get this little one a bath and get all this nasty old smoke off her, then we'll feed her, and comfort her until her mama can come get her."

Hud looked over at Rose, expecting at least a little resistance to Luna's idea.

"That poor mama. I bet she's terrified even now. First a fire and then having a stranger take her baby. We're closer to the hospital than your ranch, so we can take her to see her mama more often, just in case Dixie has to stay longer than a day." Rose hugged the baby closer to her chest when the poor little darling started to whimper. "Looks like she's bonded with you, so here's the deal—we'll keep her but you have to stay here, too."

"Thank you," Hud said.

Luna took the baby from Rose and swayed back and forth with her. "She's settling down. I'm going to give her a bath. While I do that, the two of you run to the store and get her something clean to wear. There's a notepad right there on the credenza. Write what I tell you. Start with diapers."

He followed instructions. "Are you serious about me staying here?"

Rose nodded. "There's five extra bedrooms upstairs. You can have your choice," Rose told him as she went through the diaper bag. "We need a car seat, and write down this formula." She held up a sample bottle from the bag. "And four or five sets of clothing in size..." She cocked her head to one side and stared at the baby.

"I'm not sure I'll be very good at pickin' all that kind of thing out," he said.

"Three- to six-month size," Luna said. "I might not have kids, but, honey, I've sure helped with a lot of them when I owned the carnival. And when Dixie gets out of the hospital, we'll go to a local church clothes closet and get her whatever she needs."

"I'll gladly pay for a couple of nights for her." Hud wished that he didn't smell like smoke. "She's got no place to go, no money, and a baby. I couldn't just let the baby go to foster care."

"Of course you couldn't," Luna said. "Now get on out of here and hurry back. My shift ends when you two get home. Then y'all can play at being parents."

Rose walked beside him to the truck. "The room is empty, and I'm sure Aunt Molly would take care of that poor woman until she could get on her feet, so no problem. This has been a day, hasn't it?"

He opened the door for her. "You probably don't ever want to see me again. I bring bad luck with me."

"But there sure isn't a dull moment when you're around." Rose smiled.

Chapter Four

Hud followed Rose around Walmart and helped her load the cart with baby things. Lord have mercy! He never realized a child needed so much, and Rose said these were the bare necessities. He marveled at how tiny the cute little outfits were, and wondered if someday he'd be picking out things with ducks and kittens printed on them for his own child. He picked up an outfit with a tractor on the front.

Rose shook her head, and he put it back on the rack. "How do you know so much about babies?"

"I was raised in a commune for most of my life," she said. "I was babysitting when I was eight years old. Of course, I had an older girl around to train me in how to take care of a baby.

"What about you? Where did you learn about babies?" she asked.

"I don't know a damn thing about them. Only time I ever held one was when our foreman's wife had a newborn.

It threw up on me, and I never asked to hold one again," he said.

"Well, get ready to learn a few things." She grinned.

He didn't know whether to run for the nearest mesquite thicket and hide out like a scared rabbit, or to bless the stars for giving him an excuse to stay at the B&B with Rose for a couple of days.

They checked out, drove back to the B&B, and had just gotten everything unloaded when Hud got a phone call.

"We've got a bull out of the pasture, and my brother needs me to come home right now. I can pick up some things while I'm out there, then come back to stay the night," he offered. "I hate to walk off and leave you."

"We'll take the first shift, and you can have the one when you get back." Rose got out of the truck and got the two bags from the backseat. "And, Hud, you really don't have to pay for that girl's room. Aunt Molly has a big heart, and she'd be real upset with me if I didn't help out here."

"Thanks," Hud said. "I've got an idea about a job for her if she wants to stay around this area for a while."

That cowboy has a heart of gold, Rose thought as she stood on the porch and watched him leave the house. When she was inside, she heard Luna singing a lullaby in the living room.

"I hope you brought this child something to wear," Luna called out. "She's a good little thing. I'd guess her at about three months old, and I'll be willin' to bet her mama ain't very big."

"Why's that?" Rose eyed the baby.

"She's got a delicate face."

"I should call her mama and let her know that Sally is okay. That we're going to take care of her until Dixie is released."

"Good idea," Luna said.

Rose found the number to the hospital and in only a couple of minutes she was connected to Dixie's room. The phone rang three times before Dixie answered.

"Hello?" Her voice sounded cautious.

"This is Rose O'Malley. My aunt and I are helping Hud Baker take care of your baby girl. I just wanted to reassure you that she's fine. We've gotten her cleaned up and she's had a bottle. Is there anything else we should know?" Rose asked.

"Thank you, ma'am," she said. "I'm so grateful that y'all didn't hand her over to the system."

"You just get well, and don't worry about a thing." For some crazy reason, Rose thought of her mother and made a mental note to call her later that evening. "If you feel up to it, we could bring Sally to see you."

"I'd love that. Can you come now?" Dixie sobbed between words.

"Be there in half an hour," Rose answered. The girl sounded so pitiful that Rose couldn't tell her that she'd really thought about bringing the baby later—like after supper.

"Be where?" Luna asked as she held Sally up in a cute little pink outfit.

"Looks like we're going to the hospital so Dixie can see her child..." Rose answered.

Once at the hospital, they found Dixie's room easily enough. Dixie had evidently just gotten out of the shower because her dark brown hair still had water droplets hanging on it, and dark lashes framed her blue eyes. She was thinner than Rose, and the hospital gown hung on her frame like a feed sack on a broomstick, but she was sitting in a rocking chair beside the bed. She stood up and reached for Sally.

Rose put Sally in her arms and sat down on the edge of the bed. "I'm Rose O'Malley and this is my aunt Luna."

"Y'all are angels," Dixie whispered. "Look at you, sweet girl," she crooned over Sally. "You smell so sweet and clean."

"How did you get here to Bowie?" Luna sat down in a chair on the other side of the bed.

"I don't like to talk about it," Dixie said. "But you deserve to know, since you've been so good to help me and Sally. My real name is Dixie Boudreaux. I ran away from home last year with my boyfriend. We used to live in Louisiana, but Mama moved us to Sweetwater, Texas. I was seventeen when Derrick and I ran off to San Antonio, and we had big plans."

She paused and kissed Sally on the hand. "Truth is, I was pregnant, and it all sounded good at the time. We'd run away and get jobs, get us a little apartment and have our baby. But Derrick"—she paused—"he hated working at fast-food joints and that's all the jobs we could get." She sighed. "And then I had the baby, and sitters cost as much as I was making, so we was living on his paycheck. He came from a pretty good family. Not rich but real comfortable. Me—not so much. When times got real, real bad, he called his mama, and she sent money for him to come on back home and go back to school."

"And the sumbitch went without you?" Luna frowned.

"He left me a note," Dixie said. "Said that he just couldn't do it anymore. I only had ten dollars in my purse, so I used it to buy diapers, and I hitched a ride with a nice couple from San Antonio to Bowie. They even bought me food twice on the trip. I was going to sleep in the park, even though it was cold, but I saw that empty house. It didn't have heat, but the electricity was still on, so we had light."

"And then it caught on fire?" Luna said.

Dixie nodded. "That nice cowboy, the one who rescued Sally, let me call Mama on his phone, but she said I can't come home. I don't know what I'll do, but I'll do any kind of work I can to support me and Sally. I'd scrub floors, and I can do waitress work if I can find a babysitter that don't cost too much."

"We'll worry about that when they let you out of this place." Luna stood up and patted her on the shoulder. "Do you cook? Maybe you could work for us at the B&B."

"I grew up in southern Louisiana, and I can make Cajun food. My grandmamma taught me before she died. Mama hated anything that had to do with the kitchen, so I did all the cooking"—she blushed—"well, until I ran away."

"I'm only going to be in Bowie for a little while longer," Rose said, "but you and Sally are welcome to stay there until you can find a job. You can pay for your keep by helping us cook."

"For real?" Dixie's face lit up like a little kid's eyes at Christmas.

Rose smiled. "I hate the kitchen."

"And all I can make is breakfast food," Luna said.

"I can't believe that you're going to give me a job, just like that." She snapped her fingers. "I ain't never had this kind of luck before in my life."

Luck, Rose thought. Was winding up in the same town with Hud, who'd been her teenage crush, her bit of good luck?

* * *

"Here comes the Montague County Hero," Tag teased when Hud reached the ranch. "I've been trying to get this damn bull to cooperate for an hour. You get back in your truck and herd him to the pasture. Then we'll fix the broken fence."

Tag and Hud were twins, but not identical. They were both six feet tall, but Tag's eyes were blue and Hud's were green. Hud was a little more muscular than his brother, but Tag had always been the daredevil and the ladies' man.

When Hud found the bull, the critter was eating grass in a ditch, and no amount of honking fazed him. Finally, Hud got out of his truck and ran at the big black fellow. The bull lowered his head, pawed the ground, and took off after him like he was starving and the cowboy was supper. He managed to keep ahead of him and yelled at his brother when he saw him on the other side of the fence.

"I'm bringing him in. Get that post ready to sit up straight. He's pretty mad," Hud hollered.

The second the bull cleared the hole in the fence, Tag drove the new metal post into the ground. The poor old animal didn't realize he'd been penned until he saw the rest of the herd. He lost his momentum, snorted a few times, and glared at Hud.

"Guess you got your exercise for the day." Tag chuckled as he helped Hud stretch the barbed wire. "First you go rescuing a woman and a baby, and now you've played matador."

"How'd you know about that burning house?" Hud asked.

"Nikki called me," Tag said. "And it was on the radio news at noon out of Bowie."

"Are you kiddin' me?" Hud asked.

"Nope," Tag shook his head. "So where's the baby?"

"Rose and her aunt are helping me out while I came to get the bull." He removed his cowboy hat and mopped the sweat from his face with the sleeve of his jacket. Then he went on to tell his twin brother the whole story. "And now I've got to pack a bag and go back there to help until Dixie gets out of the hospital."

"Don't forget to pack your cape," Tag laughed. "According to the news, everybody's singing your praises and hailing you as the volunteer fireman of the year. You might as well be Superman. Look." Tag held out his phone. "You're all over YouTube."

Hud hit the PLAY button. The audio was grainy, but the commentator said the fire chief praised Hud for what he'd done and warned homeless people about staying in abandoned houses. The fire had started in the attic, he thought, when rats had chewed through electrical wires, so no arson charges would be filed against the woman who'd been in the house.

Hud handed the phone back to his brother. "I just did what needed to be done."

"So what happens to the woman when she gets out of the hospital?" Tag asked.

Hud shrugged. "I was wonderin' if maybe Claire still wants to hire someone at her quilt shop."

"She mentioned it last week," Tag said. "You could ask her."

"All jokin' aside, brother." Tag clamped a hand on his shoulder. "We're proud of you. It took courage to go into a burning house to save that baby."

"Thanks." Hud didn't tell them that it took far more courage to walk into the Rose Garden Bed-and-Breakfast and see Rose for the first time than it did to run into a burning building and rescue Dixie and Sally.

* * *

Rose was rocking the baby when her phone rang that afternoon. She picked it up from the end table right beside her and smiled when she saw her mother's number. "Hello, Mama, great minds must think alike. I was going to call you this evening."

"You are still coming to Kentucky when Aunt Molly gets home, right?" Echo asked.

"Plannin' on it. Bet you can't guess what I'm doin' right now," Rose chuckled.

"I hear a squeaky rocking chair," Echo replied. "Are you reading a book or studying another language?"

"I'm rockin' a baby," Rose said.

"Yours?" Echo gasped.

"No, Mama, I wouldn't do that to you. When I have a baby, you'll know all about it before it's born." Rose told her and then gave her the full story from the first time Hud came into the shop until that moment.

"If she's interested in a commune, I'll take her in," Echo said. "I miss having a daughter in the house."

"It's been ten years," Rose reminded her.

"Once a mother, always a mother," Echo said. "But now tell me more about this cowboy. Is he that young boy you had a crush on in Tulia? I still think that's why your dad made us move to Daisy. He always had it in the back of his mind that you'd marry someone at the commune."

"That's the same one," Rose told her. "Seeing him again doesn't mean I'm going to marry him."

"You never forget a first love. If you could, I wouldn't be living where I am today." Echo's laughter seemed more than a little brittle.

"Speaking of the cowboy, I hear him out in the foyer. Got to go. Call you again in a couple of days. Love you, Mama," Rose said.

"I hear your dad coming in for supper. Love you right back."

The call ended abruptly. Rose didn't even have to shut her eyes to know that her mother was in the bathroom, hiding the cell phone in among things that her father would never, ever look inside.

"Hello?" Hud called out.

Rose stood up and headed toward the foyer. He'd smelled like a smokestack when he left. Now that he'd cleaned up, something woodsy with a slight hint of musk floated across the room toward her. His dark hair was combed back, and he held his hat in one hand and an army-green canvas bag in the other.

"Where do I put this?" he asked.

"Drop it over there by the credenza. I've ordered a pizza for supper, and then we can talk about Dixie's future. Aunt Luna and I took the baby to see her. They're probably going to release her tomorrow, so we went by Aunt Molly's church closet and then the Walmart store to get her a few things." Rose led the way back to the living room. "I've offered her a job here until I leave."

"I think I've found her a job working in a quilt shop with..." He paused.

"With who?" Rose wondered if the quilt shop lady was one of Hud's old girlfriends. Not that it was any of her business, but still she did wonder.

"Levi is the foreman over on the ranch next to mine—where Emily lives—and he's married to Claire, who has a quilt shop and is pregnant. She's been looking for help, like in not temporary, but if..."

"Hey," Rose said, "I just want her to not be homeless. She can stay here until she and Claire talk."

"Thank you." Hud stood in the middle of the floor.

"If we're going to be parents for a day, then you can make yourself at home," she said. "In your wildest dreams, did you ever figure you'd find yourself in this situation?" Rose put the baby on a pallet on the floor.

"Not one time." Hud sat down beside Sally. "You sure are a pretty little girl."

Sally gave him a big grin.

The doorbell rang and Aunt Luna yelled, "Supper is here. I'll bring it on back to the kitchen."

Passing the evening with a baby and an old aunt full of sass, Rose and Hud had little time to talk to each other. She was able to steal several long looks at him, and for a cowboy who didn't know anything about babies, he was pretty dang good at making Sally giggle. When bedtime came, he looked over at Rose with those deep green eyes that had mesmerized her even back in junior high school.

"Whose room is Sally sleeping in tonight?" he asked.

"You brought her in, so she's all yours for the night." Luna yawned. "I'm going to bed. See you kids in the morning. I'll make breakfast and then maybe we'll get the call to go get Dixie. So don't worry, Hud, it's only for one night." She waved good night to them as she left the room.

"You've got that deer-in-the-headlights look." Rose laid a hand on his arm. "How about we both watch her through the night right here in the living room?"

Hud wiped his brow. "Thank you—again—only this time from the depths of my soul. I'm not afraid of snakes, spiders, or wild women, but babies terrify me."

She giggled. "Okay, then, let's do it this way. I'll take the couch and you can have the recliner. We'll..." She threw up a hand when Chester came out from his little igloo home behind the sofa. "I forgot about the cat."

"We should've bought that little bed-thing with a zippered net over it. Walmart is open twenty-four hours. I can go back and get it. Then we can put her in it, and she'll..."

"That sounds great," Rose said. "You can be there and back in the time it takes me to give her a night bottle."

He'd barely made it out the door when her phone rang. She reached for it and accidentally knocked it across the floor. Chester grabbed it up in his mouth and carried it back to his igloo, and she had to fight him for it. She finally got a hold on it on the fifth ring, swearing the whole time that she was buying a case not made of soft plastic next time.

"Hello," she panted. "Please don't tell me they've sold the last one."

"Why are you out of breath? And what did they sell the last one of?" Aunt Molly asked. "It sounds like you've been running. Girl, it's not safe for a woman to be out jogging at this time of night."

"The phone fell, and Chester grabbed it and carried it to his igloo, and I had to battle him for it," Rose explained. "I'm so glad you called. I've got a million things to tell you and to ask you about."

"Well, talk fast. Me and my friends are on a train. It's three in the morning here, but I couldn't sleep so I decided to call you," Molly said.

Rose told her about the fire, the rescue, and that Hud had brought Sally to the Rose Garden, and ended with, "What do you think?"

"I hate to admit that Luna was right, but if I'd been there, I'd have handled things the same way she did. You're doing just fine, Rose. What about you, honey? Have you had time to think about your future?" Molly asked.

"Not yet," Rose said. "I'm still weighing all my options. Last time I talked to Mama, she said she and Daddy would be elated if I came back to Kentucky to the commune, but that's the last thing I'd ever want to do. I've gotten a job offer to be a translator for an oil company out of Fort Worth, but I've still got a while to make up my mind."

"You'll make the right decision. You've always been stable like me, not flighty like the rest of the women in our family." Molly ended the call after she said, "Good night, darlin'. Sweet dreams."

Hud tiptoed into the room with the big box in his hands, so evidently the store still had one of those portable beds in stock. He carefully opened the end and set it up right there in the living room floor. Chester came out and jumped inside it while Rose was gently picking up the sleeping baby from the floor.

"Oh, no!" Hud picked up the big cat and set him on the sofa. "This is for baby, not for cat."

Rose laid Sally in the bed, put her pacifier in her mouth, and stretched out on the sofa. "You can have the recliner. I'll trade spaces with you in four hours and you can get some real sleep. Just try not to snore." She grinned.

"I never snore," he declared as he kicked off his boots, sat down, and threw the lever to raise the footrest. "And you can have the sofa all night. I'm fine right here. If she wakes up, what do I do?"

"Make her a bottle and rock her back to sleep." Rose tossed a throw his way. "You might need that."

"Thanks," he said and shut his eyes.

In minutes he was snoring. Not like her father, who made noises like a grizzly bear, but more like deep sighs. The sound wasn't enough to keep her awake. Her thoughts did that for her. Finally, she got up and made her way out of the living room, and to the other side of the foyer, where the dining room and kitchen were located. She was surprised to find Aunt Luna sitting at the table with a deck of cards and a cup of steaming hot tea in front of her.

"You couldn't sleep either?" Rose asked as she got the milk from the refrigerator.

"Nope." Luna laid out the cards. "There's going to be a death in the family."

"How can you know that?" Rose poured milk into a mug, added a couple of squirts of chocolate syrup, and put it in the microwave for thirty seconds.

"The cards and tea leaves never lie to me," she said. "Anytime I can't sleep, I just get out my cards and make myself a cup of real tea, not that bagged stuff that tastes like paper and lint."

The microwave bell dinged. Rose removed her warm chocolate milk and carried it to the table. "I'm sure there will be a death in the family sometime in the future. We don't all live forever."

"Don't mock me." Luna narrowed her eyes at Rose. "Last time I got this feeling, your Granny Dee died the next week. Too bad you're not having tea; I'd read your leaves."

"I don't want to know if I'm dying," Rose told her as she sat down and took the first sip of her milk.

"I don't think the cards are sayin' that you're the one that's only got a few days or weeks left." Luna sighed. "But I'm real worried that it might be Molly. She has no business traipsing around the world at her age."

"I can't believe you're worried about Aunt Molly when you were out there on the road hitchhiking," Rose said.

"Truck drivers think I'm their granny or their mama. They're not gonna hurt me," she said. "Now stop sassin' me, and I'll lay out the cards to see what your future might be."

"I'm not sure I want to know," Rose told her.

"Sure you do." Luna shuffled the cards and laid out the first one. "I see a hard decision in the near future."

"That much is right," Rose said. "I've got a fantastic job

opportunity to work as a translator for an oil company. I can speak several languages. But I can reenlist and either go to Italy or return to Washington, D.C., to work inside the Pentagon. Or Mama would love it if I came back to the commune. Do the cards tell me exactly what to do?"

"Nope, but they will guide you, and, honey, I feel for you," Luna said. "My advice is not to get in a big hurry with none of it, but *do not* go to the commune."

"Why's that?" Rose remembered days of running wild through the hills of Kentucky. Living there had had a certain freedom that she missed.

"Your daddy will try to run your life"—Luna laid out another card—"that's why, in a nutshell. He's a good man, but he likes to be in control. That's why you left the commune to begin with, if you'll remember."

Chester chose that moment to hop right up on the table and scatter the cards. Luna didn't even fuss at him but scratched his ears instead. "I miss my big old cat. Did I tell you that I had him stuffed and he sleeps forever in his little bed right at the end of the sofa?" Luna reshuffled the cards and laid out one.

Rose shivered at the visual of a dead stuffed cat in the living room. "What does that one mean?" She looked down at The High Priestess card. "Does that mean I should go into a convent?"

"No, darlin' girl." Luna shook her head and kept petting Chester. The cat was purring at about the same volume that Hud was snoring. "She symbolizes your dream world, your instincts, and your emotions. She's here to guide you through those tough decisions. She senses what's going on beneath the surface and will be there to help you. She would never tell you to go back and live with your folks. She would think that was a big mistake."

If Rose believed in all this hocus-pocus of cards, that would mean she now had two options—military or oil company job.

Luna slapped down another card. "Aha, we have The Hierophant! He will ground you in wisdom to make your choice. He's a powerful card, and you're lucky he showed up."

The first part of the word was *hero*, and that made Rose think of Hud. He'd been a hero that day. Dixie probably felt very lucky he had shown up on the scene and was watching over her child while she was in the hospital.

The next card was The Moon and put a smile on Luna's face. "This means that there's a light at the end of your tunnel. It says that you should rely on your intuition and work through your dreams to find peace and tranquility."

"Only one more," Luna said. "I only do readings with four cards because that's my lucky number." She laid out The Lovers card. "You might think this means that you are going to fall in love with a sexy cowboy, but it really means that you must make choices to get to that place where you'll have balance in your life."

"Do you ever do more than one reading for a person?" Rose asked.

"I have in the past, and you'd be surprised how often the same cards show up. In a nutshell, you've got to make up your mind—not your mama's, not mine, not that hunk of a hero in there in the living room—but you. You have to make the decisions about your life or you'll have regrets and never be at peace."

"Have you done what you really wanted with your life?" Rose asked.

"Damn straight, I did," Luna said. "And I ain't never had a single regret. Now I'm sleepy, so I'm going to bed.

Breakfast is at eight in the morning, so set your alarm. Ain't nothin' worse than cold gravy."

"Yes, ma'am." Rose picked up Luna's teacup and her empty mug, rinsed them both, and put them into the dishwasher.

Luna was already in her bedroom when Rose went back to the living room. Those crazy cards had been right in saying that she had a big decision to make, but could that Lovers card mean that once she made up her mind about the future, there would be a relationship waiting for her?

Chester jumped up on the sofa beside her and curled up in the crook of her body. His purring and Hud's snoring soon put her to sleep. But not for long. At midnight Sally awoke with a whimper at first and then a full-fledged screaming that brought both Hud and Rose out of a deep sleep.

"Is she sick? Do we need to take her back to the hospital?" Hud got to her first and picked her up. She threw herself backward so hard that he almost dropped her.

"She's probably just hungry. I'll make a bottle." Rose headed to the kitchen.

The weeping got even louder as she shook the powdered formula into the water, so she hurried back to the living room and held out her arms. She took the baby and settled into a rocking chair with her, but neither the bottle nor the rocking chair brought the poor little thing a bit of comfort.

Rose checked Sally's diaper and it was dry. "She missin' her mama. I bet she's not been away from her."

How could Aunt Luna sleep through all this? Rose wondered as she handed Sally back to Hud and suggested that he try walking her.

"I'll do anything." He yawned and held Sally close to his chest, keeping a hand firmly on her back, and started pacing the floor. That didn't work, so he hummed a slow country ballad—more to keep his own sanity than to help the baby.

She settled right down, sighed heavily, and shut her little eyes. He tiptoed to the little bed and laid her down, but the minute her body hit the mattress, her eyes popped open and the screaming started all over again.

He immediately picked her up again and held her to his chest. "What did I do wrong?"

Rose took the baby from him and began to walk back and forth, but nothing worked. "Here, you see if you can work magic again." She handed Sally back to him after a few minutes, and he tried, but with no luck. Even though his expression left no doubt he was stressing, his patience with Sally impressed Rose. Suddenly, the child gave a big sigh, settled down, and went right back to sleep.

"What did you do?" Rose whispered as she threw herself back on the sofa.

"Hummed," he said softly as he sat down in the recliner with Sally still in his arms. He threw the lever and leaned back so that he was stretched out.

Rose listened carefully to the soft humming and recognized the song as one by Randy Travis, "Forever and Ever, Amen."

"Whatever you're doin', don't stop," Rose told him.

"What if I fall asleep?" he asked.

"Then pray that she doesn't wake up," Rose said.

Hud closed his eyes and kept humming. In a few minutes the noise turned to his deep, even breathing, and Sally kept sleeping. Rose propped herself up on an elbow and took in her fill of Hud lying there with a baby on his chest. Someday, that cowboy was going to be a mighty fine father.

Chapter Five

Hud awoke to the squeak of a rocking chair. He opened his eyes slowly to see Rose sitting on the other side of the room. Sally was in her arms, and she was singing a sweet lullaby to the baby as she gave her a bottle.

"Good mornin'," he said.

"Mornin' to you." Sun rays filtered through lace curtains, putting highlights into her light red hair. The sight fairly well took his breath away. "You were supposed to wake me if she needed anything."

"She slept through the night and only woke up a few minutes ago. Aunt Luna is making breakfast. Dixie will be ready to come home in half an hour. They're getting the release papers ready at the hospital now," Rose said. "When you've had a cup of coffee, you can go get her."

"Forget the coffee." He picked up his phone and called Claire and asked her about the job.

"With all the support I've had through my pregnancy, I

can't imagine being all alone and sleeping in an abandoned house," Claire said. "Where is the baby now? Did you take her home with you?"

"No, I took her to the Rose Garden B&B, but I wondered if maybe you could talk to her mother," Hud said. "You've been looking for someone to help out at the quilt shop. I have no idea if she knows anything at all about fabric or quilting, but..."

"Sure, I will," Claire said. "Thanks for thinking of me, Hud."

"Thank you for even considering it," Hud said. "I appreciate you giving her a chance."

"We all need a helping hand at times. I'll be there about eight thirty, before my doctor appointment," Claire told him.

"What was that all about?" Rose asked.

"That job thing for Dixie. My friend says she'll be here about eight thirty. I guess I'd better get my boots on and go get Dixie so she can talk to Claire." He stole long sideways looks over toward Rose. The sun rays had moved, but that was quite a picture of her with a baby in her arms.

The dream he'd had the night before filtered through his mind as he pulled on his boots. He and Rose were having a picnic at the creek that ran along the backside of the ranch. He could remember every detail—from the way the spring wind blew her red hair across her face, to the tiny sprinkling of freckles across her nose. Most of all, he remembered how happy they both had been, and how much he craved that feeling to be in his heart forever.

Suddenly the sun disappeared and it started raining. He was headed for the door when the first clap of thunder hit.

"Take an umbrella and that bag of clothing I set aside for that girl," Luna yelled.

"Yes, ma'am," he said over his shoulder as he picked up the bag.

When he arrived, Dixie was sitting on the side of the bed in a hospital gown. Her eyes were bloodshot, but she looked a lot better than she had the day before. "Luna sent these things for you. I'll wait outside while you get dressed."

"Bless her heart." Dixie teared up. "Did Sally do all right during the night?"

"She did fine. Slept all night," Hud replied.

"I feel like I need to pinch myself to see if I'm dreamin'. Rose just called and told me not to eat breakfast—that Luna was cooking."

"It smelled pretty good." Hud's stomach grumbled as he left the room.

He'd barely sat down in a chair when she came out of the room. She was dressed in a pair of jeans, a sweatshirt, and worn tennis shoes, and her brown hair was pulled up in a ponytail.

"That was sure quick," he said.

"I'm ready to go see Sally. I ain't never been away from her this long," she said. "And truth is I'm hungry."

The nurse appeared with a wheelchair, and despite Dixie's argument, she rolled her out the front doors to Hud's truck. The rain was still pouring, but the awning kept Dixie from getting wet.

"I want to thank you, again, for everything," Dixie said as she settled into the passenger seat.

"Well, I guess there's no time like the present to tell you that my good friend Claire is coming to see you in about half an hour. She's been looking for someone to work in her quilt shop, and I think you might be just the right fit," Hud said.

"Oh, my!" Dixie sucked in a long breath. "Tell me more about her."

Hud shook his head. "Nope, you need to make your own opinion."

"Right now, I'm just glad that those folks giving me a lift put me out here in Bowie," she whispered.

After Hud got Dixie into the house, he decided to forgo breakfast and go on home. He didn't want to be there when Claire arrived. That was something the ladies needed to discuss, and besides, he and his foreman planned to do some ranch work that day.

"My sweet baby." Dixie reached for Sally the moment she was in the door. The baby wiggled against her mama's shoulder and looked up at her as if she couldn't believe that she was there.

"I think she's missed you," Rose said.

"Not as much as I missed her." Dixie kissed the baby all over her face. "I'm glad we're both alive, and I promise to never take you in an abandoned house again."

"We've got someone in the kitchen that wants to meet you," Luna said.

"I'm going to leave you ladies to this," Hud whispered to Rose.

"Will you come back later?" she asked.

"Of course I will," he said. "Call me when Claire leaves and let me know what Dixie decides."

He wanted to hear more than the news about the baby, but just hearing Rose's voice about anything would do for starters.

* * *

The yellow line in the road was barely visible as he drove home to the ranch that morning. It sounded like pellets hitting the windshield and hadn't let up a bit when he parked his truck. It beat down on his body like BBs as he ran from his vehicle to the house.

Paxton was just coming out of his bedroom when Hud opened the front door. "I didn't mean to sleep in this late, but when I woke up and heard the rain, I knew we wouldn't be plowing today. I'd rather have snow than this stuff," he groaned. "I hate being in the house all day."

"Guess we can catch up on laundry or get the place cleaned up," Hud suggested.

Paxton just grunted and headed for the bathroom at the end of the short hallway. He'd never been a morning person, but neither was Hud, so they made pretty good roommates. At least there were only two of them in the little two-bedroom house these days. Last year all four of them—Paxton, Maverick, Hud, and Tag—had lived in the place. Some mornings it had been like four old bears were coming out of hibernation until they got their first cups of coffee.

Hud tossed his hat and wet coat on a chair just inside the door and headed to the kitchen. He put on a pot of coffee, then got out a can of biscuits, popped it on the edge of the cabinet, and put all eight of them in the oven. He was whipping up a dozen eggs when Paxton arrived and went straight to the coffeepot.

"Want me to get out a couple of steaks and cook 'em to go with those eggs?" he asked.

"Yep," Hud said.

Paxton put a cast-iron skillet on the burner, let it get hot, and then slapped two thick sirloin steaks in it. "I'm jealous as hell of my brother and yours."

"Because you miss their cookin', or because they woke up this mornin' with a woman in their arms?" Hud asked.

"Both," Paxton said. "I thought us four would be chasin' skirts and two-steppin' at the bars until we was at least forty."

"Times change," Hud said. "Maverick told me that Alana,

the tall blond woman over in Daisy, has a thing for you. If you want a wife, maybe you should chase her down when you get back that way this summer."

"Whew!" Paxton wiped his forehead in a dramatic gesture. "Don't think so. That woman scares the bejesus right out of me."

"Why?" Hud asked.

"She can outdo everything I ever tried." Paxton let the steaks sizzle on one side for a few minutes and then flipped them over. "I want a woman who will at least see me as a little bit of a hero."

"And Alana ain't that woman?" Hud asked.

"Nope," Paxton said.

"You decided when you're moving out?" Hud asked. Paxton and his brother, Maverick, had inherited the family ranch over in the Panhandle, near a little town called Daisy. Their grandmother had deeded it over to them a few weeks ago, about the time that Maverick got married.

"Maverick needs me." Paxton rubbed his chin. "He's workin' from daylight to midnight. I feel guilty that I haven't gone out over there, but..."

"Hey." Hud laid a hand on his friend's shoulder. "I've got Tag, and we can hire a couple of local boys to help out on weekends and for the summer. You should go home."

"You sure about that?" Paxton asked.

"Very sure," Hud said.

"Thanks." Paxton put the steaks on two separate plates. "Maybe I'll get things together and go the first of next week, then."

"We'll miss you, but you got to do what you gotta do," Hud said. "What I'll miss the most is your steaks."

Paxton pulled the pan of biscuits that he'd put into the oven earlier and shared them between the two plates. "Eat up! A hero has to keep up his strength in case he has to run into another burning building."

"I'll miss you and your steaks, but not your smart-ass mouth," Hud teased.

* * *

"Mornin'." Dixie smiled as she entered the kitchen. "Sounds like we got us one more storm out there. Thank y'all for sending me some clothes to wear. I was beginning to think I either had to wear those dirty things from the fire or else that hospital gown."

Dixie sure looked better than she had in the hospital the night before. It was amazing what a little sleep and clean clothes, even if they were used, could do for a woman. Rose remembered basic training and having to crawl through mud puddles under a barbed wire fence. A shower had never felt so good as it did that night.

Reluctantly, Dixie laid the baby in the bed. "This is so pretty. She's always slept in a wooden crate I found behind the café where I cooked. She looks like a little princess."

Rose peeked into the portable bed. Sally curled up on her side in her pink gown. She had a thumb in her cute little mouth, and her dark hair, which had been almost gray with smoke the day before, was sticking up in all directions. Rose reached down into the crib and touched her soft, chubby cheeks. Something inside her stirred, telling her that her biological clock was ticking pretty loudly.

I've still got time. She sighed. *But someday I want kids. I never liked being the only child, so I want at least two.*

She'd learned years ago that she didn't need anything more than a good job and the ability to travel. She lived in the barracks, ate in the mess hall, and worked fourteen hours some days, but now she'd begun to yearn for more—a relationship, a family, and maybe even roots instead of wings.

Did she even want to think about that job in Fort Worth? It would mean renting an apartment, buying furniture and dishes, and all that kind of thing. Reenlisting would be so much easier. All she'd have to do was sign her name on the dotted line, move her suitcases back into a room, and go back to what she already knew. It would be going against what her heart was telling her, but it would be the easy way out.

"What do you think, Rose?" Dixie asked.

"I'm so sorry. I was woolgathering. What do I think about what?" Rose asked.

"About fate being real? I was just tellin' Luna that I never believed in fate until now," Dixie said.

A loud knock on the door made all three women look toward the foyer. "Hold that thought," Rose said and headed toward the door. She smiled at the short pregnant woman with light brown hair and kind eyes on the other side of the threshold. "I'm Rose O'Malley. You must be Claire. Come on in out of that horrible rain. Hud told me you'd be coming by. Have you had breakfast?"

"Yes, ma'am, I'm Claire, and I did have a piece of toast, but I'm pregnant, so I'm always hungry."

"I had a friend in the service who said the same thing," Rose said. "When are you due?"

"In a month," Claire answered. "I'm seeing the doctor once a week now. Thank you for letting me stop by today. I'm really excited about meetin' Dixie."

"Can I help you with your coat?" Rose asked.

"Yes, thank you," Claire said.

"Aunt Luna's got the food on the table. We were just about to sit down. We can visit while we eat," Rose said.

Claire removed her coat. "Lead the way."

Luna had put out pancakes, bacon, eggs, and toast on the bar separating the kitchen and dining area. "Y'all help yourselves. I'll get down another plate. I expect that you are Claire. Hud told us you'd be droppin' by."

"Yes, ma'am, and thanks for inviting me to breakfast." Claire laid a hand on her stomach. "This little boy is always hungry, and this all looks so, so good."

"I'm Dixie Boudreaux, and I remember those days when I couldn't get enough to eat," Dixie said. "When are you due?"

"In a month, but the doctor says the baby is big, so he could come a little early." Claire helped her plate and stopped to look at Sally. "Your little girl is precious. How old is she?"

Dixie's eyes lit up. "She's three months old, and her name is Sally."

"Did Hud tell you about the job?" Claire asked.

Rose poured a mug full of coffee and set it in front of Claire. "Yes, he did."

Claire buttered her pancakes and topped them with warm maple syrup. "I've been lookin' for over a month for someone to help me out in my quilt shop. I'm going to need extra hands when the baby is born."

"I helped my granny quilt a few times when I was a little girl," Dixie said. "I'm a fast learner at anything you want me to do."

"It would be full-time and as long as you want it. If you're interested, you could start right away, and if we're both satisfied with the way things are working out, we'll make it permanent. My shop used to be a house, so you'd have a bedroom and bathroom all to yourself, and a kitchen. I'm open from nine to five and have quilting classes one evening a week, and I'd pay you minimum wage here at first," Claire said.

"Can I talk to Miz Luna and Rose about it before I say yes?" Dixie asked.

"Of course," Claire said, "just let me know when you decide." Claire turned her attention to Rose. "I remember seeing you at Maverick and Bridget's wedding out in Daisy, but I don't think we were introduced."

"My best friend was the maid of honor, and I was visitin' with her, so I kinda crashed the reception," Rose said.

"And Miz Molly talked you into helping out at the B&B while she's off on her dream vacation? She and our friends the Fab Five have been talking about this for months. None of them have been on a real vacation in years," Claire explained.

"Who's the Fab Five?" Rose asked.

"Five elderly folks who bought a house in Sunset and moved into it together. All of us love them and have included them in our extended family. They're just a little older than Molly, but she's gotten to be good friends with them since they attend the same church."

"That's so sweet," Rose said. "But now, how do you know Hud?"

"I'm married to Levi, the foreman at the Longhorn Canyon ranch. Justin Maguire, who co-owns the ranch, is married to Hud and Tag's sister, Emily. She worked at the assisted-living facility where the Fab Five used to live. It's kind of like an extended family on the two ranches," Claire answered.

"Wow, everyone really does know everyone here, huh?" Rose said.

"It's true," Claire laughed.

"More pancakes?" Luna asked.

"No, but thank you," Claire answered. "I hate to eat and run, but my doctor's visit is in a few minutes. I've got to be going." She fumbled in her purse and laid a business card on the table. "My cell number and the business number are on that. You can give me a call when you make up your mind, Dixie. I sure hope you say yes and can come to the shop soon. That way, you'll be settled in when I go into labor and have the baby."

"Will I be able to keep Sally with me while I'm workin'?" Dixie asked.

"Sure. There's even a baby bed and a playpen already in the bedroom. I put them in there so when I have this child, I'll have a place to keep him, but I can always clean out the storage room and make another nursery." Claire stood up. "Lord, I feel like a waddling duck these days."

Dixie giggled. "Yep, I remember that feeling too."

As soon as Claire was out of the house, Dixie looked over at Luna and Rose. "This job feels like a present from heaven. I'd have a place to live, a steady income, and I can even keep Sally with me."

"I think it's fate," Luna said. "You was dropped off here for a reason, and that was to help Claire in her business. And she started that business however long ago, so she'd be here to help you when you needed a job."

"Rose?" Dixie asked.

"I'd never stand in your way. If you want this job, call her. If you want to go back to the quilt shop with her today, we'll load up your things and hold the umbrella over your head so Sally won't get wet." Rose hated to see her go, since she could cook. "It sounds like a fantastic opportunity for you."

"I just can't believe all y'all are so nice to me when you don't even know me." Dixie wiped away a tear. "First

Hud, and then y'all, and now Claire. It's like I walked up out of hell into heaven. 'Thank you' don't seem like nearly enough, but it's straight from my heart."

"Then it's plenty of thanks." Luna patted her hand. "I never got around to asking. Just how old are you?"

"I was eighteen last week," she answered. "I was just seventeen when I had Sally, the same age as my mama when she had me."

That meant her mother was only seven years older than Rose. As cute as Sally was, she could barely think about being a mother, much less a grandmother at thirty-four.

"You reckon it'd be all right if I called Claire now?" Dixie asked.

"I think that would be fine. That way, you can get started today." Luna pulled a twenty-dollar bill from her bra. "This is for you. You'll need diapers and maybe some personal things for yourself before your first paycheck."

"I'll only take it if I can pay it back when I get that first check," Dixie said.

"Deal," Luna said.

She might be downright weird, and she definitely looked like a bag lady, Rose thought, but Luna had a heart of gold, and Rose was glad that she'd shown up the day before.

Chapter Six

The rain continued all through the night, but when Rose awoke on Friday morning, the sun was shining brightly into her bedroom window. The smell of coffee floated up the stairs. That meant Luna was already up and around, and probably had a big breakfast waiting on the bar.

Today, Rose decided, they'd go out at noon. Maybe to that little Italian restaurant where she and Hud had gone the first day he had showed up in her shop. The thought that she might see him warmed her face more than the sun rays coming through her window. She sat up in bed and stretched.

Then she flopped back and stared at the ceiling, focusing on nothing, and just like she'd done in junior high school, she wished that she'd had a life like Hud's—stable parents, a big ranch to explore, and most of all, siblings. She'd been dealt a whole different set of life cards, so maybe re-enlistment was the answer. The idea looked pretty good that morning. At least she wouldn't wake up to leaky pipes, and she would have room and board, and a really nice pay-check each month. She could understand exactly why Dixie had jumped on the job that Claire offered. Security brought peace of mind.

"Muffins are coming out of the oven in five minutes," Luna yelled from the bottom of the stairs.

"Be right down." Rose threw back the covers just as Chester jumped up on her bed from the other side. She thought he had a toy in his mouth, but when he dropped it and the gray, furry thing ran, she realized he'd caught a mouse—and the damned thing was running right toward her hand. She felt like she was moving in warp speed when she left the bed and was suddenly standing on a ladder-back chair.

"Get that thing off my bed!" she screamed.

As if he understood, Chester grabbed the mouse, carried it to the middle of the bed, then let it go again. When it ran to Rose's pillow, he quickly slapped it off onto the floor.

Rose's heart thumped around in her chest like it was try-ing to find a way out of a box when the critter came right at her, scaled the legs of the chair, and scampered across her feet. With one leap she was back on the bed.

That's when Luna came into the room, pistol in hand. "Who's in your bed, and what's happening?"

Rose pointed to the mouse, who was now on top of the back of the chair. Luna zeroed in on the thing and pulled the trigger. The mouse fell onto the floor and Chester grabbed him up and went back to the bed with it, but the poor animal was dead and wouldn't run from him.

Luna picked it up by the tail. "No blood. Guess I gave the damned thing a heart attack." She slung it out into the hall-way. Chester retrieved it and took off down the steps with it in his mouth.

Rose shivered as she carefully got off the bed, her eyes

still on the big hole in the wall with light coming through it. She went to the next room to find that the bullet had busted up a lamp on its way to break the glass and stick right in the eye of a poor sheep in the picture.

Luna chuckled behind her. "I was aimin' at a mouse and done killed me a sheep."

"What're we goin' to do about all this damage?" Rose muttered.

"Wonder if Hud knows anything about patchin' holes in walls?" Luna shrugged. "We can ask him when he comes to get his bag that he left in the foyer. Right now we're goin' to have breakfast, then I'm going to clean Madam. You got to take care of your weapons in case another vicious mouse gets in the house. And Chester better damn well eat that whole mouse. If I find part of it layin' somewhere, that cat may get my next bullet."

"I can't ask Hud to fix the walls," Rose said. "That would be taking advantage."

"Not if you pay him with kisses," Luna grinned.

* * *

On his way into town to get another roll of barbed wire, Hud passed by the little Italian café where he'd taken Rose for dinner. He realized that it was past noon, and he hadn't eaten anything since that bowl of cereal he'd had for breakfast sometime before daylight. As if on cue, his stomach grumbled loudly, so he whipped into a parking spot, got out of his truck, and went inside.

The moment he walked in, Luna waved at him from a booth. "Join us. We've got room," she called out.

He locked eyes with Rose, and she smiled. He felt like his cowboy boots were six inches off the ground as he headed toward their booth. Her smile always affected him that way—even back in junior high school. The first day of school he'd caught her staring at him and she'd flashed a big grin. She didn't blush or turn away, but just kept right on smiling until they were out in the hallway.

He thought for sure that as soon as Tag came up to them, her attention would shift, but she'd barely said hello and turned back to Hud. When she put her hand on his arm, his skin had tingled and his heart had skipped a beat. Strange thing was that he'd never known strong vibes since then—not until he helped her get up out of that bowl of water.

"Good afternoon, ladies." He hung his cowboy hat on the rack at the end of the booth. "What brings you to town this cold day?" He slid into the booth beside Rose.

"We're hungry for something other than breakfast," Luna told him. Today, she was dressed in bibbed overalls and a red flannel shirt, and had pulled her hair up into something that looked vaguely like a hay mow that someone had spilled purple grape juice on. "That's all I know how to cook, and Rose don't even know that much. About all she can do is open a can or put something in a microwave, but I can't bitch about that, since it's my limit too after breakfast is over."

"I guess the cat is out of the bag about my culinary skills." Rose shrugged.

"He had to know sometime, darlin'." Luna's old eyes twinkled. "Just think about it. If he hadn't found out until after he asked you to move in with him, he might kick you out."

"Aunt Luna!" Rose gasped.

"I'm old and eccentric"—Luna shook her forefinger at Rose—"so I can say what I damn well please, so don't you *Aunt Luna* me in that tone."

"Well, you need to put a filter on your mouth. Just because

you *think* something doesn't give you the right to spit it out for the whole world to hear," Rose told her.

Luna laughed out loud. "Your sass makes up for the fact that you can't boil water without setting off the smoke alarm. I'd rather have sass as fancy dinners and supper. We can always order out or heat up something in the microwave."

Listening to Luna made Hud homesick for his own grandmother, who lived out on a ranch out near Tulia, Texas. He'd seen her for a short time at Maverick's wedding, but it hadn't been nearly long enough.

"I guess I've outed Rose." Luna continued to giggle. "How about you, Hud? Do you cook?"

"I make a mean omelet, a fantastic peanut butter and jelly sandwich, and I've been known to grill up a pretty good steak."

The waitress finally made it to their booth with menus and three sets of silverware wrapped in dark-green cloth napkins.

"Kylie not working today?" Hud asked.

"No, she quit yesterday," the lady said. "Got a night job working the bar at the Rusty Spur. I hear the tips are pretty good."

"Bet y'all will miss her around here," he said.

"I'm sure, but it gives me more hours, so I'm kind of happy for that and for her," the waitress said.

"I'll have sweet tea," Luna said as she looked over the menu, "and spaghetti with mushrooms, and a takeout dinner of the same, and then a side salad with French dressing."

"Water with lime," Rose said, "and I'll have the lasagna. House dressing on my salad."

"Coors on tap, and the manicotti, and I'll have ranch dressing on my salad." Hud handed his menu back to the lady.

"Be right out with your drinks," she said and hurried over to another table.

Hud was very aware that his hip was right next to Rose's. The room suddenly seemed ten degrees warmer.

"So, what brought you to town today?" Luna asked.

"We need more barbed wire, so I got elected to come get it," he said. Where was that waitress? His throat was totally parched. "Thought we'd bought enough last time, but we're still short a couple of rolls."

The waitress appeared at his elbow and set the drinks, their salads, and a basket of bread on the table. "Your food is almost ready," she told them but didn't stick around long, since the place was filling up fast.

Hud took a long drink of beer from the mug. "And I thought I'd stop back by your shop and pick up those candles."

"You sure you want to chance it." Rose turned to face him.

"You told me the third time's the charm." He grinned. "I'm hoping you're right."

"Shhhh," Luna scolded, "don't even talk like that. But we do have a little project for you to look at. You ever fixed holes in walls or put new glass in a picture?"

"Yes to both. What's happened?"

"I missed a rat and killed a sheep." Luna giggled.

Hud turned his head so he could see Rose and raised an eyebrow.

"It's like this..." Rose sighed and started to tell the story.

Luna broke after the first sentence and told the tale with a lot more spice. "So I wasn't lyin' about shootin' a mouse."

By the time she finished, Hud was wiping his eyes on a big green napkin. "I'll be glad to look at the walls and the picture. But once the wall is patched, we may have to do some painting. I can't imagine that we'll be able to match the color that's on there now."

"This has been one disaster after another, ever since I moved in," Rose sighed.

"Yeah, and most of it happened since I first came in the shop." Hud turned back to explain to Luna. "I thought I could buy my sister, Emily, a birthday present at the Rose Garden gift shop. That morning, Rose and I both got soaked." He didn't mention that was the same day Luna had arrived. "I came back to get the present and that time I got called out to a house fire before I could pay for the candles. Now all we got left is a power outage or a tornado."

"I'd forgotten about tornadoes in Texas." Rose shivered.

He almost threw his arm around her but stopped himself. "Honey, tornadoes are almost unheard of in January. They mainly come to visit Texas in the spring. You have nothing to worry about."

"Good," she said and set about eating her salad. "I'll be long gone by spring."

"Gone where?" Hud asked.

"Don't worry about tornadoes, Rose, darlin'. I done scared them things off with my gun," Luna said.

"Either back to the army for another four to six years or to Fort Worth to work as a translator for an oil company," she answered between bites. "The army is sounding better and better when I think about tornadoes."

"What makes you so afraid of them?" Hud asked.

"One hit Kentucky the last year I was home. It almost wiped out the commune. Trailer house roofs were blown off and dead chickens were everywhere. Daddy put me and Mama in the bathtub and covered us with the mattress off my bed, and he got in a closet." She shivered again. "When that thing came over our trailer, it was the most horrible noise I've ever heard."

"Me and Wilbur had us an experience with a hurricane

in Florida," Luna said. "We moved to Alabama, and be damned if the very next spring, a tornado didn't come through our campsite. It was the craziest thing. It tore up travel trailers all around us, but the only thing that happened to us was a tree limb broke the bedroom window."

"Which one was worse? The tornado or the hurricane?" Hud asked.

"The tornado, but I'd kind of settled in to our little place in Alabama," Luna answered. "When I get real lonesome for the sound of the beach, I can always hitch a ride down to Mobile."

"Don't think you'll be seeing any storms other than rain and lightning until spring around here." Talk of tornadoes and hurricanes made him think of the unrest in his own body that sitting so close to Rose caused.

* * *

Rose held out her hand for the bill when the waitress brought it by, but Hud reached over her head and got it first.

"But you paid last time," Rose argued.

"My granny would take a switch to me, even if I am twenty-eight years old, if I let a lady pay for dinner," he said. "I'll stop by and pick up those candles on my way home."

"They're in a gift bag and ready"—Rose clamped a hand on his forearm—"and thank you for dinner."

Little heated shivers chased up her arm, all the way to her neck and then down her backbone. She couldn't help but wonder if he'd felt the same thing. If he did, they'd have to be careful. The next disaster might be a fire at the B&B.

"Y'all are very welcome," he said.

Rose couldn't keep her eyes off him as he paid the bill at the counter and then left the café. His swagger and the tilt of his hat, the way he filled out his jeans and his biceps threatening to burst the seams of his knit shirt—all of it put an extra few beats in her pulse. It had been all she could do not to pick up the dessert menu at the end of the table and fan herself with it during the meal. He must not have felt what she did, she thought, but then he probably hadn't been in love with her from back when they were only fourteen.

When Aunt Luna's takeout order came, they went to the counter to pay for it only to find that Hud had picked up the tab for that as well.

"Now wasn't that sweet of him," Luna said as she made her way to Rose's car. "You should flirt with that man. He's a real gentleman."

Rose got in behind the wheel. Flirting like she'd done earlier was one thing, but she didn't dare go further than that. "Why get involved with him when I'll be gone in only a few weeks? Why start something that would only end badly?"

"Honey, you got to loosen up." Luna fastened her seat belt. "If life can make a complete turnaround in five seconds, just think what it can do before Molly gets home. Hud is coming by the shop before he leaves town to check on that little dustup I had with that wicked rat. Flirt a little. Maybe you'll at least get laid."

"Good God, Aunt Luna!" Rose gasped.

"God isn't good. God is great, beer is good, and people are crazy." She threw back her head and cackled.

"That's from a Billy Currington song," Rose said. "I might've lived on a lot of overseas places for a while, but I still love country music."

"It sums up life," Luna said. "I wish Wilbur would call. I love being here with you, darlin', but I miss that old sumbitch. That song reminds me of him. I guess he's still mad at me, but it was all his fault. He shouldn't have encouraged that hussy clerk at the grocery store."

Rose's phone rang before she could respond to Luna. She put it on speaker and said, "Hello, Aunt Molly. I've got you on speaker, and Aunt Luna is right here in the car with me. We're just about a block from the Rose Garden."

"We're packing up to go to our next country, and I forgot to tell you that I run an after-Christmas sale every year. You need to put everything in the shop on sale for fifty percent off. Drag stuff out of the storeroom and sell what you can. That'll give me room to put out the new stock that's been ordered. Molly stopped for a breath. "How long are you plannin' on staying, Luna?"

"Until Wilbur calls, like always," Luna answered. "If he don't call you may be stuck with me forever, even though I never did like Texas."

"We'd kill each other after a week," Molly said.

"Probably so," Luna agreed. "We're home now, and I'm taking my food and myself into the house. You should put all that junk in the shop on half of half. People like that kind of sale."

"Junk!" Molly's voice shot up. "That's expensive stuff, not garage sale junk like you decorate your trailer with."

"It's all stuff, whether you pay a dime for it at a yard sale or fifty bucks for it in a shop like yours. Goodbye, sister." Luna got out and slammed the door.

"Is she gone?" Molly asked.

"Yep, she's nearly to the porch," Rose said. "You want me to start the sale today?"

"Yes, I do," Molly answered, "and, honey, I'm sorry you have to put up with Luna. She's always had a few screws loose, just like your Granny Dee did."

"She's not so bad," Rose said. "Honest, she kind of entertains me."

"What happened to the girl that y'all took in? Is she still there?" Molly asked.

"No, Claire gave her a job at her quilt shop and she left. I kind of miss the baby, even if we did only have her for that one night." Rose explained about the time she and Hud had had with the baby and then about Chester bringing the mouse to her bed.

"Holy crap!" Aunt Molly fumed. "My sister is dangerous without a gun. With one she's trouble waiting to happen. I'll call Wilbur, myself, if she's not gone in a couple of days." Molly said. "Got to go now, darlin'. I'll call again in a few days, but if things get too bad with Luna there, cancel all the appointments, and drive her to Alabama in my car."

"I don't think it'll get that bad," Rose laughed. "Honestly, Aunt Molly, she's not so hard to live with, and she tells the most amazing stories."

"Don't believe a one of them," Molly said. "Bye now."

The call ended and Rose put her phone back in her purse. She got out of the car, went inside and hung her coat on the rack inside the door, flipped the sign on the gift store from CLOSED to OPEN, and turned on the lights. There were over a hundred scented candles in addition to lots of figurines and small gift items ranging from blinged-out pens and key chains to silk scarves and fancy gloves in the store's inventory.

She wondered if she should put an ad in the local newspaper about the sale as she went into the storeroom and opened still yet another box marked PUT OUT FOR VALENTINE'S DAY in Aunt Molly's neat handwriting.

"Hey, come and see this..." Luna yelled from her bedroom. "Your boyfriend is a hero. He's done got his picture on the front page of the newspaper." She'd already crossed the foyer and had the paper spread out on the checkout counter when Rose came out of the storage room. "There he is, carrying little Sally out in one arm and he's got Dixie hangin' on his shoulder like a bag of chicken feed. We gotta save this for when Molly gets home."

"Where'd you get that paper?" Rose asked.

"There's one on the porch every day about this time. I picked it up on my way in the house. You should give your feller a kiss for being such a big hero," Luna said.

"He's not my feller," Rose argued.

"And he ain't never goin' to be unless you make a move." Luna raised one of her perfectly arched gray eyebrows.

The sound of a truck door slamming caused both of them to stop talking.

"Sounds like he's here," Luna said. "Yep, that's boots on wood that I hear. He's goin' to knock on the door any minute."

Sure enough, he knocked and then stuck his head inside to yell, "Anyone here?"

"The woman in a relationship is always the one in charge," Luna whispered. "She sets the mood for the whole house. We only let the menfolks think that they're the ones handling everything."

"Then why are you here and not at home with Wilbur?" Rose asked.

Luna chuckled. "There's that sass that I like again. I'm here because every so often, I get lonesome for my sister, and I usually start a fight so I'll have a reason to come see her. But, honey"—she winked at Rose—"I always make him think it's his fault, and this time it is. He needs to stop flirtin' with that two-bit hussy at the store."

"Hello!" Hud called out again as he opened the front door, wiped his feet on the mat, and then stepped into the small gift shop.

"I've got your candles—" Rose started to say, and then the electricity went out.

"I didn't touch a thing," Hud said immediately.

If it hadn't been for the sunlight shining in the windows, the place would have been pitch-black.

"I can't ring your candles up," Rose said. "The cash register runs on electricity."

"Might just be a fuse in an old house like this," Hud said. "Is the fuse box—"

"It's in the basement," Luna butted in. "I'll get my flashlight and lead the way down there to it. Me and Molly had to replace a couple the last time I was here. I been tellin' her for years that this old place needs rewiring and new plumbing. Hell's bells! It needed that done when she bought the business forty years ago." She talked the whole way across the foyer and into her bedroom. She came out with a tiny flashlight in her hand and her big denim hobo bag thrown over her shoulder.

"I don't think you'll need your purse," Rose told her.

"Never know when looters might break in and steal it while we're in the basement. Better to be safe than sorry, and besides, I got my important stuff in here." Luna opened the door under the staircase and led the way down the narrow steps into a dark, damp, pungent-smelling room with a dirt floor.

"I've never been down here. Didn't even know it was here. Why does it have a dirt floor?" Rose was very aware of poor old Hud practically filling the stairwell and ducking to keep from hitting his head on the ceiling. She shuddered when she walked through a spiderweb, but she managed not to scream.

"I expect that the original owners planned to finish the floor someday, but that day never got here." Luna shined her little light on the breaker box. "Well, would you look at that? She's replaced the old round fuses with circuit breakers. I'll just flip this one and . . ."

When she switched it to the ON position, Rose was looking up at the lightbulb that was swinging from a cord hanging from the ceiling. The light almost blinded her, and then she saw a big black spider on the water pipe right above her head. She squealed and turned to make a mad dash for the stairs and ran right into Hud's broad, hard chest. There were two things that scared the bejesus right out of her— rats were one and spiders were the next.

Before she could get past him, she heard a loud bang that echoed off the walls of the tiny basement. Water spewed out of the pipe right above her and Hud, soaking both of them, and a squished spider fell right on the toes of her boots. She jumped straight up and wrapped both her legs around Hud's waist and hung on to him like a monkey with her arms around his neck.

"I hate rats and mice. Give me a snake any day of the week rather than those creatures," Rose muttered.

"Didn't need to waste ammunition on that varmint"— Luna held up a shovel—"and if the other one comes sniffin' around here, I'll kill his sorry ass too."

"Aunt Luna, you busted a hole in the water pipe," Rose said.

"Pipes can be fixed. That big old mother could have laid a thousand eggs and would have taken over the whole place."

"Guess I'd better go get my toolbox again." Hud took a few steps to the side to get them out of the spewing stream.

"I can call a plumber," Rose whispered.

"This one will be easy to fix, but the water will be off in the house for about thirty minutes." Hud started up the stairs with her still wrapped around his body.

Before they got to the top step, another spider swung down from a thin thread, and landed on Hud's shoulder. It ran across Rose's hand before it floated down to the floor.

"It touched me, Hud!" Her voice went high and squeaky. "That damned thing ran across my hand."

"Just a couple more steps, and you can get the feel of it washed off your skin," he said.

He hurried through the open door, straightened up, and she slid off him. Her body was still pressed against his, and his eyes were on her lips. She was sure he was about to kiss her, so she instinctively moistened her lips with the tip of her tongue. His eyes slowly closed, and then that damned spider crawled up the wall and was staring right at her. Chester came out of nowhere and took off after it like a lion chasing a gazelle.

A loud boom right behind her startled Rose so badly that she dropped to her knees and put her hands over her ears. Sure, she'd had combat training, and she'd done a couple of tours in Afghanistan, but she had always worked as a translator. She'd never been in combat, and the sound of a shovel hitting a spider sounded like gunfire.

"Two down," Luna said. "If there's another sumbitch down there, it better light a shuck for another state, because I'm a sure shot with the backside of a shovel." She looked at the black spot on the wall and said, "I'll get the cleaner and get rid of the nasty stuff now. Y'all go on and finish that kiss I interrupted."

Rose's face instantly turned crimson. Hud helped her to her feet and kissed her on the forehead. "I'll get on to fixing that leak before it turns the basement into a mud lolly."

"With all the excitement, I'd forgotten about that." Rose was still quivering inside. The spiders had scared the devil out of her, but now, all she could think about was that sweet kiss he had brushed across her forehead.

Chapter Seven

That afternoon, Rose made a quick trip to Walmart for a bouquet of flowers to put in the guest room that would be occupied that night. She picked up a box of chocolates and planned to arrange them on a cute little three-tiered crystal stand that she'd found in the kitchen. Then she found a bottle of champagne to set down in the ice bucket that matched the crystal, and planned to use the wine flutes she'd located in the cabinet.

When she got home, Luna was waiting on more than half a dozen customers in the gift shop. Evidently, she'd told a couple of ladies that everything was half price and they'd gotten on their cell phones and put the word out. Rose took her purchases to the kitchen, shoved the flowers down into a tea glass full of water, and rushed back to help Luna. In an hour, they'd sold almost seven hundred dollars' worth of merchandise, leaving space on the shelves to unload two boxes of Valentine things.

"Oh, I almost forgot," Luna said. "The folks that were going to stay here tonight called about thirty minutes ago. The husband died and his funeral was today. They won't be joining us tonight."

"And I just bought flowers, champagne, and chocolates to put in their room." Rose groaned.

"I told you someone was going to die, didn't I?" Luna whispered. "We will have a wake tonight with the champagne and chocolate for the dear old man. We can warm up the spaghetti for supper, and then we'll throw a quilt on the living room floor, steal one of these candles"—she motioned toward the display of jar candles—"light it, and have us a good old Irish wake. We can't waste what you already spent money on."

"You're not Irish," Rose told her.

"Yes, but you are, and I can't let you mourn alone," Luna said.

Word spreads quickly in a small town, and with Valentine's Day right around the corner, people arrived at the shop all afternoon. By six o'clock, when the store closed, Rose had unpacked all but two small boxes out of the storeroom. She'd made more in that afternoon than she'd made in the whole two previous weeks she'd been in Bowie.

"Whew!" She wiped her brow dramatically, locked both the shop door and the front door, put out the CLOSED sign, and sat down on the bottom step of the staircase. Aunt Luna came out of her bedroom. She'd changed from her overalls into a muumuu printed with bright yellow flowers and shamrocks and with a matching turban tied around her head.

"It's got shamrocks and they're green, so I expect it's Irish enough for our wake," she said as she spread a quilt out on the foyer floor. "Are you going to change?"

"Nope," Rose answered. "How do we even know the man was Irish?"

"His name was O'Cleary," Luna said, "so he was Irish, whether he knew it or not. I'm going to heat up the spätzle, and you can get the champagne to cooling and open up the chocolates. We'll say an Irish blessing for the dearly departed."

"Aunt Luna, I've been to Ireland"—Rose rolled her eyes—"and spätzle and spaghetti are two very different things."

"It's all noodles, so I'll call it whatever I want." Luna adjusted her turban and headed for the kitchen.

Not even sucking on a lemon could have kept the grin off Rose's face. She'd been almost kissed, and Aunt Luna was a hoot. Lord, she wished that woman had come around more often when she was growing up.

They sat cross-legged on the quilt and shared the spaghetti with a bottle of beer while the champagne chilled in the crystal ice bucket. When they'd gotten down to the last bite, Luna shoved the plastic container over to Rose and raised the beer up. "Mr. Ralph O'Cleary, I have no idea if you were a good man or a regular old sumbitch, but here's to you. May you have been in heaven three hours before the devil knew you were dead."

Rose poured each of them a flute of champagne and opened up the box of chocolates. She touched her glass to Luna's and said, "Mr. Ralph, I hope that you lived a good full life, and that sometime during the last months of your life you repented of all your sins."

"Now that's a good one." Luna threw back the champagne like it was a shot of cheap whiskey and held out her glass for more.

Rose refilled it as well as her own. "How about this one?

If life is just a story, then I hope the last chapter was your best one, Mr. Ralph O'Cleary."

They started on the chocolates about the time that the champagne was finished, and the chocolates were half gone. "Too bad that we can't eat the flowers," Rose said with a giggle, "but we could put them on Mr. Ralph's grave if we knew where he was buried."

"We should say a prayer for Mrs. O'Cleary." Luna bowed her head and said, "Lord, give the grievin' widow some peace and help her lean on happy memories. And while I've got your ear, will you please make Wilbur call me. Amen." She raised her head. "It's a shame to waste such pretty daisies. Now, if your feller had brought them to you, that would be a different matter, but I believe it might be a sin to buy them for a guest and not use them wisely." She burped loudly. "Not bad manners, just good champagne and spaghetti, I mean spätzle." She rolled her eyes toward the ceiling. "Pardon me, Mr. O'Cleary, for calling your wake food by an Italian name."

The woman was goofy as hell, but Rose couldn't remember when she'd had such a buzz on or had been so entertained. She got up too fast and had to hold on to the railing for a moment before she went into the kitchen and came back with the bouquet of bright-colored daisies.

Luna was already standing and had a bottle of Jack Daniel's in her hand. "Let us celebrate the life of a good Irishman. We don't know where he's buried, but we can go out in the backyard and put these flowers in front of that cute little angel yard ornament that Molly likes so well. And if Wilbur don't call soon, I may knock him in the head with that angel."

"I'm sorry, Aunt Luna," Rose said. "Maybe he'll call real soon."

The sun had long since gone down and a cold blast of wind met them as they made their way out onto the screened-in back porch. Luna grabbed a quilt from the back of a settee and carried it with her out into the yard. Rose sat down on the sidewalk right beside the concrete angel. Luna laid the flowers in front of the ornament.

"Rest in peace, Mr. O'Cleary," Luna said.

"Aunt Molly said she's the sane one of you three girls," Rose whispered.

"In the realm of all things great and good, she always was the sanest one of us. My sister Devine, your Granny Dee, thought she was either an angel or a witch. We never knew whether to pray with her or help her concoct a potion to pour on someone's yard who'd done evil to us. Did you know that I met Wilbur at a carnival? One came to town, and I fell in love with the guy who ran one of the rides. When the carnival left town, I went with him. He got me a job getting all dressed up and telling fortunes. I loved it, but we got bored with that kind of life after a couple of years, and when they closed it down for the winter that year, we went back to Florida, to the warm, sandy beaches."

Rose shivered against the cold wind. "Never heard that story. So that's why you can work with the Tarot cards?"

"Yep, and tea leaves," Luna said. "You're freezing. Let's wrap up in this quilt. We'll have us a little nip of Jack to keep us warm, and you can tell me the whole story of your sexy cowboy and you. Did he kiss you today?"

"Just almost," Rose said.

"How does someone *almost* kiss you?" Luna spread out the quilt and sat down on the very edge. She patted the place beside her. "Sit beside me and tell me about it."

Rose moved closer to Luna, who pulled the rest of the quilt up over them until only their faces were uncovered.

Luna brought one hand out from under the covers, took a long swig from the bottle of Jack, and passed it over to Rose.

"It was a forehead kiss. It was sexier just being plastered to his body with my legs and arms around him." Rose took a sip and passed it back to Luna. Champagne was good, but it didn't have the warmth that a good gulp of whiskey had. "I fell in love with him when I was fourteen. It was love at first sight. He helped me find my first class and was so nice. His twin brother was one of those bad-boy types back then, struttin' around like a little banty rooster. He always had a girl on his arm and a gleam in his eye, but Hud was different. Just as sexy, only in a different way, and he was so sweet to me. I still think that Daddy found out I had a crush on Hud, and that's the reason he made us move after I finished the school year. I've dated a lot of guys, and even been in a relationship or two, but no one ever made my body tingle like Hud Baker did and"—she paused and took another drink—"and still does."

"You never forget your first love," Luna said. "What was it about him that got your blood boilin'? Lord, you wasn't but thirteen or fourteen."

"I don't know if I can put it into words, but from the time we looked at each other, there was this connection. He was so kind and sweet, showing me where homeroom was, and then staying close by those first days. His twin brother, Tag, was the ladies' man at the school, but Hud..." She stopped and searched for words.

"Every time we held hands, I got all hot and bothered, and I didn't even know what the feeling was back then. I dreamed about him and couldn't wait to get to school every day." She'd begun to slur her words. "Dammit, Aunt Luna, I still get hot when he's around, and I can't wait to be around him. And why are you fussin' at me for feelin' like that when I was fourteen. You wasn't much older than that when you ran off with Wilbur."

"I was seventeen and he was nineteen," Luna said.

"Holy crap on a cracker," Rose spit out.

"We been together more'n sixty years," Luna said. "We've bought and sold two carnivals, lived just the way we wanted, and now we got us a trailer in Alabama that we call home…" She stopped and wiped away another tear. "I miss him."

"Oh, Luna. I'm sure he'll call soon." Rose squeezed Luna's hand.

"He'd better." Luna sniffled. "But right now let's talk some more about Hud Baker. I like that cowboy."

"So do I," Rose admitted. "I like him a lot."

* * *

The next morning, Rose's head was pounding like there were a hundred little men with bass drums inside it. She sat up, kind of remembered the wake from the night before, and frowned when she tasted whiskey and spaghetti in a burp. Then she grabbed her aching head with both hands and groaned.

"Aunt Molly will kill me…" she said and then she heard whistling and pots and pans rattling in the kitchen. "Praise the lord, Aunt Luna isn't dead."

Her phone rang and she scrambled to find it in the back pocket of the jeans she'd worn yesterday. "Hello, Aunt Molly. She's not dead. It was Mr. O'Cleary."

"What are you talkin' about?" Molly asked.

"Me and Aunt Luna got pretty drunk, and I didn't check to see if she made it in the house. I was afraid she'd died in her sleep, but I hear her in the kitchen. She's whistling," Rose explained.

"Some days, not even a good Christian woman can catch a break," Molly said. "I should've told you about her years ago. She cusses like a sailor, and, honey, she's got two hollow legs when it comes to booze. She gets plastered and never, ever has to suffer for it. Told me that hangovers are for sissies. If I didn't know better, I'd swear my mama had her by artificial means and they preserved the embryo in straight moonshine. Why in the name of God did you have a wake for someone that neither of you even knew?"

Each word was like a hammer beating on Rose's forehead. "It seemed like a good idea after the rats."

"Rats? What rats?" Molly yelled even louder.

Rose explained everything in as much detail as she could, from the electricity going out, to the mouse and spiders, and even the kiss Hud had given her on the forehead.

Molly sighed. "Lord have mercy!"

"Sorry," Rose said.

"Oh, honey, none of this is your fault. I've been meanin' to get the place rewired, and the holes the bullets made can be patched. Don't worry about repainting. I was going to do that this spring anyway. Already got the painters lined up to come in the first of March," Molly said. "Patsy just stuck her head in the door, so we're ready for the excursion. But don't you be worryin' about anything, or even about Luna."

"I love you, Aunt Molly," Rose said.

"Love you more. Talk to you later," Molly said and the call ended.

"Breakfast is ready," Luna called out cheerfully.

Rose threw back the covers, jerked on a pair of faded pajama pants that had Miss Piggy printed on them and a T-shirt that hung halfway to her knees and would have fit a baby elephant, and made her way downstairs in her bare feet. She hoped that Aunt Luna had made only muffins. The thought of eggs made her gag.

She thought she heard voices as she crossed the foyer into the kitchen, but Aunt Luna talked to herself all the time. Maybe that's why she and Wilbur had an argument every so often—he got tired of hearing her constant chatter.

She stopped in the doorway and rubbed her eyes. Never before had she had hallucinations with a hangover, but there was Hud, in all his sexy glory, sitting at the end of the table.

"Good mornin'." He smiled at her, and there were those vibes again.

What was he doing in her kitchen for breakfast? Sweet Lord!

"Good mornin'," she whispered.

"Hud came by to get those candles that he's been trying to pick up for days," Luna said. "Poor boy hadn't had breakfast, and he's done so much for us that I invited him to stay. Sit down, darlin'." She motioned toward the chair to Hud's right. "A good breakfast and two cups of black coffee will take care of that hangover."

Hud got to his feet and pulled the chair out for her. She slumped into it. The smell of bacon and eggs, sausage gravy and biscuits, and a big stack of pancakes might have looked good any other day, but it sure didn't right then.

She picked up the coffeepot and poured a cup, then it dawned on her what she was wearing. If all the catastrophic things that had happened in the bed-and-breakfast hadn't scared Hud off by now, seeing her in the condition she was in that morning surely would. One peek at her reflection in the mirror above the buffet verified that she could easily be a bag lady stoned on drugs. Her red hair looked like she'd just grabbed hold of a bare electric wire. Her eyes were bloodshot, and her mascara had run down her cheeks—probably the result of laughing so hard the night before.

"Honey, hammered owl crap would be pretty compared to you this morning." Luna laughed and passed the platter of bacon and eggs across to her. "Eat at least two eggs and some bacon. It'll help get rid of the hangover. And then you need a banana—I put them in the pancakes—and put some honey on them. But leave the gravy alone. No milk products this morning."

"Aunt Molly said you don't get hangovers." Rose took a small portion of eggs and bacon and passed the platter on to Hud. When their hands brushed in the passing process, she glanced over at him. Their eyes locked, and for a few seconds that seemed like hours, she felt as if he was making love to her with his eyes.

"Wilbur." Luna broke the spell with one word. "God love his soul." She glanced up at the ceiling. "He loves the taste of Jack Daniel's or Jameson, but the poor old darlin' gets a hanger every single time he drinks. It don't even have to be as much as we put away last night. Two shots, and he thinks he can sing just like Hank Williams. I learned a long time ago how to cure his headaches the next morning. Eat your eggs. They're not good cold."

"So you've got a good hangover recipe?" Hud asked.

"I thought you were a choirboy," Rose muttered. "Why would you need a hangover remedy?"

"I'm a good little boy on Sunday morning when I go to church to ask for forgiveness for what happened on Saturday." He grinned. "But I still like to blow off a little steam and do a little two-steppin' after a hard week's work. So what were you drinkin' last night, or can you just not hold your liquor?"

"Aunt Luna and I shared a beer, then a bottle of champagne, and after that, we took a bottle of Jack out to put flowers out for Mr. O'Cleary." She went on to tell him about the angel lawn ornament and the daisies.

"Sounds like I missed a good time." Hud finished off his bacon and eggs and slid four pancakes onto his plate.

"It seemed like it last night, but this morning, not so much." Rose clamped a hand over her mouth.

"Sick?" Luna asked.

"No, I just thought about how crazy we were." Rose was amazed that her headache was already feeling better.

"Into every life a little insanity must come," Hud chuckled. "And speaking of crazy, I miss the Fab Five."

"Is that a shop or a bar?" Luna asked.

"No, it's the name five senior citizens have given themselves. They're on that tour with Molly. Emily used to work at an assisted living center where they lived, and they kind of adopted her. When she married Justin and moved out to his ranch, they all bought a house together in Sunset and moved into it." He finished off his pancakes and pushed his chair back. "Thank you for the breakfast. It was sure nice to sit down with you ladies."

Luna kicked Rose under the table and drew her eyes down.

"What?" Rose asked.

Walk him out, Luna mouthed and then smiled at Hud. "Honey, we owe you lots of breakfasts after what all you've done around here, and for you picking up the bill on our dinner yesterday. So you come around anytime"—she chuckled—"at least while I'm here. If you wait until it's just Rose, you'll get microwaved breakfast biscuits or maybe them waffles that you put in the toaster."

"Yes, ma'am, and thank you again," he said.

"I'll walk you to the door." Rose pushed back her chair.

She caught her reflection in the floor-length mirror in the foyer and shuddered. There was no doubt in her mind that this morning would be the last time she ever saw Hud Baker.

"I wouldn't have come down to breakfast..." she started.

He tipped up her chin with his fist and smiled. "I think you look adorable, even with a hangover." His lips touched hers in a sweet kiss. "See you this evening. After I get finished at the ranch, I'll come by and we'll see about fixing those holes in the walls."

She was shocked totally speechless as she watched him walk down the sidewalk to his truck. Either he was a good liar or he was stone-cold blind. She took a step back and looked in the mirror again—nope, she hadn't turned into Cinderella. She wasn't wearing a pretty ball gown. Her hair wasn't all done up in curls, and she damn sure didn't have on glass slippers.

She twirled around twice, holding out an imaginary skirt tail, with a big smile on her face. She might not be a princess on the outside, but the way Hud had looked down into her soul, she sure felt like one.

Chapter Eight

Plowing put Hud in a tractor alone with nothing but the radio and his own thoughts playing all day. He remembered those days of eighth grade when Cactus Rose came to Tulia Junior High School. From that first handshake, something had passed between them. She wasn't prettier than the other girls. She was smarter than most kids in the class, but that wasn't it either—Misty Dawson was the smartest kid in school, and she didn't take his eye.

He couldn't put his finger on it then, or now, but just being in the same room with Rose jacked up his pulse and made his heart skip beats. Maybe it was that their hearts needed the other one to be truly happy—like they each had only half a heart without the other one, kind of like that necklace that Tag gave his first girlfriend. His name on the half that Daronda Smith wore, and hers on the half he wore around his neck.

Hud remembered that he'd invited Cactus Rose to the

winter formal, but she'd said that her dad didn't let her date. He asked her to the Valentine's dance, but the answer was the same. They saw each other at school and rode the bus home together, but that was as far as it went—until that last day of school and he'd kissed her just before she got off the bus.

He'd figured it would be a long summer, since her folks didn't have a telephone, much less a cell phone, but it had gone by fast. He couldn't wait to get to homeroom on the first day of his freshman year. Maybe Cactus Rose was old enough to date now. Maybe she'd let him take her to church if nothing else, and her dad would let her go home to Sunday dinner with him.

She wasn't there—and his heart felt like it had rocks on top of it for weeks. Even now, as he drove back home from the fields, Hud remembered how miserable he'd been all those years ago.

Paxton looked up at him from the kitchen table, where he was having a bowl of leftover chili for supper. "You look like you just lost your best friend. Did someone die?"

"No, but"—Hud hung up his coat and hat and dipped up the last of the chili for himself—"past memories and feelings."

Paxton nodded. "Been there. Done that. I'm going to the Rusty Spur tonight. Go with me and dance those thoughts right out of your head."

"Not tonight," Hud replied. "I've got some bullet holes to patch up at the Rose Garden B&B."

"You've got to what?" Paxton asked. "Who got shot?"

"A mouse," Hud answered.

"For real?" Paxton asked.

"You remember meeting Alana's friend at Maverick's wedding—Cactus Rose?"

"Wasn't that your first girlfriend?" Paxton asked. "The one that you told me about last year?"

"I'm not sure you could call her a girlfriend. We were fourteen, and the only time I saw her was at school. She couldn't date, and I wasn't old enough to drive." Hud told him about the past week's experiences. "And tonight we're going to patch up holes and see what I can do about a picture that got shot up."

"Man, you must really have a case of that first-love crap"—Paxton shook his head in disbelief—"to do that for a woman that you ain't even hooked up with yet."

"Would you do something like that for Alana?" Hud asked.

"Sure, but I've known her my whole life," Paxton said. "When you get done with your drywall job, come on out to the bar. I'll buy your first beer."

"Maybe I will." Hud headed out to the barn to get the supplies he'd need.

When he had everything loaded in the back of his truck, he drove from the ranch to Bowie. He carried an armload of tools up to the porch, and knocked.

Luna slung the door open and motioned to him. "Come right on in," Luna said. "Rose is upstairs already, so you can go on up there. I'm not climbing the stairs. My knees are hurting tonight. I bet there's rain on the way. But if you'd like to take Madam with you—just in case another rat comes around—I'll trust you with her."

"Who?" Hud asked.

"My pistol," Luna whispered. "It hurts her feelings when I don't refer to her by her name."

"I think I can manage without her, but thank you for putting so much trust in me," he said.

"I'm a damn fine judge of character." Luna patted him on the shoulder.

"I appreciate that." Hud started up the stairs with Chester right behind him. "Besides, a mouse would have to be suicidal to come out in the open with old Chester here to protect us."

Luna giggled and waved over her shoulder as she went back to the living room.

"I'm in here," Rose called out from a room at the head of the stairs.

He peeked into the room, and there she was, taking a picture off the wall. "Looks like it knocked a hole behind it too. Who'd have thought one bullet could travel so far?"

Her hair was twisted up and held in place with a long clasp, but a few strands had escaped. She kept blowing them away from her face, much like she did that first day when they were just young teenagers in homeroom. His gaze traveled down her body and back up again. Her waist nipped in from a perfectly rounded butt. She'd tied her T-shirt into a knot at the back so that it hugged her curves. His eyes went to her lips—so full and sweet tasting.

"What?" she asked.

"You're beautiful," he whispered.

She turned toward him. "I picked this outfit out special for you. The T-shirt and the jeans are vintage, and my hair was done by the wind when I stepped outside for a breath of fresh air."

He chuckled. "Age didn't rob you of your sense of humor."

"You sayin' I'm old." She marched up to his chest and wrapped her arms around his neck.

The toolbox and supplies hit the floor with a thud. He cupped her cheeks in his hands, got lost in her eyes until they fluttered shut, and then his lips were on hers. The kiss started out sweet, but soon it deepened into more and got hotter and hotter with every second. They were both panting when she finally took a step back.

"That should prove that I'm not old," she said.

"I'm not so sure," he teased. "Maybe we should give it another try."

"One more kiss like that, and, honey, I'll be nothing but a melted pile of hormones layin' on the floor, whining for more," she joked right back at him.

"I'd sure love to see and hear that." He drew her back to his chest and hugged her tightly. "But I suppose if that happened, Aunt Luna would be charging up the stairs with Madam and we'd have even more holes to patch."

"You're smart as well as sexy," Rose told him.

"You think I'm sexy?" He leaned back and smiled down at her.

"Honey, I thought that the first time I laid eyes on you, and I damn sure haven't changed my mind, not one bit!"

Hud had never been as outgoing as his wild twin brother, but he'd never had trouble with a flirty comeback—at least not until right then.

"I guess we'd best get to work," Rose said. "I don't know jack crap about drywall or fixing bullet holes, but if you'll tell me what to do, I'll be glad to help."

"Well, darlin', if I run out of steam, you could kiss me again." He finally found his voice.

"It's a deal." Her eyes twinkled with mischief. "You're a good man, Hud Baker, for helping take care of this, but if you have something you need to be doing, I'm sure the folks that Aunt Molly has hired to paint the place can patch the holes."

"You going to kiss them if they run out of steam?" he asked.

She air-slapped his arm. "Of course not. I only kiss

handsome cowboys that pull me up out of nasty bowls of water, and who save me from rats."

"Well, that's good to know." He opened up his toolbox and went to work on the two holes in that room. "Looks to me like that picture may be shot. Unless it's sentimental to Molly or an antique, I'd just replace it with another one."

That sure didn't sound romantic, but his heart was still pounding like he'd ridden a bull for eight seconds. If he didn't get his mind off how much kissing her had aroused him, he'd shut and lock the door.

"I'll ask her about it next time we talk. How long have you known Aunt Molly?" Rose asked.

"Not very long and not very well," he answered as he cut away a six-inch square of drywall around the hole. "Met her at church when she sat on the pew with the Fab Five once, but I'm sure she'll appreciate what we're doing."

Chester dragged a sock into the room and laid it at Rose's feet. She bent to get it and then changed her mind. "That's a man's sock. Where did you get it?"

"Maybe Molly has some secrets," Hud suggested.

Rose crossed her arms over her chest. "Guess maybe I'd better talk to her about that too."

"I wouldn't if I was you." He cut a square of drywall from the scrap piece he'd brought with him and fit it into the hole he'd made. "She's a consenting adult, and if she's got a love life, then pat her on the back—don't fuss at her."

Rose narrowed her eyes at him. "Are you telling me what to do?"

"No, ma'am, just telling you what I'd do if a man's sock showed up in my grandmother's house," he replied. "Now on to the next hole in the wall. I'll get them all patched and then I'll bed and tape. Have to come back later to sand."

* * *

Rose wanted to dance a jig right there in the bedroom. Hud had a good excuse to come back later—not that he needed one in her book. "Want a beer when you get finished?"

"Sure." He nodded, and then threw the hammer on the floor and grabbed his thumb. "Dammit! I swear, bad luck crawls out of the walls of this place."

Chester let out a howl and took off down the stairs, carrying his dark brown sock with him. Aunt Luna yelled up from the foyer, "Y'all okay up there?"

"We're fine. Just dropped a hammer," Rose hollered as she picked up Hud's hand and kissed his thumb. "I'm sorry. Looks like you just got the edge, so there won't be a blood blister under your nail. Let's go get that beer now and do this another time."

"Hell, no!" Hud shook his head. "I won't let a hammer win the war. It won't take much longer to finish up, and besides, your kiss made it all better."

"Okay, then," Rose agreed. "Let's get it done."

Hud had been right about it only taking a little while longer in that room, and then they went to the next room, her bedroom. Chester came bounding back up the stairs with his dark sock still in his mouth, hopped up on the bed, and laid it on her pillow.

Hud raised an eyebrow. "Maybe Miz Molly needs to have a talk with you, instead of the other way around. Is Chester putting that sock back where he found it?"

"The only person who knows for sure is Chester, and he ain't talkin'," Rose said.

The crazy cat chose that moment to meow several times, pick up his sock, and march out of the room.

"Too bad I don't understand cat language. I think he just told on you." Hud set about patching up the last wall.

"Even though he's a tattletale, I'd gladly adopt him if Aunt Molly would let me," Rose said. "I always wanted a pet, but Daddy wouldn't let me have one. He said I was too sentimental, and I'd cry when it died."

"I did," Hud admitted.

"You did what?" Rose asked.

"I cried when Willie died. He was a Catahoula puppy, I got him for Christmas when I was four. He died when I was a senior in high school. They'd wrapped him in the horse blanket he'd slept on in the barn and buried him under a shade tree. I spent the rest of that day at the back side of the ranch crying."

"I'm sorry." Rose's heart broke a little at the thought of a big tough cowboy like Hud crying.

Luna poked her head in the door. "I've made some banana nut muffins to go with coffee when y'all get done up here. I heard what you said about your dog. Wilbur adopted an ugly old stray mutt that came around the last carnival we had. We named him Beggar because that's what he did—begged for food from everyone in the carnival. When he died, we had a funeral for him, and one of our friends recited a poem called 'The Rainbow Bridge.' It seemed like a nice thing to do. I wouldn't be surprised if Molly don't have a funeral for Chester when he dies."

"All finished," Hud said. "I'll bring some bedding tape and mud over tomorrow evening and finish up this job."

Luna started for the stairs. "Wilbur should've called by now. It's about time for him to apologize. Besides I'm gettin' homesick."

"Aunt Luna, I hate to see you leave," Rose said, "but I can always take you to the bus station and get you a ticket back to Alabama if you're ready to go home."

"We'll see about that tomorrow." Luna nodded. "I've got money, darlin', so I don't need to hitch rides. I just like truck drivers. Me and Wilbur drove our own trucks back during the years when we owned our carnival. I liked sitting up high and the excitement of going from one place to the other. And, Hud, you ain't comin' back here tomorrow to work."

"Why not?" Hud asked.

"Because tomorrow is Sunday and according to Molly, if you work on Sunday God is sure to send lightning bolts from heaven to strike you graveyard dead. You can mud and tape on Monday," Luna answered with a wink at both of them. "Muffins are on the cabinet. Coffee is made. I'm going to my room and watch television. Be quiet when you leave, Hud. Wilbur says I can hear a mouse chewin' cheese at fifty yards. I wouldn't want to think you was an intruder and shoot you."

* * *

"Would it be rude for us to bypass the muffins and coffee and go to the Rusty Spur for a beer and a few dances?" Hud asked.

"Yes," she answered without hesitation, and picked a short leather jacket from off the coatrack inside the door. "I'll just leave a note on the credenza for Aunt Luna in case she gets up and can't find me."

When they got to the truck, he opened the door for her, and Rose hesitated. "Maybe I should change into something more western."

"I told you before, you're beautiful. I'll have to fight off the competition as it is," he said as he shut the door and rounded the front side.

"How far is it to the bar?" she asked when he was behind the wheel.

"Maybe ten minutes," he answered.

They'd gone about two miles when blue lights began to flash behind Hud's truck. He slowed down and pulled over to the side to let the officer go on by, but the police car pulled right in behind him and turned on the sirens.

"Was I speeding?" Hud asked.

"I have no idea," Rose answered.

Hud rolled down the window and the policeman asked for his driver's license and registration. He pulled out his wallet and got the papers from the glove box, and handed them out the window.

"Step out of the vehicle." He called for backup and a second officer got out of the car and came running toward the passenger side.

"You, too, ma'am," the second one said. "Put both your hands out of the truck so I can see them."

Holy smokin' hell! she thought. There was no way Hud was going so fast that they should be treated like drunks or serial killers, but she did what she was told.

"So where's the drugs, and why did you have to pistol-whip poor old Truman Wheeler?" the first officer said.

"I did what?" Hud frowned.

"You robbed the drugstore, and the pharmacist is in the emergency room getting stitches in his forehead right now," the second one said. "Truman might have had blood in his eyes, but he saw a black pickup truck speeding away and he got the first three license plate numbers. You can tell us where the drugs are now, or we can rip this truck apart."

"How many black trucks do you reckon are in this county, and how many of them have license plates that start with those three numbers?" Rose asked.

"Don't you get sassy with me, woman," the officer said. "We'll sort all this out at the station. Give Officer Turnbull your keys so we can impound this truck."

"Do y'all know Molly Wilson?" Rose asked. "She owns the Rose Garden Bed-and-Breakfast, and she's my aunt."

"Lady, I don't care if the mother of Jesus is your aunt," he said, "it looks to me like y'all have just got caught after robbing the drugstore in town. I don't know why, but we're going to get this all straightened out at the station, so get in the back of the patrol car."

Hud was already in the backseat when she got in. "At least they didn't handcuff us."

"They're going to be embarrassed when we call Luna and she tells them we've been at the B&B all evening," he whispered.

Officer Turnbull drove them to the station in Bowie, and opened the back door. "Don't either of you run."

"Wouldn't dream of it, but I would like to make a phone call," Rose said.

"After we get inside," he said. "But it sure looks like you're guilty of something when you want to call a lawyer before we even ask our questions."

"I'm not calling a lawyer," she told him.

Turnbull kept one hand on his holstered gun as he ushered them inside the station and told them to sit down behind a desk. "If you want to make that call, you can do it now before we fingerprint the both of you."

Rose drew in a sharp breath. If the army found out she'd been taken in for questioning, it might have a bearing on her reenlistment. She hit the speed-dial number for the bed-and-breakfast and sent up a silent prayer that Aunt Luna wasn't in the bathtub or sleeping.

"Hello, Wilbur," Luna answered. "It's about time you called."

"Aunt Luna, this is Rose." She went on to tell her what had happened. "Can you get a taxi to bring you down here to tell these people that we didn't rob the drugstore? That we were at the B&B and you were with us all evening?"

"Hell, no!" Luna screeched. "You're only four blocks from me, so I'll walk. Ain't no use in payin' for a taxi, and I damn sure need the time to cool my temper. Them policemen had better have me a place cleaned off, because Luna is on her way and she's bringin' hell with her."

"She'll be here in fifteen minutes," Rose told Hud and sincerely hoped that Luna left Madam at home.

Her great-aunt stormed through the door in ten minutes, and the poor policeman's eyes popped out of his head so far that Rose was afraid they'd be rolling around on the floor any minute. Luna had not taken her hair out of its customary braids with the beads that made a clacking sound every time she did a head roll. She was wearing a floral flowing skirt and a striped blouse, boots that looked like they'd come right out of Granny Clampett's closet, and a cowboy hat crammed down on her head. The hat was either Molly's or one that a visitor had left behind, but Rose had seen it on the rack that stood just inside the front door of the B&B. The boots were about two sizes too big and muddy around the bottom edge where she'd probably waded right through mud puddles on the way to the station.

She came into the station with a full head of steam, and her forefinger waggling. She leaned over the desk and got nose to nose with the officer. "You sumbitches are about to get a lawsuit slapped on your sorry asses for this. My niece wouldn't be robbin' no damn store. She's just served her country in the army for the past ten years, and Hud Baker is a respectable citizen of Montague County. He owns a ranch over there."

"Aunt Luna, just tell them that we were at the B&B all evening. He needs to know that you were with us," Rose said.

Hud slipped his arm around Rose's shoulders. "It could just be an honest mistake. We were on our way to the Rusty Spur to do some dancing, officer. We haven't been drinking and we sure didn't rob a store."

"Excuse me, sir." The second officer popped his head in the door. "We had the drug dog sniff out the truck, and we didn't find anything."

"Can we please just go now?" Rose asked.

"Not without an apology for all this crap you've put us through. It's supposed to be innocent until proven guilty, right?" Hud's tone was cold as ice.

Luna started toward the new officer with blood in her eye and her hand in the pocket of the oversize coat. "Are you the other fool who thinks he's some kind of hero? Well, right here sits the real hero." She turned and pointed at Hud. "He's the one who rescues babies from burning buildings. He don't rob drugstores. This is just one of the reasons I hate Texas."

The officer slammed the door in her face before she could back him up into a corner. "Run, you little sumbitch!" she yelled. "Just shows that you don't deserve that badge when you can't stand up to an eighty-year-old woman." She returned to the desk and started in on Officer Turnbull again. "Is there a law in this gawd-forsaken town about havin' a black pickup truck?" Daggers shot from her eyes straight at him.

"No, ma'am." Officer Turnbull shook his head.

"Why did you stop Hud in the first place?"

"He was going a few miles over the speed limit, and

we was only going to give him a warning," the officer answered.

The young officer opened the door again. "We did find traces of fertilizer in the truck. You reckon these two were makin' a bomb?"

"You ain't nothing but a baby-faced kid," Luna said. "Hud is a rancher. Of course he has traces of fertilizer in his truck. Did you find any explosives? How long have you been on the force?"

"This is my first day, ma'am," he answered. "And no, I didn't find anything but a few grains of fertilizer."

"Like the lady said, I'm a rancher." Hud's tone hadn't warmed a bit. "I hauled ten bags of fertilizer in that truck a few days ago. You can check with the feed store if you want to verify that."

Luna narrowed her eyes at the officer behind the desk. "You were training him on how to make a stop and write out a warning, and then realized that the truck was the same color as the one that was used in a robbery. Are you crazy or just plain stupid?"

"No...well...I don't have to..." the officer muttered, and then cleared his throat.

Luna gave him a go-to-hell look. Rose bit back a giggle, and Hud chuckled under his breath.

"Your truck is in impound," the younger officer said.

"Then you can go get it out," Luna turned on him. "This is your stupid mistake, and Hud's not paying you one single dime."

The young man looked over at Officer Turnbull. The older man shrugged. "Go on and do it." Then he turned his attention back to Hud. "You are both free to go with our apologies. I didn't recognize you as the firefighter who saved that kid."

"Thank you," Rose said.

Hud leaned over the desk and stared the man right in the eye. "You might want to give a person a chance to explain things a little more before you haul them in to the station."

"That wasn't much of an apology, and it don't make up for the fact that you've done such a stupid thing," Luna said. "I'm going home now. If I missed my call from Wilbur, I'll be back to give you another piece of my mind. I'll be waiting out front. I don't like this place." She stormed out of the police station and slammed the door behind her.

"She's hell on wheels, isn't she?" the officer said.

"Oh, yeah," Rose agreed. "Just be glad that she wasn't really mad."

In less than ten minutes, they were free to go. Luna was sitting on a bench, smoking a cigarette. When she saw them, she threw it on the ground and put it out with the heel of her boot. "I give up smokin' five years ago, and only have one when I'm mad. You kids can take me back to the house. If Wilbur called while I was gone, I may sue this city yet."

"He can call back, can't he?" Rose asked as she helped Luna into the backseat of the truck.

"Not until tomorrow. The office at the trailer park where we live closes up tight at eight o'clock." Luna chuckled and then it grew to a full-fledged laugh. "I'm callin' Molly soon as I get back in the house. She's got to hear this story." She stopped long enough to wipe her eyes, and then went on, "I swear to God, I wish I'd had one of y'all's fancy phones so I could have taken a picture of them policemen's faces when I cornered them; she would've loved it."

Rose laughed with her, but she didn't know if it was nerves or if the situation was really that funny. Then she suddenly stopped. "What does the trailer park office have to do with y'all calling each other?"

"We ain't got a phone"—Luna wiped her eyes again—"never saw no need for one. Me and Molly like to write and get letters, and she's the only one I'd ever call, so payin' a phone bill seems like a waste of money."

Hud pulled to a stop in front of the B&B and unfastened his seat belt. "You can stay in the truck if it's too cold for you."

"Honey, I ain't no weakling," Luna told him as she opened the door, "and I don't need you to walk me to the door, either. It might make Rose jealous." She cackled, "So you just go on and do some dancin' and maybe even some makin' out on the way home."

Hud waited until she was inside the B&B before he backed out of the driveway and started toward town one more time. "That was a real circus back there."

"I almost felt sorry for the policemen," Rose said. "I bet they didn't know what hit them and still don't. First Luna comes in and goes crazy on them, and then you deliver a dose of cowboy pride. I bet they stop and consider before pulling over someone on a trumped-up charge again."

"As for me, I'm wondering if you and I will ever have a date that doesn't involve a catastrophe."

"I think we've covered a lot of them." She smiled as they passed the place where they'd been stopped before.

"There's still hail, floods, and tornadoes," he said.

"Shhh." She shook her head at him. "Don't say that out loud."

She'd always wondered what Hud Baker would become, even when she'd known him as a lanky teenager. Now she'd had a little taste of the answer, and she'd never felt more alive in her entire twenty-eight years. Nothing was ever humdrum around him, and catastrophes seemed to follow him everywhere he went.

"You ever had this much bad luck in one week?" she asked.

"Nope," he replied with a head shake, "or this much good luck, either. Guess one comes with the other."

"Good luck?" she asked, incredulously.

"Got to go through all of them with you, didn't I? Do you have your heart set on going dancing?"

"Not really," she answered, honestly. "I just wanted to spend some time with you."

"Then let's go to the Dairy Queen and have some ice cream. I'd rather talk until they run us out than have to yell above the jukebox at the Rusty Spur," he said.

"Or we could go out to your ranch and let me see where you live." It might be brazen, but a girl didn't get anywhere by being shy. She'd proven that more times than one.

"I've got ice cream in the freezer and cold beers in the refrigerator." He turned the pickup around and headed in the opposite direction.

* * *

Hud's hands shook a little when he turned into the lane leading up to the small ranch house. Everyone in Tulia knew that the Bakers had a ranch as big as a small third-world country, so what was she going to think about the little two-bedroom house he now lived in?

"Oh! My! Goodness!" Rose exclaimed. "Your place looks like something out of a magazine with the fence and all. When I retire, I want something just like this."

"You really like something this small?" Hud had been reluctant to tell her too much about the run-down ranch that he half-owned. She deserved so much more than what he could offer. She'd been all over the world, and she spoke however many languages. Surely her dream home was more than a little ranch-style, clapboard frame house.

"Love it!" she said as she got out of the truck before he could even open his door. "I've always lived in small spaces. In the commune, it was a trailer. The two years I went to public school, we rented a house about this size, and now, I live in a dorm room in the army barracks. This is perfect."

"Well, it does have about seven hundred acres surrounding it," he said as he got out of the vehicle.

Rose had already let herself out when he reached her door. "That's bigger than our whole commune. Do you make a garden? I love to putter about in the dirt, and I really like fresh vegetables."

"We haven't got one yet, but we've talked about putting one in this spring."

"Do you realize that it's only been since Wednesday that we've actually reconnected? Seems like I've known you forever," she told him.

"I know," he replied. "It's kind of crazy, isn't it? We did have that year together out in the Panhandle, even if we were just kids, and we saw each other at Maverick's wedding the first of the month," he said. "One thing for sure, there doesn't seem to be a dull moment when we're together."

"Amen to that." She started for the porch.

Suddenly, Hud couldn't wait to show her his place. He beat her to the door and opened it for her. "Welcome to my house. Actually, I share it with Paxton right now, but he'll be leaving soon to go back out around Daisy." He reached around the door and flipped on the light, and a dog scooted in past both of them. The animal yipped once and then took off for the kitchen.

"That would be Red. He's a little rude tonight, not stoppin' to even say hello," Hud said. "But it's past his supper-time, and from the way he's actin', he didn't catch a rabbit or even a squirrel."

"Then I guess we'd better feed him, hadn't we?" She marched through the living room and straight into the kitchen.

Lord, that girl had spirit and spunk. Nothing seemed to faze her, and yet that shouldn't surprise him. From what he already knew, she'd grown up pretty much in a conservative commune. She'd had the nerve to join the military without telling her father until she'd already signed the papers. He'd just bet she'd locked horns with her dad on more than one occasion.

He hung up his coat and, when he made it to the kitchen, found her dropped down on her knees, scratching Red's ears. "He's named after the dog in Blake Shelton's song. Since he looked a little like the hound in the video, we thought it was a fitting name," he said as he filled a bowl with dry food.

"I love dogs." She stood up when Red bounded off into the utility room to scarf down his supper.

"I thought you were going to adopt Chester." Hud got the ice cream from the freezer and filled two bowls. "We've got caramel and chocolate toppings. Which one?"

"Both, please." She stood up. "And I'd gladly take a dog *and* a cat, long as they didn't kill each other." She squeezed out caramel first and then chocolate onto her ice cream.

"Living room or kitchen?" he asked.

"Let's take it to the living room." She picked up her bowl and headed in that direction. "Think we might start a blaze in the fireplace."

"That's easy enough." He set his ice cream on the end table and turned a knob to one side of the bricks. "The logs are fake and it's gas powered."

"I don't care if it's solar powered," she said. "I just love to look at it while I'm eating ice cream."

"Did you have one in your house?"

She shook her head. "Nope. Never even done this before, but I always imagined it in my head as a little bit romantic."

So she wanted romantic? Hud could give her that for sure.

She sat down on the sofa, and he settled in beside her, and pulled a quilt over both of them. "Is this the way you imagined it?"

"Yep," she replied. "Only we were fourteen, not almost thirty. I used to lay awake at night and think about how it would be if we went on a real date. That was my favorite scenario. Did you even think about me when the day ended?"

He set his ice cream to the side and pulled her in even closer to him. "I've dreamed about you for years and years, darlin'."

"That sounds like a pickup line to me, but I like it." She put her bowl on the coffee table, and snuggled up closer to him. "What did you dream?"

"That you were back in my life, and that we had times just like this," he answered. "Sometimes in my dreams we were having a picnic by a creek, other times we were sitting on the porch watching kids playing in the yard."

"How did you feel when you woke up from those dreams?" she asked.

"At peace," he replied. "How'd your imaginations about a fireplace make you feel?"

"Excited." She shifted her position so that she was sitting in his lap.

Her tongue darted out to moisten her lips, and then her eyes fluttered shut. The kisses started out with enough steam to fog the windows in the living room, and got hotter and hotter. She unbuttoned his shirt, and the touch of her hands on his bare chest made the pressure behind his zipper unbearable. He slipped his hands under her shirt and unfastened the hooks of her bra, and then moved around to cup her breast with his hand.

"Sweet Jesus!" she muttered. "I hope you have protection somewhere in this house because I'm not on the pill."

That's the moment when Red decided to jump on the couch and lick Rose from her chin up to her forehead in one long swipe. She wiped at her face with the back of her hand and then began to laugh. "Ask and ye shall receive."

"What's that got to do with anything?" Hud asked.

"I asked for protection. I wasn't expecting it in the form of dog slobbers, but that sure ruined the mood," she said.

He chuckled with her. "I guess it did. Maybe Red knows that it's too soon for us to..."

"Have sex," she finished the sentence for him. "Well, I usually do wait until the fifth or maybe even the sixth date. How about you?"

"I don't think I've ever been on a third date," he answered, honestly. "Most of my dates"—he air quoted that last word—"have been one-night stands that I picked up at the bars."

"Then we probably do need to slow down a little." She threw back the quilt and picked up both bowls of melted ice cream.

"How long is a little?" he asked.

"Who knows," she answered. "When Red don't interrupt us, maybe?"

He followed her into the kitchen. "Does this mean you're ready for me to take you home?"

"I think it does." She headed for the front door. "Aunt Luna mentioned church tomorrow. Are you going?"

"I attend every week. Can I pick you up?" He helped her put her coat on.

"What time?" she asked as she got into the truck.

"Starts at eleven. I could get you at ten thirty. Emily and the rest of us go to the little church just down the road from here," he said.

"Think it's safe?" she asked. "With the luck we're having, just being together on a church pew could cause a major fire or something."

"Surely we'll be safe in church," he said.

"If something happens there, I'm going to take it as a sign that Fate definitely doesn't want us to be together," she said.

"Maybe Fate has a sense of humor, and she's just throwing obstacles at us to see how serious we are?" Hud turned the key and then switched the heat on high.

"Guess we'll find out tomorrow," Rose said.

Before they got out of Sunset, dark clouds had gathered overhead, and a hard rain started pouring from the sky in great sheets. When they reached the B&B, he insisted on walking her to the door, gave her a good night kiss, and then jogged back to his truck.

This had been the craziest week he'd ever spent. If it could go wrong, it did. If it couldn't, it did anyway. He was soaked to the skin, cold to the bone, and yet singing with Blake Shelton to "Honey Bee" on the way back to his ranch—and he'd never felt so good in his whole life.

Chapter Nine

When she'd lived in the commune, Rose had gone to the dining hall on Sunday morning along with everyone else. That was one of the rules—a spiritual time on Sunday morning at nine o'clock, and three meals a day shared by everyone.

The service consisted mostly of singing hymns, but occasionally someone would read from the scripture. She'd loved the singing, but she had trouble staying focused on what was being read.

Going to chapel during basic training had been a whole new experience. The congregation might be asked to sing one hymn, but mostly the choir presented the music. A chaplain delivered the sermon and tried to make it fit the current issues of the day. Those services hadn't moved her as much as the hymns they sang at the commune. She'd always loved the tambourines and the guitar music that had been used as accompaniment.

She'd been to other church services since she'd left the commune. They'd sing a song or two, hear the church announcements, and then the preacher would deliver his sermon. To this day, she couldn't remember a single thing or feeling that she left with from the preacher's message, but she could shut her eyes and know the peace she'd felt from the singing. She hoped that there was more congregational singing that morning as she got dressed.

She'd tried on six outfits and rejected them all. Some were too dressy, some too casual. She was now standing in front of the dresser in nothing but her lacy bra and matching underpants, trying to figure out exactly what to wear to go to church with Hud.

Luna stuck her head in the door, glanced at the pile of clothing, and asked, "You about to start packing, or are you giving all that stuff away?"

"Neither." Rose threw up her hands in defeat. "I don't know what to wear to church this morning. I've been to a conventional church a few times in my life, but I don't know how to dress for this place."

"I'd say just be yourself, and if the people there don't like what you're wearing, then they can take it up with God. I hear He's not much interested in what a person wears anyway, but He looks on the heart," Luna told her.

"I hope so." Rose pulled a long, brown plaid skirt from the pile of clothing and topped it with a cream-colored sweater. Then she picked up a brush from her dresser and ran it through her long hair.

"You look beautiful," Luna said. "If I was going, I'd wear something to brighten the congregation's day."

"What do you mean? If you were going?" Rose laid the brush down.

"Today, I'm staying home, Rosie-Posey," Luna told her.

"That's what I called you when you were a tiny baby and I got to hold you. Miz Rosie-Posey with the pretty red hair. I told you that you'd grow up to be a beautiful woman, and I was right."

"Why aren't you going to church?" Rose asked.

"I'm getting a little worried about Wilbur. He usually calls by now. I hope he's not sick. He's such a big baby when he's even got a little cold," she said.

"You could always call him," Rose suggested.

Luna just glared at her. "Bah."

"Well, since you aren't going with us, I'll pick up something for our Sunday dinner and bring it home. Fried chicken, okay?" she asked.

"Now that's a real Sunday dinner." Luna's grin deepened all the wrinkles in her cheeks. "It's almost time for Prince Charming to come for you, so we'd better go on downstairs. You go first. I'm slow with this old crippled-up knee. If I'd known that all that heavy lifting from the carnival business would invite arthritis into my bones, I might not have done it. But hey, you got to first be young and stupid to have something to bitch and moan about when you're old."

Rose crossed the room and gave her a hug. "You are amazing, Aunt Luna."

"I appreciate that, darlin'." She wrapped her arms around Rose and kissed her on the cheek. "Now, let's try to get down the stairs without falling over our own two feet. Us Wilson girls never had a lick of grace. I always hoped you'd be graceful, and if you did fall, a sexy cowboy like Hud would be there to catch you."

"I've got my share of clumsy." Rose slipped on a pair of brown high-heeled shoes. "You could have given me something nicer, like fewer freckles or maybe blue eyes."

"If you're going to wear those, then it's a good thing

you're going before me." Luna waited until Rose had started down, and then she got a firm grip on the banister.

"Why's that?" Rose asked over her shoulder.

"Because if you started to fall, we'd both go ass over boobs all the way to the bottom," Luna replied.

"You're too funny," Rose giggled.

They were both in the foyer when Hud rapped on the door. Rose glanced at the clock—ten thirty. Hud was right on time. She opened the door and her breath caught in her chest when he swaggered inside. The smell of his shaving lotion, something woodsy with a hint of musk, sent her senses swirling. Snug jeans hugged his thighs and bunched up over the tops of his boots. A plaid shirt peeked out from under a black leather, western-cut coat that stopped at his knees, and his black cowboy hat sat just right. She wanted to melt into his arms and kiss him until they were both breathless.

"You look beautiful," he said.

Rose could feel the blush creep up her cheeks as she took her coat from the rack beside the door. "Thank you."

Hud helped her into her coat and turned to Luna. "Ready?" he asked.

"I ain't goin'," she said. "Me and God decided a long time ago that we don't need a church house building to have our conversations. You kids go on, and don't be makin' out on the back pew. And don't forget to get a couple of extra chicken legs for our dinner."

"Aunt Luna!" Rose scolded.

"I'll be a gentleman," Hud chuckled. "And I'll be sure to take care of that chicken."

"I'm sorry about that," Rose said on the way to the truck. "Sometimes she's funny, and other times—"

"And other times," he butted in, "she's hilarious. I hope

when I get old, I'm just as ornery as she is." Hud tucked her hand into his.

Warmth spread through her body. No one had ever made her feel the way Hud did by simply holding her hand.

He settled her into the passenger seat and rounded the back of the truck, whistling a tune she didn't recognize.

Loving someone and being in love with someone are two different things, Granny Dee had told her more than once. *Have the patience to wait until you can find someone that you are in love with and then you'll not only have peace in your heart but also a wonderful life.*

"Good advice," Rose muttered.

* * *

Hud hadn't told any of the extended family about Rose, except Paxton and Claire, so he was a little nervous that morning as he drove from the B&B back to Sunset to the little white church.

"Do you go to church every Sunday, even if you've been out dancing until two in the morning?" Rose asked.

"Yes, ma'am. Mama made us go to church no matter what. That was the rule, and it kind of stuck, even after we moved over to this part of the state on our own. How about you?"

"Haven't been to a church in years and years," she answered. "We had a service at the commune that was geared mainly to singing, and playing musical instruments, and I attended a few churches through the years, but nothing to speak of."

"Well, then I welcome you to the Sunset Community Church. I got to admit the singing is my favorite part, and too many times I don't listen like I should to the preachin'," he said.

"I'm still a little worried. The way things have been going for us the congregation might blame us if the church exploded or lightning came shooting down through the rafters." She smiled across the console at him.

"The sky is clear. No clouds in sight. I think we're safe." He pointed toward the windshield. "If it starts to look like something's about to go down, we'll hurry outside and leave."

"Fair enough," she said.

It only took a few minutes to reach the church, and Hud snagged a parking space not far from the front door. He and Rose were walking across the parking lot when he heard someone call his name. He looked over his shoulder to see Levi, Claire, Dixie, and the baby.

"Wait up," Levi called out.

"Hud!" Dixie almost squealed as she handed the baby carrier off to Levi and ran across the lot to hug both him and Rose. "I'm so glad to see you today. I can't thank you enough for everything. I love my job, and Claire and everyone has been so nice."

Her words and enthusiasm meant far more to him than getting his name mentioned on the news or his picture in the local newspaper.

"That's great," Hud said.

She left Hud and hugged Rose. "You and Luna were so good to me. I'll never forget it."

"Maybe someday I can drive over and visit you and Sally." Rose's voice caught in her throat.

"I'd love that." Dixie took the baby carrier from Levi.

"Hey." Levi grinned at him. "You going to introduce me to your friend?"

"Sorry," Hud said. "This is Rose O'Malley. She and I knew each other when she went to school in Tulia. And this is Levi, Claire's husband, and the foreman of the Longhorn Canyon Ranch."

"Small world, ain't it?" Levi tipped his hat toward her.

"Yes, it is." Rose gave him a head nod. "Never thought I'd look up and see Hud at a wedding in the Texas panhandle, or in my gift shop this past week, either."

"I'm so happy to be going to church today, and guess what, Rose." Dixie inhaled deeply before she went on. "They've invited me out to their ranch for Sunday dinner. If I'm dreaming, don't pinch me. I don't want to wake up."

"One cowboy's courage saved her life and gave her a brand-new start," Rose whispered as they followed the others inside the church.

Hud took her hand in his and squeezed it gently. "Thank you, but I only did what I needed to do."

His grandpa and his father had always told him not to gloat over success, but he couldn't help but feel a little pride sneaking into his heart and soul when he thought about what Rose had said. With her by his side, he felt ten feet tall as he walked down the center aisle that Sunday morning.

When they sat, Rose was between him and Claire. Then Tag and Nikki arrived, and everyone slid down so that they could join them on the pew.

"Tag and his wife," Hud whispered to Rose.

Most women got all moony-eyed when they saw his brother—even now that Tag was married—but not Rose. She glanced toward him and then went back to whispering to Claire. Hud loved his brother, but for the first time that he could remember, he truly felt like he'd just come in ahead of him.

Bowie was a fairly small town where rumors got around pretty fast, but in Sunset, with its small population, gossip spread faster than the speed of light. Hud could hear the buzz of whispers all around him and wondered how many of them concerned him and Rose.

The room went quiet when the choir director took her place behind the podium and gave out the number for a congregational hymn. Sharing a songbook with Rose seemed even more personal than sitting so close to her that no light could get between their hips. He wondered if anyone else in the church could feel the heat from the sparks dancing all around them.

When they'd finished singing, the preacher took his place. He cleared his throat, and a loud clap of thunder came out of nowhere to rattle the windows and startle young and old alike. Rose elbowed Hud in the ribs and whispered, "You think maybe we should leave?"

"The lightning isn't coming through the rafters yet, so maybe we're safe," he answered in a low voice.

"Well, I believe I've got your attention now," the preacher chuckled. "I guess the good Lord knows what I'm about to speak on this morning, and that's hearing His voice when He speaks to us. It might be a whisper in our ear, or it could be a raging storm in our soul, but God will speak."

Raging storm. Hud's thoughts went off on their own.

He and Tag had originally planned to have the ranch up and going good before either of them settled down. Now Tag was married, and Paxton was leaving them, so a lot of responsibility fell on Hud. Could he do right by a woman, spend enough time with her, and still not slack on all his ranching duties?

He was still thinking about all that when the sermon ended on another loud clap of thunder, and a hard rain started to beat against the church windows. The preacher leaned into the microphone and said, "I'll give the ending prayer this morning, and y'all can all hurry on out to your vehicles without shaking my hand at the door. I truly hope that you got a message from the Lord into your own hearts this morning. Now let us pray."

Hud gave silent thanks for the downpour because all his extended family made a mad dash toward the door. Introducing Rose to all of them wouldn't be an embarrassment, but it would be nice to do it a little at a time. Today, it had been Levi, and pointing out Tag and Nikki. Maybe next week it would be Retta and Cade.

"I should've brought an umbrella," he said.

"I'm not sugar or salt," she said. "I proved that last night when we got wet running from your truck to the B&B, and I didn't melt. We'll just run between the raindrops."

* * *

As Rose held on to Hud's hand and ran through the rain to the truck, she had a crazy vision of stopping right there in the parking lot and dancing. An old song by Tanya Tucker called "Would You Lay with Me" played through her mind, but she changed the lyrics to say, would you dance with me in the pouring rain.

She was humming the song when she crawled into the truck. Her coat had done little to keep her skin dry, but the truck had a fine heater, so by the time they reached the drive-by window at the chicken place, she was toasty warm. When he parked at the B&B, Rose got out and tried to run across the grass, but the heels of her shoes kept sinking into the wet ground, and then one of her heels sank into the mud, throwing her off balance.

She turned slightly and ran smack into Hud. Her hands shot out to grasp anything at all and landed on Hud's broad chest. He scooped her up in his arms and carried her back to the porch.

"Don't you dare carry me over the threshold." She laid her head on his chest and listened to the rhythm of his heartbeat. Hers seemed to be thumping a lot faster than his, but then she'd nearly fallen, and she was in his arms.

"Why not?" he asked.

"Aunt Luna would never let me hear the end of it. She'd say it was as good as jumping over the broom, like she and Uncle Wilbur did." She began to hum the song that was still in her head. She didn't care if her hair was lying in wet strands hanging down her back, she slipped her arms around his neck and began to sing, "Would you dance with me in the pouring rain?" to the tune of "Would You Lay with Me."

"Yes, ma'am." He slipped his arms around her waist and two-stepped with her on the porch. When she stopped singing, he tipped her chin up with his fist and kissed her— long, hard, and passionately.

She was so hot on the inside that she didn't even mind the cold rainwater streaming down her cheeks and sneaking under her coat collar to inch its way down her spine. One kiss led to another and another and yet another, until finally, he pulled away and opened the door for her.

"Your Aunt Luna will get out her pistol if you get pneumonia from making out with me in this weather," he whispered.

"Maybe so, but what a way to die," she laughed.

"Amen!" He kissed her once more and then ran around the front of the truck and grabbed the sacks with the food inside. When he'd jogged back, he said, "Glad I left that bag here with a change of clothes in it."

"Maybe Chester will steal one of your socks," Rose said as she opened the door and the two of them rushed inside.

Luna met them with a couple of towels in her hands.

"Y'all best get dried before we sit down to eat. Did you get extra chicken drumsticks?"

"Yes, but I forgot to ask Hud if he was a leg man." Rose dried her hair and face, and headed for the stairs. "I'll only be a minute. Hud, you can change in the shop."

"Thanks, and I'm not a leg man," he chuckled. "I'm a breast guy."

She blushed in spite of the chill and forced herself not to look down at her own chest, which was average size, and wondered if her boobs were too big or too small. It was a crazy thought, because other than a few kisses, whatever this was with Hud couldn't go anywhere permanent until she made up her mind about her own future. It wouldn't be fair to a great guy like him to ever lead him on for weeks and then reenlist. The army only knew where her next duty station would be, but it sure wouldn't be anywhere close to Bowie, Texas.

She shivered the whole time that she changed, and hadn't warmed up yet when she started back down the stairs. Her pulse jacked up a few notches when she realized Hud was standing at the bottom of the steps, watching her. Just the way he looked at her heated up her insides more than any sweater in her closet.

Luna walked up behind Hud and poked him on the shoulder with a bony finger. "Y'all quit makin' moony eyes at each other, and get on in here to the table before the gravy gets cold. Nothin' worse than cold gravy."

"Yes, ma'am." Hud held out his hand toward Rose.

He didn't drop it until he pulled out a chair for her. "So, what's your favorite piece of chicken?" he asked as he rounded the table and seated Luna.

"Legs," Rose answered. "Daddy used to tell me that he needed to perfect a breed of chicken that had three legs."

"My granny used to tell Tag the same thing," Hud said.

Luna bowed her head. "Thank you, God, for this food. Amen."

"We've never said grace before," Rose said.

"It's Sunday," Luna said bluntly and took two legs out of the box of chicken before she passed it on to Hud. "Now let's eat."

"What was your favorite thing about living in a commune?" He removed a breast and a wing.

"I think it was the land. Although the commune owned only maybe thirty or forty acres, it had a nice stream bordering it on one side and a mountain on the other. I loved running wild and free, wading in the clear water or taking a sandwich up into the trees and having a picnic with the squirrels," she answered honestly. "What did you like about growing up on a ranch?"

"Pretty much what you said." He spooned some mashed potatoes out onto his plate and handed the container to her. Vibes passed between them when their fingertips touched—but that wasn't a surprise, since it happened every single time they were even close to each other. "After me and Tag would get done with chores, we'd either go to the creek running on the Rockin' B Ranch property or we'd play rodeo cowboys. We about wore out a bull Grandpa made us from a tractor tire and hung from a big old scrub oak tree in our backyard. I'd ride while he pulled on the rope to make it buck, and then we'd trade places. The best thing was when Daddy or Grandpa came out there and jerked the rope around, because the bull got really rowdy then."

"The boys had one of those at the commune," Rose said. "I tried it one time, but I only stayed on a couple of seconds. That ended my rodeo career right there."

"Not mine," Hud said between bites. "I still ride bulls whenever I get a chance."

"Ever been hurt?"

"Few times," he admitted.

"Wilbur used to get a wild hair up his butt and want to do rodeo stuff. I told him that we had a carnival and riding the Ferris wheel or the Tilt-A-Whirl was enough excitement for him," Luna said and changed the subject. "How'd y'all fare at the two-steppin' last night?"

"We didn't go," Rose replied. "We went out to Hud's ranch and I got to see his house and meet his dog, Red. He kind of reminds me of Daddy's redbone hound named Merle. He's a big pet, for the most part, but he hates coyotes, so when one comes around lookin' for a chicken or a newborn calf or baby goat, Merle puts them goin' pretty fast."

"Is he named after Merle Haggard?" Luna asked.

"Yep, and Red is after that song by Blake Shelton," Rose told her.

Rose glanced up at her reflection in the mirror hanging above an old washstand on the other side of the kitchen. Her makeup was completely washed away, leaving her eyebrows and eyelashes the same strawberry blond color as her hair. Every freckle was shining, and her full lips still looked slightly bee-stung from the make-out session. Hud had kissed her when she looked like a runaway street person, so evidently, he really did like her.

"Well, I got to meet them dogs someday," Luna said, smacking her lips. "This is some fine chicken. Reminds me of what your mama made for me the last time I saw her. Only thing I like better than fried chicken is catfish. We had that on the table the day I went to see her too. Man, was that some good food."

"When spring comes, we should go fishing in one of our farm ponds," Hud suggested. "They've been stocked with catfish, and the old guy we bought the place from said no one has fished in them for several years. That means they might be good eatin' sized."

When spring rolled around, Rose could easily be thousands and thousands of miles away, or then again, she could only be a couple of hours down the road if she took the job in Fort Worth.

"I haven't been fishing in years." She put the thoughts of where she'd be in two months away, and focused on the memories of the commune. "Daddy and I often went on Sunday afternoons, and if we caught something, we'd cook it over an open fire right there on the creek bank and eat it."

"Did you feel guilty that you didn't take it back to share with the others?" Hud asked.

She shook her head. "Me and Daddy called it an afternoon snack. There wasn't enough for everyone in the commune to even have a taste. The way I figured, it was that if they wanted plenty to feed the crowd, then they should be out there helping us. We all worked together in the huge garden, picked the fruit from the orchard, and took care of the livestock, so it was either fish and eat or not fish and have whatever was left over in the kitchen for snacks."

"Sounds like pretty sound thinking to me," he agreed.

"I thought so." She stole looks over at him.

"Where was your favorite place to be stationed when you were in the army?" he asked.

"I'm not sure," she replied. "I loved each place, even the tours over in Afghanistan. There was something eerily beautiful about that place, but I have to admit I got sick of the sand. There was no way to keep it out of everything, from your clothes to your bedsheets. That part I didn't like at all. What about you? You've worked on your folks' big ranch, and now this smaller one. Which is your favorite?"

Hud hesitated for so long that she wondered if he'd ever answer. Then he gave a brief nod, as if he'd found the most truthful one. "I'd have to say the Canyon Creek ranch is my favorite. Tag and I are working toward something that we can be proud of and, hopefully, add to as land around us comes up for sale. What my folks have is huge, but my great-grandparents started small like we're doing and built the ranch into an empire. We want to do the same for our future generations. It takes long hours and lots of elbow grease, but there's a lot of pride in getting a fence built, or a barn roof put on, or even a pasture full of hay baled. And that's not even talking about the excitement of a new calf on the ranch."

She loved the enthusiasm in his voice. She wanted to feel the same way when she made up her mind about what step to take next in her own life.

Chapter Ten

Paxton called just as they were finishing Sunday dinner and told Hud that a dozen cows were out on the road. "Evidently, all this rain has left those old rotted fence posts easy to push over. There's about four of them down on the ground. Reckon you could get on back here and help me get them back inside the pasture?" he asked.

"I'm on my way," Hud said and ended the call. "Ladies, I hate to eat and run, but Pax needs my help right away."

"Get on out of here." Luna waved him away. "But before you leave, don't make plans for Wednesday night. We're all three goin' square-dancin' down at the VFW. I saw an ad for it in the newspaper this mornin', and they said everyone was invited. So put on your dancin' boots, and we'll go have us a good time. That is if Wilbur don't call between now and then."

"If he does, we'll let you know," Rose told him.

"Thanks," Hud said as he disappeared out of the kitchen.

At least the rain had slacked off to a slow drizzle when he got back to the ranch that afternoon. He made another dash through the house to change into work clothes and boots and called Paxton on his way back to the truck to see exactly where he should go.

"I'm at the back side of the ranch on the far side of Canyon Creek," Paxton answered. "I've got them herded up together, but the old cow in the lead won't budge, so the whole lot of them are being stubborn. Bring Red with you. Maybe he can get them moving."

When he whistled, the dog came running and barely slowed down enough to jump onto the passenger's seat.

"We're both on the way," Hud said.

When he reached Paxton's truck, he pulled over beside it and opened the door. Red bailed out and headed right for the cows. He went to the lead heifer and barked at her. She didn't take even a half step, so he nipped at her heels. That set her in motion, and she headed into the narrow strip of land between the fence and the creek. The herd rolled their eyes and bellowed, but they followed her until they were all crammed up in a huddle, still afraid to step into the rolling creek waters. Finally, Red got them moving single file toward a small bridge up the creek a ways.

"Well, we got them going, but getting that old cow to cross the footbridge might be another thing," Paxton said.

"Let's get this fence patched," Hud told him. "They could live on this little piece of dirt until the water recedes. How do you figure they got across anyway?"

"They either came over before the water got deep or one of them led the herd across the bridge." Paxton got what they needed out of his truck.

"It'll seem strange to be working with just me and Maverick," Paxton said as he tossed one of the old rotted fence posts off to the side. "The four of us have been a team for a decade now."

Hud drove a metal post where the old one had been. "We'd try to talk you into staying if it would do any good."

"Can't stay, now." Paxton grinned. "Emily and the family have a big surprise going-away party for me tonight at her place. I can't disappoint her."

"How'd you know about that?" Hud asked. "I don't talk in my sleep, do I?"

"Nope." Paxton kicked another post out of the way. "I hate goodbyes, so I was going to slip away this morning. Then Tag came by. He had to let the cat out of the bag so I'd stay for the party. Ain't no way I'm going to disappoint Emily and Justin after all they've done for us."

Hud understood Paxton completely, because he'd been dreading telling his roommate and best friend goodbye the next morning too. However, the strip of land separating the creek from the road seemed to strike a nerve in Hud's thoughts.

"This strip of land is a little oasis between the past, with all the raging water, and the future, which is the road out there," he said.

"When did you become a philosopher?" Paxton asked.

"Since Rose showed up in Bowie, I guess." He set another metal post and moved on down to the next place. "I'm happy on my ranch, but I wonder about Rose. Where will the future road take her?"

"That's pretty deep thinkin' for us old cowboys." Paxton got out the barbed wire and started stretching it from post to post. "But I reckon it'll be up to her. You gettin' serious about that woman?"

"I can see it going that way if she doesn't leave in a few

weeks." Hud followed along behind him with another row of wire.

"Well, would you look at that?" Paxton pointed across the creek where the whole herd of cows had their heads bent, getting drinks from the creek.

Red ran up and down the creek, yipping at Hud. Finally, he jumped in and started paddling to their side. The current took him downstream a little ways, but when he reached the grassy shore, he bounded back to Paxton and Hud, shook water all over them, and then barked at the cows across the creek.

Hud rubbed the dog's ears and said, "I don't know how you got them across that little bridge but you did good, old boy."

"You might want to put up a gate so they don't come across it during high water times," Paxton told Hud.

"Great idea," Hud agreed.

"Now, what do we do with the rest of the afternoon?" Paxton asked.

"How about we get into some dry clothing, grab a couple of beers, and watch some Sunday afternoon football until it's time to go for your surprise party," Hud suggested.

"Sounds good to me," Paxton said. "Meet you at the barn, and we'll get the feeding chores done early so we won't have to do them in the dark after my party. Come on, Red. You can go with me. Might be the last time we get to see each other for a while."

Hud had been so wrapped up in Rose that he hadn't really thought about Paxton leaving until that moment. For the first time in his life, starting tomorrow, he would be living alone. He'd lived in the big ranch house on his folks' ranch until he was eighteen, and then he and Tag had moved out into the bunkhouse on the Rockin' B Ranch.

They had declared that they wanted to be grown-ups, but in actuality, what they really wanted was to be free to go to bars and bring women home with them. Then when they moved to Sunset, they'd lived in the house together until Tag moved out into the little cabin over on Longhorn Canyon and wound up getting married. After that, he still had Paxton in the house. Now it would be empty except for him and Red.

When he and Tag had lived in the bunkhouse, and then again in the little two-bedroom ranch house with Maverick and Paxton, he'd sworn that he would give his right arm for some peace and quiet. Now that it was coming tomorrow morning, he wasn't so sure he was ready for it.

He didn't even realize he'd gone past the turn to the ranch until he was almost to Sunset. "Dammit!" he muttered as he turned the truck around and headed back. When he topped the hill, he saw the most beautiful rainbow he'd ever laid eyes on. He pulled over to the side of the road and called Rose.

"Need some help with those ornery cows?" she asked.

"Go outside and look to the east," he told her. "There's a gorgeous rainbow."

He could hear the front door opening and then her gasp. "Oh. My. Goodness! It's so bright and beautiful," she said.

Her reaction made him feel like he'd just laid the moon at her feet. "I thought you might like that. Glad I got your number so I could show it to you."

"Me too," Rose said. "I wish we could be standing together at the end of the rainbow."

"So we could find the pot of gold together?" he asked.

"No, so we could discover what was there together," she replied. "It might be answers to all our questions instead of a pot of gold."

"Wouldn't that be great?" Hud caught a movement in his peripheral vision and turned to look to his right. Paxton had pulled up beside him and was motioning for him to roll down his window.

"It's starting to fade. I've got to go get Aunt Luna and show it to her," Rose said.

"Talk to you later," Hud told her as he hit a button and the passenger-side window started moving downward.

"Got trouble?" Paxton asked.

"No, I just pulled over to look at that rainbow," Hud told him.

"Awww, that's romantic," Paxton teased.

"If that's the case, maybe you should write a poem about it and send it to Alana," Hud shot back.

"Now, you're gettin' downright mean. I bet I can beat you home, and if there's only one beer, I'm not goin' to share it." Paxton rolled up his window and left a long black streak on the wet road.

Hud chuckled and followed along behind him at the speed limit. He wasn't worried about losing the race, and he knew there was a whole six-pack of beer in the fridge because he'd put it there the day before.

Getting the cows back onto ranch property, repairing the fence, and then doing all the chores had taken Paxton and Hud longer than they'd thought it would. They listened to the kickoff of a football game as they got dressed for Paxton's surprise party. Hud had known about it all week, and his job was to deliver Paxton when Emily called to tell him that it was time.

He'd just gotten his boots on and was combing his hair when his cell rang. Expecting it to be Emily, he answered, "Timing is just right."

"For what?" Rose asked.

"To talk to you," he answered. "What's up?"

"Aunt Luna is depressed because Uncle Wilbur hasn't called," she said. "I was wondering if you could come over and play a game of dominoes with us to cheer her up."

"I'd love to, but this is Paxton's last night here, and my sister is giving him a going-away party." He bit back a groan.

This was the first time she'd called him, and the only time she'd asked for his help—every other time he'd helped her out had been nothing but coincidence. "But, hey, why don't you join us at the party? Y'all can be my plus two. It's nothing formal. Just a buffet supper and some visiting with Paxton, since he's leaving tomorrow morning."

"Are you sure?" Rose asked. "I don't want to crash a family gathering."

"I'm positive," he said. "Remember how to get to the ranch?"

"Yes," she answered. "But..."

"It's the first right on the road after you turn off from Sunset. My ranch is the second one, so if you get as far as the Canyon Creek, then turn around and go back a quarter mile. No, I've got a better idea. Y'all come here to my ranch, and we'll go together"—he looked at the clock beside his bed—"say in about thirty minutes."

"If you're absolutely sure," she said. "Aunt Luna would probably love a party and being around people right now."

"I'm positive," he assured her, again.

"Thanks, Hud. We'll be there." She ended the call.

His phone rang as soon as he'd gotten it tucked into his hip pocket. Emily's picture popped up, and he groaned as he answered it. "We're runnin' a little behind. Had to fix a broke-down fence and..."

Emily giggled. "That's what I'm calling to tell you. We're

doin' the same over here. I should've planned it for six, but we'll be ready right after five thirty. Will that work?"

"Perfectly, sis." He smiled. "And can I bring a couple of guests?"

"Rose?" Emily asked.

"And her aunt," he answered.

"Sure," Emily agreed. "The more the merrier, and I've been wanting to catch up with Rose anyway. I remember her being at our school in Tulia when I was a senior and she was either a freshman or sophomore. It'll be fun to catch up. Claire says her aunt is a hoot. See you soon, and don't forget that you're down to bring a case of beer."

He had forgotten—totally—and he sure didn't have time to run back into town, but if he could catch Rose and Luna in time, maybe they'd be willing to stop by a convenience store for him. He made the call, and waited through three rings, four rings, and finally on the fifth one, Rose answered.

"I have a huge favor to ask," he said. "Have you left town yet?"

"No, we're just pulling out of the driveway," she said.

"My only job was to pick up a case of beer and I forgot," he said. "Could you—"

"What kind? Bottles or cans?" She butted in before he could finish.

"Cans are fine. Could you get Coors out of the cooler so they're already cold?" he replied.

"Do you need ice too?" she asked.

He hadn't thought of that. "Good idea. Why don't you get a bag, just in case."

"No problem."

"Thank you. You're a lifesaver."

"See you soon!" she trilled.

The call ended, and he shoved the phone into his hip pocket.

When he opened his bedroom door, Paxton was just coming out into the hallway. Hud could see boxes stacked everywhere. Some were still open, but several were taped shut.

"You reckon you'll be able to get all those in your truck?" Hud asked.

"I think so," Paxton said. "I've got the whole backseat, plus the extra one in the front, unless you want to send Red with me."

"Naw." Hud grinned. "I'll need him here to keep me company. When you get over there in the flat country, you won't have all these mesquite trees to hide behind. I reckon in six months, Alana will have lassoed you and dragged you to the altar."

"I bet you a hundred dollars you are standin' in front of a preacher before I am," Paxton countered.

Hud stuck out his hand. "You're on, and you can pay me right after y'all get married."

They shook on it, and Paxton headed toward the door.

"Not yet," Hud said. "They're not ready over at Emily's, and Rose is bringing the beer that I forgot to get. I invited her and Luna to the party."

Paxton chuckled, then laughed and then roared. "I'm going to spend my hundred dollars buying beers for everyone in the honky-tonk. I'm definitely going to be the last bachelor among us for sure."

"We'll see about that," Hud told him, but he figured it might be the best hundred dollars he'd ever spend if Paxton was right.

* * *

Rose dashed into the convenience store, bought a case of Coors, a six-pack of Bud Light, and a bag of ice. She tipped the young guy behind the checkout counter when he carried it all out to her car for her.

"Just how big is this party?" Aunt Luna asked.

"I'm not sure, but I'm kind of guessing that there'll be about a dozen people there, and I know that you are partial to Bud Light, so I got that six-pack for us," she said as she drove south to Sunset.

Luna turned on the radio and sang the words she knew to an old country music tune by Waylon and Willie called "Mammas Don't Let Your Babies Grow Up to Be Cowboys."

When the song ended, Luna glanced over at Rose. "You know you could marry a doctor or a lawyer instead of a cowboy. You're a smart girl."

"So are you, and you married a carnie." Rose turned off the road and headed east toward the ranch.

"But I wanted excitement and adventure," Luna argued.

Rose mentally relived the excitement of the rainbow phone call. "You think that being in a relationship with a cowboy wouldn't be an adventure?"

"I'm thinkin' about *you*, darlin'," Luna told her. "The way you've traveled around the world and had a new life at each duty station. Can you imagine being tied down to a ranch and dealing with small-town politics? It'd be kinda like eternity with cows, calves, and a man who comes home every night smelling like bullshit and has hay all up in his hair."

Rose pulled into the lane leading back to the ranch. The next song on the radio was Travis Tritt's "Where Corn Don't Grow."

"This is more my song," Rose said. "I couldn't wait to get out of the commune and get to see the big cities, and now that I've been away so long, I kind of miss some of it.

I liked living in the country. It was just those rigid rules that drove me crazy."

"Just be sure that you know how deep the water is before you jump in with both feet." Luna pointed toward the small house. "That's cute as a button."

"I know," Rose agreed. "And a cowboy comes with it."

"Two cowboys." Luna nodded toward the house where two men were coming out of the house.

"That's Paxton. He's leaving tomorrow to go back to West Texas, so the party is for him tonight," Rose explained.

"If I don't hear from Wilbur right soon, I might follow that one out to the panhandle," Luna giggled. "Look at the way he fills out them jeans, and that swagger. All he'd have to do is wink, and a woman would fall backward on the bed and pull him down on top of her."

"Aunt Luna!" Rose scolded.

"Truth is truth, no matter how much bullshit you spread on top of it," Luna told her. "And that cowboy that's been givin' your heart a hard time don't come in far behind him for looks."

Far behind him? Rose thought. *The sun hasn't come up on a day that Paxton Callahan could outdo Hud Baker for sexiness.*

Hud crossed the yard and tapped on the window. She rolled it down. He propped his elbows on the edge of the window and leaned into the car just slightly. The woodsy scent of his cologne and his lips that close sent her senses reeling.

"Y'all want to ride with me or follow me?" he asked.

"We'll just follow. That way, we'll have our car there when it's time to leave," Rose said. "You got a cooler to put the beer and ice into?"

"I forgot that. I'll go back in and get it," he said and then yelled at Paxton, "Don't go in until I get there."

Paxton gave him a thumbs-up and then got into his truck. Hud jogged back to the house and brought out a big red and white cooler. He carried it to the back of her car and opened the back door. He dumped all the cans into the cooler and then added the bag of ice. "That should keep them cold. I can't thank you enough for picking all this up for me."

"No problem." Rose watched him lift the heavy cooler up as if it weighed two pounds. She couldn't see his biceps under the suede jacket, but she had no doubt that they were bulging. Hudson Baker was a real cowboy, and he got his muscles from hard work on the ranch, not from a set of weights in a gym. He didn't just put on cowboy boots on Saturday night to go to the honky-tonk—no, sir, he wore them all week, no matter if he was shoveling bullshit, as Aunt Luna would say, or if he was sitting on a church pew.

Luna laid a hand over her heart. "I don't know if I can survive so much testosterone in one place. I'm used to old men sitting out on the trailer park picnic table. It would take all four of them to pick up that cooler, and they would have to call out two more to lift it over the top of that pickup bed."

"You're funny," Rose said. "Do they play chess?"

"Oh, hell no!" Luna shook her head. "Honey, they relive the carnie days. Just about all the folks in the park are our old carnival friends. I'm startin' to miss them pretty bad."

Rose patted her shoulder. "I bet that he's getting pretty lonesome to see you."

"I hope so," Luna sighed. "But for now get this buggy turned around and follow that cowboy. I'm thirsty for one of them Bud Lights."

They were at the other ranch in only a couple of minutes. Rose parked right beside Hud. She and Luna got out of the car and followed him onto the porch. Paxton hung back, like he was listening to a song on the radio. Emily came to the door and motioned them inside.

"We're so glad y'all could come with Hud," she said. "We've been dyin' to get to spend some time with you, Rose. I remember you from the year you were in Tulia, but I didn't know that you were friends with Alana until Maverick's wedding."

"How did you know Alana?" Rose asked.

"We were the kids growin' up on ranches in the same area, so we saw each other at all the functions—parties, stock sales, you name it." Emily led the way into the living room. "Put that cooler in the dining room at the end of the table, Hud. I'll introduce Luna and Rose to everyone." She pointed over to a tall cowboy with light brown hair, steely blue eyes, and a square jaw. "This is my husband, Justin. The guy beside him is his brother, Cade."

Believing that the two men were brothers was no problem. Cade's eyes were a little lighter and he might have been an inch or two taller, but they had the same face shape and both were tall.

"The lady sitting on the end of the sofa with the baby is Cade's wife, Retta, and the baby is Annie." Rose could tell that Retta, even though she was sitting down, was tall. Her chestnut-colored hair was pulled up in a ponytail, and her big brown eyes glittered with happiness.

"I heard that you've met Levi and Claire, and Dixie and Sally," Emily said, bypassing the next four folks in the room, "and that you sat beside Tag and Nikki in church this morning. That's everyone, except Paxton, who'll be coming in any minute. He thinks it's bad luck to not finish listening to a song on the radio." Emily smiled. "Everyone, this is Rose O'Malley and her aunt Luna. Luna is Miz Molly's sister, one of the other ladies on the tour with our Fab Five."

As if on cue, Paxton came in the door and yelled, "Hey, Emily, Hud said you needed to see me before I left?"

"In the living room," Emily called out.

Hud slipped inside and crossed the room to stand beside Rose. When Paxton entered the room, everyone there yelled, "Surprise!"

"Whose birthday is it?" Paxton asked.

"It's your going-away supper." Emily pointed toward a banner with *We'll Miss You* written in glitter with a set of twinkling Christmas lights around it. "We couldn't let you leave us without throwing a party."

Leaving without a party—the thought stuck in Rose's mind. When she'd left the commune to go to the army, there had been no party. Her father rode to work with another guy that morning, and her mother had driven her into town. Normally, the women only got away from the commune once a month for necessary items they couldn't supply themselves—like feminine items or maybe quilting fabric if they could afford it.

She wondered what kind of concession her mother had made for the privilege of taking her to the recruiter's office that day.

"This is too much," Paxton said. "Y'all know I hate goodbyes. You're liable to see me cry over all this."

"Well, don't start boo-hooing right now," Hud said. "Emily's been cooking all your favorites all day, so what do you say we kick this party off with food, and since it's your party, you can even go first. Just leave a little rigatoni for me, please."

"And don't go too hard on those hot yeast rolls." Claire stood up with the help of a hand from her husband. "I've been craving them for a week."

"Now this is a party," Luna whispered to Rose and then

leaned around to look up at Hud. "Thank you for inviting us."

"My pleasure." Hud took Rose's hand in his. "Let me show you where the food and drinks are, and don't be shy. My sister cooks for an army."

"That comes from dealing with three big strapping brothers my whole life," Emily said. "We didn't even start breakfast if we didn't have three dozen eggs in the house."

"And two pounds of sausage," Tag added as he picked up a plate at the end of the buffet line. "And you should see Hud put away pancakes. He can put the Hulk to shame."

That word, *goodbye*, had stuck in Rose's mind. It wouldn't be long until she had to leave Texas and make the trip to Kentucky. Just thinking about leaving Hud put a lump in her throat.

Chapter Eleven

Monday turned out to be a decent day—cold but the sun was shining, so Hud and Tag worked all day getting a section of new fence put in and the old wood posts that were mostly rotten and the sagging barbed wire redone. At noon Hud went back to Tag's house, where Nikki had left a slow cooker full of beef stew for them that day. Tag dipped it up into two bowls while Hud sliced a loaf of homemade bread.

"She was a cute kid, but she's turned into a pretty woman," Tag said as he sat down at the table.

"Who?"

"Come on now," Tag teased. "You know exactly who I'm talking about. I saw the way you looked at her in church yesterday, and I heard about your trip to the jailhouse on Saturday night."

"I don't know about being a hero, or if I was if it would do any good." Hud set the bread on the table, pulled out a chair, and eased down into it. "She'll most likely be leaving in a few weeks to reenlist. I might never see her again."

"That's a half-empty-bottle-of-beer attitude." Tag slathered a piece of bread with butter. "Think of it more like a half full bottle of beer. As in you've got a few weeks to change her mind. Believe me, I had a hard time changing Nikki's mind. You weren't nearly as wild as I was, so it might be easier on you. What is it about her that makes you want her to stay? You can kick any mesquite bush between here and Oklahoma and a dozen women will come runnin' toward you, so why Rose?"

Hud removed his hat and ran his hands through his hair. "I can't put it into words. It's something in here." He touched his chest.

"Then she's the one. That's the way I felt about Nikki," Tag said.

"I don't want to rush things, and I'm afraid that she couldn't find work around here even if she didn't reenlist." Hud sighed.

"What'd she do in the army?" Tag asked.

"She speaks a gazillion languages, so she translated. She's been everywhere, including two tours in Afghanistan."

"There's not much call for that sort of thing in this part of the country unless she can speak cow language."

Hud shook his head and frowned. "Don't think she knows that one."

"Too bad," Tag said. "If she did, I'd hire her to work here."

They finished eating and then went back out to take care of more fencing until dark. Hud was used to hard work. He'd been putting up fence, hauling hay, and plowing fields since before he was a teenager. His muscles might ache at the end of the day, but it was a good tired, as his grandpa used to say. One that could see progress. That evening his muscles told him that he'd put in a long day, but his mind was just as weary as his body. He'd thought all afternoon about the conversation he'd had with Tag. He tried to figure out more reasons why he loved being with Rose, and it all came back to what he felt in his heart.

After he'd taken a long, hot shower, he put on a pair of pajama pants and sent Rose a text: *Busy?*

She replied: *Not really? Want to talk?*

He called her and she answered on the first ring. "Thank you so much for last night," she said. "It really helped Aunt Luna to get out, but she's gone back into a pout. I swear, if I had Uncle Wilbur's number, I'd get in touch with him and tell him that it was time to end this argument."

"I wanted to kiss you good night, but there were so many people that..." He paused.

"I would have blushed for sure, and Aunt Luna would have teased me all the way home. Speaking of embarrassment, I hope Aunt Luna didn't..." She hesitated.

"Honey, she was the life of the party," Hud cut in. "We all love getting together, and Emily likes to entertain, so we celebrate everything. I sure miss Paxton this evening. Want to come out here and keep an old cowboy company?"

"Can't tonight." She sighed. "Aunt Luna won't get far away from the phone, so I should stay with her. I don't know what she'll do if Wilbur doesn't call in the next couple of days."

"So, no square dancing on Wednesday night if he doesn't call?" Hud asked.

"She says we're going to that dance for sure, and he can just wait until the next day. That'll be his punishment for not calling when she's here. But I'm a little worried," Rose said. "It's crazy the way I feel all protective of her. I haven't even known her a whole week, but we've been through so much together."

"They say that blood is thicker than water. What did they fight about anyway?" he asked.

"I'm not real sure, but I'd bet it was over some checker at the grocery store who's been makin' eyes at her Wilbur," Rose replied.

"Sure about what?" He heard Luna say and then there was a distant buzz of conversation that he couldn't make out.

"It's Aunt Molly on the house phone," Rose told him. "I'd better go. Aunt Luna needs me to show her how to put the phone on speaker so we can both talk."

"Good night," Hud said.

"Night to you." She ended the call.

* * *

Luna handed the receiver over to Rose. "Fix it so we can all talk. Some of her friends are in her room too."

Rose pushed the speaker button and laid the phone back on the base. "Hello, everyone. Luna and I are on this end."

"Patsy, Bess, Sarah, Otis, and Larry are here with me," Molly said. "We're all homesick for gossip, so talk to us. I've already told them about Dixie and the baby. We can't wait to get home so we can get acquainted with them."

"Patsy here," a husky voice said, "what's this about Paxton going back out to West Texas?"

"We had his going-away party last night," Luna said. "It was fabulous."

"Otis here," a masculine voice said. "Hud's going to be real lonesome out there by himself. Tag's married, and now Paxton's gone."

"This is Sarah," another feminine voice said. "Honey, you should spend some time with that poor old lonesome cowboy."

"All right, enough about us," Rose said. "Tell me and Luna about your travels."

"It's been wonderful, but we should've only booked the month-long vacation instead of the six-week one," Molly said. "I'm ready to come home. Have you heard from Wilbur yet, Luna? I've been meanin' to ask you what did y'all fight about this time, anyway?"

"Ain't heard from him yet, and like you, I'm ready to go home. I love our niece, but I miss my friends and the trailer park," Luna replied. "I'm getting a bus ticket for next Monday whether he calls or not. And we had a big blowup because he's been flirting with a woman down at the grocery store. She can't be a day over fifty, and I got jealous."

"Good God," Molly giggled, "Wilbur is eighty years old. What would a woman thirty years younger want with him?"

"Darlin', they make something called Viagra now, and like Mr. Toby Keith sings about, he might not be as good as he once was, but believe me, he's as good once as he ever was. The doctor said as long as his heart is good, he can have one of them little pills every day," Luna told her.

"And you left him in her clutches? You think that was smart?" Molly asked.

"I'm testin' him, and, honey, I counted the pills left in his Viagra bottle before I left. If there's any gone when I get home, they ain't never goin' to find his or her bodies," Luna said. "I'm sorry you wasn't here to visit with me, but you could write me a letter every so often," Luna told her.

"If you will, I will," Molly said.

"It's a deal. Isn't it really late there?" Luna asked.

"It's two o'clock in the morning," Molly answered. "We just came home from dancing in a pub and having a late-night supper at an all-night café."

"Well, hot damn!" Luna clapped her hands. "You might be old as dirt, but you're finally livin' just a little bit."

"Oh, hush," Molly said. "Good night to both of you."

"Night," Luna and Rose said in unison.

Rose ended the call and glanced over at Luna. "Do you really think that Uncle Wilbur was interested in that woman, or was he just trying to make you jealous?"

Luna shook her head. "Oh, he was interested all right. He's always been a big flirt, but this time, he went too far."

"How's that?" Rose asked.

"She's got a grandson livin' with her. Kid must be about ten years old, and she needed a babysitter one day. Be damned, if Wilbur didn't offer to keep the boy and then he bought him a BB gun with our money. That's when we had the fight. I'm not a mean person when it comes to kids, but Wilbur should've talked to me as well as that kid's mama about letting him have any kind of gun before he bought the damn thing," Luna said.

"I might have been mad about that too." Rose draped an arm around her aunt, and the two of them headed out of the room.

She went to her room and watched reruns of *Longmire* on the television. Branch Connally, the deputy sheriff in the western show, reminded her of Hud. Not as much in looks as in the way he walked, and his attitude. Suddenly, every incident from the time she saw Hud at the wedding out in West Texas passed through her mind at warp speed, only slowing down when she concentrated on special moments— like when Hud kissed her or tucked her hand into his. How could so much happen in such a short length of time?

In another few days everything would change again, because Aunt Luna had said she was going home, no matter what. To everything there is a season. She thought of those words, which her mother had spoken the only time she'd ever seen her stand and say anything in a Sunday morning service at the commune.

The episode ended and Rose realized that she had been staring at the screen but seeing or hearing very little. She hit the POWER button to turn off the television and just lay there, staring at the ceiling. Was this her season to be out of the army for good? Or was it just a short season to help her decide to be absolutely sure what she wanted to do with the rest of her life?

Her phone rang and, figuring it would be Hud, she answered without even looking at the caller ID. "Hello, I'm so glad you called."

"You must've been thinking about me," her mother said.

"I guess I was in a roundabout way. I'm glad to hear from you," Rose said. "Mama, I don't know what to do about reenlisting."

"You've still got some time, so think about it some more, but you know what Granny Dee used to say—'if you ain't in peace, then it ain't for you.' If it don't seem right in your heart, then don't do it. Something that does bring you happiness will come along, but you've got to wait for it."

"I've never been good at that waiting business." Rose sighed. "What I'd like to do is use my skills in some way to help people, but how does what I know fit into that?"

"You never know, honey," Echo said. "It will all be revealed to you in some way, and the way it makes you feel will be the right thing for you to do. Now, when are you coming to see me?"

"Depends on when Aunt Molly gets home," she said.

"Well, just between me and you, I hope she cuts her trip short. Good night, my child. I'm so looking forward to seeing you, and so are your friends," Echo said.

"Good night, Mama," Rose said.

The room felt as if the walls were closing in on her, so

she went back downstairs, thinking maybe she'd make herself a cup of hot chocolate. She found Luna watching old reruns of *Gunsmoke* on the television and crying. She sat down beside her and slung an arm around Luna's shoulders. "What's wrong?" she asked.

"Me and Wilbur watch this every night together." She wiped her eyes on the back of her hand. "I miss that old sumbitch. Why hasn't he called and apologized to me for what he did?"

"He'll call soon," Rose assured her. "Mama called."

"I've always loved Echo. She's an old soul. I just wish she hadn't fallen in love with Paul," Luna sighed. "I'm sure she's told you about how they met, hasn't she?"

"He was raised out in the commune by his uncle who was the overseer there, and he worked in Harlan," Rose answered. "Daddy was in the open-air market where she was selling produce for her grandpa, and he bought a watermelon from her. She says it was love at first sight."

"It had to be, for her to put up with Paul," Luna said. "He's a tyrant, but she picks her battles. Most of them have always been about you."

"I know that." Rose nodded. "He's a hard man, and it's not easy livin' with him, but he needs Mama to smooth out all those sharp edges. I'd hate to see what kind of man he'd be without her."

"The military has been good for you." Luna turned off the television. "I worried about you when you enlisted, but I got to admit, I admired your spunk in standing up to Paul the way you did."

"I wanted to see more of the world." Rose leaned down and gave Luna a kiss on the forehead, and started up to her room. "Good night."

"Night, darlin' girl," Luna said.

Rose's phone pinged as she climbed the stairs. She slipped it out of her hip pocket to find a text from Hud.

It was just a link to a song, "You Make It Easy," by Jason Aldean. She smiled all through the lyrics and then sent back a heart emoji to him, and then she listened to it a dozen more times before she finally fell asleep with the phone on the pillow beside her.

* * *

Tuesday was one of those never-ending days for Hud. He and Tag worked all day long, plowing up fields to get ready for spring planting. His grandpa used to tell them that a ranch was only as good as its fences, and that they were supposed to be bull tight.

That evening, he flopped down on the sofa. He had been one of the first to complain about four grown men in a small house, but now he wished they were all back. Another of his grandpa's sayings came to mind—"you don't know what you've got until it's gone." He picked up his cell from the coffee table and sent a text to Paxton: *How's things?*

He got one right back: *Great to be here. Still adjusting. Lots of work.*

He sent back one more: *Call when you have time.*

Paxton sent back a thumbs-up emoji.

Hud had felt like he'd lost a brother instead of a distant cousin when Maverick left to go help out his grandmother when she'd broken a hip. Maverick was only supposed to be gone a month or so, but things changed when the grandmother gave her ranch to him and Paxton. Hud couldn't wish anything but the best for them, but he wasn't used to an empty house, and he really didn't like it. He missed the way Mav was always teasing, and the conversations he'd had with Paxton when Tag moved into the little cabin over on Longhorn Canyon. Living alone was downright lonely.

He fell asleep on the sofa and woke up after midnight with a kink in his neck. He stood up and rolled his head, stretched his arms upward, and went to the kitchen for a snack before he went on to bed. When he laid his phone on the counter, he noticed he had two messages. One was from Paxton saying that he'd be on a tractor all day tomorrow and would call him then. The other was from Rose, asking if he was going to make it to the square-dancing event with Aunt Luna.

He sent Rose a message: *Yes, ma'am. Six thirty, right?*

Then he fired one off to Paxton: *Anytime tomorrow. I'll be on a tractor too.*

Hud ate a handful of chocolate cookies and drank a glass of milk, then went on to bed. He slept poorly the rest of the night, dreaming and waking up in a cold sweat, then going back to sleep and having another dream and waking up freezing. The next morning when the alarm went off, he felt more tired than he had when he'd gone to bed. He dragged himself to the kitchen, ate a bowl of cold cereal, and had three cups of coffee. Then he filled his thermos with four more cups and made himself a peanut butter and jelly sandwich to eat at noon in the tractor.

Paxton called him before he had made the first long trip around the forty-acre field. "You on the tractor yet?"

"Yep," Hud answered. "You seen Alana yet?"

"Nope, I still got two good legs, and I can run." Paxton laughed. "So have you seen Rose since the party?"

"Nope, but we're taking her aunt square-dancing tonight." He braked when he saw Red running toward him. When he opened the tractor door, the dog used the step as a springboard, hopped across his lap, and sat in the passenger seat. "Had to stop and let Red in. Guess he wants to be a rancher."

Paxton laughed. "Ducky's little legs are so short, he'd have to get a ladder to get to the first step on a tractor. He's pretty good at herdin' cows, though. I can't believe you're goin' square dancin'."

"Iris didn't take Ducky with her to the assisted living place?" Hud asked.

"Nope," Paxton replied. "She gave him to Bridget and the cat Dolly to Laela. My granny is a wise woman. She knew that Bridget couldn't take them two animals to Ireland with her, and she couldn't leave them behind." Paxton chuckled. "Mav and Bridget are so danged happy, it makes me want to settle down."

"That's a lot of happy." Hud laughed.

"How about you?" Paxton asked. "Am I fixin' to win that money and whiskey?"

"I'm not sure," Hud told him. "I feel something for her that I've never felt with any other woman."

"I could see that from the beginnin', but here's the problem as I see it. Like the rest of us four who've shared bunkhouses and ranches together, you never have seriously dated. You've had lots of one-night stands with bar bunnies, and some even went over into a whole weekend, but to really date? Not so much. Don't you think you should do a little of that before you dive into a committed relationship?" Paxton asked.

"Maverick didn't, and neither did Tag," Hud argued.

"Maverick kind of knew Bridget from Ireland, and Tag had met Nikki when she came home with Emily that time," Paxton reminded him.

"And I went to school with Rose, so I kind of know her," Hud argued.

"Just be careful," Paxton cautioned. "Since we've seen our older brothers so happy and settling down, it's kind of given us both the fever. We need to let a little time pass so we're sure of what we want to do. I'm going to the Wild Cowboy Bar this weekend. That'll cure all these crazy feelings about living with one woman the rest of my life."

"Maybe I should go to the Rusty Spur and see if it works for me," Hud chuckled.

"We got to be strong," Paxton said. "One of us can't fold, or who'll be there to support the other one?"

"You're just afraid you'll stumble and fall, and Alana will lasso you," Hud told him.

"And I'll lose a hundred dollars," Paxton reminded him. "I hate to lose money. Got to go. Got a call coming in from Maverick."

Hud put the phone in his shirt pocket. He didn't like losing either, but for the same kind of happiness Tag had, he'd gladly fork over a hundred-dollar bill.

Chapter Twelve

Rose hadn't done any square dancing since she left Kentucky, so she was a little nervous about it that night. Luna told her to just watch her and do what the caller said and the most important thing was to have fun.

"Wear a skirt, the fuller the better," she said. "When me and Wilbur got all involved with it right after we moved to Alabama, I had a whole outfit made up, and one for Wilbur to match. We got pretty good at it."

Rose found a gauze skirt with layers in her closet and paired it with a bright, turquoise knit shirt. "What about shoes?" she called down the staircase.

"Cowboy boots," Aunt Luna yelled.

Aunt Luna was waiting for her at the bottom of the stairs when Rose started down. "You look great, and not to worry. Y'all can even sit the first one out to get the hang of it, but you ain't goin' to be wallflowers all night. I want to see the two of you dance."

"I'll do my best," Rose agreed just as the doorbell rang.

Luna grabbed her coat from the rack on the way to answer it, and then looked over her shoulder. "Our golden chariot is here. Let's don't keep Prince Charming waiting." She opened the door and stepped out onto the porch.

"I don't mind being Prince Charming." Hud's eyes twinkled when he saw Rose. "Especially when I get to escort Cinderella to the ball." He slung an arm around Rose's shoulders and pulled her against his side.

"If I'm Cinderella then I'll have to be home before midnight," Rose told him.

"Honey, the do-si-do stuff ends at ten," Luna told her.

"And"—Hud walked Rose to the truck—"I figure that'll give us time to get some ice cream and still get you home before midnight. If you lose a shoe, I'll be by tomorrow to see if it fits you."

"And if it does?" she asked.

"Then I'll have to carry you off to my mansion on Canyon Creek, where you'll be a princess forever and ever amen," he replied.

"Lord, help my soul." Aunt Luna threw a hand over her heart. "That's the most romantic thing I've heard in years."

Rose felt the heat start at her neck and work its way up to her cheeks. By the time Hud was in the driver's seat, the temperature in the truck had jacked up at least ten degrees— maybe even a few more when she took a second look at him in his ironed jeans, pearl snap shirt the color of his eyes, and his polished black boots. Prince Charming didn't have a thing on Hudson Baker that night!

When they arrived at the VFW, Rose glanced up at the clear night sky. Stars looked like diamonds lying on a bed of black velvet. A gentle breeze blew her hair to the side as they went from the truck to the building. They could hear lots of noise and the caller singsonging the dance steps before they even opened the door. The minute they were inside, Aunt Luna went over to a group of elderly gentlemen, said a few words, and in seconds she and one of them had joined a group that needed one more couple.

"We're about to do a rip and snort," Luna told Rose and Hud. "Y'all watch close and you can do it the next time around."

"Yeah, right." Rose grinned as she and Hud each took a chair along the wall. Before the dance set was half done, Rose was tapping her foot to the fiddle, banjo, and guitar music.

"Looks like you're gettin' into it," Hud said.

"I'm trying to remember what he's saying and how to do the steps, so I don't embarrass you," she said.

He leaned over and whispered softly in her ear, "You could stumble and fall right into my arms, and I wouldn't care, as long as I can spend time with you. I was thinkin' maybe we could go dancing at the Rusty Spur on Saturday night. I'm a little better at two-steppin' than I am at square dancing, and besides I'd like to hold you close to me, not swing you out."

His warm breath on the sensitive part of her neck sent shivers down her spine. She turned toward him so that her mouth was next to his ear. "I haven't been to a honky-tonk in years."

He whipped his head around and kissed her right there in public. "Then you'll go with me?"

"Yes, Hud, I'd love to go."

The first dance ended, and the dancers who'd been on the floor headed for the bar to get drinks. Aunt Luna winked at Rose when she passed her and nodded out to the floor at a group that was looking around for another couple.

"Well, I guess this is it." Hud took her hand in his. "If I'd realized there was a bar back there, I might have had a beer to loosen me up a little before we started this."

"I'd have had a double shot of Jack." She smiled up at him.

"Y'all new at this," one of the older gentlemen asked, "or are you old veterans?"

"I'm technically not a veteran yet," Rose answered. "I'm trying to decide whether to reenlist after my leave is up. And it's been years since I've square-danced, so you'll have to bear with me," Rose said.

"It's all right, honey." The man's wrinkles deepened when he smiled. "These other two couples here with me and Mama ain't never done the dancin' before either, so it'll be a learnin' experience for all y'all. And thank you for your service, darlin'."

"You are so welcome," Rose said just as the fiddle music started.

The caller said to circle to the left and then to the right, and then to swing your partner high and low. Hud got all involved with that part, swinging her out and back again and then dipping her before he went back to the circle. Square dancing was a little like riding a bicycle—after a couple of rounds, it was all coming back to her. At the end of the set, the caller said to promenade her off the floor.

Hud wrapped his arm around her shoulder and danced her right over to the bar. They passed Luna on the way, and she grabbed the old guy's hand that she'd danced with before.

"I love the auctioneer dance, and Teddy here tells me he's the best at it. I'm about to show him up," she told Rose.

"What're you havin'?" the bartender asked.

"Coors in a bottle," Hud answered and then looked over at Rose.

"The same," she said, still a little breathless from those *swing your partner wide* parts of the dance, and just from being that near to Hud through the whole dance. Strange thing was that when they changed partners and another cowboy not much older than Hud had held her hand, there had been no electricity between them. When Hud had grabbed her hand again, she'd felt the vibes all the way to her toes.

"I thought you wanted a double shot of Jack," Hud said.

"That was to get me loosened up to dance," she told him. "Beer is because I'm thirsty, and I don't mix the two, especially after last weekend."

"So did you like square dancing?" he asked.

"Not as much as I do two-stepping," she told him. "I really love an old country waltz or swing dancing, but I'm sure I'm pretty rusty at both."

"I have no doubt that as quick as you picked up the steps to square dancin', that you'll do fine with two-stepping or waltzing." His gaze locked with hers and she felt as if he could see to the bottom of her soul. "I could get lost in your green eyes, Rose. When I'm with you and can just stare into your eyes all I want, it's like swimming in a river of peace."

"You've got quite a way with words, cowboy," Rose said. "Wouldn't peace be nice, though?" She brought her bottle to her lips for another sip. "I see that you're settling into your ranch, and I want the peace and contentment that you have."

"Then stick around this area," he suggested.

"There's not much call for my skill set in Bowie, Texas," she said.

"Do you have to get a job right away? Can you take a few weeks to look around? I'm sure you could live with your Aunt Molly for a while," he suggested.

"Not for very long," she said. "I love her and love visiting with her, but living with her for more than a week wouldn't be a good idea. She's too bossy. If I want someone like that, I can just go back to the commune and let my dad run my life."

"He did that?" Hud asked.

She nodded. "Daddy is the overseer of the whole commune. His word is law, and in his world, women obey their husbands," she said. "I'm not much at that submit stuff, so he and I clashed horns."

"Shut your eyes, Rose," he said.

"I told you, I don't obey too well," she told him.

"It's just a little test," he told her. "I'm not ordering you to do it, but I'm trying to help you make a decision."

She closed her eyes. "Okay, now what?"

"Imagine yourself on a beach with the sound of the waves," he said. "But don't open your eyes yet. Now think about being in the mountains with the cool, crisp mornings. Next think about the commune and your family there. Then last think about Bowie, Texas, and the rolling hills and kissing me."

Her eyes popped wide open.

"Which one did you like best?" He leaned over to the side and kissed her ever so sweetly.

"Your kisses—those were the very best. If you're talking about places, I loved them all when I was there, but part of me is afraid I'll get bored in one place," she admitted.

He continued to stare into her eyes, but he didn't say a word.

Dammit! She wanted him to tell her that he'd be ecstatic if she stayed in Bowie, and to say that would give them longer to get to really know each other. Sometimes trying to read him was like staring at a big stone.

* * *

Hud thought his poor old heart would jump right out of his chest when she said she might stay in Bowie for a while.

"Rose O'Malley calling Hudson Baker," she said over the noise.

"I'm sorry," he apologized. "My mind was floating out there in space somewhere."

"I noticed." Her tone was slightly cool. "Am I boring you?"

"No, darlin', you definitely are not. Do you want to dance or have another beer?" he asked.

"Another beer," she told him. "I motioned for the bartender and already paid for this round."

"Shhh..." He put his finger on her lips. "The Texas wind will carry your words right to my mama and granny's ears, and they'll pick a switch off the scrub oak in the front yard and whip my butt if they find out."

"This is the modern world where women ask men out on dates, and they pay for the drinks or even the food," she told him.

"But us rough old cowboys still live by the code," he said.

"What code?" she asked as the bartender set two more beers on the bar.

He held up one finger. "Live each day with courage."

Then another finger shot up. "Take pride in your work."

One more finger came up with each sentence. "When you make a promise keep it. Ride for the brand. Do what has to be done. Finish what you start. Be tough, but fair. Talk less, say more. Remember that some things ain't for sale. Know where to draw the line. Respect women." He stopped for a breath. "And that means being a gentleman and paying for drinks. And always, always love your wife, because that teaches the children that she's the important thing in your life."

"Is that really the code?" she asked.

He nodded seriously. "Only my grandpa added those last two things about respecting women and loving your wife. He said that they were the most important items in the code for a cowboy, so that's why I ran out of fingers."

"Sounds to me like the code should be a way of life for everyone, not just cowboys," she told him.

"Sure make this old earth an easier place to live in if they did, wouldn't it? Was there a soldier's code that you went by in the army?" he asked.

"I guess so." She shrugged.

"How did it go?" he asked.

"It said that I'm a member of a team, and that I serve the people of the United States. That I live the army values, will always place the mission first, and never accept defeat. I will never leave a fallen comrade behind, and that I'll guard the freedom and the American way of life. I'm not sure I got all that in the right order," she said.

"It's different words, but it pretty much says the same thing, doesn't it?" He took a long drink from the bottle. "Did you always put the mission first?"

"I did, but I'm struggling with that right now. I need to know what my mission in life is before I can put it first, and that takes making a decision," she replied. "At first it wasn't so hard for me. No kids, no ties, just my folks and Aunt Molly, and every blue moon I'd see Aunt Luna, but spending two tours in the Middle East taught me that I love green grass and am not fond of sand in everything," she told him.

"Ever get PTSD?" he asked.

"Nope, but I did have trouble sleeping when I first got there. There was always noise, and tent living quarters didn't make for great sleeping quarters. Then when I got home, it was so quiet that I finally bought one of those little wind machines to put beside my bed," she answered.

He could have sat there until dawn just talking to her and listening to her soft southern voice, but when ten o'clock rolled around the square dance caller told everyone that this was the last set.

"Shall we dance this one, or just watch Aunt Luna?" he asked.

"Let's give up our barstools and go sit in our original chairs. That way when it's over, we'll be ready to take her home," Rose answered.

By the time they had walked around the perimeter of the room, the caller was telling the dancers to escort the ladies off the floor. Luna came right over to them and said, "This was so much fun. I just wish Wilbur was here with me, but truth be told, Teddy was better at the dance than Wilbur. I'm going to get me a shot of Jameson to help me sleep like a baby."

She declared that she didn't even want ice cream when they reached the truck, so Hud drove straight to the B&B. Luna slung the back door open, and said, "All right, kids, y'all can sit out here and make out, but at midnight Cinderella turns from a princess into a scrub girl again. She ain't lost a shoe, so you don't have a reason to show up tomorrow, Hud, so you'd best make the most of the rest of the night." She giggled as she started toward the house. When she got halfway there, she turned and came back. "Give me the key. I'll leave the door open for you."

Rose fumbled in her purse, brought out a hot-pink fluffy key chain, and handed it off to her aunt.

When Luna was in the house, Hud leaned across the console, cupped Rose's cheeks in his hands, and kissed her. He teased her mouth open with his tongue and had just begun to get into the kiss when she pulled away.

"Charley horse in my ribs from this damned console," she said. "Walk me to the porch and let's sit on the swing."

"In the cold?" he asked.

"You're warming me up pretty damn good, cowboy." She grinned.

He hurried out of the truck, but she already had the door open and was sliding out of the seat when he got to her side. He tucked her hand into his and led her to the porch. He sat down first and pulled her down onto his lap. The chains creaked with each movement, but he didn't care, not as long as his lips were on hers. He slipped his hands under her coat and pulled her body close to his. The only noise was the whisper of the wind as it blew through the bare pecan tree limbs and the beating of their hearts as they tried to sync up with one another. Her arms went around his neck, and she took off his hat, laid it to the side, and then tangled her fingers in his hair. He moved one of his hands from her back to hold her head steady for the next kiss.

Finally, she pulled away. "Darlin', one more kiss, and we're either going to see if this swing will support a wild bout of sex or we're going to set this whole house on fire."

"I'll repair the swing if we break it," he offered.

She traced his jawline with her finger. "I hate to even say it, but we'd better call it a night. I can't tell you when I've had more fun. Sitting on the barstool and talking to you was so..." She seemed to be reaching for the right word.

"Comfortable and yet romantic." His lips zeroed in on hers, and they were making out again.

She kissed him back until they had to stop for breath, and she stood up, held out her hand, and said, "Walk me to the door, and kiss me once more."

"That sounds like an old Ray Price tune that my grandpa used to sing," he said.

"I thought Conway Twitty laid claim to that one." She pulled at his hand.

"He covered it a few years after Ray did it. It was a faster tune. Let's do Ray's version, since it's slower." He got to his feet and wrapped both arms around Rose's waist. "One kiss, one step."

Ten kisses later they were at the door. "I need a couple more to get me home. I may not see you again until Saturday night."

"Maybe three to hold me until then," she breathed into his ear.

Half a dozen kisses later, she handed him his hat and finally went inside. He hummed "Honey Bee" and danced all the way to the truck. He'd couldn't wait to tell Paxton that there was a possibility she'd be living in Bowie.

* * *

Thursday Rose uncovered more boxes of stuff in the storage room, and put out Easter items on one display shelf, and Mother's Day on another one. She got the first text from Hud when she was arranging cute little plaques and necklaces that had to do with mothers.

He asked: *Busy?*

She shot one back: *Yep. No end to gift shop stuff.*

One came back: *Call you tonight?*

She sent back a smiley face with hearts for eyes.

So many things reminded her of the last Mother's Day she'd spent with her own mother three years ago. She'd come home on a week's leave and had gotten her mother a tabletop mixer. She'd known that her mother, Echo, would take it to the dining room for everyone in the commune to use, but that was okay with Rose, because her mother was the primary cook. When she was a little girl, she'd always picked a bouquet of wildflowers from the fields of Kentucky, and later when she was a teenager, she'd made her a necklace from a smooth river rock hanging on braided strips of cloth.

Seeing all those little Mother's Day things made her miss her mama so much. She sat down on the dusty wooden floor of the storage room, put her head in her hands, and let the tears flow. When she had children, she wanted them to live so close that she could see them every year on Mother's Day. She hoped they would bring her bouquets and maybe little handmade things that she could keep forever.

She wiped her tears away with the back of her hand and hurried into the shop to answer the phone. "Rose Garden Bed-and-Breakfast."

"Miz Molly?" a thin little high-pitched voice asked.

"This is her niece, Rose. Miz Molly is out of town on vacation, and I'm taking care of things for her," she said.

"Well, darlin', this is Edna Davis, and we have reservations for tomorrow night. I'm just calling to make sure that everything is still good for us to arrive after three," Edna said.

"That's perfectly all right," Rose said.

"Well, we had a wonderful honeymoon there many years ago and we always come back to the B&B to relive it. Tell Miz Molly hello for us," she said.

"Yes, ma'am," Rose said.

"Bye now," Edna said and the call ended.

"Who was that?" Luna poked her head in the door.

"We've got guests coming tomorrow night. I guess Aunt Molly didn't get a few of them called to cancel reservations before she left," Rose told her.

"Well, dammit! I thought maybe someone died." Luna's eyes twinkled.

"Aunt Luna!" Rose scolded.

Luna shrugged. "I was only teasing, but I do like a good wake."

Luna came into the room and peeked inside a box of Christmas items. "I'll help you get this crap put out. Folks is going to swarm in here like flies on cow patties soon as they hear we've got more stuff at half price."

"You're pretty good at selling stuff," Rose told her.

"Comes from hawkin' stuffed animals and other trinkets at the carnival." She carried two snow globes at a time toward an empty shelf.

"I thought you were a fortune-teller," Rose said.

"I was until I got tired of it. I tried everything there was to do in the carnival before we sold the thing. Sometimes I wish me and Wilbur woulda kept it until we died." She came back for a couple more snow globes and wound each one up before she put it on the shelf. "Why on earth would people collect these things?"

Rose started setting out Mother's Day things. "I don't know. We didn't have room at the commune to have much that couldn't be shared with everyone else. When I got into the military, I didn't want to surround myself with stuff I'd have to move."

The phone rang again, and Rose ran from the back of the shop to the checkout counter. She grabbed it on the third ring, and answered it.

"Hello, this is a friend of Luna's. Would she be around?" A man with a deep southern drawl asked. Was it finally Wilbur? Rose wondered. Or perhaps it might be Teddy from the square dancing the night before.

"Sure thing. Just hold on," she said.

"You will need to deposit another two dollars and thirty cents," the tinny voice of a telephone operator said.

"Aunt Luna, it's for you, and it's from a pay phone," Rose said.

"Thank God!" Luna had just wound up another snow globe, and she carried it back to the checkout with her. She took the phone from Rose and said, "Wilbur, you old sumbitch, why'd you wait so long to call me?"

She listened for a minute while Rose went back to unload the rest of her box of Mother's Day things, and then there was a crash. Rose peeked around the end of the shelving to see that Luna had dropped the snow globe on the floor. All the color had drained from her face, and she was slowly sliding down the back side of the counter toward the floor. Rose had started to run toward her when she noticed that Luna's eyes were rolling back in her head. She barely made it before her aunt fell right into the pile of broken glass. The music box in the snow globe was still playing "Blue Christmas."

"Aunt Luna, open your eyes, and talk to me," Rose said as she reached for her phone to call 911.

Tears flowed down her aunt's face as she opened her eyes just enough to look up at Rose. "That sumbitch married that woman from the grocery store. He flat-out married her in a courthouse wedding, and he's moved out of our trailer and in with her. And he didn't even call me and tell me his self. One of the guys from the trailer park called. He wouldn't marry me or give me a weddin' ring, and now she's got both."

Chapter Thirteen

Rose had held Luna close, their tears blending together and dripping off their faces onto their shirts. "I'm so, so sorry. Why would he do that so quickly? You've only been gone a little while."

"Must've been happening right under my nose, and he just waited for me to get mad and leave," she whimpered.

"He took the car too, since that was in his name and not mine, and so is the trailer. Reuben, that's my friend at the trailer park, he said that the trailer is up for sale. Wilbur told him that if I want to pay for it, then I can call him." Luna pushed Rose away and narrowed her eyes. "I ain't shellin' out a single dime of my money."

"Aunt Luna, where are you going to live?"

"After I go home and make a trip to the bank, I'll make up my mind then. I bet he's forgot that all the money we got from the sale of the carnival was put in my name," Luna said.

"Why would you do that?" Rose asked.

"We retired because he got colon cancer, and we put everything in my name just in case he didn't make it. He got over it in a few months, and we just never did get around to changin' things. When we took out the money for the car and trailer and put some in a fund to live on, he laughed and said that he should have those things fixed in his name," she explained. "'Course, I did have it fixed so that if I died, it was all his. That's what I've got to go fix."

The music box finally stopped playing and Luna slapped the top of the counter. Another note or two sounded but then it quit again. Even a broken music box was afraid to cross Aunt Luna when she was angry.

"If you could do the business over the phone with the bank, you could just stay here," Rose suggested.

"Oh, hell, no!" Luna dried her eyes and glared across the room as if she was looking at something—or someone. "Tomorrow I'm getting on a bus, and I'm going home to take care of things in person. Put a CLOSED sign on the door, and go get a bottle of whiskey. I need a drink even if it is only ten o'clock in the morning. When I get home, I intend to hunt that old sumbitch down and give him a piece of my mind."

"Will you promise me that you'll leave Madam at home?" Rose had sworn she'd never drink with Luna again, but she went to the kitchen and took a half-full bottle of Jameson from the cabinet and a full one of Old Rip Van Winkle, the whiskey Aunt Molly saved for very special occasions. By damn, this was the time for it.

"I give you my word. I'm going to refill his Viagra for him and take it to him for a weddin' present," Luna said. "I found some little blue candy a while back that looks just like them pills. I intend to swap them out. We'll see how much that hussy likes him when nothing will pop up."

When she got back, Luna had cleaned up all the glass from the broken snow globe. "I had to do something or else I would have put a curse on Wilbur, and I need to think about just how mean I want to be when I conjure up my spell."

"Whatever you need, I'm right here to do it with you," Rose assured her.

"Then call us in a pizza. We ain't had breakfast and we'll need something in our stomachs before we get too far into the bottle. Not even Luna Ferry Wilson can hold that lot of whiskey on an empty stomach."

"Fairy?" Rose frowned.

"Not as in little critters with wings, but as in a big flat boat that carries people from one side of the river to the other." She took the Old Van Winkle from Rose, opened it, and took a long swig. "Molly will pass little green apples when she comes home and finds that we drank all her best whiskey."

Rose reached for the bottle, and Luna handed it over.

"Then we'll make a green apple pie." Rose turned it up for a swallow. "Damn, that is some smooth whiskey."

"Yep," Luna said. "You'd best call in that pizza now, because once I get started, I just keep on drinkin' and drinkin', like that song on the radio."

Rose made the call and asked them to deliver it to the back door, and then she plopped down on the sofa beside Luna. "I'm going to miss you. Do you really have to go?"

"Yes, honey, I do," Luna said. "I'll come visit you when you and Hud have your first child. Maybe you'll even let me name her."

"No, ma'am, I will not ever put my daughter through the teasing that I got because you named me Cactus," Rose told her.

"Honey, your grandma's name was Devine. Your mama's name is Echo. We couldn't very well name you Susie or Kathy, now could we?" Luna asked her.

"Well, I'm going to break with tradition," Rose declared.

"How long after you and Hud get married are you going to start a family? You know you're already older than your grandmother was when she had Echo and your mother when she had you," Luna said.

"Aunt Luna, this is about you getting over Wilbur marryin' another woman, not about me and Hud. Can he even do that legally? I mean isn't it considered common law when you've been together as long as y'all have?" Rose put the bottle to her mouth and pretended to take a sip and then handed it to her aunt.

"To Wilbur." Luna held up the bottle. "May you and your new woman fight every day and be miserable until the day you both die."

Rose took the bottle and said, "To Wilbur. I hope that you regret the day you left my aunt for that other woman." She set the bottle on the table.

Luna picked it up again and kissed the side of it. "I remember the first time Wilbur kissed me and the last. The first time rocked my world, as you kids say. I was only seventeen and he kissed me out behind one of the tents. The last time, it was a peck on the forehead, because we were arguing. He said that he'd see me when I got over my snit." She put her lips to the bottle and took another drink. "He ain't never goin' to see me again, because I refuse to go to hell, and after this stunt God ain't goin' to let him into heaven."

Tears began to roll down her cheeks again, settling in the wrinkles until they were full and then going on to drip off her jaw. "We even made a pact that we'd go together like in that movie *The Notebook*, so neither one of us would have to grieve, and look what he's done."

"I've heard there's many steps to grief, and the first one is denial, and it's for divorce and death alike," Rose said.

Luna dried her eyes and cheeks on the tail of her shirt. "He's not dead. Put the cap on that bottle. Wilbur is about to see the wrath of Luna Ferry Wilson. Call the bus station and put me on the first one going east, and don't let me forget Madam." She hopped up and headed for the bedroom.

"What are you fixing to do?" Rose asked.

"Pack," Luna threw over her shoulder as she left the room. "I want to be ready when the next bus leaves Bowie."

Rose looked up the phone number, made the call, and charged the ticket to her own credit card. One was leaving at eleven thirty that morning and would arrive in Sweet Water, Alabama, at nine o'clock that night. She picked up the two bottles of liquor and put them away. She'd started toward Aunt Luna's bedroom when someone knocked on the back door.

"Pizza!" She slapped her forehead as she grabbed up her purse and headed toward the door. She paid the delivery girl and carried it with her to Aunt Luna's bedroom. "Next bus leaves in half an hour, and then there's not another one until tomorrow. I went ahead and booked you a ticket."

"Thank you, darlin'. You can cancel the reservation that I made for Monday. I'm just about packed. Us carnie folks know how to travel light." She smiled for the first time since she'd gotten the news of Wilbur's marriage. "Gimme a piece of that pizza to eat right now. Then while I finish up, you can wrap up a couple more for me to eat on while I'm riding."

Rose opened the box and Luna took out a slice, folded it lengthwise, and took a bite. "Anything else I can fix for you? Maybe a bottle of water or some cookies?"

"Honey, you just make me up whatever you think I might need or want, and I'll be real happy with it." Luna laid her slice of pizza on the dresser and hugged Rose. "I'm really glad I finally got to spend some time with you. We've made lots of good memories that we can both hold on to, and now, you got to promise me that you'll write me a letter once a month and tell me what all's going on around here."

"What makes you think I'll stay here?" Rose remembered the feeling she'd had when she thought about the beach or the mountains. "I can live anywhere."

"Your heart is here," Luna answered. "Now, get on out there and make me up a tote bag of goodies. I like to eat when I'm riding. It helps pass the time."

Rose went on to the kitchen, found a zippered lunch box in the cabinet—probably something that Aunt Molly carried cold food to a church potluck in—and packed it full.

When she got back to the foyer, Aunt Luna was waiting with her suitcase right beside her. "We only got fifteen minutes so we'd better get movin'. I hate to leave you on such short notice. I didn't even have time to read the cards for you again."

Rose carried Luna's suitcase to the car, and put it in the backseat, then drove straight to the bus stop. She pulled up to the curb right behind where the bus had already parked, went inside, and brought Luna's ticket back to her.

"What do I owe you?" Luna began to dig in her purse.

"Nothing, they were giving away tickets free today to anyone over thirty-nine." Rose leaned across the console and kissed Luna on the cheek.

"You are full of bullshit"—Luna laughed—"but thank you for this and for the whole time I've been here. Now help me get my baggage out on the sidewalk and then leave. Goodbyes are not my thing."

"Aunt Luna"—Rose got past the lump in her throat—"I hate goodbyes too, but I'm going to give you a 'see you later' hug. I want you to call me as soon as you get to Alabama tonight so I know you're safe. One more thing, promise me no more hitchhiking. Ride the bus when you want to come see me or Aunt Molly."

"A hug is fine, but I'll make no promises," Luna said as she got out of the car.

Rose got the suitcase out first, rolled it up onto the sidewalk, and then hung the tote bag full of snacks over Luna's shoulder. She gave her aunt a brief hug and turned and walked back to the car. She watched to be sure that Luna didn't have problems with her ticket or with getting on the bus, but it was with tears flowing down her face.

You came into my life in a whirlwind, and now you're leaving the same way. I'll miss you, Aunt Luna.

When she got back to the B&B, the driveway and parking space out to the back were filled with cars. She'd forgotten and left the front door unlocked, so there were dozens of people in the shop, some already lined up to check out.

"Crap!" she muttered as she rushed inside. She'd wanted some time to repair her makeup and to get control of herself. "I'm so sorry," she said as she hurried to the counter. "I had to take my aunt to the bus station. I hope y'all are finding things all right."

"Honey, this is a small town," one lady said. "We understand these things, and besides, Miz Molly often lets us just browse and ring the bell when we were ready to check out."

By the middle of the afternoon the cash register was full, the shop was finally empty, and Rose finally had time to sit down and eat a slice of cold pizza. At five o'clock, she flipped the sign from OPEN to CLOSED and went into Aunt Luna's bedroom. She fell back on the bed, inhaling the vanilla scent of her aunt's perfume, which was still on the pillow. In only a few more hours, Luna would be home in Sweet Water.

She sat up enough to get her phone out of her back pocket and called her mother.

"Hello, darlin'. Are you on your way to Kentucky?"

"Not right now, Mama. Aunt Luna left this morning and I wanted to hear your voice because I'm all alone in this big empty place," Rose said.

"Shut it down and come home," Echo said.

"Can't. I have guests coming for a night, and I'm keeping the shop open," she said. "But I am getting homesick to see you."

"And your father?"

"Maybe a little bit," Rose admitted. "How is Daddy?"

"Strong as a horse and running the commune like always," Echo answered. "I have to go now. Be safe. Love you."

"You too and love you right back." Rose ended the call.

She stared at the ceiling for several minutes and wished they could have talked longer. If her father ever found the cell phone, there would be a war in the commune, so she understood why her mother had to go so quickly. Rose had decided long ago that she would never defer to a man like all the wives in the commune did.

Only one time had her father, Paul, let her mother have her way about something, and then he was hypocritical about it. When Echo wanted to let Rose have a year or two in public school, Paul had agreed. Rose knew the real reason he agreed was because of the argument she'd overheard the day before they'd all three left Kentucky. Her father and his uncle, the overseer, had had a big argument, and it had ended with the older man kicking her father out of the group. Two years later, the people that Paul stayed in touch with asked him to come back and be their leader when his uncle had passed away.

Rose sat up and then slung her legs off the side of the bed. "I'm still not going to live my life walking two steps behind a man."

She went back to the shop, got the pizza box, and carried it to the kitchen. She pulled the tab on a can of Bud Light and took a long swallow. Hud liked Coors. Was that a sign that they were incompatible? That they shouldn't be making out on the front porch like loved-starved teenagers? Was the universe trying to tell her that they were too different? His background was far different from hers, but hers was a helluva lot more colorful. That thought brought on a visual of Aunt Luna that first day that she'd showed up in Bowie. Putting her family and his together at a wedding would be like mixing cow patties and caviar.

As if on cue, her phone rang, and the name that popped up was Hudson Baker.

"Hello," she said. "How'd your day go?"

"Busy, but then we're a helper short, so we've been pulling some long hours. I thought I might have to come into town for a part to fix the tractor or some barbed wire, but I didn't have to. I was a little disappointed because I was hoping to see you while I was there," he said. "How'd your day go?"

"*Crazy* is the only word I can think of." She told him about the whole morning and then all the customers.

"Has Luna called? Is she there yet?" Hud asked.

"She won't get there until nine and then she'll have to go to the trailer park. I have no idea how far away from town that is," Rose said. "I just felt so sorry for her. Lord, they've been together for more than sixty years."

"Do you want me to come to town and be there with you when she calls?" Hud asked.

"I'm a big girl," Rose said. "You sound exhausted, and we both know if you come here, it'll turn into another make-out session."

"That might revive me," he chuckled, "but you're right."

"I'm used to being mentally weary, but I think going through this day with Aunt Luna has drained me emotionally."

"No doubt about that," Hud said. "But I sure do like that old gal. She's so full of spit and vinegar that she lights up the whole universe. I kinda feel sorry for Wilbur when she sees him the next time."

"What if, hypothetically speaking of course, you were to have to introduce your family to her?" Rose asked.

"Tag and Emily are part of my family, and they thought she was a hoot. My grandmother and mother would adore her spunk," Hud answered. "Why are you asking me that, anyway?"

"My first thought when I saw her sitting on her suitcase was that she was a bag lady looking for a handout. I just wondered what kind of reaction your family might have to her," she said.

"Well, Emily wants her to come to Sunday dinner. I was supposed to ask y'all tonight. That was to be my reason for calling."

"Hud, you don't need a reason to call me, or even to stop by. The door is always open to you," she said.

"Well, thank you, darlin'," he drawled. "And my door is always open to you too."

As usual, when he used that endearment, she got a warm feeling in the pit of her stomach. "The landline is ringing. Got to go. Talk to you later." She ended the call and ran across the floor to get the phone hanging on the kitchen wall.

"Hello," she said.

"Will you accept collect charges from Luna Wilson in Sweet Water, Alabama," a lady asked.

"Of course," Rose said.

"Go ahead," the woman said.

That's when Luna began to screech. "He's off on a honeymoon with that woman."

"Settle down, Aunt Luna," Rose said. "You're going to have a heart attack or a stroke."

"Not until Madam and I have a talk with him." Luna's voice had dropped to a whisper.

"Leave it alone," Rose said. "That'll do no good and will just create a dust storm. Pack up what you want out of the trailer and come back here. He's not worth spending the rest of your life in prison."

"You're right, but I got to be mad at someone," Luna said. "This is costing Molly a lot of money so I'm going to hang up."

"Have you got a pencil or something to write with?" Rose asked. "I need to give you my cell phone number. And I need your address. I'm going to send you a prepaid cell phone, and I want you to call me on it. I'll have it sent overnight so you'll have it tomorrow."

"Farm Road Two Thousand, Box two hundred," Luna said.

Rose rattled off her cell number as she wrote the address on a paper napkin. "When it arrives you call me and we'll visit."

"Maybe the smoke from Madam's barrel will be cooled down by then." Luna hung up the phone.

Rose left her beer sitting on the counter beside the pizza box, picked up her purse, and drove straight to Hud's place.

She wanted to talk to him in person, not on a phone, and if he fell asleep while they were sitting together, that was all right. She just couldn't be alone that night. She didn't only *want* to be with someone, she *needed* to be, and her heart said that someone was Hud.

Rose parked beside his truck and got out. Red met her on the porch, and she stooped down long enough to rub his ears before she rapped on the door.

Hud yelled, "Come on in."

She eased the door open and stepped inside a small foyer with a hallway leading off to the right. A couple more steps and she could see into the living room, dining room, and kitchen area—all one big room, divided by floor type—off-white tile in the kitchen, hardwood in the dining room, and a light brown carpet in the living area. He'd been stretched out on the sofa, but when he saw her he jumped up and met her in the middle of the floor.

He wore a pair of loose-fitting, plaid pajama pants and a faded tank top. When he opened his muscular arms, she walked right into them and laid her cheek against his hard, broad chest.

"Are you all right? You look like you just lost your best friend," he asked.

"I can't wrap my head around why Wilbur would do that. Aunt Luna is so mad that I'm afraid she'll have a heart attack."

He wrapped his arms around her and cradled the back of her head in his hand. "I'm sorry, darlin', but pain and grief are strange things. They affect everyone different. How are you holding up?" He helped her remove her jacket and then led her to the sofa.

"I've only just gotten reacquainted with Aunt Luna, so why am I so sad?"

They sat down at the same time, but he didn't let go of her hand. "What is it that you're really sad about? Find that and you'll know what's triggering your emotions."

"When did you get to be a therapist?" She laid her head on his shoulder.

"I'm not, but I've kind of been in Luna's shoes. When my grandpa died, I loved him too much to blame him for leaving me in a world without him, so I got mad at the doctors for not saving him when he had the heart attack," he told her. "You're afraid of losing your aunt, and maybe feelin' a little like..."

She put a finger over his lips. "If a love that lasted more than sixty years falls apart, what chance does anyone have? I'm tellin' you, Hud, they'd have to sedate me for days and maybe even hospitalize me if that happened to me."

"I hope that when I get married, I go first," Hud said. "I can't imagine the pain of losing someone I love, either to divorce or death."

"But that's selfish," Rose whispered. "That's leaving behind someone to endure the pain like Luna is doing now."

"Call it self-preservation. I've kind of always hoped that if and when I ever get married, my wife and I will go together." He let go of her hand, slipped an arm around her shoulders, and pulled her even closer to his side.

"That's what Aunt Luna said." Rose sighed. "She and Wilbur had watched *The Notebook* and they made a pact to die the same night. Guess that some loves have an end to them that doesn't involve death."

"Guess Luna and Wilbur forgot to include God and that other woman in the plan," Hud said.

"Looks like it, but meeting her and then this—it's teaching me to value each day, not give a damn what other people think, and to live today like there's no tomorrow," she said.

"That reminds me of Tag's motto. He got it from a Tim McGraw song called 'Live Like You Were Dying.' Only he took it to extremes a lot of the time," Hud told her.

"I remember that song." She sat up straighter. "That's what I should do. Not take it to extremes but not be afraid to take risks."

"That's a beautiful attitude. Congratulations on deciding." He tipped up her chin and kissed her. "I kind of made the same one when we moved here from Tulia. I wasn't going to regret living in this little house or working from daylight to dark, because Tag and I were paving the way for future generations. Someday they'd look at what we'd made and be grateful we had it to pass down to them."

"And that's beautiful too." She snuggled down into his arms. "You wouldn't by any chance have *The Notebook*, or could maybe find it on Netflix?"

"I have it," Hud said. "It's one of Tag's favorites, but don't tattle on me. He tells everyone he only watches action films. Want something to drink? I've got sweet tea, beer, milk, orange juice. I'll get you something before I get the movie."

"Love a glass of tea." She got to her feet. "But I can pour it while you find the movie."

She went to the kitchen and only had to open two doors before she found the glasses. She filled them with ice and tea, then carried them to the living room. She'd barely sat down on the sofa when he returned with the movie in his hands.

"We don't have cable TV out here so we brought a closetful of movies with us when we moved." He put the disc into the DVD player and picked up the remote. Then he sat down so close to her that air couldn't force itself between their bodies. Sparks danced around the room like fireworks on the Fourth of July, and Rose loved the feeling.

Sometime during the movie, she fell asleep. When she

awoke, she and Hud were cuddled up together on the sofa and the sun was pouring into the room. She checked the clock on the wall and jumped to her feet, startling poor Hud so badly that he fell off the sofa.

"It's eight thirty." She gasped. "The gift store opens at nine. I've got to get home."

Hud braced his back against the sofa. "Tag is never going to let me live this down."

"Did I hear my name?" Tag asked as he came through the back door. "We've got fencin' to do...oh, so you had company last night?" He grinned.

"We fell asleep in the middle of the..." Rose stammered.

"No one falls asleep watching *The Notebook*." Tag's grin got bigger.

"Well, we did." Hud stood up, walked across the floor, and kissed Rose. "Sorry, darlin'. I should've set an alarm. Call me when you have time."

"I will, and Tag, don't be judgin' your brother by yourself." She nodded as she put on her shoes. "Y'all have a good day!"

"Ouch!" Tag said.

She heard Hud chuckling as she closed the door.

She left the house with every shred of her dignity intact, and when she got into the car, she started to giggle, and she laughed all the way home. She'd just spent the night with Hud. They hadn't had sex, but if they had, she wouldn't have been embarrassed. She was comfortable with Hud. Just being with him was comforting and exciting both at the same time. For the first time since she'd been a teenager in Tulia, Texas, she could just let go and relax around a guy.

Chapter Fourteen

By Friday afternoon, Rose had put a pretty crystal candy dish filled with chocolates in one of the bedrooms—one that did not have a patched hole from bullet holes. She'd arranged a lovely bouquet of mixed flowers in a vase for the dresser, turned down the bed, and had a bottle of champagne cooling in a pretty bucket filled with ice. She was busy chasing Chester out of the room and off the bed again when she heard a rapping on the door.

When the Davises arrived, she met them at the door and even carried their suitcase up the stairs for them. With his tail held high, Chester followed her up the steps, like he was the butler. She showed the sweet little lady with gray hair, and her dignified-looking husband with wire-rimmed glasses and a head of silver hair, to the room.

"If y'all need anything, just call me," Rose said as she shooed Chester out—again.

"This is the very room that we stayed in our first night," Edna said.

"Only then, I had the strength to carry you over the threshold, darlin'," her husband said.

"Well, darlin'," Edna giggled. "I was sixty pounds smaller then too." She turned back to Rose. "We'll rest a little while and then we plan on meeting up with some friends for supper and maybe a movie. It's the couple that was our best man and maid of honor at our wedding. We'll be back by eleven at the latest."

"Thanks for letting me know. Your room key will let you in the front door if you get back early, and breakfast will be ready at eight," Rose said as she closed the door.

Chester raced ahead of her and went straight to the kitchen. He sat in front of the refrigerator door until she got out his daily piece of fish, cut it up, and put it on his plate. He ate all that, and then batted one of his toys around the living room while she looked up simple recipes for muffins. Her plan was to make muffins and serve them with a side of fresh fruit the next morning. If they flopped, she'd rush down to the pastry shop and buy a dozen, but she'd love to tell Aunt Molly that she managed for at least one day.

Chester dashed behind the sofa and brought out an argyle sock, fought with it for a few minutes, then dragged it back to where he'd found it. In a couple of minutes, he brought out a bright pink sock with black cats all over it.

"What have you got back there?" Rose asked as she stood up and pulled the sofa out from the wall. There was a whole pile of socks—every color, every style from men's to ladies'. "Good grief, you're a sock thief. I bet Aunt Molly doesn't know about this."

Chester jumped up on the sofa, bounded over the back, and looked like a flying squirrel spreading out over his pile of contraband. He looked up at her with his yellow eyes as if asking her to keep his secret.

"I won't tattle if you don't tell on me," she whispered.

Chester meowed at her.

"Okay, then, deal." She stuck her hand down over the back of the sofa, and he slapped at it.

"Be careful, boy," she warned. "I can show all this to Aunt Molly."

Her phone rang and Chester took off like he'd been shot. Rose was giggling when she answered it. "You'll never believe what a stash I've found."

"What kind? Liquor or chocolate, or maybe a cheesecake in the freezer?" Hud chuckled.

"Socks," she said and told him what she'd found. "Evidently Chester is a thief. I wonder if the folks who stay here think the place is haunted by a sock-stealing ghost."

"How does he get into the rooms?"

"He has to be a sly critter," she said. "I've got guests tonight. They're here because they spent their honeymoon in this place years ago."

"That's romantic," Hud said.

"It is, isn't it?" She sighed.

"How long have they been married?" he asked.

"I didn't ask, but I'd guess maybe forty or fifty years."

"Out of all the places where you've been, where would you like to honeymoon?"

Wherever you are, she thought, but she said, "That would depend on who I marry."

"Fair enough," Hud said. "What I called for, other than to hear your voice, is to ask if seven is okay to pick you up tomorrow evening."

"That's fine," she said.

"Hey, you want me to come over in the morning and help you make breakfast?" he asked.

"Yes," she said without hesitation.

"I'll stop by the store and bring what I need to make omelets and waffles," he told her.

"Thank you so much. I've got fresh fruit cut up and thought I'd make muffins," she said.

"That sounds good. What kind of muffins?" he asked.

"I was just lookin' at recipes," she said.

"I'm not much at baking, but..."

"Hey, if you're willing to help me, I'm good with whatever you want to make. I told them I'd serve it at eight. Is that too early?" She'd rather be talking about things more romantic than cooking, but if working in the kitchen meant she could spend time with him, then that was fine.

"Okay, then, eight in the morning, and seven tomorrow evening. Getting to see you twice in one day is great," he said.

"You could come over this evening and keep me company," she suggested.

"I'll be there in twenty minutes," he said.

"See you then. Don't knock. Just come on in. I don't want to disturb the guests." She ended the call and pushed the sofa back with her knees.

Chester peeked around the door and dragged what Rose hoped was another sock and not a dead mouse across the floor. He dashed behind the sofa with his prize and set up a loud meowing.

Edna poked her head into the room. "I hate to bother you, but that cat sneaked into our room when I opened the door, and grabbed one of Abe's socks. I chased him down here, but he's a fast critter."

Rose pulled the sofa out again. She and Edna put their knees on the cushions and peered over the back.

"Take your choice," Rose said.

Edna laughed. "The argyle is the one we lost last year on our anniversary, and that dark red one is the one I was chasing the cat for tonight. What's funny is that the argyle is the socks that he was wearing when we married, and he only wears them on anniversary time. He was disappointed that he didn't have both of them to wear this year. I'm glad to find it."

She reached down and got both socks. "You'll think we're crazy, but I saved that single sock even when we thought this one was lost."

"No, ma'am, I think it's kind of sweet," Rose told her.

"I can't wait to get back up to our room. This is a fantastic anniversary present." Edna hurried out of the room.

She'd barely disappeared when Rose heard the front door open. Hud carried in a bag of groceries and went straight for the kitchen. "I didn't have to go to the store. Had everything at the house." He put the eggs and sausage in the refrigerator, and set a small waffle maker on the cabinet.

"Chester stole another sock, and..." She told him all about the argyle. "Would you do something like that?"

"Sure I would." He nodded. "It sounds like a really neat thing to do. I wonder if she wears something that she wore to the wedding too."

"I bet it's that little brooch she had on her dress. It was shaped like a double heart, and she kept touching it," Rose whispered.

"You're probably right." He removed his phone from his hip pocket, toyed with the front of it a little bit, and laid it on the cabinet. "You said it had been a while since you've been out to a honky-tonk." He picked up her hand and said, "May I have this dance, ma'am?"

Her arms snaked up around his neck and his went to her waist. They were the only ones in the whole world as they danced to "I Cross My Heart" by George Strait. He sang the words with George, and she believed every one of them. That song ended and another one began.

"I kinda made a playlist while I was plowing this morning," he said.

After half an hour, Lonestar finished up the concert with "Amazed."

She stepped back, stood on her tiptoes, and kissed him on the cheek. "Thank you for a lovely evening. Want a beer?"

"Only if we can take it outside and look at the stars," he said.

"It's cold out there," she said.

"We can keep each other warm."

She believed him. Just looking up into his eyes warmed her from the inside out. "I'll get the beers. You get the quilt from the back of the sofa. We might want it to sit on."

"Or wrap up in it and pretend that we're the only people on Earth."

Now that was romantic for sure, and it echoed exactly what she was thinking. She pulled two beers from the refrigerator and followed him to the foyer, where he helped her put on her coat. Chester did his best to get out of the house, but she managed to shove him back inside and close the door.

They sat down on the swing and he covered them both with the quilt. "Once a year let's celebrate this night by wrapping up in a quilt and sharing a couple of beers."

"I like that idea a lot," she said.

"No matter where we are in our life, let's remember the good times," he whispered as he kissed her for the first time that evening.

Words weren't necessary that cold winter night. They made out until they were breathless and then she fell asleep in his arms. When she awoke, she was lying on the sofa, with Chester staring down at her from the arm. The smell of coffee and sausage filled the air. The clock on the far wall said that it was seven thirty.

She sat up so fast that she got light-headed. Chester took off in a flash, and then Hud was right there, holding a cup of coffee out toward her.

"Good mornin'." He sat down beside her and kissed her on the cheek. "It was nearly dawn when I woke up, so I just brought you in and started the coffee."

She almost told him right then that she loved him, but the words wouldn't come out of her mouth.

"I'll have to leave soon as breakfast is served. Tag and I are still plowing fields," he whispered.

"Thank you," she said. "You're a lifesaver."

"So are you," he told her.

* * *

The Davis couple left right after breakfast that morning. Hud offered to stick around and help with cleanup, but Rose shooed him out of the house and called her mother.

"Can you talk?" Rose asked.

"It's a great time," Echo told her. "Your father is over in Harlan finishin' up a project and won't be home until suppertime."

"I might be in love," Rose blurted out.

"I'm not surprised," Echo told her. "Hud Baker stole your heart when we were in Texas, and he never gave it back."

"But, Mama, I was just a kid then. I'm a full-grown adult now. Times have changed. I have changed," she argued.

"Honey, the heart doesn't change, and when it gets set on something, that's what it wants," Echo told her.

"What if he doesn't feel the same way?" Rose paced back and forth across the living room floor.

"You can't do anything about the way he feels," Echo replied. "The only emotions you're in control of are yours."

Rose almost stumbled over Chester when he ran across the room. "Dammit!"

"Sorry, but that's the way it is." Echo giggled.

"I wasn't talking to you. Chester just about tripped me," Rose explained. "But don't you sometimes wish you could control Daddy—just a little bit."

Echo laughed out loud. "I'm not sure anyone, including Paul O'Malley, can get that job done. Maybe you need to get out of the forest so you can see the trees. Come home for a few days or weeks. Get a fresh perspective on things."

"I'll be coming that way soon as Aunt Molly gets back," Rose said.

"I can hardly wait," Echo told her. "But right now I should go out to the kitchen and get the chocolate cakes made for supper. I love you, Cactus Rose."

"Love you," Rose said as she ended the call.

That word, *home,* stuck in her mind. She'd read that home is where the heart is, so where was it located?

"Well, it's damn sure not in a place where they call me Cactus," she muttered.

* * *

Rose wore the same cowboy boots that she'd worn the night they'd gone square dancing. She brushed them off with a tissue, pulled on a pair of skinny jeans, and topped them off with a form-fitted shirt that had lots of black lace inserts. She spent a little extra time on her makeup and curled her long hair. Then she put the boots on, and was all the way to the bottom of the stairs when she heard Hud's knock.

When she opened the door, Hud said, "Well, dammit! I left my handcuffs at home."

"Why would you need cuffs?" she asked.

"Because it's a crime to look that good, sweetheart," he replied. "I'll be the luckiest cowboy at the Rusty Spur."

"I've got cuffs if you don't mind pink velvet," she teased.

Hud's eyes just about popped right out of his head. "Are you serious?"

"I do keep a few secrets." She handed him her jacket and winked.

He helped her get it on and then escorted her out to the truck with his hand on her lower back. When he opened the door for her, he asked, "What other secrets have you got hidden away?"

"It would take a lifetime to tell you all of them." She hopped into the passenger seat and fastened her seat belt. "Do you have secrets?"

"A few, but I'd like to make a bunch more with you." He shut the door and whistled all the way around the front end of the truck.

He'd left the engine running, so the headlights lit up the way he filled out those snug jeans. Beneath his suede jacket he wore a light green western shirt with pearl snaps. Her fingers longed to start at the top of his throat and pull hard enough that all the snaps popped open one by one. Or better yet, undo them slowly one at a time and run her hands through the soft brown hair on his chest. By the time he got behind the wheel, her wild imagination had her wishing that she really did own velvet handcuffs.

"How far is it to the Rusty Spur?" she asked.

"Not far," he answered. "Maybe ten minutes. Tell me one of your secrets on the way."

"Only if you tell me one of yours first," she told him.

"Fair enough. This isn't really a secret, but no one would believe me, so it kind of is the same thing. You are the first woman I've ever taken to a honky-tonk," he said.

"Good lord, Hud!" It was her turn to go all buggy eyed. "Are you serious?"

He raised a hand. "As serious and as sober as a judge. I usually go with the guys. Sometimes, I get lucky and go home with a lady, or take one home with me. I'm not a saint, Rose."

"I haven't located any wings or a halo, so I wasn't thinking you were," she said.

"Now your turn," he said.

"All right, but it's a big secret," she whispered. "I'm not a saint, either. That said, though, I don't do one-night stands. If there's not a possibility of some kind of future with a guy, I don't lead him on."

"That's pretty honest," he said with a nod, "and you may not be a saint, but I swear I can see a halo above your head tonight, so you must be an angel."

"If I am, it's a honky-tonk angel," she said. "Hey, Elvis Presley sang about that, I think."

"Are you going to be my honky-tonk angel tonight?" Hud pulled into a gravel parking lot with a metal building set at the back of the property.

She'd lived in Texas as a teenager and in her travels, she'd seen lots of honky-tonks, and after she'd enlisted, she'd even been in a few. But the old rustic building in front of her looked more like something she'd seen in the movies with its swinging doors and a wide front porch with a hitching rail.

"This is the Rusty Spur?" she asked.

"Yep, disappointed?" he asked.

"No, just surprised." She unfastened her seat belt. "What's it look like inside?"

"Rather than tell you, I'll show you, but promise me that you'll save the last dance for me." He turned the engine off.

"Every dance belongs to you," she told him, "unless you want to dance with another woman."

"No way, darlin'. I've got the most beautiful girl in Texas with me tonight, and I'm spending all the time I can with her." He got out of the truck and came around to open her door.

She looped her arm into his, and they crossed the parking lot together. "Well, I do believe I'm with the sexiest cowboy in all of Texas."

"Awww, shucks." He grinned as he paid the man at the door the entry fee for both of them.

A dozen barstools lined up in front of a long, shiny bar to her right that stretched from one end of the building to the other. Bottles of liquor on shelves lined the wall behind it, and there were two beer stations, one on either end.

She tiptoed so she could talk to Hud above the loud juke-box music. "Now, this is a honky-tonk."

"What does that mean?"

"I've been to bars and clubs, but nothing like this," she said above the noise of a full house. Only one table was empty among the half a dozen lining the far walls. At least twenty people were on the sawdust-covered floor, doing a line dance to "Boot Scootin' Boogie" by Brooks & Dunn.

He helped her out of her jacket and hung it on the back of a chair and did the same with his coat. Then he held out his hand. "May I have this dance, ma'am."

Blake Shelton's "God Gave Me You" started to play when she put her hand in his, and he twirled her around once before he brought her back to his chest. With one hand on his shoulder and the other tucked into his hand, she was amazed that she could keep up with his smooth moves.

"This is my song to you, tonight," Hud whispered. "Like the words say, I really need you to stay beside me as the storms blow through."

She looked up into his green eyes. "Well, honey, we sure have had some storms already, haven't we?"

He sang along when the lyrics said that God had given her to him for the ups and downs. She made up her mind right there on the dance floor that she was going to walk down the aisle to that song when and if she ever got married.

The next one up on the jukebox was "Walk Me Down the Middle" by The Band Perry. It was slower than the previous tune and talked about being a misfit. When she got to go to public school, her daddy still had strict rules. She hadn't been allowed to wear makeup. She wasn't permitted to have a cell phone or even a phone at home to talk to friends. She had to dress modestly. Jeans and shirts were fine, but none of that had intimidated her. She was like a free bird out in the big wide world, and she had a lot to discover.

"Would you do that—walk me down the middle of the county fair?" Rose asked.

"Darlin', I'd walk you anywhere you want to go and be proud to hold your hand for the whole world to see," he vowed.

The look in his eyes told her that he was telling the truth, and she felt like she was floating on air for the rest of the night.

* * *

It was past midnight when Hud walked Rose to the door of the B&B. True to her word, she'd danced only with him all evening, and between times, she'd held hands with him across the table.

"I'm too wired up to sleep." She turned back to him when she'd unlocked the door. "Want to come in for a cup of hot chocolate, and maybe some doughnuts? I think there's some of those little white powdered ones left. Aunt Luna was partial to them."

"Love to," he said.

She stepped inside, dropped her coat on a ladder-back chair in the foyer, and headed to the kitchen. "I never learned to cook, but I can make a mean cup of hot chocolate."

"Are you hungry?" He followed behind her.

"Starving," she said. "I was too nervous to eat supper."

"Why were you nervous? Got news from Aunt Luna?" he asked.

"Nope." She shook her head. "I didn't want to disappoint you."

He wrapped his arms around her. "I've got a confession. I was afraid of the same thing. I worried more about what shirt to wear tonight than I ever have before. I played through dozens of scenarios in my head—from what would I do if some other cowboy swept you off your feet, to how would I react if you hated the Rusty Spur and never wanted to talk to me again."

"I didn't know guys even thought like that." She tiptoed and kissed him—long and lingering.

When the kiss ended, he took a step back. "Darlin', very many more of those and we'll burn this house down with the heat, which I got to say, wouldn't be a bad way to go."

He went to the refrigerator and brought out peppers, cheese, eggs, and sausage.

"Instead of hot chocolate, I'll make a pot of coffee." She bent over to get the container from the bottom shelf of the fridge. There was her perfectly rounded butt, only a few inches him, and he had a carton of eggs in one hand and a block of cheese in the other. Sometimes a cowboy just couldn't win.

When he'd finished making the omelets, they sat down at the small kitchen table. "Why didn't you ever learn to cook?" he asked.

"It was my one act of rebellion. I liked going to school, and didn't even mind Mama homeschooling me, but I didn't want to live in the commune. So when all the other girls went with the women to the kitchen to learn how to cook, I'd run off to the woods and study my languages," she told him between bites.

"How? Did you have books for that?" Hud took a sip of coffee, made just to his taste—strong and black.

"No, I actually had a CD player. Of course, I wasn't allowed to use it for vanity—like music—but I had the CDs for different languages. When we lived on the beach and down near the bayou, Mama learned a couple with me, during my homeschooling lessons, but Daddy didn't like it so much, so she quit," Rose answered.

"How many did you learn?" Hud asked.

"Seven, plus English." She buttered a second piece of toast and then smeared grape jelly on it. "No, six. I learned Farsi after I got into the army. I know seven now and, of course, English makes eight." Her eyes twinkled. "Unless you count Kentucky Redneck as a language. If so, that would make nine."

He chuckled. "I guess that means you can cuss me out seven ways to Sunday, and I won't know what you're sayin'."

"You'll know by the tone." She stood up and held out her hand. "Let's go to the living room. I'll take care of the cleanup later. My feet hurt from so much dancing. I'm going to kick off my shoes and—"

He took her hand in his and kissed the palm, then scooped her up in his arms and carried her to the living room. He put her down on one end of the sofa, and removed her shoes, then he sat on the other end and put both her feet in his lap. He picked up the left one and began to gently massage her heel and slowly moved up to the ball of her foot.

Rose moaned. "That feels so good."

When he finished with that foot, he kissed it, then met her gaze and slowly crawled up her body until he was lying on top of her. His lips came down on hers in a long, hard kiss. One led to another until they were both breathless.

"What are we doing, Rose? Where is this headed?" he asked.

"We're making out, and I was thinking that we'd move it up to my bedroom and get out those handcuffs you've been thinkin' about all night," she teased.

He propped up on his elbows. "You've really got cuffs?"

"No, but, honey, I don't think that we'll need any kinky stuff." She wiggled her way out from under him and led him across the floor. On the first step she stopped to unsnap his shirt in one easy motion. He was already about to break the zipper in his jeans, and when she ran her hands over his chest, he groaned out loud.

She moved up a couple of steps. He placed one of his boots on the first step, making her lips and his on the same level. While he smothered her with more kisses, he unfastened her shirt and cupped a breast in his hand. God, she felt so good.

"Sweet lord," she muttered when he removed her shirt and bra and kissed both breasts. By the time they reached the top of the stairs, they were both naked and Hud was on fire.

"Which one is your bedroom?" He pushed her hair back with his hands, cupped her cheeks, and stared into her eyes.

She took him by the hand and led him across the hallway

to a bedroom. Moonlight flowed through the window at the head of the bed, giving him just enough light to see her expressions.

He laid her on the bed. "You are so beautiful, Rose. I dreamed for years about this night, but never thought it would happen."

"I've ached for you," she said. "Take me, please."

"Got to get out some protection," he said.

"I've started taking the pill," she told him as she pulled him even closer.

He entered her and they began to work together in a perfect rhythm. He brought her to the edge of a climax, then slowed down, kissing her neck, her ears, her eyelids all the while. He wanted to last a long time, but things sped up so fast that he finally whispered her name in a hoarse Texas drawl, and then collapsed on her for a few seconds.

"Sweet Jesus!" she moaned.

"I'm sorry it didn't last longer." He rolled to the side but kept her in his arms. She pulled the chenille bedspread up around them, creating a cocoon where only the two of them existed.

"One more second and there would have been nothing left of us but bones and ashes. That was...no words. Just feeling and it was amazing." She cuddled up closer to his side and closed her eyes. "Don't leave me. Stay the night."

Hud kissed her on the forehead. "I'm not going anywhere, darlin'."

Chapter Fifteen

The sound of rain on the windows and the drip in the bucket in the room across the hall awoke Rose the next morning. She'd fallen asleep against Hud's chest, his arm holding her tightly, and they were in the same position when she awoke. She rose up on an elbow to find him already awake.

"Good mornin', gorgeous," he whispered and brushed a sweet kiss across her forehead.

She'd heard it said that home was where the heart was. It wasn't a town or a particular house, or even a country. If that was true, she was home, because her heart was happy that morning. "Good mornin' to you, sexy cowboy." She gave him a peck on the lips.

"Want a repeat of last night before we get ready for church?" he asked.

"If we start that, we might not make it to church." She bailed out of bed and headed straight for the bathroom. "Want to join me in the shower?"

Hud threw back the covers and beat her to the bathroom. He'd already adjusted the water to the right temperature when she arrived, and he helped her step over the edge of the bathtub. "Are you going to wash your hair?" he asked.

"Yep." She nodded.

"Then turn around and let me do it for you." He picked up the shampoo, washed her hair, and then massaged her scalp.

"That's even more wonderful than the foot massage," she told him.

"We still have conditioner to do." He did a repeat of the previous process, and not once did he get soap in her eyes. Now it was her turn. She picked up a washcloth, soaped it up, started with his face, and worked her way down his body—slowly, savoring every single moment.

Having a guy wash her hair and then stand still and let her touch him like this was the best thing next to sex that she'd ever experienced. She could sure get used to a permanent commitment, she thought, if this was what that meant.

When she'd rinsed him off, she looped her arms around his neck and pressed her body against his. "Ever had shower sex?"

"Nope," he said.

"Me either. Want to give up our shower sex virginity?" With a little hop she wrapped her legs around his body.

His lips landed on hers and he took a couple of steps forward to brace her back against the wall of the tub on the far end. "Yes, ma'am, I'd love that." He maneuvered a hand between them and in a few thrusts, it was all over for both of them.

He turned around until *his* back was against the wall, and slid down with her still in his lap. "Wow! Too quick, but wow!"

"Amazing! We've got to do that again, sometime." She wiggled free of his embrace, stood up, rinsed off, and then stepped out of the shower. "If we're going to make it to church and pray for our sins, we'd better not do it right now, though."

She wrapped a white towel around her hair and one around her body. He reached out of the tub and tugged at the one from her body. "I'll take a chance on getting struck by lightning if you're willin' to stay in this morning and take another shower with me."

"Not me." She snatched the towel from his hands and wrapped it back around herself. "I'll meet you in the foyer in fifteen minutes. I'll be dressed for church, and you'll just have time to get out to the ranch and change."

"But I'm hungry," he whined with a grin on his face.

"I'll bring along that package of doughnuts." She waved at the door. "You can eat them on the way."

She dried her hair and twisted it up into a pile of curls on top of her head, slipped on underwear, and then put on a long-sleeved, dark blue dress. Her feet still hurt from the night of dancing, and combat boots or even her one pair of dress boots didn't look right with the Sunday dress, so she went downstairs in her bare feet to get her flats. She passed Hud on the bottom step where he was putting on his shirt.

"First time I ever got dressed one piece of clothing at a time on the stairs," he told her.

"Lots of firsts last night and this morning," she said. "Maybe I should mark them all on the calendar so we won't forget."

"Honey, everything about last night and this morning is branded into my brain. No way I'll ever lose these memories." He reached out and brought her to him for another hard kiss.

"Mine too," she told him as she pulled away and went for her shoes—and the doughnuts.

They were in the truck and headed toward Sunset when Hud's phone rang. He pulled it out of his hip pocket and answered it, "Good mornin', brother. I'll take over the feeding chores—"

Hud's eyes went wide and he glanced up in the rearview mirror. "Holy smokin' hell! Yes, yes, yes, we're going to have to outrun it. Meet you and Nikki in the cellar."

"What?" Rose asked.

"Turn around and look behind us," Hud told her.

"Is that what I think it is?" she asked.

"It's a tornado and it's coming right through Bowie. Tag says that there's another one on the ground at Park Springs coming toward Sunset. The closest shelter is the storm cellar at the ranch." He talked faster than the speedometer, which kept climbing all the way to ninety miles an hour.

The storm behind them was still visible when they went through Sunset and made the turn to head to the ranch, but now Rose could see the second one out her window. It was swirling with a long, wide tail that was busy throwing all kinds of debris around. Hud made the final turn into the lane to the ranch on two wheels and gunned it all the way to the house. He slammed on the brakes and came to a long, greasy stop.

"Go run around to the back of the house," he said. "I'll be right behind you."

Rose didn't need to be told twice. She stepped out into an eerie quietness where everything had a slightly green cast. It all changed when she reached the porch and started around the house. Suddenly, it sounded like a freight train was coming right at her. She froze for a second, and then she was flying. She landed hard on Hud's shoulder with her arms and legs flopping in the hard wind like a rag doll. She saw a piece of sheet metal blow past her head, and then a child's teddy bear brushed her cheek.

All she could do was hang on until he set her down at the top of a set of narrow stairs, and she rushed down into a cellar. Red bounded over to her and raised up on his hind legs, putting his paws on her stomach. Hud came right in behind her, pulled the door down, pushed the dog back into the cellar, and grabbed her by the shoulders.

"Are you hurt? Did anything hit you?" He checked her face, and her arms, and scanned the rest of her body.

"I'm fine," she told him. "I think a teddy bear went past me, but it was all so fast."

"Glad y'all made it, but that was way too close of a call. We were worried that you'd be right in the eye of it. Didn't you check the weather this morning?" Tag let out a big lungful of air as he sat down beside Nikki.

"Didn't even think about the weather," Hud said. "We were just coming out here so I could get ready for church when you called. I hope we don't get too much damage."

"We'll be lucky if we've got houses when we get out of here," Nikki said. "I expect that as soon as it's over I'd better call the hospital and see if I'm needed."

"And me and Tag will be out with the fire department, taking care of downed trees and electrical lines," Hud said.

"I'm a translator, if anyone needs one," Rose offered.

"If you're serious, you can come with me," Nikki said. "We have a huge Mexican population around here. It would be good to have someone who speaks Spanish on hand."

"I'd be glad to help." Rose slumped down into a metal folding chair. "That was scary."

"Tornados always are," Hud yelled above the noise of debris hitting the sheet metal covering the door to the cellar.

In some ways, it seemed like they'd been in the small underground place forever, and yet it was really less than fifteen minutes. Everything went strangely quiet after the storm had passed through, and then the first drops of rain began to ping on the cellar door.

Tag raised the door, and Red ran out ahead of everyone else. He made a beeline for the back porch and yipped for someone to hurry up and let him inside. Tag and Nikki went out next, and Tag called out that the house was still standing, but there were lots of shingles strewn about the ground.

Hud and Rose were the last ones to leave, and he closed the cellar door behind him. He pointed to a huge tree, now down with its roots sticking up every which way. "Looks like we'll be cuttin' up that one for firewood."

Rose ran toward the porch and let the dog inside. She followed him with Nikki right behind her. Nikki was making a call on her phone before she even made it through the utility room and into the kitchen.

She listened for a few seconds, ended the call, and turned to Rose. "It's all hands on deck, so don't even take your coat off."

Hud and Tag came in, shed their coats, and both of them looked up at the ceiling. "We'll be lucky if we don't have leaks," Tag said.

"Rose and I are going to the hospital." Nikki stopped long enough to give Tag a quick peck on the lips and then ran out toward a truck.

"See you later," Rose said as she followed her and got into a vehicle pretty similar to Hud's.

On the way to Sunset, she and Nikki saw a lot of barn roofs that had been torn off. They made it up to the turnoff for Bowie, and that's where the real destruction began to show its ugly face. A house would be flattened and the two on either side of it would only have a few shingles blown off their roofs. A convenience store had no outside walls, and yet bottles of wine were still sitting intact on the shelves. The bare trees were covered in wet paper and clothing, and Rose even saw a teddy bear like the one that had swiped past her face.

She held her breath when they got near the Rose Garden Bed-and-Breakfast, and let it out in a long whoosh when she saw the damage. "Sweet Jesus and all the angels in heaven," she whispered. The place was still standing, but shingles were missing and the porch swing was tangled up in the oak tree in the front yard. Aunt Molly's car was wrapped around a pecan tree across the street.

"Do you need to stop and check the inside?" Nikki asked.

"Not in this rain. I can check on it later," she answered. "But I do need to call my aunt."

Molly answered on the first ring. "We're just about to go out for an early supper. What's up?"

Rose explained what had happened in as few words as she could. "We're lucky, Aunt Molly. The house beside the B&B was flattened and all of the ones across the street have massive damage."

"Yes, we are, and if anyone needs a place to sleep, you give them a room free of charge," Molly said. "I think I should come home. Me and the Fab Five are getting bored and homesick. I'm going to talk to them, and we'll book the first flight we can get."

"I can't even come and get you," Rose told her.

"Not to worry. A car and a porch swing can be replaced. I'm just glad the B&B is still standing," Molly said. "Where were you when it hit? Are you hurt? Did you go to the basement?"

"Hud and I were on the way to church," Rose said. "We barely made it to his ranch and into the cellar when all hell broke loose. I've never seen anything quite like this."

"Where are you right now?" Molly asked.

"In the car with Nikki. I'm going to help out at the hospital," she replied.

"That's good. I'll be home in two days, tops, maybe even late tomorrow night," Molly told her. "And don't worry about anything. God works in mysterious ways."

"What did she say?" Nikki asked as she parked her car in the employee part of the hospital parking lot.

"That God works in mysterious ways. I thought there would be crying and gnashing of teeth, but she was pretty cool about it." Rose filled her in on the rest of the conversation.

"I want to grow up to be just like her and the Fab Five. Nothing fazes them, and they usually make a big joke about things we'd have a meltdown over." Nikki picked up her purse and headed toward the emergency room entrance.

They walked into chaos—people in the waiting room, the emergency room cubicles full, and a receptionist who didn't speak a word of Spanish. Nikki went to get a visitor's badge for Rose, while Rose got straight to work translating for the beleaguered staff.

Her phone pinged with a message from Hud: *Have you seen the B&B? Are you OK?*

She sent back one: *Yes. It's still standing, and Aunt Molly is coming home. I'm fine.*

Nikki returned with a clip-on badge, then led her back to a cubicle where a little boy had gotten separated from his parents during the storm. She sat down beside him, took his hand in hers, and translated his French for the doctor.

"He's from Haiti and he's five years old," Rose said. "Is

it all right if I go out into the waiting room and see if I can locate his mother?"

"Sure it is," the doctor said. "I need her permission to treat him."

Rose hurried down the hall, busted through the double doors, and called out in French about the little boy looking for his mama. With tears in her eyes, a small woman pushed her way through the crowd, asking if her son was all right. Rose took her by the hand and led her back to the cubicle where Nikki, the doctor, and the little boy waited. The child opened his arms and his mother went right to him.

"Now they need you back in the waiting area," Nikki said. "You are a godsend today, Rose."

"Glad to help out," she said.

And I thought my skills were so limited, she thought as she ran down the short hallway.

Chapter Sixteen

How can the sun shine on so much devastation? Rose wondered as she stood in the yard of the B&B and stared at all the destruction around it.

Hud put his arm around her waist and pulled her close to his side. "Are you all right?"

"Do you realize that if we'd left for church thirty minutes later, we could have been killed?" She shook her head, still in disbelief.

"Darlin', we can't do anything about the damage around us, but we can go see what's been damaged inside." He dropped his arm and took her hand.

She stopped inside the door and looked around at the mess. Evidently a tornado shook things up as much as an earthquake, because there was glass all over the floor of the shop, and poor old Chester was sitting on top of the credenza howling at them.

"He's either blaming us or trying to convince us that he didn't cause all this," Rose said as she went from room to room, checking the windows and ceiling for water leaks. In some rooms, lamps and chairs were turned over. In others, everything was intact.

"We can get this cleaned up in no time," Hud said.

"Not until I call Aunt Molly." She pulled her phone from her hip pocket.

"What's the damage?" Molly asked.

"Glass everywhere. The shop is a mess, but we can clean it up. The walls and windows look all right. You'll probably need a new roof, but other than that, it's not too bad. I expected a few broken windows at least."

"How's Chester?"

"Following me around like he's afraid I'm going to blame him for all this," Rose said.

"Don't touch a single thing. I'll call the insurance company to come do an estimate. And don't let anyone stay there tonight, either. If they were to get cut or hurt, I'd be liable. I want you to lock Chester in whatever bedroom isn't damaged and you go stay with Nikki or Emily," Molly told her. "And tell Hud to go on and turn off the electricity and the water, just as a precaution."

She went into her bedroom to find the only thing out of place was the small wooden box she kept on the dresser, which was on the floor. Chester hopped up on the bed and finally stopped yowling.

"Poor old boy." Hud sat down beside him and scratched his ears. "Did you think the end of the world had come?"

Chester started to purr and curled up on a pillow.

"Looks like he'll be content in this room." Rose went to the closet and put a couple of changes of clothing into a tote bag. "I'll need to bring up his litter pan and his food and water."

"I can do that while you pack, and you can stay with me, Rose," he said.

"Thank you. I was going to ask Emily, but I'd rather stay with you." She opened a drawer and removed what she needed. Then she picked up the little wooden box and put it in the bag. Thinking about her prized possessions being in that box brought to mind the pile of socks behind the sofa.

"You stay right here," she told Chester as she shut the door behind her. She met Hud coming up the stairs and said, "Be right back. Don't let him out of the room, or we'll have to chase him down."

She gingerly made her way around all the mess until she got to the sofa. Pulling it out, she discovered that the pile of socks hadn't been disturbed. She gathered them all up in her arms and carried them up to her bedroom. Hud must've heard her because he had the door open. With one eye on the cat, and the other eyebrow raised, he asked, "What's that all about?"

"This is his comfort stuff. If he's got to be locked in one room, he should have his things around him." She tossed them on the bed.

"You could take him to the ranch with us," Hud suggested.

"I'm afraid he and Red wouldn't get along," she said. "And besides, Aunt Molly brought him to the B&B when he was just a baby. He's never even been outside. The trip alone would traumatize him. But thanks for the offer."

Chester hopped up and rolled around in the socks, purring the whole time. After a few seconds, he chose a white one and carried it back to the pillow and curled up around it.

"See, he's happy here," she said.

"Thinking of that was pretty sweet," Hud said.

"There was this little boy in the emergency room," she whispered, "who held on to a ratty old teddy bear. To him that toy was his last link to the way his life had been. I think all the noise terrified old Chester, and he needs his stash of socks to remind him that everything will be all right."

"I feel so sorry for the folks who've lost their homes and possessions, but I'm glad we didn't have any deaths." Hud picked up her suitcase and gently closed the door behind them as they left. He set the baggage down at the bottom of the steps. "I'm going down to the basement to turn off the electricity and water. Maybe you'd better wait on the porch. It's going to get dark real soon, and there's lots of glass on the floor."

She stood in the middle of the foyer and looked around. A tornado truly was a weird thing when it could shake a house like an earthquake and not break a window. The sun peeked out from behind closed doors every so often, and provided a little bit of light in the house, but that was gone in a flash.

"I thought you'd be outside," Hud said when he was back in the foyer.

"I was trying to figure this tornado thing out." She removed a yellow coat from the rack as they went outside and tossed it the backseat of his truck on top of her suitcase. A small giggle escaped as she did so. "That coat reminds me so much of..."

"Luna coming to the police station?" He finished the sentence for her.

"I shouldn't be laughing when we're surrounded by such horrible destruction," she said.

He tipped up her chin for a long kiss. "Probably not, but I get tickled every time I think about Luna blasting into that police station."

"Maybe we've got that memory to help us get us through this mess." She shivered in spite of his arms around her.

"I've heard them called an act of God, but right now we need to get you out of this cold wind." He helped her get settled in the passenger seat.

Her phone rang before he could even get the engine started. She removed her hospital badge from the pocket of her jacket and answered it.

"Hello, Aunt Molly," she said.

"Is Chester all right?" Molly asked.

"He's fine. I put him in my bedroom. I'm staying with Hud tonight, but something is strange about the B&B. No windows are broken and yet it looks like the house was shaken—almost like an earthquake."

Molly chuckled. "That's a tornado for you. They're bat-crap crazy. The Fab Five and I are at the airport. We'll be home tomorrow evening. Got a couple of layovers, but if we make all our flights, we'll be there by suppertime. Long as you and Chester are all right, everything is good. They're calling for us to board now. See you soon."

"I'll see you tomorrow night then?"

"Yes, you will," Molly said.

Hud started the engine and headed out of town.

He made the turn to go toward the ranch and laid a hand on her shoulder. "It's been a long day, and I'm starving. While you take a shower, I'll hustle us up some food."

"Thank you, again, for everything." She covered a second yawn with her hand. "I felt so sorry for those folks in the hospital. I wished I could do more."

He parked the truck, and she got out without waiting for him. Red met her on the porch and followed the two of them into the house.

"Nikki said you were a big help, and she was going to yell at you again if they needed someone with your skill set."

"I'm always glad to volunteer." Rose set the computer case on the floor inside the door and took the bag from him. "I'll only be a few minutes, and then I'll help you cook, but you'll have to tell me what to do."

"I'm just going to heat up a can of chili and make us Frito chili pies. They'll taste pretty good on a cold night like this," he said. "And there's rocky road ice cream for dessert."

"That sounds great." She carried her bag to the bathroom. *Yes, ma'am, it wouldn't take a very hard push for her to be head over heels in love with Hudson Baker.*

* * *

Hud had the food ready and on the table when Rose made it to the kitchen. She wore a pair of cute little green pajama pants with a matching tank top, and her wet hair was tied up in a towel on top of her head. "Well, now, don't you look like a model for a fancy lingerie company? And you smell wonderful, but, darlin', I'm wiped out tonight."

"Me too." She sat down and picked up a spoon. "And hungry, and sleepy. I'm not up for another round like the one we had last night."

"Sleep," he sighed. "All cuddled up with you sounds like heaven to me."

"Tell me about your day," she said.

"We put out an electrical fire at a trailer house to start off the morning," he said between bites.

"And then?" she asked.

"We had to dig an old couple out of the debris. They had enough sense to get in the bathtub and cover up with a mattress, but a huge dresser was holding them down," he answered. "There was a little boy in the shed behind the trailer. He had a shard of glass in his arm. We put him in an ambulance with his mother. Did you see him?" he asked.

"I did, and Nikki stitched up his arm. He cried, not for the pain, but for his daddy. I located him out in the emergency room. He had a concussion, but they treated him and let him go home," Rose answered. "I heard they'd opened the churches in town for shelters. Do you know how many houses got hit?"

"Ten trailers in a park on the south side of town, the B&B, two convenience stores, and a car dealership on the west side, and lots of roof damage and fallen trees. It'll be a while before it's all cleaned up, but Texans are a resilient bunch of folks. There'll be donations to the church clothes closets and food banks, and you can bet that the people who have rental property will be lowering the first three months' rent to help out those who are left with nothing," he answered. "Now, your turn. Tell me more about your day."

"Mostly, I just translated from Spanish to English, but I did have one little guy from Haiti, and I got to use my French," she told him. "But in a couple of instances I held someone's hand while the doctor stitched them up—and assured them in whatever language they spoke that it would be all right."

"That's really special of you to do that," he said.

"It's pretty awesome of you to volunteer as a firefighter," she shot right back.

"Tag and I volunteered out in Tulia, so when we came here, we just told the fire chief that we'd be glad to help out." He carried his bowl to the sink and rinsed it. "Help yourself to the ice cream. I'll get mine when I get out of the shower."

Hud washed away what felt like a week's worth of smoke and grime. He took time to shave and splash on some cologne and then dressed in a pair of pajama pants and a white T-shirt. If Rose hadn't said that she was hungry, he would have taken a shower before he heated up the chili.

He found her curled up on the end of the sofa with a half a bottle of beer in her hand. She handed it to him, and he took a long swig before he sat down beside her. "Thanks. Want to watch a movie until bedtime?"

"Let's watch reruns of whatever cop show is on television. That way, if we fall asleep it won't matter," she said.

He picked up the remote and hit the POWER button, then surfed through the three or four channels until he found reruns of *Friends*. "This all right?" he asked.

"I love that show." She moved closer to him and laid her head on his shoulder.

"Me too." He kissed her on top of her head.

If the contentment he felt right then was what he could look forward to with Rose on a long-term basis, then he was already looking forward to it. To come home after a long day at work just to sit together with a woman who was satisfied just to be near him was something he'd never known before. To know that tomorrow he'd wake up with her by his side was pretty great.

* * *

Rose awoke the next morning before dawn, realized where she was, and reached out for Hud, but all she got was a handful of pillow. Thinking that she might have been dreaming, she sat straight up in bed, just in time to see Hud coming through the door with a wooden tray in his hands.

"I thought we'd have breakfast in bed before we go back to work. Nikki already called and asked if you'd help out at the hospital today. She'll pick you up at seven. Tag and I'll have to start repairing our roof, and then we'll go over to Emily's and help Justin with that one. Seems like the other two over there didn't even get a single shingle blown off," he said as he set the tray down on the bed. "By the way, darlin', you sure look cute with bedroom hair and no makeup."

She couldn't keep the smile off her face. "Did you forget to put your contact lenses in this morning?"

"Honey, I've got twenty-twenty vision, and I'm speaking the guaran-damn-teed truth." He sat down beside her and picked up a piece of crisp bacon with his fingers with the intention of feeding it to her. She snatched it from him and popped the whole strip into her mouth.

"Cooked just right," she said. "And those pancakes look amazing."

"They're my special butter pecan recipe," he told her.

She cut off a bite with the edge of her fork and popped it into her mouth. "Oh, my God! Will you marry me?"

"Is that the best pickup line you've got?" he asked.

"Short of getting down on one knee and proposing, it's all I've got," she replied as she handed him a fork. "Let's share. You've got enough on this plate for an army."

Never, not one time, had a man brought her breakfast in bed. Sharing a plate of food with Hud was so romantic that she got a little misty eyed.

When they'd finished off everything on the tray, including a four-cup pot of coffee, she cupped his cheeks in her hands and kissed him. "Mmmm, bacon and maple syrup kisses are almost as good as whiskey kisses on the dance floor."

"I was just thinking the same thing," he told her as he tossed his truck keys on the bed. "Nikki will be here soon. If you'd rather have a vehicle of your own, you can use my truck. I won't need it all day, so if you need to run any errands or maybe stop by and see Dixie, feel free to use it."

"A woman doesn't usually come between a cowboy and his truck," she said.

"You're right special to this cowboy, ma'am." He picked up the tray and headed out of the room. When he got to the door, he turned back and winked. "Matter of fact, you're real special, darlin'."

"So are you." She blew him a kiss.

Chapter Seventeen

Rose was walking out of the hospital with Nikki that afternoon when her phone rang. Molly had made it home and was in Sunset with the Fab Five.

"Hello, darlin' girl," Molly said. "We went by the B&B, and I've got Chester with me in Sunset. The Fab Five insisted I stay with them until we can figure out what happened. The insurance adjuster is coming at four. You're right—it looks more like earthquake damage than tornado."

"I just finished volunteering for a day at the hospital." She glanced at the clock on the dashboard. "I'll have Nikki drop me at the B&B."

"See you in a few minutes then." Molly's voice sounded weary. "I've got Chester settled and the folks here said I can borrow the van to drive over."

"I heard most of that." Nikki made a right-hand turn toward the B&B. "Either or both of you could stay with us, or I'm sure Emily would let y'all use the cabin. And one more thing, the hospital administrator asked me if you'd be interested in a job. He could use someone with your skills. You'd probably be working in the admissions office in addition to translating."

"I promised my mother I'd come to Kentucky for a visit. Does he need an answer right away?" Rose asked.

Nikki pulled up next to the curb. "I don't think so, but please think about it."

"I will." Rose nodded. "And you can tell him that I'm very interested."

"Fair enough," Nikki said. "Want me to come in with you?"

"No, Aunt Molly and the adjuster will be here in ten minutes, and Tag is probably waiting for you. Thanks for everything, Nikki." Rose got out of the car and headed across the lawn toward the house.

She had to really work on getting the key in the lock that afternoon, and then she had to put her shoulder to the door to open it. She hadn't had that kind of trouble the day before, but maybe it had something to do with the damage. She picked her way through the glass on the floor, and peeked into the shop. The place looked even worse than it had before—all that lovely crystal shattered into pieces and scattered everywhere on the floor. From there she went to the dining room. The china cupboard was still standing, but only the framework remained. The glass sides were gone, right along with all of Aunt Molly's antique glassware.

Molly came in the door like a whirlwind, grabbed Rose in a bear hug, and held on to her for a long time. "I'm so glad to see you, child, and I'm glad you were gone when this happened. Have you ever seen such a mess?"

"Can't say as I have, but we can clean it all up and then you can get back into business." Rose patted Molly's back. "I'll see to it that it's all done before I leave for Kentucky."

A hard rap on the door broke up the hug, and Molly yelled, "Come on in."

Molly wrapped her hand around Rose's arm, and the two of them crossed the floor together. "We're in here, Marvin."

"Miss Molly." An older gentleman tipped his cowboy hat toward her. "I'm right sorry about all this, and I'll take lots of pictures and look around, but I can tell you that you'd better be looking for another house to live in. Seeing the gap between the porch and the house tells me exactly what happened here."

"And that is?" Molly asked.

"The tornado picked up the house and then set it right back down. I've seen this a few times in my career. The only trouble is that the storm doesn't get the house set back on the foundation right. Come on out here in the yard, and let me show you," Marvin said.

"I'm so sorry." Molly must've suddenly remembered her manners. "This is my great-niece, Rose, and this is my insurance adjuster and my Sunday school teacher, Marvin Conners."

"Pleased to meet you." Marvin tipped his hat again.

"Likewise," Rose said.

They followed him outside, and he showed them the problem. "See how the house is set back on the foundation a good three inches right here at the front? Now come on around to the backside." He pointed toward the overhang. "This is structurally unsound and will have to be condemned. I'm putting in papers for it to be totaled, which means that you'll receive a check for the insured amount for the business, plus the contents. And you paid extra for any case like this, so we'll have it torn down. Then you'll just have to sell the land or rebuild."

"Holy crap!" Molly gasped.

"That's why it looked like an earthquake rather than a tornado," Rose said.

"You're right," Marvin said. "Only thing is I'd expect a few broken windows, but then one never knows about tornadoes. They're a phenomenon all of their own. I'll go on inside now and take some pictures, and again, I'm sorry."

"Can we go inside and get our personal belongings?" Molly asked.

"Sure, but be careful." Marvin started back around the house, snapping pictures with his camera the whole way.

Molly sat down on a back porch step and put her head in her hands. "I've been thinkin' about retirin' and sellin' the place, but I sure didn't think it would be forced on me like this."

Except for the hair—Molly's was gray and cut into a pageboy—she and Luna could have been twins. They were both on the slim side, had the same face shape, and their voices sounded enough alike that it would be difficult to know which one was talking.

Rose sat down beside her and draped an arm around her shoulders. "I'm so sorry. Maybe we can salvage some of the furniture."

"Nope." Molly shook her head. "I've had to dust all that stuff for years. If I'm startin' all over, then I'll do it from scratch, and get comfortable furniture. And I'll buy a small house in Sunset. There are two or three for sale over there that's close to my church and my friends."

"Won't you be a little sad after living here so long?" Rose asked.

"Ain't no use in cryin' over spilt milk." Molly sighed. "The Lord works in mysterious ways. Evidently, He had to get pretty loud to get my attention and tell me it was time to retire. We'll pack up what we want and not even look back when we leave. You need to go see your mama. By the time you get back, me and Chester will be settled into a new place."

"Maybe I'll catch a bus to Kentucky tomorrow, if you're sure you don't want me to stick around and help with things," Rose said.

"Catch a bus, my ass," Molly said. "I'm buying us both a new car, but only if you promise to come back to Bowie and see my new place before you reenlist."

"I may not do that." Rose told her about the job opportunity at the hospital.

"Does Hud Baker have anything to do with your decision?" Molly asked.

"Did I hear my name?" Hud asked as he rounded the back corner of the house.

"Well, good evening, Hud Baker." Molly stood up. "First night back and a good-lookin' cowboy comes to see me. Did Marvin tell you the news?"

Hud's jeans had holes in the knees, and his T-shirt was stained. His hair stuck out from around a sweat-stained black cowboy hat that he removed and held in his hands. "I saw Marvin when I knocked on the door. I'm right sorry about all this, Miss Molly. You ladies need anything?"

"Thank you, but it could be a blessin' in disguise. I should've quit the business years ago," Molly answered.

"You going to rebuild?" Hud asked.

"Nope. I'm going to buy a house in Sunset. Rose and I are fixin' to get our things out of the house, and I'm going back to stay with the Fab Five for a few days until I can get things arranged."

"Rose can stay with me," Hud said.

"That's what I figured." Molly motioned toward the house. "It's sad, but sometimes it takes a little sadness in the soul to make us appreciate the rainbows more. I'm already liking the idea of living near my friends and my church."

When she was out of sight, Hud gave Rose a quick peck on the lips. "I'm too dirty and smelly to give you a hug. I'll see you later tonight."

He settled his hat back on his head and waved over his shoulder as he left. Rose touched her lips to see if they were as hot as they felt.

* * *

An hour later, the van that Molly was driving was packed full of their clothing, and they were on their way to the car dealership right there in Bowie. Molly took one long look at the B&B before she pulled away from the curb. "It's a shame that it had to go the way it did, but it's a blessing at the same time. I've got a lot of good memories from that place."

The place would always be special to Rose, since that's where she and Hud had spent... She blushed at the pictures of the two of them all tangled up in the bed and in the shower. Even if things never worked out for them, she'd carry her beautiful memories with her forever.

"Maybe after we buy cars, we should celebrate by having dinner together," Molly said.

"Aunt Molly, I can't let you buy me a vehicle. I don't even know what I'm going to do with my life. I may or may not need a car," Rose said.

"I know what you'll do with your life, but I'll let you figure it out. But I will tell you that you need one to drive to Kentucky and haul the babies around in when you have them," Molly said.

"Aunt Molly!" Rose gasped.

"Don't fuss at me." Molly waggled a finger at her. "When I die, you're going to get everything I own, so you can have it now or have it when I'm dead. Your choice. Just pick out what you like."

"But—" Rose protested.

"Shhh!" Molly interrupted. "If I'm buying two cars, I should get a real good deal, right?" She looked at the salesman expectantly.

Two hours later they were walking off the lot, keys in hand.

Molly giggled. "Saved fifteen thousand dollars. Luna ain't got a thing on me when it comes to making deals."

"Why would you say that?" Rose asked.

"She sold that carnival for twice what it was really worth, and then she invested her money. She called me on that cheap cell phone you gave her. She told me that she's leaving whatever is left of her money to you, just like I am. By the time you're fifty, you'll be able to buy a ranch of your own if you want one." Molly slid behind the wheel of her car and turned the key.

"But why, if she's got all that money, does she live like she does?" Rose could feel her eyes getting so wide that they hurt.

"Money don't mean jack crap to her, and it means even less to me." Molly giggled. "We both just like to think we've made a good deal and know that we've got a giant nest egg if we ever need it. How do you think your folks keep that commune going? Your Granny Dee left them her money."

"Daddy runs the construction crew too," Rose said.

"I'm not saying that Paul ain't a hardworkin' man, but his damned pride just about caused him to refuse that money when Devine died. Your mama threatened to leave his sorry ass and take you with her, if she couldn't at least live in a decent trailer and have money for your schoolin'." Molly's finger shot up again. "And don't you dare tell her that I told you that."

"It can be our secret," Rose whispered.

"Now, you unload what's yours out of this van, get in your car, and go out to the ranch and show it off to Hud, and go on and tell him what I said about babies." Molly laughed as she slammed the door.

"I will not!" Rose yelled at her through the window. "I thought we were going to dinner."

"We'll celebrate when you get back from Kentucky," Molly said.

"What about the Fab Five's van?"

"I know the dealer here. He's going to take it back to Sunset today." Molly waved and drove away.

Rose loved the feel of the car and the way it handled and especially the seat warmers. She drove below the speed limit all the way to the ranch just so she could savor the first moments of owning her very own car for the first time.

Hud and Tag were on the roof when she first got there, but when Hud saw her get out of the vehicle, he climbed down the ladder that was propped up at the end of the house. "Hey, is that Molly's new car or the rental?"

"It's *my* new car," she said. "I wanted to show it to you first."

"Well, it's almost, but not quite, as pretty as you are." He peeked inside and then took her by the hand and walked all around it. "Got a whole lot of room. Does this mean you aren't going to the army after all?"

She nodded. "Probably, but I'm still thinkin' about what I want to do." "I just had to show it off, since this is my very first vehicle."

"You're kiddin' me," he said.

"Nope, didn't need one at the commune, since I never went anywhere. When I was in the army, I didn't need one because I never knew how long I'd be anywhere," she said. "But now I do. Oh, and day after tomorrow, I'm leaving for Kentucky for about a week. I got a call on the way here from a lady at the hospital. We're meeting tomorrow morning to talk about a job."

"How about I grill us some steaks to celebrate your new car?" He grinned. "And maybe your new position?"

"Sounds wonderful," she said, but in reality she was already missing him—and she hadn't even left yet.

He gave her a quick kiss, but even that much made her knees a little weak.

Chapter Eighteen

Rose sipped on a cup of hot chocolate as she waited in the back booth of the Dairy Queen for the woman from the hospital to arrive. Every time the door opened she looked up from the book she was reading, a romance that had been translated into German. At exactly the right time, a lady walked in and scanned the restaurant. Rose stood and met the lady in the middle of the floor.

"I'm Rose O'Malley." She extended a hand.

"Danielle White." The lady shook her hand. "I just wanted to meet you and talk about the job opportunity at the hospital before you leave."

Danielle was shorter than Rose by a couple of inches and older by a couple of decades. She had piercing brown eyes and long black hair that hung down her back. She wore black leggings and a flowing floral tunic, black boots that reached her knees, and a turquoise necklace that Echo would love.

"Can I order you a cup of coffee, a hot chocolate, or something to eat?" Rose asked.

"I'd love a hot chocolate," Danielle said.

By the time Rose got back to the booth with the woman's order, Danielle had a folder and her laptop sitting on the table. Rose set the hot chocolate down and slid into her side. "Why are we meeting here and not at the hospital?"

"I'm doing this on my lunch hour," Danielle said. "The hospital administrator, Timothy Wallace, and I saw what you did those couple of days when you volunteered. He asked me to sit down with you and kind of lay out what we need, since it'll probably start off as part-time work. You can be thinking about it while you're gone."

"All right then, shall we get down to business?" Rose said.

"With your skill set and what a help you'll be in admissions, we can pay you well, and it can work into a full-time job."

"The job sounds like something I'd sure be interested in doing, but may I ask, is it mainly Spanish speaking that you'd need?"

"Five years ago I would have said yes to that question, but today, we need more. That's why Mr. Wallace and I are so interested in creating a position for you," Danielle said. "I just wanted to visit with you and make you understand that we're serious. Here's my business card with my number and Mr. Wallace's on it. If you have any questions call either of us."

Rose didn't even know Molly was in the restaurant until she'd slid into the seat that Danielle had vacated. "Well, where did you come from?" Rose asked.

"I dropped right down out of heaven," Molly joked. "I had to leave my wings and halo in my new car, which is parked out there beside yours. I've been all over town this morning taking care of business. Been to the insurance place about the house and the car, and then to the wrecking company that's going to take the house down and leave an empty lot."

"Well, I just got my first official job offer," Rose said.

"Where?" Molly asked.

"The hospital right here in Bowie. Part-time at first, but it could work into more," Rose answered. "I'd be using my language skills to admit people to the hospital, and to translate wherever I'm needed. I liked working with Nikki—felt like I was helping people."

"Well, hot damn!" Molly slapped the table so hard that the salt and pepper shakers rattled. "That's the best news I've had in years. You can live with me until you find a place. I've already picked out my new home over in Sunset." She wiggled her eyebrows. "And that ain't far from Hud."

"Win. Win. Win." Rose grinned at her aunt. "And I'd be doing a job that I love."

"Let's celebrate by ordering something to eat. I haven't had a good taco in a month." Molly slid out of the booth. "What do you want? My treat because I wanted you to take this job so you can live close to me."

"Tacos sound good to me, and thank you." Rose was learning that arguing with Luna or Molly did as much good as fighting with a stop sign.

"I should be thanking you for making this decision," Molly said as she headed toward the counter.

"I haven't agreed to it yet. I've got to go see Mama first," Rose said.

"Well, once you spend a week at the commune, you'll be hurrying back here," Molly teased.

"You just might be right."

* * *

Hud couldn't sleep, not even after sex that had left him and Rose both breathless, so he raised up on one elbow and stared his fill of her. Never in his wildest imagination would he have dreamed that someday he and Cactus Rose O'Malley would be in bed together. Seeing her at the Christmas party had been a pure miracle, and then to get to spend so much time with her was magic.

He wanted to kiss every freckle on her face, but that would wake her, and she needed her rest for the long trip she had to Kentucky the next day. She slowly opened her eyes and pulled his lips down for a kiss.

"Is it morning?" she muttered.

"No, darlin', it's just a little past midnight," he whispered.

"Hold me until I have to go, and be here when I get back," she said.

"That's a promise." He drew her over closer to him and kept an arm around her when she laid her head on his chest. When he finally went to sleep, he dreamed of her.

She had white streaks in her strawberry blond hair. She was standing in the kitchen with a baby on her hip when he came in from evening chores.

"Take your grandson, darlin', so I can get the bread out of the oven." She smiled up at him.

He kissed her first and then took the baby from her.

When he awoke, dawn was just breaking up the night, and she was sitting up in bed, staring at him. "You talked in your sleep," she said.

"What did I say?" he asked.

"You were mumbling about a baby," she answered.

"Just a crazy dream," he said, but oh, how his heart ached for it to come true.

"Shall we have a muffin and a cup of coffee before I get on the road?" she asked.

He grinned as he pulled her back down beside him. "I'd rather have dessert in bed before you leave."

"Oh, honey, that's the main course," she giggled. "The muffin is just dessert."

"I like your way of thinkin'." He pulled her over on top of him and started stringing red hot kisses from that soft, sensitive spot on her neck to her lips.

A couple of hours later, he walked her out to her car, held her close, and whispered, "Come back to me, Rose. Promise me that."

"I give you my word," she told him. "The commune is a great place to visit, but it's not where my heart is."

He raised her chin with his knuckles and stared down into her eyes for several minutes before he kissed her goodbye. "Text me when you can, and call me tonight?"

"You do the same." She hugged him one more time and got into her car. He closed the door and watched her drive away until he couldn't see her anymore.

When he started back toward the house, Tag stepped out on the porch. "Cupid has bitten pretty bad, hasn't he, and it's not even Valentine's Day yet."

"Yep, just like you were with Nikki," Hud said.

* * *

Rose made good time and had reached Memphis by suppertime. According to Agnes, the name she'd given her GPS lady, she was a little more than halfway to Miracle, Kentucky, barely a dot on the map.

She checked into a hotel right off the highway and called Molly for a few minutes of FaceTime. "I'm safe and in a room."

"That's great," Molly told her. "Crazy, ain't it. You used to travel all over the world, and I never worried about you. Now that you're close to me, I fret if I don't know you're safe. I like being able to see you."

"Me too, and now I've got to call Hud." Rose smiled.

"Before you go," Molly said, "you should know that Luna is at the commune. She has no idea that you're on the way."

"I bet Mama just loves that." Rose rolled her eyes. "How'd you find this out?"

"She's makin' good use of that cell phone you got her. And she's bought a car, too—an old 1960 Cadillac that probably eats more gas than an army tank. She drove herself from Alabama to Miracle, and when she called, she said that she just might buy a trailer and live up in those hills," Molly informed her. "Just thought you should know."

"Thanks for the heads-up. Love you," Rose said as she ended the call and hit the icon on her phone for Hud's number.

"Hey!" Hud answered the call on the first ring. "You look tired, darlin'. Did you make it all the way to Memphis?"

"Yep, and I'm in a hotel room, in my pajamas, and not planning to go out until tomorrow morning." She yawned. "Sorry about that. I've had lots of coffee and sugar, and yet I'm still sleepy."

"I wouldn't know why," Hud teased. "You did get a good night's sleep last night, right?"

"Hell, no!" She smiled. "This sexy cowboy kept me awake half the night, first by having mind-blowing sex with me and after that by talking in his sleep about babies. You absolutely sure you don't have a skeleton in the closet that we need to talk about?"

"Nope," he said. "Where exactly in Kentucky are you going?"

He changed the subject so fast that she wondered what she'd find if she really did open his virtual closet doors. That he knew his way around a king-size bed suggested that he'd been with lots of women, but hopefully none of those nights had netted a baby.

"Miracle is the closest town, but it's really tiny. I cross over the Cumberland River there, and go several miles along the river to the end of the road, take a dirt path back into the hills and hollers about three miles, and there's the commune. It sits down in a pretty little valley between two mountains, but it's narrow, so some of the trailers in the commune are on a hillside. Mama and Daddy have one of the two or three in the actual holler," she explained. "You should've come with me. We could've stayed in a hotel in Harlan instead of at the commune. I miss you, Hud."

"I miss you too." His drawl seemed deeper. "A week seems like forever."

"You've got lots of work to keep you busy," she told him.

"And you've got to think about that job offer," he said, "but that don't make the nights any shorter. I'm already dreading going to bed without you to cuddle with."

"Me too." She blew him a kiss.

"Call me tomorrow morning before you get on the road again?"

"Of course," she agreed.

They ended the call at the same time, and she opened the bag with her food, turned on the television to reruns of *Friends*, and wished that Hud was with her on the big king-size bed.

Chapter Nineteen

The next day Rose hit a snag in traffic and was held up for an hour between the Tennessee and Kentucky borders. That meant she had to drive the last few miles in the dark, causing her to almost miss the turnoff to the commune. She parked her car beside a big blue Caddy in front of her folks' trailer. Nothing much had changed. Her mama's flowerbeds were full of pansies, and a mama cat was nestled down in a basket at the corner of the porch. Rose stopped to count five kittens, and wondered if she could get home to Bowie with one or two. Now that she was settling down, Rose thought she would love to have a pet.

All right, she scolded herself, you've put it off long enough. *Open the door and go inside.*

Before she could straighten up, the front door flew open and her father's silhouette filled the space. He had a double-barreled, sawed-off shotgun pointed right at her. "Didn't you see those NO TRESPASSING signs on the fence out there?

We don't cotton to outsiders here." Then he dropped the gun and cocked his head to one side. "Cactus Rose, darlin', is that you?"

"Surprise, Daddy," she said.

"Echo!" her father yelled over his shoulder. "Cactus Rose is home."

"Well, quit hollerin' and get out of the way." Echo's husky voice got louder with each word as she pushed him to the side and grabbed her daughter in a fierce hug. Taller than Rose by several inches, Echo had the same strawberry blond hair, green eyes, and full lips. She carried about twenty or thirty pounds more than Rose, but it looked good on her with her height.

Paul set his gun down behind the door and made it a three-way hug. "Why didn't you let us know you were comin'?"

"I'd have made a chocolate cake if you'd told me exactly when you were getting here." Echo kept an arm around Rose's shoulder and walked with her into the double-wide trailer.

Paul came in behind them. "Luna's been tellin' us that you're seeing a cowboy from Texas. Is that true? When are you bringin' him home to meet us?"

"Where is Aunt Luna?" Rose asked.

"She's out in the community room, entertaining folks by reading the cards for them," Echo said.

Rose could feel her body tense. There was no way when she had been living at home that Paul O'Malley would have allowed such a frivolous thing in the community hall. Luna would have been burned at the stake—not really, but pretty damn close—if she'd played fortune-teller when Rose lived there.

Paul's expression looked like he'd just gotten a whiff of a

skunk. She glanced at her mother, and Echo sent a sly wink her way.

"She'll be here in a little bit. Lights out at nine, remember?" Echo said.

"I hear from Aunt Molly that she's thinkin' about stayin' here." Rose sat down on the sofa. Everything was the same, from the well-worn brown couch, to the pictures hanging on the walls. There wasn't a single photo of her in her uniform, because her father believed women didn't belong in the military. That's why she never wore her uniform home after that first time.

"About this cowboy?" Paul persisted.

"Do you remember the Baker boys from Tulia?" Rose looked up at her tall father. Dark eyebrows were drawn down in a scowl. His jet-black hair hung down to his shirt collar, and his arms stretched the knit of an oatmeal-colored shirt.

"Those wild kids with weird names? Taggart and Hudson, right?" Paul's frown deepened.

"That's right. They have a ranch not far from Bowie, where Aunt Molly lived. Tag is married to a nurse, and I helped her in the hospital, but that's another story. Hud is the cowboy I've been seeing these past few weeks. He's a really nice guy, Daddy. If things get serious, I might even bring him home to meet you," she said.

Paul crossed his arms over his chest. "Well, don't be expectin' me to come to Texas to walk you down the aisle if things get serious, as you say. You can come home and get married in the community room like all the other kids here have done."

"Wouldn't dream of making you come to Texas," Rose said with a smile on her face that didn't come close to reaching her heart. "So y'all tell me what all—"

Luna burst into the house before she could finish the sentence. "Well, hot damn!" She ran to the sofa and plopped down beside Rose, gave her a sideways hug, and said, "This is a wonderful surprise. I was goin' to call you tonight on my new cell phone and tell you that I was here. I'm buyin' a trailer and an acre of ground from the commune to park it on. It ain't new or as big as the one me and Wilbur had, but that's not important. You're the center of attention here. Tell me about Hud and Molly and Dixie."

"Molly is home and in her new house. I dropped by Claire's quilt shop on Monday. Claire looks like she's carrying a baby elephant. Dixie and the baby are thriving, and I've got a job offer from the hospital. I'd work in admissions, but I'd also be all over the hospital as a translator. Hud is fine. I just talked to him a little while ago." She spouted off the news to keep from having to deal with her father.

"We're glad to have Luna in the commune with us," Echo said.

Rose glanced over at her father, but his face didn't give away anything.

"Last time I was here"—Rose steered the conversation in another direction— "the trees and mountains were green. It's been years since I've been back in the winter. Things look different. How're things with the construction business, Daddy?"

"Booming." Paul's expression went from angry to happy in a split second. "The young men that you turned down have married and joined the business. We were able to buy forty more acres for the commune recently. When can we frame up a house for you?"

"I think I'll settle in Bowie for a while," she said. "Are you putting your trailer on the new forty, Aunt Luna?"

"Yep, I'm the first one in that section, and I have a place

for a garden and it's pretty close to the Cumberland River, so I can take my cane pole down there and fish," Luna told her.

"You sure you'll be happy in a commune?" Rose asked.

"Honey, I've lived in one ever since I was a teenager. A carnival is just a glorified commune, and then when we retired, we kind of made another one in the trailer park," Luna replied. "If you're here on Saturday, they're bringin' my new home in and gettin' it set up and leveled. And anytime you want to come live with me, you are welcome."

"If I can talk her into coming home, she'll live right here," Paul said. "Is your suitcase in that car out there? I'll go get it for you if you'll give me the keys."

"It's open, Daddy." Rose looked up at the clock on the wall. "It's been a long two days on the road. I'd like to have a shower and crawl into bed."

"Good thing I put fresh sheets on the bed yesterday. Line dried too, just how you like them," Echo said.

As soon as her father was out the door, she stood and gave her mother another hug. "He don't change much, does he?"

Luna sighed. "He's a sumbitch, but he's Echo's sumbitch, and she loves him. And he loves you, girl, even if he ain't real good at showin' it."

"I know, Aunt Luna." Rose smiled. "I can't believe that you drove up here all by yourself and that you're using the cell phone I gave you."

She put a finger over her lips. "The phone was going to be my secret, but you know me and my big mouth. I done told Paul about it. And I told your mama that she can use it whenever she wants."

Echo shot a look toward Rose and shook her head ever so slightly, as if telling her that she didn't know how to handle Luna, either.

Rose couldn't wait to get into her room that evening. She

sent Hud a quick text telling him that she'd arrived and then called Aunt Molly.

"I'm here," she whispered.

"Why are you whispering? Oh, yeah, no cell phones, right? That would be bringing the world into the camp, and that's an unforgivable sin," Aunt Molly said. "Want me to call Hud? Did you warn him about the rules there—no phones or televisions?"

"No, I didn't. I don't want to scare him away from ever coming to visit my folks," she answered. "I'll give him a quick call tonight, and then we'll probably just text each other."

"Texting is a great thing about technology, but I do like to hear your voice," Molly told her. "Glad to know you're safe."

"Good night. See you in a week," Rose told her. "Or maybe even sooner."

The last thing she heard before the call ended was Molly's giggle.

She closed her eyes and visualized Hud in his pajama pants and snug-fitting T-shirt as she waited on him to answer the phone. When he did, the first thing he asked was about FaceTime so he could see her gorgeous face.

"Phones of any kind, except the one in the communal kitchen, are forbidden," she said in a soft voice. "If anyone heard your deep drawl, there'd be trouble. It would probably be better if we text most of the time."

"Whatever works best for you," Hud said. "I just want you to have a good week, and then come home."

"I haven't felt like I had a real home in a very long time. Something was always missing when I was a kid in the commune. I loved being with Mama, and the quietness of the hills and hollers, but I felt like I was in limbo, waiting for my real life to begin. That's why I joined the army, but I didn't feel whole there either."

"Do you now here in Bowie?" Hud asked.

"Almost," she answered, honestly. "Maybe when I get my own place, I'll really be home."

"I hope so, because I missed you more today than I did yesterday. That old saying about being out of sight, out of mind, is a crock of bull crap," Hud said.

Rose was glad they weren't FaceTiming, because she did a fist pump.

"What is that noise?" Hud asked.

"Aunt Luna is in the next bedroom, and she's snoring," Rose told him. "I never heard her do that in the B&B, not one time."

"Maybe it's all that mountain air. If you snore when you get back home to Sunset, I promise I won't kick you out of bed," he said.

Sunset? Home? She hadn't thought of renting something in the tiny little town of Sunset. She figured she'd have to get an apartment over in Bowie, but Sunset made more sense. Aunt Molly lived there, and it was closer to Tag and Hud's ranch.

"On that note, and with that vision in my head, I'm going to tell you good night," Rose said.

"Good night, darlin'. Talk to you tomorrow," Hud said.

Just hearing his deep, sexy drawl made her wish that she was back in Sunset, cuddled up next to him in the ranch house.

* * *

Mornings started way before daylight in the communal kitchen. Breakfast had to be ready and served before the men left for work. Then the women had cows to milk and chickens to feed, and when spring came, gardens to plant and take care of. If they had children, they also had to homeschool them, and train them to enjoy the work. Older boys were taught to milk cows and take care of livestock. Girls were taught the fine arts of quilt making, sewing and cooking, plus keeping house. It was all incredibly traditional, and Rose had been a part of it—except for the cooking part. She didn't mind working in the garden, milking cows, or throwing corn out for the chickens, but kitchen work was not her thing.

Everyone seemed happy, and there were no strings holding the young people there if they decided to leave. If they did go their own way, as Rose had done, they were welcome to come home for visits. Several had changed their minds once they'd tried life outside, and the commune took them right back in without questions.

Rose went to the kitchen with her mother that morning. Aunt Luna had gotten the huge pots of coffee brewing and was already sipping on her first cup.

"Good mornin'!" She held up her cup in greeting.

"Mornin'." Rose headed toward the pot to pour herself a cup.

Echo went straight to the stove, lit two burners, and set two big cast-iron skillets on the fire. She took five pounds of sausage from one of the refrigerators and divided it between the two pans.

"Can I help you, Mama?" Rose asked.

"No, honey, you go on in there and keep Aunt Luna company. I've got help coming any minute"—Echo nodded toward the door—"there's Grace now. She and I work really well together."

"And besides, you're afraid I'll burn the biscuits or scorch the eggs, right?" Rose said.

"Well, there is that." Echo stopped what she was doing and gave Rose a quick hug.

"If I wanted to learn how to cook, how would I start?" Rose asked.

"Read the recipes and follow them to the letter," Echo answered.

"Y'all still got pecans in the freezer from last year's crop? Maybe I'll make a pecan pie. I've been hungry for one." Rose remembered seeing a recipe for one in a magazine that called for two tablespoons of Jack Daniel's whiskey.

"That's easy enough," Echo said. "Maybe you could make several for supper before you leave."

"I can manage that, but you'll have to make the crust for me," Rose said.

"I'll be glad to," Echo offered.

"Well, hello!" Grace crossed the kitchen floor and grabbed Rose in a fierce hug. "Echo didn't tell me you were coming. This is a wonderful surprise. We'll talk later, though. It's my week to help in the kitchen. Come by my house after lunch. You can meet my newest baby girl, Jennifer."

"How many do you have?" Rose asked her childhood friend.

"Jennifer makes the fourth girl. We're hoping the next one will be a boy." Grace, a tall brunette with pretty brown eyes, hurried to the kitchen. She covered her jeans and shirt with a bibbed apron and went to work browning the sausage in one of the pans.

"Just think," Luna said out of the side of her mouth, "you could have four kids by now and be thinking about a fifth. You and Hud are going to have to get busy to catch up. And by the way, you're welcome."

"I'm glad my friend is happy with her lot, but I'm also

glad I didn't marry at eighteen and have four kids right now. And I'm welcome for what?" Rose asked.

"My snoring," Luna said. "I don't snore. Molly does and Devine did, but I don't, but last night I heard your dad say something about noises in your bedroom, and he said that he bet you had a damned cell phone in there, so I started snoring. Echo told him that was what he heard, and all was well, but be careful when he's home. He has to maintain a standard, you know. If no one else can have a phone, then it wouldn't be right for him to overlook yours."

"I realize that, but how come you get to keep yours?" Rose asked.

Luna patted her pocket. "Because I don't use it except when he's away at work, and if he doesn't like it, he can take it up with Madam."

"Aunt Luna!" Rose threw a hand over her mouth. "What brought you here anyway? Especially when you know how Daddy is?"

"Reminds me of the carnival, only without all the rides and hawkers. We ate together and we worked together, and we were a happy lot," Luna said.

"Did you buy that forty acres Daddy was bragging about?"

"Yep, I did, and that's my price to live here until I die. I get to be near your mama, so it's a fair deal. Things just ain't the same in Alabama without Wilbur, and I got a little taste of being near family when I stayed at the B&B. I liked it, plus I get my meals cooked, and when I get too old to take care of my trailer, I can pay some of the young ladies to do it for me," Luna said.

"Why didn't you move to Sunset?" Rose asked.

"Me and Molly can stand each other for about a week, and then it's the beginning of war. Your mama is easier to live around, and like I said, I like the commune idea. It fits me," Luna explained. "This way we both have family, and I promise I'll come visit," she giggled, "...and I won't snore."

Life as the commune knew it was about to change, Rose thought. Her father had talked about that forty acres separating the camp from the river for years. Now it belonged to the group, but it had not come at a cheap price.

As if he heard her thoughts, he came into the dining hall with half a dozen men behind him. They all smiled and waved at her as they headed to the coffeepot. More people drifted in, right up until six thirty, when Grace and Echo put big bowls of sausage gravy and biscuits on the buffet counter. They set out several large pans of what Rose recognized as her mother's special breakfast casserole.

"Are you going into town this week?" Rose asked Luna.

"Tomorrow, to take care of some banking business," Luna answered.

"Reckon you could pick up a bottle of Jack Daniel's for me?"

Luna leaned forward and propped her elbows on the table. "You only been here one night. Why would you need Jack?"

"I'm going to make pecan pies," Rose whispered. "I'll have to sneak it into the pies. You know the rules about liquor here."

"Yep, and I intend to follow them to the T." Luna moved back and slapped her thigh. "If you believe that, then I'll sell you the Cumberland River. I'll pick up a bottle for you, and, honey, I love bourbon pecan pies."

Paul sat down at the table. "Feels right and good to be home, don't it?"

"I've always loved having breakfast with everyone."

Rose sidestepped the question. "I'm making pecan pies one night for supper."

"When did you take an interest in cooking?" Paul asked.

"Figured if I'm going to live alone without benefit of communal dining or an army mess hall, then I'd better learn a few things," she answered. "Aunt Molly says anyone can cook. All you got to do is follow directions."

"Yeah, right." Paul almost snorted. "Anyone can read directions and frame up a house too, but there's technique involved to get it done right, just like in cooking. Your mama could teach you if you'd stay home where you belong."

"Hey, Echo is about to ring the bell," Luna said.

Rose could have kissed Luna's shiny red-and-white-checkered rain boots right then. Maybe, just maybe, life would be easier when she came for visits, since her aunt had moved there.

After breakfast, Luna drove away in her big boat of a car, and Rose cleaned the whole trailer for her mother. She'd always enjoyed things being neat and in their place—that had sure made it easy to get along in the military. By the time she finished, it was lunchtime, so she headed back to the dining room. A squirrel fussed at her from a tree limb, and the mama cat that she'd petted on the porch left her kittens and followed her.

There were few things that Rose truly loved about the whole communal thing, but mealtimes were the highlight of her visits. She loved breakfast because she felt like it started off the day with a family reunion, but lunchtime was her favorite part of the day. That's when the womenfolk gathered together with the children and had time to visit with no men around. Being with them was like enjoying one big coffee klatch—only it was every day rather than once a month.

At noon she took time to go out to the dining hall for a sandwich and a bowl of potato soup. Her childhood friend, Grace, sat down beside her with a sweet little baby girl in her arms. "This is Jennifer. Amelia, Charity, and Rachel are right over there. Desmond Bennett's older girls help out with them at lunchtime."

"They're all beautiful girls." Looking at the baby, Rose was amazed at the yearning in her heart to hold a child of her own. Could it be that the roots she was putting down in Texas were causing her to have a feeling that she'd never had before?

"Thank you," Grace said. "When are you going to start a family?"

"I guess I should have a husband before I have a child, right?"

Grace's face turned bright red. "I'd hope so. Paul might never let you come home if you had a baby out of wedlock."

Well, there is that. Rose echoed her mother's earlier words and bit back a giggle.

"Do you ever regret not leaving the commune, just to visit the outside world?" Rose asked Grace.

"Not once," Grace answered without a second's hesitation. "I was born here. I'm happy right where I am with the love of my life and the children that we've produced. This is where I belong. I don't even like going to Harlan every few weeks. When we do go, I can't wait to get back home." She stopped long enough to unbutton her shirt and take out a breast to feed the baby. "How long are you going to wander around out there before you decide to come home?"

"I'm still trying to decide where home is," Rose admitted, honestly. "I've pretty well made up my mind to live in Texas. Luna's sister Molly lives there. I'd be close to her, and I have a job offer to work in a hospital as a translator."

"That's not like having your mama and daddy right next door." Grace's tone bordered on scolding.

"I guess it's not," Rose said. "It's been great visitin' with you, but I should at least go help Mama with the dishes. We'll see each other again at suppertime."

"That's the beautiful part of being here." Grace smiled. "We get to share in everything."

To have been so close that they could finish each other's sentences when they were little girls, she and Grace had surely grown apart. Yet, in a small way, Rose was jealous of Grace for being content with her life.

* * *

Friday morning Rose awoke and didn't want to go to breakfast. That had been her prerogative in the army. Sometimes all she had wanted was an extra hour of sleep and an energy bar before she got dressed for work. When her mother knocked on her door, she wanted to pull the covers up over her head.

When in Rome, that niggling little voice in her head reminded her.

"If I was in Rome, I'd be my own boss," she mumbled as she slung her legs over the side of the bed and stood up. "Hell's bells! If I was in Bowie, I'd be my own boss."

Like the day before, Luna was in the dining hall when Echo and Rose arrived. She waved from her place at one of the long tables and held up a doughnut. Today she'd braided her hair into two long ropes with beads and tiny yellow silk flowers interwoven in them. She wore a pair of bibbed overalls and a yellow-and-black-plaid shirt and had a bibbed apron over the top.

"I gave Grace the day off," she said. "I'm damn good

help in the kitchen at breakfast time, and little Jennifer wasn't doin' so well when I visited them last night. Poor little thing had a low-grade fever."

Echo's expression said she didn't like that Luna was taking such liberties as giving Grace the day off without asking permission, or even helping in the kitchen when Paul hadn't given the okay. If Paul found out Luna was usurping his authority, he'd have a meeting with the ladies, and that woudn't be a good thing. Rose bit the inside of her lip to keep from smiling. Luna had bought property. She had an agreement that said she could stay until death, and now she was taking the first baby step at changing something that had been the same for at least three generations.

Good luck with that, Rose thought as she picked up a doughnut from the box that had only two left.

"Aunt Luna, you know that we aren't supposed to bring food to the kitchen from the outside," Echo reminded her. "We either grow or make our own from scratch."

"Then you'd best eat this last one before Paul finds it," Luna said and gave her an innocent look.

Echo grabbed the box and carried it to the kitchen with her. She laid the last doughnut to the side and tore the box into little pieces before she put it into the garbage can. Then she picked up the doughnut, ate every bit of it, and licked her fingers.

"That was delicious," Echo said, "but don't bring anything in here again."

"Yes, ma'am." Luna saluted her smartly. "Let's make pancakes."

"Today is bacon-and-scrambled-egg day with blueberry muffins on the side," Echo reminded her.

"All right," Luna sighed and then shot a wink toward Rose. "Then I'll make the muffins. You can start the bacon to frying in the oven and whip up some eggs. If there's batter left over from the muffins, I'll just make a few blueberry pancakes out of it, so we don't waste anything."

* * *

All day long, people kept stopping by to visit with Rose. She barely even had time to read and answer Hud's text messages before lights-out at nine o'clock, and she'd only managed to get in one more call to him—when Aunt Luna started to do some high-powered, fake snoring on Friday night.

Then on Saturday, in between cooking duties, she'd helped her mother with the laundry. They washed the bedsheets and hung them out to dry, and even washed the windows, since the temperature was above freezing that day.

When they were finished, Echo pulled out a chair across the table from Rose. "Have you called the hospital with an answer yet?"

"Not yet, but..." Rose laid a hand on her mother's hand. "Mama, I can never thank you enough for introducing me to foreign languages. Looking back, I can see that you had a fight on your hands with Daddy about that."

"That's been my biggest regret about raising you." Echo sighed. "If we hadn't lived next to a French-speaking family in Louisiana, I wouldn't have thought of helping you learn a different language. I wanted to be able to visit with the lady, so we kind of learned from each other."

"Why would you regret it? I've been able to see the world because of my skills," Rose said.

"Because of what you just said." Echo drew in a long breath and let it out in another sigh. "You left us and went out into the world, and now I feel in my heart that you're never coming back."

Rose laid her hands on her mother's. "I love you, Mama, but you're right, I'm probably never coming back to the commune except for visits. If and when I get married, will you leave Kentucky to come to my wedding?"

Echo slowly shook her head. "That's not our way. But you will bring my grandchildren to see me here, won't you?"

"Of course I will." Rose gently squeezed Echo's hands. "And they can run in the hills and wade in the creeks like I did when I was a little girl." She looked into her mother's sad eyes. "Mama, why did you buy the programs for me to learn other languages if you already regretted teaching me Spanish and French?"

"You loved that kind of thing. You were a different child from birth. You were so inquisitive and learned so fast in the homeschool program. You wanted more and more, and I wanted you to have a little something for yourself. I hoped that by giving you something of your very own, I could get you to stay with us," Echo said. "And there was the fact that Aunt Luna had run off with a carnival. I feared that a boy from outside would catch your eye when we went to Harlan, and you'd run off with him."

"Kind of like you did when you met Daddy?" Rose asked. "You left your family to move to the commune."

"That thought did go through my mind," Echo said.

"But, Mama, I love you, and even though he's an old bear at times, I love Daddy. I don't love the commune. I knew, as a little girl, that I wanted to be a part of something bigger." She drew her hand back, stood, and got each of them a glass of sweet tea from the refrigerator. "Why did you let me go to public schools those two years in Texas?"

"Your father and the man who was overseer here at the time had a falling-out over rules. The overseer thought we shouldn't let anyone, other than our own following, into the camp. Paul said that if someone wanted to join us and was willing to obey our rules, then they should be allowed to come into the commune. I was in agreement with your father. After all, before long, we'd have cousins marrying cousins, and that would bring on all kinds of problems." Echo took a long drink of her tea and went on. "Besides, I wanted you to go to public school so you would see that it wasn't for you."

"It really wasn't." Rose smiled. "I liked being home-schooled so I could move ahead faster."

"Well, at least that one worked." Echo said.

"And I loved spending the time with you," Rose told her.

"I know it's going against your father's wishes, but I love having the cell phone so I can talk to you more."

"I have to leave in the morning. I want to get back to Texas and get settled, and I really do want that job at the hospital," Rose said.

"I understand," Echo told her. "Oh, and your father has called a meeting of the womenfolk right after supper. Just giving you a heads-up."

"I figured that was coming when Aunt Luna took Grace's place yesterday morning. You do know that they're going to butt heads real often, right?"

Echo just nodded. "Every choice has a consequence. He wanted that land, but he forgot to figure in the price of Luna being a part of the commune. I tried to tell him it wasn't a good idea, but he wouldn't listen."

If Rose hadn't already made up her mind about the commune, she did so right then. There were too many rules and laws, and she'd be damned if any man or any set of rules said that Rose couldn't attend her daughter's wedding—if she ever was blessed with a daughter.

* * *

The women filed into the dining building a few at a time, picked up some cookies and milk, and sat down at the long tables to visit while they waited on Paul. This wasn't the first time Rose had sat in on one of these meetings, but she vowed it would be the last. It was the commune's law that all females over the age of twelve had to attend the women's meetings when Paul scheduled one.

He came in the side door and nodded at each of them as he passed. When he reached Luna, he gave her a look that was meant to fry her on the spot and leave nothing but little yellow silk flowers and a pile of bones on the floor. She just smiled back at him like he had no more authority than any one of the little girls in the room—and then she turned and gave Rose a sly wink.

"Ladies, we are gathered here together tonight to go over the rules. Luna, here"—he pointed to her as if he was sending her straight to hell on a rusty poker—"is new, so maybe she doesn't understand the laws we live by. When someone is assigned to do a duty, then they do it unless they are sick nigh unto death. Grace, you can call on one of the older girls, or even Luna, to take care of one of your sick girls, but if you are able to get to the kitchen, it's your responsibility to be there. Is that understood?" Rather than the way he'd looked at Luna, he gazed at Grace as if he were a loving father reprimanding his daughter.

"Yes, sir. No excuses. It won't happen again," Grace said.

"And how is Jennifer?" Paul asked.

"Doing much better. No fever now. I think she's cutting teeth." Grace smiled.

"Do we need to go over all the rules, Luna?" Paul asked in a stern tone.

"Nope, I got the message loud and clear." She glared at Paul. "But you need to wake up and see that this isn't the dark ages."

"Then this meeting is finished. You ladies enjoy another half hour, and then it's lights-out and time to go home." Paul ignored what she'd said and left by the same way he'd come into the dining hall.

Rose knew her father loved her, but she wanted more in a relationship than rules and regulations. She wanted someone like Hud, someone who didn't have laws and rules, and if she had a sick baby, he'd probably stay home with her and help take care of the child.

"I think I've belonged with him ever since I was fourteen," she mumbled.

Aunt Luna jerked her head around and asked, "Were you talking to me?"

"No, I was figuring some things out for myself. I wasn't aware I'd said anything out loud," Rose said.

"Love and change take time and patience," Luna whispered.

Rose couldn't have agreed more.

Chapter Twenty

Hud and Tag finished with the roof repairs on both ranches before the weekend, and then went back to building fence on Monday morning. Hud had lots of time to think—and to miss Rose. Molly and the Fab Five had kept the phone lines hot between them and him since Rose had left. They told him they'd found Rose a house right there in Sunset, but he had other ideas.

"What are you thinking about?" Tag asked as they stretched the last length of barbed wire for the day.

"I'm going to ask Rose to move in with me," he said.

"Don't you think that's movin' kind of fast?" Tag asked.

"Not any faster than you and Nikki," Hud reminded him.

"I guess not." Tag chuckled. "I had to move fast or she might've found out even more about my past, and kicked me to the curb." He grew serious. "You love her, don't you?"

"I think I just might." Hud finished the last of the job and removed his heavy work gloves. "I miss her a lot, and the house is so empty when it's just me there by myself. I feel like I'm going home to a tomb every evening."

Tag propped a hip on the pickup's open tailgate. "I remember having that feeling after Nikki and I had spent time together over in the cabin. But, brother, you got to *know* you love her, not just *think* it, before you ask her to live with you, and you got to tell her. It's not easy to say the words, but you have to do it if that's the way you feel."

Hud hopped up on the tailgate and sat beside Tag. "I wanted to tell her before she left, but I just couldn't. I'm afraid every night that she's going to tell me that she's decided to stay in Kentucky."

"If she does, you'll just have to go get her." Tag grinned.

"Like you did Nikki when she got kidnapped?" Hud asked.

"Yep, now let's go home. Nikki and I are going over to Emily's for a game of—Well, rats, that's the ringtone I've set up for when we have a fire." Tag answered the phone. "It's an old trailer house just north of Sunset. We'd better get going. You can ride with me."

"I thought maybe I'd go to the Rusty Spur tonight, but I guess that's out of the question," Hud said as he got into the truck and buckled his seat belt.

"You ain't in love with Rose, brother." Tag put the gas pedal on the floor and slid around the corner when they reached the end of the lane. "If you were, you wouldn't still be chasin' skirts."

"I wasn't thinkin' about tryin' to get lucky. Besides, the place is nearly empty on a Monday night," Hud protested. "It's just that, not long ago, Rose and I spent a lot of time on the dance floor and at the bar, and well, this sounds kind of dumb, but I was just looking for memories."

"Then go to your bedroom, not the bar," Tag advised as

he slung gravel everywhere when he made a turn toward the north.

One end of the trailer was ablaze when they arrived onsite. A woman was standing in the front yard screaming that she had to go back into the house. Her four-year-old son had run back in to rescue his kitten. The fire chief was telling her that she had to let them do their jobs.

Without thinking, Hud took off in a dead run to the front porch, pushed his way into the house, and grabbed the little boy, who was holding a little gray kitten close to his chest. The little guy's eyes were watering, and he was coughing so hard that he kept gagging, but he held on to that squirming cat like it was a lifeline.

The mother broke through the firemen who were holding her back and grabbed the kid as soon as she saw Hud coming through the smoke with him in his arms. "I told you not to let go of my hand."

"I had to get Rascal, Mommy," the child said.

"Boy, you are either the craziest fireman I've ever known or the most courageous," the fire chief said, "but if you don't stop doing things like that without—"

An explosion shot flames from the trailer's doors and windows and caught the dormant mesquite trees surrounding it on fire. The mother of the child dropped to her knees and wrapped herself around the little boy and his kitten.

"Somebody get that damned gas line turned off...now!" the fire chief yelled. "And get those hoses on the trees before we burn down the whole damn town." He turned back to Hud. "You ain't suited up, so you take care of that woman."

Hud hurried over to the lady, who was so shaken that she could hardly speak. "My husband is coming home tomorrow." Tears rolled down her cheeks, and she waved her arms around to take in the whole mess. "To this. To nothing."

"Where's he coming from?" Hud asked.

"He's just getting out of the military, and he just did a six-month tour in Kuwait. Everything is lost but my phone." She hugged the little boy tighter.

"Mommy hurting me," the little guy said.

"I'm sorry, baby." She kissed him on the forehead and loosened her hold.

"Do you have family around here? Anyone I can call?" Hud asked.

"Nope, my folks moved to Tulsa last month. I guess we'll have to go to Bowie and get a room."

"I'll do you better than that," Hud said. "I'll take you to my house. It'll be more comfortable for you than a hotel. Have you had supper?"

She shook her head. "I should tell you no, but my husband will be home tomorrow, and it'll only be for one night, and I know my son will be..." She started to weep again.

"Hey, my girlfriend just got out of the service," Hud told her. "She's away visiting her folks right now, but she'd kick me all the way across the Red River if I didn't help out a military family."

"My husband, Josh, and I were going to load up and move to Oklahoma in a couple of days. He's got a job in Tulsa with a security firm. I guess we'll be moving sooner than that, now," she said.

"Is that your car?" He pointed to a small, older-model vehicle out by the road.

She nodded.

"I rode here with my brother," he said, "so if you don't mind, I'll be glad to drive it to the ranch. You can text your husband on the way."

Her hands shook as she handed him her purse. "My name is Millie Swisher. The keys are in the side pocket. I'm glad I grabbed it when I ran out the door. It's got all our important stuff in it."

"Well, Millie, you did good," Hud reassured her. "Now, let's get you and your little boy to the ranch and get some food into you and..." He glanced over at the little boy, who was still holding the kitten.

"Lucas," Millie said. "Lucas is his name."

"And this is Rascal." Lucas held up the kitten.

"We'll get you and Lucas some supper fixed up and then you can get a good night's sleep," Hud said.

She was a tall woman with clear blue eyes that were still swimming in tears. "Thank you for doing this. I'm so rattled that I'm jittery inside."

"No problem," Hud assured her again. "By tomorrow, you'll feel lots better."

* * *

Rose hummed as she drove toward Sunset that Monday evening. Only a couple more hours and she'd be at the ranch. She'd deliberately avoided Hud's calls that afternoon because she wanted to surprise him. If he heard the road noise, he'd figure out that she was on the way home.

There was that word again: *home.*

Her mother had a cute little pillow stitched with the words HOME IS WHERE THE HEART IS. Rose could relate to that as she kept time to the music on the radio, tapping her thumbs on the steering wheel.

After traveling around much of the world, Rose had found her place, and the feeling in her heart was somewhere between peace and exhilaration. She couldn't wait to get home and tell Hud that she loved him.

She'd gotten a late start on Sunday because her parents

insisted that she go to church with them that morning. When the sun had dropped below the horizon, she had another two hours to drive, but she'd still be there well before ten o'clock. She visualized Hud opening the door, picking her up, and swinging her around in circles until they were both dizzy. Then he'd carry her to the bedroom, where they'd make wild, passionate love.

The clock on the dashboard read nine thirty when she got to the Sunset city limit sign. She switched off her head-lights when she made a right-hand turn up the lane toward the house and slowed down to a crawl so he wouldn't hear her.

Light poured from both the living room and the guest room windows, leaving yellow streaks on the yard and the bushes around the front of the house. She cut off the engine and coasted to a stop, got out of the car, and closed the door as quietly as possible. She'd made it halfway across the yard when a movement caught her attention. Hud had evidently been sitting on the sofa, and he stood up.

She stopped and smiled at what was practically a sil-houette of him framed perfectly in the living room window. Then a tall woman's body appeared and she wrapped her arms around Hud's neck and hugged him. Rose could easily tell that it wasn't Emily, Claire, or Retta. For a second or two, she tried to convince herself that it was Alana, but the woman who had hugged Hud and was now beside him as they headed out of the room was shorter than Alana. Hud switched the light out when he left the living room, and in a minute or two, the guest room light went dark too.

Rose went completely still. Her feet wouldn't move. Her brain ran in circles so fast that she couldn't catch a thought before it was gone. How she finally got from the place where she was standing back to her car was a mystery. One minute, time stood still, and she thought she might faint. The next, she was in her car and driving. She almost flipped over in the ditch when she made the left turn to go back to Sunset. When she reached the highway, she started to head toward Aunt Molly's but decided she didn't want to talk to anyone or see anyone. She just wanted to run away and never look back, and she had the means to do just that.

She made it to the liquor store in Bowie five minutes before they closed, then managed to check into a hotel without crying. When she got up to her room, she slid down the back of the door, drew her knees up to her chest, and let it all out in wracking sobs. She'd been a complete fool to think that Hud could ever love her. That "out of sight, out of mind" saying had definitely been true. She'd been gone six days, and he was already shacked up with another woman.

Chapter Twenty-One

The hangover the next morning was far worse than the one she'd had when she and her aunt had had the wake for a man neither of them even knew. Just the air conditioner clicking on sent sharp pains shooting through her head. With a night and half a bottle of whiskey behind her, she couldn't get that vision of the spare bedroom going dark out of her head. Hot tears ran down her cheeks and soaked the hotel pillow. She needed to eat, yet the thought of putting food in her mouth made her gag.

Still, she couldn't wallow in self-pity any longer. *So, you've been played*, she told herself. Just suck it up and get on with your life. But she'd have to face Hud first.

She made herself get out of the bed, take a shower, get dressed in clean jeans and a shirt, and go to the hotel dining room for breakfast. When she'd downed two cups of coffee, and taken two aspirin, she had a waffle and a plate of scrambled eggs. Her head still pounded, but at least she could stand a little bit of light.

When she turned on her phone, she saw fifty-two messages—several from Aunt Luna, a couple from Molly, and forty-one from Hud.

She read Aunt Luna's first. She and Echo were worried about her, since she hadn't texted them to say she'd arrived in Sunset. Luna threatened to call Highway Patrol in every state of her route if Rose didn't respond ASAP. Aunt Molly's messages were both dated after midnight the night before. She too was worried and had even called Hud to see if maybe Rose had stopped out there and forgot to message.

Rose sent Luna a text saying that she'd gotten in late and gone to a hotel in Bowie, that she was fine, and she'd call her sometime tomorrow. Then she sent Molly one that said all was under control.

She didn't want to talk to Hud or read whatever messages he'd sent. She cried every time she thought about him, and she sure didn't want to see him. She tossed her phone over on the bed and picked up the morning paper, and right there on the front page was a big bold headline: COWBOY SHOWS COURAGE SECOND TIME.

The picture wasn't sharp, but there was no doubt it was Hudson Baker, carrying a little boy with a kitten clutched in his arms out of a burning trailer house. The story said that on Monday evening, a trailer had caught on fire in southern Montague County, and Hudson Baker of the Sunset Volunteer Fire Department had been a hero for the second time in only a few weeks. Little Lucas Swisher and his mother had gotten safely out of the trailer, but Lucas had run back inside to get his kitten. Fireman Baker had dashed in to bring the child to safety seconds before the trailer had exploded.

Millie Swisher, the little boy's mother, told firemen that her husband, Josh, was coming home the next day from a six-month deployment to Kuwait, and that they'd planned to move to Oklahoma. The story went on for another three or four inches, praising the firemen and their ability to put the blaze out quickly, even though it had spread to the mesquite trees that surrounded the trailer.

"He used to be *my* courageous cowboy," she muttered.

She sucked in a lungful of air and picked up her phone, expecting to read a message from Hud that told her he had found a new woman. *Sorry, Cactus Rose, but I'm not ready for a lifetime commitment.*

Instead, the messages told her that he wished she was there, that he'd put out a fire that night, that he brought the woman and her son and his kitten to the ranch until her husband arrived home the next day—which would be today.

Her brain was totally scrambled as she tried to sort through the emotions. While she was still holding her phone, it rang and startled her so badly that she threw the thing halfway across the room. She stared at it as if it were a fire-breathing dragon until it went to voice mail.

His deep drawl came through so clear that she could've sworn he was sitting beside her on the bed. "Rose, darlin', where are you? Luna has called three times this morning, and Molly has called twice. They said you left Kentucky before noon on Sunday. You should have been here by now. Please, please call me. I'm worried out of my mind."

She continued to stare at the phone. How could he be worried when he'd gone to bed with another woman the night before? Seconds passed, and then minutes, before she crossed the room and picked up her phone, which now had a long crack down the face.

"Good God!" She fell back on the bed when she realized what had really happened. The woman had been giving Hud a thank-you hug for saving her child's life, like any good Texas lady would do. She and the little boy were sleeping in the guest room, and the mother had turned off the light, and Hud had gone on to his room at the end of the hall.

She checked the timing of the messages and saw that the one had come in right after she'd seen the lights go out. It said: *I'm lying here in bed wishing you were next to me. I miss you so much.*

If only she had read her messages instead of letting stupid imagined scenarios color her judgment, she might not have a hangover this morning. But oh, no! She'd let her own insecurities and worry about her past get in the way and had jumped to the wrong conclusions.

She called him without even thinking about what she'd say. He answered on the first ring. "Are you all right? What happened? Talk to me, darlin'."

"I'm fine," she said. "I'd rather tell you in person, alone with just the two of us in the room. Has your company left yet?"

"Yes," he answered. "I'll be waiting with open arms whenever you can get here."

You may not want to hug me when I tell you what I have to say, she thought as she ended the call.

* * *

Hud paced the floor in the living room for fifteen minutes. When the fifteen minutes had passed, he put on his coat and went outside to wait for her. The sky was completely gray, as if it could either rain or drop a foot of snow at any minute. Could that be an omen? Was he about to have his heart broken by the same girl twice? Once, when she moved away, and now when she went back to the commune?

He heard the car before he saw it and didn't even realize he was holding his breath until she got out of the vehicle and started toward him. It all came out in a whoosh, leaving a cloud of vapor like a huge puff of cigarette smoke in the cold air. True to his word, Hud opened his arms.

She stopped at the bottom step and looked up at him with bloodshot eyes. "I don't think I deserve a hug until you hear me out, and then you can decide. Can we go inside where it's warm? I'm freezing, and I have one helluva hangover."

"Of course." He nodded as he opened the door for her. "Why do you have a hangover?"

"It's a long story, but if we're ever to have a relationship, I have to start out on an honest foot," she told him.

"What have you done so bad that you had to tie one on before you could tell me? Had a fling with someone at the commune?" He followed her into the living room, wondering the whole time if he could forgive her if that was the case.

"No, never!" She slumped down on the sofa. "I didn't trust you. That's my big sin. I judged you without even giving you a chance to explain, and I'm so sorry, Hud."

"Go on." He sat down beside her and took her hand in his.

She told him about every detail of the previous day—how she'd planned to surprise him and what had happened when she arrived at the ranch. "I turned my phone off at noon yesterday. I didn't want to be tempted to answer it while I was driving, and I wanted to surprise you."

"Whew!" He wiped his forehead. "I thought you were going to tell me you'd found another guy at the commune, and you were going back there. This ain't nothing, honey, but a misunderstanding." He moved closer to her, raised her chin with the back of his hand, and looked deeply into her bloodshot eyes. "Darlin', as long as we're honest with each other, we'll be fine."

Her arms snaked up around his neck and tugged his lips down to hers in a steamy, hot kiss. "Just hold me, Hud. I want your face to be the last thing I see every night and the first thing I see every morning."

"I think I can manage that just fine." He scooped her up like a bride, carried her down the hall into his bedroom, and kicked the door shut with his heel.

Chapter Twenty-Two

Rose stood in the middle of the little garage apartment and closed her eyes. She wanted to feel like this was the right place and not just take it because it was convenient. Molly said that Nikki had lived here for several years before she moved into a cabin over on Longhorn Canyon.

The apartment had a tiny living room, a galley kitchen barely big enough to be called a kitchen, and a bedroom. She could buy a small table to work on, set it right there in the kitchen, and it would be just fine, but it didn't feel right. Maybe she had too much of Luna in her and not enough Molly. Emotional versus practicality. Mind over matter. She had never even considered her heart when she made her decisions before, but now it seemed to be the most important thing. Evidently, Luna had made more of an impact on her than she realized.

Rose tried to imagine furniture put here and there, but it still didn't seem like the right place for her. She walked out,

went down the stairs, and returned the keys to the sweet little lady who owned it.

"Do you like it?" the woman asked.

"Very much, but I've got another one to look at. I'll call
you this evening and let you know one way or another,"
Rose said.

Two apartments later, and none of the three felt right.
Why couldn't that *third time is the charm* thing work for her
that day? She drove to the Dairy Queen and ordered an ice-
cream cone, sat in a booth with a notepad, and wrote down
the pros and cons of each place.

She was down to the cone part of the ice-cream cone
when her phone rang. Thinking it was Hud, and he'd have
some insight into which place she should rent, she answered
it without even looking at the caller ID.

"I've looked at three apartments and I don't like any of
them." She almost groaned.

"Good," a female voice said. "This is Emily. My brother
dropped by today and said that you were looking at apartments. I've got one more for you to check out before you
decide. If you'll drive out here to Longhorn Canyon, I'll be
glad to show it to you."

"I'll be there in twenty minutes." Rose slid out of the
booth, dumped the rest of her ice cream in the trash on her
way out, and sent up a silent prayer that this place would be
the right one. It had been dark when she and Luna had gone
to Emily's house for Paxton's going-away party. She wasn't
sure how to get there in the daylight, so she called Emily
when she turned into the lane leading up to the house.

Emily answered on the first ring. "I'm sitting at the ranch
house in a red car. Just follow me. The path might get a little
bumpy, so we'll go slow."

"I see you. See you there." Rose ended the call and

tossed the phone over on the passenger seat. She began to wonder if Emily was teasing her when they drove past a huge barn, and a mile down the road, she still hadn't seen an apartment of any kind. The trees in this area were small and gnarly, not at all like the sugar maples, sweet birch, poplars, and beautiful magnolias in Kentucky. The land didn't have hills and hollers, but somehow it felt the same.

The road curved to the left and Emily pulled up in front of a rustic cabin. She got out of her car and stood beside it. Rose turned off the engine, opened her car door, and sat staring at the cabin. Wagging his tail so hard that it was a blur, Red came from the porch to greet her.

"He was just a pup when he showed up over on my brothers' ranch, and in those days, Tag lived here in the cabin, so Red thinks both places are his home," Emily explained. "The door is always open, but I have the key right here. We've never charged rent because only family and very close friends have lived in it, so it's yours if you want it. I thought it might be a nice quiet place for you to work." She pointed to her right. "That barbed wire fence separates our ranch from my brothers'. If you were standing on top of the cabin, you could be able to see Hud's house. It's less than a quarter mile as the crow flies, but if you're driving, it's maybe three miles."

"Can I go inside now?" Rose asked.

"Of course!" Emily handed off the key and started back to her car.

"Aren't you going in with me?" she asked.

"Nope." Emily smiled. "You need to see it and get a feel for it without anyone around. I will tell you that it's got a reputation, though. Justin and I lived in it before we married. Levi and Claire met here, and Tag and Nikki lived here. We all believe that the place has magical love powers, and it *is* pretty close to Valentine's Day, so you might get a double dose of Cupid's power."

"Aunt Luna would love that story." Rose smiled. "Thank you so much, but I don't expect miracles."

"Neither did I." Emily laughed as she got into her car. "Call me when you decide."

Rose nodded as she walked up on the porch. When she swung the door open she was surprised to see that the cabin was furnished. She reached for the light switch, but there wasn't one. Surely she wouldn't have to work by candlelight, would she? Then she remembered how the lights got turned on in the place where she and her folks had lived in Louisiana and looked up. Sure enough, there was a string hanging from a bare bulb in the middle of the living area. She crossed the floor, tiptoed just slightly, and got a grip on the wooden spool hanging from the string. When she tugged on it, she had light.

A sturdy coffee table with dents and dings sat in front of a well-worn brown sofa with a quilt thrown over the back of it. Red bounded inside and sniffed around the fireplace and then looked up at her.

"I bet you're used to having a blaze in it, aren't you?" Rose asked.

He wagged his tail, jumped up on the sofa, and went to sleep.

She took a couple more steps and saw four mismatched chairs pushed up under an old wooden table with another light bulb above it. A tiny kitchen area was against the far wall. A king-size bed over to the side was covered with a lovely quilt. She went to the refrigerator and opened it to find a six-pack of beer and a withered apple, but the freezer was packed with roasts, steaks, and even a package of frozen burritos. Dishes were stacked in the upper cabinets, which had no doors, and the lower ones held a few pots and pans, along with a pretty good stock of canned goods.

She left the cabin, went outside, and looked around. The only noises she heard were a few birds chirping and a squirrel fussing at her from the top of a scrub oak. The place took the best parts of the commune—the sweet freedom and the peace of being away from the world—and set it right down in the middle of a Texas ranch where none of the rules and laws imposed on the folks at the commune applied.

She noticed firewood stacked up at the west end of the place and figured maybe she'd start a fire to ward off the chill. She picked up her phone and called Emily.

"So, how do you like it?" Emily asked without any preamble.

"It's perfect, but I really have to pay rent. There's electricity and gas and someone has to put wood out there for the fireplace," Rose told her.

"No, ma'am," Emily protested. "The utilities are tied in with the ranch, and we'd have no idea how much to charge for them. The wood is just the by-product of when we clear the land. We all have fireplaces, so the guys keep us stocked. Have you even seen the bathroom?"

"No, but I'll go look at it now." Rose carried her phone with her.

"Oh, my!" she gasped when she opened the door to the tiniest bathroom she'd ever seen in life. The toilet and wall-hung sink were on one wall, and a narrow shower on the other.

"Still want to live there?" Emily giggled. "You should have seen me in that shower with my height and size."

"Of course I want to live here." Rose told her about how much work she'd gotten done that morning. "I was just surprised. The cabin is small but roomy—I love it here."

"The bathroom was the one thing I hated, and I wanted you to see it before you said yes," Emily said.

"Do I sign a contract?" Rose asked.

"Of course not," Emily told her. "We're almost family. When you move out, just leave it like it is right now for the next folks."

"*Thank you* seems like so little, but it's coming from my heart." Rose could hardly believe her good fortune and couldn't wait to send pictures to Molly, Luna, and her mother. She could already hear Luna giggling and saying that there wouldn't be room for Rose and Hud both in that itty-bitty shower.

"Hud is here, and champing at the bit to know if you like the place," Emily said. "Want to talk to him?"

"Just tell him to come be my first visitor," Rose replied.

* * *

Emily had told Hud she was going to offer the cabin to Rose, and he'd been antsy about it all morning as he plowed up the final field, getting it ready to plant alfalfa for a hay crop. He'd been afraid to get his hopes up.

"I thought she was moving in with you," Tag said as Hud started for the door.

"I took your advice and decided it might be too early." Hud settled his black cowboy hat on his head. "She needs time to adjust to her decision not to reenlist. Besides"—he smiled—"I still know how to jump a barbed wire fence."

He jogged out to his truck and drove down the rutted lane to the old cabin and parked behind Rose's new car. The brittle winter grass crunched under his boots as he started toward the porch. The cold north wind had picked up and practically blew his hat off. He reached up to hold it down and noticed a movement in his peripheral vision. He whipped around, and there was his Rose.

The wind whipped her hair across her face. She wore a pair of skinny jeans and a T-shirt that hugged her curves. His mouth went dry just looking at her. When she finally noticed that he was there, she flashed a bright smile his way that warmed his heart and soul.

She dropped the load of wood in her arms and ran across the yard to meet him, wrapping her arms around his neck and tiptoeing for a long kiss. "I've missed you so much," she said when the kiss ended.

"Oh, honey"—he breathed into her hair—"this time away from you seems like years instead of days."

"Welcome to my new home." Rose hugged him again. "I thought we might start a fire. Red keeps going to the fireplace and whining. Have you had dinner? I've got some chicken noodle soup on the stove."

"I thought you couldn't cook." Hud picked up the firewood.

"I can open a can, and I'm a guru at the microwave business." She grinned as she opened the door for him. "I've managed to survive for almost twenty-nine years."

"April first, if I remember right from junior high." Hud unloaded the firewood on the rug in front of the fireplace, stood up and took her in his arms for a long kiss. "I love your new place, but it's cold in here. We do need a little blaze."

"You remember my birthday?" she asked. "I don't know that I ever knew yours."

"That's because mine is in the summer, and we weren't in school. Our English teacher used to tell when it was anybody's birthday, and I wrote yours down. I was planning to give you a rose the next year, but you were gone by then," he said.

"That is so sweet." She rolled up on her tiptoes for another kiss.

He glanced longingly at the bed, but he'd promised Tag he'd meet him at the barn in thirty minutes. He'd already used up half that time, and he really should start a fire for Rose before he left.

As if she could read his mind, she said, "We've both got work to do, but when the day is done…"

"My place or yours tonight?" he asked.

"Mine, to celebrate me having such a beautiful new home," she replied, "but be forewarned, the shower is too small for both of us."

"We'll see about that when the time comes." He got to his feet and crossed the room to build a fire. "I'll show you how…"

"I know how to build and keep a fire going," she told him. "We had to use a woodstove for heat and to cook when we lived in Louisiana. Best grilled crawdads in the world came from the top of that old thing."

Hud wondered if he'd ever discover all of Rose's secrets. Maybe not, but he was willing to give it a try—even if it took a lifetime.

Chapter Twenty-Three

It had only taken Rose a couple of hours to get moved into her new little cabin, but within the next few days, more and more of her things got transported over to the ranch house. By the first week in February, she was spending all her time at the ranch house with Hud—at least when she wasn't at her new job at the hospital.

That morning was her day off, though, and she'd walked to the cabin to get a book she'd left there. Red ran along ahead of her, and when she arrived at the cabin, he dashed inside.

She was all but living with Hud, and yet neither of them had said those three words *I love you*. They'd skirted around them by saying "love ya" in the morning when she left to walk from the ranch house across the pasture to the stile that he'd installed for her to cross over the fence. She'd planned to tell him that she didn't only love him, but that she was in love with him when she came home from Kentucky, but somehow the moment never seemed just right.

A south wind whipped through the dormant mesquite trees, and dark clouds began to gather in the distance. When she sat down on the sofa, Red laid his head on her lap and looked up at her with big, brown, understanding eyes.

"Don't give me that look." She scratched his ears. "You've never had trouble telling people that you love them. That wagging tail and those big floppy ears let them know pretty quick how they stand with you."

Just speak your mind and be honest. Granny Dee's words came back to her.

That sounded like good advice, but Rose had never told a man that she was in love with him—not even in the semi-serious relationship where she had considered moving in with a guy. Should she just blurt it out over supper one evening? After sex didn't seem like the right time—being in love went beyond a romp in the sheets.

"All this worry isn't getting anything done," she told Red as she picked up the book and headed back to the ranch house. "I guess we'll both open up and say what's in our hearts when the time is right." Red ambled across the yard, his nose to the ground, as if he was checking for vicious grasshoppers or tracking a wild raccoon, and then he belly crawled under the barbed wire fence and took off like he was chasing a wily fox.

"If reincarnation is real, then I want to come back as a dog like Red or a cat like Rascal." She sighed. "They don't have to worry about stuff as much as humans do."

"Hey!" Hud yelled from the other side of the fence.

His voice startled her so much that she stumbled and had to grab a porch post to keep from falling. Hud put a hand on a wooden fence post and jumped over the top strand of barbed wire and then jogged over to the porch. He took her in his arms and kissed her with so much heat and passion that it made her knees weak.

Without ending the kisses, he backed her across the lawn and into the cabin. Then he sat down and pulled her onto his lap. A loud clap of thunder made both of them jump, and then rain came down hard enough that it sounded like bullets hitting the cabin's metal roof. "Where did that come from?" She laid her cheek against his chest.

"Been on the way all morning," he replied. "We've been watching the radar on our phones. We barely got the last of the fencing done when the weather forecast said we had about fifteen minutes before it hit. I decided to jog over here rather than go to the ranch house. It's going to rain all day and through the night. Think you can put up with me that long?" he asked.

"I'll do my best to endure it." She smiled and pulled his face down for another kiss. "Right now, we'd better have some lunch. You're going to need your strength if I'm going to take the afternoon off."

He kissed her on her forehead. "I like the way you think."

* * *

Hard, fierce wind had joined forces with the rain by evening, but there was about five minutes of relief right around five o'clock. "Here's our chance if we want to go home," Hud told Rose. "If we don't take it, we may be spending the night right here."

"Poor little Rascal will be lonely if we stay here." Rose grabbed up her coat and purse, turned off her laptop, and headed for the door. "I still can't believe that Lucas left that kitten with you."

"He didn't want to," Hud said. "But his daddy said the place where they'd be living didn't allow pets. I told him I'd keep Rascal for him and take real good care of the kitten."

"See, you really are a hero." She tossed him the keys to her car. "You drive. I hate driving in the rain."

He caught them midair. "So you're finally going to let me drive your new car?"

"Yep, and all it took was one hellacious rainstorm. Lock the door behind you," she said over her shoulder as she ran outside.

She opened the door and crawled into the passenger's seat, giggling the whole time.

"What's so funny?" he asked as he got behind the wheel.

"I was thinking of the first time you came into the gift shop. You stepped in that pan of water, and I sat down in it. I'm surprised both of us ran as far as we did without falling in a mud puddle," she told him.

"It's a day of miracles." He grinned as he drove down the path, past the Longhorn Canyon ranch house to the road, and made a right-hand turn. In just minutes, he'd parked the car beside his truck. "It's hard to believe that this house and the cabin are so close if we walk and yet so far away if we have to go by the road."

"Kind of like us, huh?" she asked.

Lightning streaked through the sky, and thunder rolled over the ranch like a big, lazy freight train. "We'd better get inside before it starts dumping more rain on us."

She didn't wait for him to come around and open the door for her but bailed out and ran to the porch. Red came out from around the house, did one of those doggy shivers to shake the water off him, and ran inside the second she opened the door.

"At least he did the equivalent of wiping his feet," she said.

"He's a pretty good old boy, but what did you mean when you said that the cabin and house are like us?" Hud ran into the house behind her. He helped her with her coat and hung it on the back of a chair. Then he did the same with his.

Rascal came out of the kitchen and bristled up at Red like a little gray porcupine. The dog ignored her and went straight to his favorite spot in the living room. Rose picked up the kitten and held her close to her chest.

"Poor baby," she crooned. "It's a tough job having to hold down a house when we leave, and we appreciate you takin' care of that for us."

The kitten snuggled down into her arms and started to purr. Rose carried her to the sofa and sat down close to Hud.

"Now to your question," she said. "We're close. We love spending time together, and we're fantastic in bed."

He nodded. "I hear a *but*, though, and it kind of scares me."

"I didn't know anything could scare you." She smiled.

"Losing you terrifies me," he admitted.

"I feel the same about you." She looked up, and their gazes caught somewhere just above the cat's tiny head. "But there's a barbed wire fence between us. I'm practically living with you and neither of us..." She paused.

"Rose O'Malley, I love you," he said without blinking, "and not only do I love you, darlin', I'm in love with you. I think I fell in love with you the first time I saw you in the Tulia Junior High hallway. But it's only been the past few weeks that I realized that I also love you. Does that take down the fence?"

"No, but this does." She set the kitten on the floor and cupped his face in her hands. "I've held you in my heart and loved you for years, but now I'm in love with you too. You complete my heart and soul."

Chapter Twenty-Four

The church Valentine Day's potluck was held on Wednesday night. Rose made two pecan pies, and Hud carried them in with pride.

"Hey, those really look good," Tag yelled from the corner of the fellowship hall. "If you were a good brother, you'd sneak one out into my truck."

"Guess I'm not a good brother," Hud teased.

When he'd set the pies on the table, Levi clamped a hand on his shoulder. "We haven't seen much of you this past month. What's been going on?"

Hud put his arm around Rose's shoulders and drew her to his side. "We've moved in together."

"Well, good for you," Levi said and moved on.

"Surprise!" Luna tapped Rose on the shoulder.

Rose shook loose from Hud and gave her aunt a hug. "I can't believe you're here."

"Me and your daddy had us a knock-down, drag-out

fight. I figured it was best if we put a little space between us for a few days, so I came to see Molly's new house," Luna said. "So you and Hud are living together? I just got one thing to say about that."

"And what's that?" Rose stepped back.

"It's about damn time," Luna giggled.

"What did you and Daddy get into it about?" Rose asked.

"Two things." Luna pushed her braids over her shoulder. "One was when he told me I had to get rid of my new phone. I told him that I owned half that damned commune, and what I did on my half was my own damned business. Then little Jennifer got pneumonia, and I took her to the doctor for medicine. He called a meeting and said that I should have asked permission. I told him that if he had a cell phone in his pocket, I might have given him a call."

Molly walked up beside them with a Bundt cake in her hands. "Luna's just traded her old sumbitch for a new one." She set the cake on the table.

"Ahh, he ain't that bad," Luna said. "He just needs a little bit of trainin', and I'm the one to take over that job. In a few years, he'll be downright likable."

"Well, we're glad you're here for a little while." Hud patted Luna on the shoulder. "You'll have to come out to the ranch and visit with us some evening. I'll grill some steaks." He walked away to talk to Levi, leaving the three ladies alone.

"I'll bring the dessert," Molly said.

Luna raised an eyebrow at her sister. "You can be my plus one if you'll bring mama's bread pudding with caramel sauce."

"That sounds good." Rose tucked her hand into Hud's. "Granny Dee used to make it, and I haven't had it since she died. Want to share the recipe with me?"

"No, she won't." Luna tipped her chin up defiantly. "She got Mama to give her the book with all our grandmother's famous recipes in it before Mama died, and she's selfish as hell with them."

"But not with you." Molly smiled sweetly at Rose. "I'll even show you how to make it."

"You're an old toot." Luna waggled a finger at Molly.

"I may be, but I've got the recipes and you don't," Molly said.

Rose giggled at the way the two of them bickered. "Give us a call when you've got a free evening, but not this Friday. This old cowboy is taking me to a fancy place for a Valentine's Day candlelight dinner."

"We're goin' to the American Legion for a few drinks and some square dancin'," Luna said. "So it'll have to be the first of the week. Oh, there's Dixie. I've got to go talk to her and see the baby."

"I hope Luna and Paul make up soon. I can only take her for a few days, and then I'm ready to strangle her," Molly sighed. "When she came before, I lived in the B&B, and there were lots of places to hide from her when I'd had enough of her shenanigans. I can't very well sneak away from her in my new house, not even for a thirty-minute nap. It's too small," Molly said. "But on a more positive note, I'm glad that you and Hud are officially together. Love is a good thing. Don't let it slip away, and don't let it die in its sleep."

"I already lost her once." Hud walked up behind Rose and slipped his arms around her waist. "I'm sure not plannin' on doin' it again."

"That's the right attitude." Molly waved as the Fab Five entered the room. "I need to talk to Patsy about the dance on Friday night. Y'all excuse me."

"It's amazing how these folks have taken me in," Rose muttered.

"Welcome to small-town Texas." Hud gently squeezed her hand. "And welcome to our extended family."

"Thank you," she said. "I've been looking for my place in the world ever since I was a child. I'm glad that it's here in Sunset, Texas."

"Well, darlin', I'm sure happy that we found each other again, and that we're together," he whispered.

Dixie crossed the room with Sally on her hip. "I wanted to let y'all see how much she's grown and how happy we are. I still feel like I climbed up out of hell and found heaven."

"I know a little of that same feeling." Rose smiled. "Let me hold that baby a minute before the Fab Five get over here. I heard that they've all but adopted her."

Dixie laughed out loud. "They're spoiling her rotten. They drop by the shop nearly every day to play with her, and most days they bring a cute little outfit or a toy for her. I can't tell them no because it brings them so much pleasure."

"She's got lots of grandparents," Hud said. "Let them dote on her. Before long Claire's little boy will be here, and then Sally will have to share."

"I doubt it," Dixie said. "They'll just spoil them both." She motioned toward the other side of the room. "You better get your lovin' now. Sarah is on the way, and then they'll fight over how long each one gets to be the grandma."

"Wonderful, isn't it?" Rose said.

"Amen," Dixie answered.

* * *

By the time the party was over and the fellowship hall was put to rights, it was well past ten o'clock. Rose could tell that something was on Hud's mind because he was so quiet. Usually, he shared everything with her, but that evening, he didn't even turn on the radio.

"Okay, spit it out," she said. "We promised when we moved in together that we'd never have secrets, and we'd be open and honest about everything."

He turned into the lane to the ranch house and shook his head. "Let's talk about it in the house. I want to be able to see your face. Did anyone ever tell you that you'd make a lousy poker player?"

"I've played poker a few times and was pretty damn good at it," she argued.

"Your expressions tell me everything you're thinking," he said.

"Oh, honey." She got out of the truck as soon as he parked it. "If you really believe that, then I've got the best poker face in the whole universe."

"Really?" He held her hand as they climbed the porch steps and didn't let go until he had to unlock the door.

"Yes, sir." She removed her coat, hung it up, picked up Rascal, and carried her to the living room. "Sit down here beside me and tell me what's on your mind."

"When Sarah came over to take Sally from you, it was like you were relieved to get rid of the baby." Hud eased down close to her. "Don't you like kids?"

Rose burst out laughing so hard that Rascal jumped out of her arms and hid behind the recliner. "I love kids, but Sally had a very smelly, dirty diaper, and I was glad to turn her over to Sarah, so she could be the one to change her."

"Ever have any experience with babies and small children?" he asked. "You were an only child, and Tag and I were the babies of the family."

"Honey, at the commune, as soon as I was old enough

to help with babies, they were part of my responsibility. The older girls helped take care of the younger ones while the mothers worked in the kitchen or in the gardens or milked the cows, or did whatever else needed done. I was babysitting by the time I was nine. It was part of our commune education," Rose explained. "So yes, I've been around babies and children enough that I could probably run a day care. If you're about to ask me if I want children, the answer is yes, and that's plural. I don't want to raise a child with no siblings. Even though I had lots of friends in the commune, I missed having a brother or a sister of my very own."

"I guess we've got that settled." Hud covered a yawn with his hand. "I've always wanted children."

"Then let's go to bed," she said. "And, honey, it's late and we're both tired, so there'll be no starting a baby tonight."

"Yes, ma'am." He picked her up like a bag of feed and threw her over his shoulder. "But we can practice. You know what they say about practice making perfect, and I sure want pretty babies."

"You're a rascal."

"No, Rascal is a cat. I'm a hero," he said. "Don't you read the papers?"

"Yes, I do, and you'll always be my hero."

* * *

Hud worried with the box in his coat pocket for two days. He just knew if he didn't stop messing with it that all the pretty red velvet would be worn off by Valentine's Day. Finally the day arrived, and he had it all planned. He'd made reservations for a romantic dinner on Lake Worth. The drive would take an hour, so they'd leave early enough to watch the sunset. He planned to ask Rose to marry him at the edge of the water with the stars shining above them.

He hadn't told a soul about his plans for fear someone would leak them to Rose. He wanted it to be a total surprise, and he couldn't wait to see the look on her face when he opened the box to reveal an engagement ring with tiny diamonds circling around an emerald, the exact color of Rose's eyes.

He finished up the day's work, took a shower, got dressed in ironed jeans, a white shirt, and his best boots. When he entered the living room, Rose was standing in front of the fireplace. She turned and all the air left his lungs. She was wearing an emerald-green velvet dress that hugged every curve of her body. The hem stopped an inch above her knees, and she had on matching green high heels. She'd left her long light-red hair down to float on her shoulders in big loose curls, and her makeup was perfect.

"I feel like a country bumpkin compared to you," he whispered.

"Welcome to my world." She crossed the floor and slipped her arms around him. "When I went to school with you, I sure felt that way. You were the handsomest boy I'd ever seen, and now, you're the sexiest man, and, honey, you sure look fine to me tonight. Where are we going?"

"That, darlin', is a surprise." He gave her a sweet kiss, helped her with her coat, made sure he had the little box in the pocket, and held her hand all the way to the truck.

"I've never had a big Valentine's Day," she said. "At the commune we only celebrate Christmas and Easter. Valentine's is just a commercial holiday, according to their rules and laws."

Hud made sure she was in the truck and settled before he leaned in and gave her another kiss. "Confession, here. I've never taken a girl out on Valentine's Day or planned a surprise for her."

"Seriously?" she asked.

He rounded the end of the truck, got behind the wheel, and started the engine. "Very serious," he said. "How about you? Have you ever been courted properly on Valentine's Day?"

"Nope," she answered.

The first part of the evening was wonderful. The sun set off to their right in a beautiful array of colors, and then dusk settled around them and the stars began to pop out. But somewhere just south of Bridgeport, there was a loud bang, and the truck veered off to the side.

Hud brought the vehicle to a stop and then slapped the steering wheel with both hands. "We've had a blowout, but don't worry. It's not going to ruin our night. I can get it changed in a few minutes."

"Can I help? I was trained to change tires when I was in Afghanistan," she said. "We never knew what might happen when they took me from one place to another to translate for them, so I learned lots of things."

"No, darlin', you sit right there and stay warm." He smiled.

True to his word, he had the old tire off, thrown in the back, and the spare put on in fifteen minutes. He managed to get a nice big black smudge on his shirt, but he could cover that with his jacket.

"Now we're on the way," he said as he pulled back out onto the road. There had to be one catastrophe, he figured—after all, this was Rose O'Malley and Hudson Baker out on the road, and their relationship had started off with him stepping into a big pan of water and her sitting down in it.

The traffic jam started north of Boyd, Texas, and by the

time they reached the other side of the small down, cars and trucks had come to a dead stop.

"Must be an accident up ahead," she said.

"Maybe they'll get it cleared out soon." He cussed himself for not taking the interstate, but he'd thought a little backwoods drive would be so much more romantic.

They listened to twelve country songs on the radio before traffic started moving again. When they reached the spot that had jammed them up, it wasn't an accident at all, but work on a bridge had closed down all but one lane.

"We'll only be a few minutes late to dinner. I allowed extra time so we could have a slow drive, and where we're going isn't far now," he told her.

Hud thought it strange that there were only four cars in the restaurant's parking lot. This was a place that only seated folks with a reservation on Friday and Saturday nights, and it should have been booming on Valentine's Day. But hey, if there weren't very many people there, then they'd be served quicker. He helped Rose out of the truck, tucked her arm into his, and patted his coat pocket. Only another hour or so, and he'd drop down on one knee and propose. He knew in his heart that she'd say yes, but he was still as nervous as the only chicken at a coyote convention. He pushed on the door to the restaurant, and it didn't budge.

"Look," she pointed. "There's a sign that said they had a grease fire in the kitchen and will be closed until repairs are made."

"Three for three." He groaned. "Some romantic evening this is."

"Darlin', we're all dressed up, and we're together. That's romantic to me." She buried her face in his chest. "Let's get a burger on the way home and spend the night in bed."

"I wanted us to have a special evening," he complained.

"You are special enough to make any evening fantastic," she told him.

"We could go to an Olive Garden or a RibCrib or somewhere other than a burger joint," he said.

"I like burgers and fries," she said with a shrug. "They're just about my favorite food. What say you that we hit that Dairy Queen we passed in Boyd, Texas, rent a movie at one of those box things beside the Dollar Store in Bowie, and go home? We can build a fire and cuddle up on the sofa with Rascal and Red, and make our own special, romantic evening. We'll even break out two beers, put on some music, and dance."

"You are the most amazing woman I've ever met," he said.

"Well, thank you, but can we please go get a burger?" she asked. "I'm starving plumb to death."

"In that case, we'd better drive back to Boyd and get you a big, old greasy burger, a double order of fries—" he said.

She butted in. "...and a chocolate milk shake."

"You got it, sweetheart."

The drive back to Boyd didn't take long. There were no mishaps along the way, so Hud thought the bad luck was over, but he was dead wrong. At the Dairy Queen he dropped a french fry loaded with ketchup on the front of his shirt, and when Rose bit into her burger, mustard shot out from the bottom onto her dress.

"We're not like other people," she laughed. "Our destiny for a romantic evening doesn't include a candlelit dinner with real napkins and violins playing in the corner."

"Evidently not." Hud left a smudge of red on his shirt when he tried to wipe the ketchup away.

Nothing had gone as he'd planned. Not one solitary, damned thing, but suddenly it didn't matter. He reached into his pocket, took out the ring box, slid out of the booth, and dropped down on one knee. "Cactus Rose O'Malley, I'm in love with you and have been for the better part of my life. Will you marry me?" He snapped the box open to reveal the ring. "An emerald because your green eyes mesmerize me. Fifty itty-bitty diamonds to represent the first fifty years of our marriage. Please say yes."

"Yes!" she squealed without a split second's hesitation.

He slipped the ring on her finger and she slid out of the booth, dropped down on both her knees to face him, and said, "I love you, Hud. This is perfect, and when we're married fifty years, you can take it to the jewelers and have them add fifty more diamonds, because we're going to be together forever."

He took her in his arms and sealed their engagement and their love with a long kiss. Neither of them thought about the other people in the Dairy Queen until they heard applause.

She hugged him and whispered, "Now, take me home. I love the sound of that word. *Home*. To the place where I belong with the love of my life."

"Yes, ma'am."

They stood up together and there was more applause when he scooped her up and carried her to the truck like a new bride.

"That was so romantic." She wiped tears from her eyes. "I can't wait to tell Aunt Luna all about it."

"But first we're going home, right?"

She held her hand up to the light on the truck ceiling. The emerald and the diamonds sparkled almost as much as the love in his eyes and the feeling in her heart. "Yes, my cowboy, we're going home."

Don't miss more about Paxton and Alana, who find a fake engagement feeling all too real in *Cowboy Strong*.

Coming in Summer 2020

Wildflower Ranch

A Novella

Carolyn Brown

Shiloh never knew what it was like to have sisters. But suddenly the father she never knew leaves his ranch to Shiloh and her two half-siblings. The only catch: to fully inherit, they must live together on the ranch for a full year. Shiloh couldn't be more different from Abby Joy, a former soldier, or Bonnie, a true wild child. But the three soon find they have more in common than they could've imagined. When a neighboring rancher catches Shiloh's eye, she'll have to decide exactly how much she's willing to sacrifice for her shot at the ranch.

Chapter One

Spring was Waylon's favorite season, when the wildflowers painted the Palo Duro Canyon with their brilliant colors. That evening, the last rays of sun lit up the red Indian paintbrush, almost the same color as the dress Shiloh was wearing. The centers of the black-eyed Susans reminded him of her dark hair, and the blue bonnets scattered here and there were the color of her eyes.

"Wildflower Ranch," he whispered and liked the way it rolled off his tongue. He'd been looking for a brand for his new ranch ever since he bought it. "I like it. Wildflower Ranch," he said again with a nod, and just like that, he'd named his place.

Since most of his friends were married, Waylon had been to lots of weddings. Like always, he found a corner where he could watch the people without having to mingle with them. He wasn't really shy or backward, but though he didn't like crowds he did like watching people. And he liked to dance some leather off his boots at the Sugar Shack, the local watering hole, on Saturday nights.

Shiloh breezed in and out of the house, appearing under the porch light to talk to someone for a few minutes, and then disappearing for a little while, only to return again. She looked different from the way she did at Ezra's funeral not quite three months ago. That day Waylon had stood off to the side as the sisters arrived one by one. Abby Joy was the last one to get there, and she looked like she had just left a military exercise in her camouflage. Shiloh might have come from a rodeo in her western getup, and Bonnie could have been a biker's woman in black leather and sporting a nose ring and tattoo. At that time he had wondered if Ezra hadn't been right when he sent all of them away right after they were born.

But ever since that morning, he hadn't been able to get Shiloh out of his mind.

Now there were only two sisters in the running to inherit the Malloy Ranch—Shiloh and Bonnie. When the sisters first came to the canyon, Waylon would have sworn that Shiloh would be the first to leave. Bonnie would follow her within a week, and Abby Joy would be there until they buried her beside old Ezra in the Malloy family cemetery right there on the ranch.

He'd sure been wrong, because that very evening Abby Joy had married his good friend Cooper and moved off Malloy ranch and over to his place. It wasn't the first time Waylon had been wrong, and it most likely wouldn't be the last time, either. He watched the two remaining Malloy sisters out of the corner of his eye. Shiloh was the taller of the two and had long dark brown hair.

In her cowboy boots and tight jeans at her father's funeral, she had looked like she was the queen of Texas. Maybe that confidence and sass was what had drawn him to her from the beginning. Not that he'd act on the attraction, not when there was so much at stake for her. Ezra had left a will behind, saying that the three sisters had to live on the Malloy Ranch together for a year. If one of them left, then they received an inheritance, but they could never have the ranch. If none of them left, then they inherited the place jointly. If they all moved off Ezra's massive spread, then Rusty, his foreman, inherited it.

Waylon had always thought that deep down Ezra wanted Rusty to have the place anyway. He'd just brought the sisters together to satisfy his own conscience for sending them away at birth because they weren't sons.

Waylon was a patient man. He didn't mind sitting back in the shadows of the wide porch and waiting for another look at Shiloh in that dress that hugged her curves. When she came back again, he sat up a little straighter so he could get a better view of her. The full moon lit her eyes up that evening like beautiful sapphires. His pulse jacked up a few notches and his heart threw in an extra fast beat. He could only imagine what kissing her or holding her in his arms would feel like—but he sure liked the picture in his head when he did.

The reception had started in the house and then poured out onto the porch and yard. That's where Shiloh was headed right then. She met up with Bonnie, and the two of them talked with their hands, gesturing toward the house and then back at the piano under a big scrub oak.

Maybe they were trying to figure out how to get the piano back inside. Waylon would be glad to help them with that, just to be near Shiloh for a little while. The chairs that had been arranged in two rows for the wedding were now scattered here and there, and Shiloh picked up one with each hand and carried them from the yard to the porch.

"Need some help?" Waylon asked when she was close enough that the porch light lit up her beautiful eyes. Ezra Malloy's three daughters hadn't gotten a physical thing from him, except the color of his eyes, and even then they were all three slightly different shades of blue.

"Hey, what are you doing hiding back here?" Bonnie, the youngest Malloy sister, pulled up a chair and sat down beside him.

"Just watching the people," Waylon answered. "You look right pretty tonight, Bonnie. When I first saw you at Ezra's funeral, you looked like maybe you were into motorcycles."

"I might have been, but they cost way too much money for me to own one. My boyfriend had one back in Harlan." Bonnie sighed. "If I'd known Abby Joy was going to wear combat boots, I would have worn my comfortable lace-up biker boots." She kicked off her shoes. "He bought me the jacket and boots, and then we broke up. He didn't want me to come out here to Texas when Ezra died. He said I was too wild to live on a ranch. I'm proving him wrong." She stopped, as if waiting for him to say something, but she hadn't asked a question. After a few seconds she went on, "Have you ever been a groomsman before? This was my first time ever to be a bridesmaid."

"No," he answered. "I've been to a lot of weddings, but I'm not usually one for big crowds."

Shiloh pushed the front door open and motioned to her sister. "Bonnie, come on. Abby Joy is getting ready to throw the bouquet."

Bonnie got up, but Waylon stayed in his chair. Shiloh's high-heeled shoes made a clicking noise on the wooden porch as she crossed it, and she crooked a finger at Waylon. "You too, cowboy. Cooper is about to take Abby Joy's garter off, and he's calling for all single men."

"Oh, no!" Waylon held up both palms. "I don't want that thing."

"I'm not catching that bouquet either. I'm superstitious, and I refuse to be the next bride in the canyon," Bonnie said. "I'm going to own a ranch in nine months. I sure don't have time for romance."

"You'll own the Malloy ranch over my dead body." Shiloh did a head wiggle. "The best you'll ever do is share it with me."

"Wanna bet?" Bonnie stopped at the door.

Shiloh stuck out her hand. "Twenty bucks?"

"How about a hundred and a bottle of good Kentucky bourbon?" Bonnie asked.

"Deal!" Shiloh shook with her.

Waylon didn't have a doubt in his mind that Bonnie would be forking over money and bourbon. Next to Abby Joy, he'd never met a woman as determined as Shiloh—or as sassy for that matter.

Shiloh surprised him when she grabbed his hand and tugged. "Come on. You can put your hands in your pockets, but you're one of the wedding party. It wouldn't be right for you not to be in on the garter toss."

He stood up, thinking she'd drop his hand, but she didn't. Sparks flittered around the porch like fireflies on a summer night. Sure, Waylon had been attracted to Shiloh since the first time he laid eyes on her, but this tingly feeling was something he'd never felt before.

She led him into the foyer, where the men were gathered over toward one end. Abby Joy was sitting about halfway up the stairs, and Cooper had begun to run his hand up her leg, searching for the garter. When he found the blue satin and white lace thing, he slipped it slowly down to her ankle. Whoops and hollers filled the room from the guys who were gathered up in a corner with their hands up. They were putting on quite a show for the lady who was filming, but then the garter wouldn't stretch far enough to go over Abby Joy's combat boot. The noise died down slightly as Cooper slowly untied the strings, pulled her boot off, and then slowly removed the garter from her foot. It got loud again when Cooper turned around backward and threw it over his shoulder. Several of the young unmarried men did their best to catch it, but it flew right past them and floated down to settle onto the top of Waylon's black cowboy hat.

"Guess you're next in line, buddy." Cooper laughed.

There was no doubt that Cooper was talking to him, and all the guys around him were laughing and pointing. He brought his hands out of his pockets and held them up to show that he had nothing. "Can't be me," Waylon said. "Which one of y'all is hiding it and teasing me?"

Shiloh reached up, removed Waylon's hat, and showed him the garter, lying there in the creases. He wanted to pick the thing up and toss it to one of the other guys, but he was mesmerized by her beautiful blue eyes, which were staring right into his.

"Fate says that you're next," she said.

"Not damn likely," he drawled.

She picked up the garter and handed him back his hat. "Give me your arm. The photographer will want a picture of you and Cooper, since you caught the garter."

He held out his arm and she stretched the blue lace garter up past his elbow. Then she held up his arm like he'd just won the trophy at a wrestling tournament. "The winner and the next groom in the canyon is Waylon Stephens!"

He played along, more to get to be near Shiloh than anything else. There was no way he'd be the next married man in the area. The only woman he was vaguely interested in was Shiloh, and he'd never knock her out of getting her share of Ezra Malloy's ranch. Maybe after she'd secured the deed, he'd ask her for a date, but not before. She'd never forgive herself—or him—if she lost her part of the ranch, and besides, as pretty as she was, she was way out of his league.

"And now the bouquet," Abby Joy said. "All you ladies get your hands up and"— she turned around backward— "here it comes." She let it fly, and it landed smack in Bonnie's hands.

"Someone take this thing from me, right now. I can't get married or leave the ranch. It would cost me a hundred dollars and a bottle of Kentucky bourbon." Bonnie tried to hand it off to the other girls, but none of them would touch it.

After the photographer took a few pictures, Waylon took a few steps back and disappeared outside again into the shadows on the porch. He'd prove them all wrong about being the next man to get married, but Bonnie wouldn't. Shiloh was going to own that ranch. Bonnie might as well face it.

* * *

The hinges on the gate into the old cemetery creaked as Shiloh opened it. She crossed over to the place where the father she had never known was buried and sat down on a concrete bench in front of his grave. A full moon lit up the lettering on her father's gray tombstone. Ezra Malloy had died less than three months ago on the first day of the year. It seemed like it had been a lot longer since she and her two sisters had sat through his graveside service. She remembered looking over at her soldier sister and thinking that she had some balls, wearing camouflage and combat boots to a funeral. Then she'd glanced to her other side to see the younger sister. She was dressed in jeans and a biker jacket and had a little diamond stud in the side of her nose. Her blond hair was limp, and what wasn't stringing down to her shoulder had a thin braid complete with beads that hung down one side of her face. In her skintight jeans and biker books, she looked like she'd dropped right out of either a hippie colony or motorcycle convention.

Shiloh had given Sister Hippie a week at the most before she'd go running back to whatever strange world she'd come from, and Sister Soldier less than a month before she was bored to death. Shiloh was going to be the last one standing at the end of a year, by damn, and nothing or no one was going to sweet-talk her off that ranch. The only thing she ever owned was the Chevy SUV that she drove. She wanted that ranch—first, to prove to the father she never knew that she could learn the business. The second reason had to do with her being so competitive. She was determined to show her two half-sisters that she couldn't be run off. They'd both eyed her that first day like she would be the weakling of the trio. Neither of them looked like they could possibly be her sister, but she'd been wrong. Not only were they sisters, but they'd also become best friends by spring.

Shiloh brushed a dead leaf from the skirt of the bright red satin dress she'd worn to her older sister's wedding that evening. The canyon was alive with wildflowers of every color and description, but the night was chilly, so she'd worn a long sweater over her dress for her walk from the house to the cemetery.

"Well, Ezra," Shiloh addressed the tombstone in her Arkansas accent, "it's down to me and Bonnie now. Bet you didn't think any of us would stick it out for this long, did you? And since she was a soldier, I imagine you figured she'd be the one to last the longest. Guess what? You were wrong. She could have gotten married, and Cooper could've moved in with her here. That way she would have kept her share, but she told me she didn't need or want it anymore, that it was like an albatross around her neck—like you were controlling her with your rules." She whispered as she pulled her sweater tighter across her chest, "I'm not sure I'll ever forgive you for throwing all three of us away because we weren't boys. I guess your punishment is that you died a lonely old man."

"I thought I might find you here." Her younger sister, Bonnie, sat down beside her.

"Damn, woman!" Shiloh shivered. "You scared the bejesus out of me."

"Is that a good thing or a bad thing?" Bonnie asked. Other than her blue eyes, she didn't look a thing like Shiloh. Tonight she wore her biker jacket over a pretty red bridesmaid dress.

"It's bad when you startle me like that, but good to think I might be a saint for a few seconds," Shiloh answered.

Bonnie shivered. "The way that north wind is whipping down the canyon, it's hard to believe that it's March and that spring is only a few days from now. I've got something to say to our father, and then I'm going home where it's warm. Did you walk? I didn't see your van when I parked."

"I did," Shiloh replied, but she didn't tell her sister that she needed a chance to think about how Waylon's nearness had been affecting her all that evening. When she'd taken his hand in hers, there had definitely been electricity flowing between them. "What have you got to say to Ezra?"

Bonnie glared at the tombstone. "Are you smiling, Ezra, because Abby Joy has left the ranch? I bet you're hopin' that Rusty winds up with it, but I'd be willin' to bet a jar of your moonshine that you thought your soldier daughter would outlast me and Shiloh. If you had let us get to know each other, then you'd have realized that she might be tough as nails on the outside, but she's got a heart of gold. So there, you won this one, but not really, because she's happy now."

"Look at us out here in a damned old graveyard talkin' to a dead man that didn't give a hoot about any of us. Paid our mothers off to go away and take us worthless girls with them," Shiloh said. "He can't hear us and would probably laugh in our faces if he could."

"And wearing our pretty dresses as if he can see us in them," Bonnie said. "I wish I didn't give a damn about him, but"—she laid the wedding bouquet in front of his tombstone—"here's something for you to think about. Abby Joy has found happiness and you never did."

"We really should get over the way we feel about him," Shiloh said.

"Maybe someday, but not anytime soon. He shouldn't have thrown us all away, and he for sure as hell should have been there to walk Abby Joy down the aisle."

"He's dead," Shiloh reminded her. "He couldn't have walked with her anyway."

"I know that, but..."—Bonnie stammered—"damn it, you know what I mean."

"Yes, I do know what you mean. I used to imagine that my father was a Navy SEAL or some other hero-type guy."

"When did you find out that you were wrong?" Bonnie asked.

"I was a teenager. I waited until Mama and her sister, my aunt Audrey, were about half lit one night and asked her about him. The truth shattered my pretty little bubble," Shiloh said.

"I knew from the time I can remember exactly who and what Ezra was. Mama just wouldn't tell me where he lived,"

Bonnie told her. "Good thing that she didn't. I might be doin' time in prison right now instead of visitin' his grave in the prettiest dress I've ever owned."

"Do you ever wish that the cemetery was on the back side of the ranch so we didn't have to look at it every time we leave or come back to the place?" Shiloh asked.

"Oh, hell, yeah, but I keep reminding myself that he probably hates to see us coming and going, and knowing that we're still here makes him want to claw his way up out of that grave and change his will," Bonnie answered.

Shiloh giggled and started to say something. Then the noise of screeching tires and the sound of metal hitting something really hard made both of them drop to a squatting position and cover their heads. The laughter had stopped and nothing but Shiloh and her sister's heavy breathing could be heard in the heavy silence.

"What in the hell was that?" Bonnie whispered.

"Someone just wrecked out on the highway," Shiloh said. "We'd better go see if we need to help."

The two of them stood up and ran toward the place where Bonnie had left her truck. "Get in." Bonnie hiked her dress up and ran around the back of her truck as she yelled, "And call 911."

Chapter Two

Waylon was the last one to leave that evening. He helped get the piano back into the house and all the chairs loaded into a cattle trailer to go back to the church before he got into his truck and drove away. He turned the radio to his favorite late-night country music program just in time to hear Cody Johnson singing "On My Way to You." The lyrics said that everything he'd been through from ditches to britches was simply taking him on his way to her. It seemed to have been written just for Waylon that night, and he kept time with the music by tapping his thumbs on the steering wheel.

He'd just rounded a sharp curve when a whole herd of deer started across the road in front of him. The squeal of his truck tires filled his ears, and the smell of hot brakes floated up to his nose. The deer scattered, and he let up on the brakes a little. Then one of his back tires blew out and sent him straight for a huge old scrub oak. He was looking out the side window, trying to swerve away from a big stump, when the airbags opened, and the seat belt tightened. None of that kept him from hitting his head on the side window hard enough to rattle his brain.

Steve Earle was singing "Copperhead Road" when everything began to blur. The lyrics of the song reminded him of the stories his great-granddad had told about outrunning the feds and the local sheriff through his moonshine-running days. His granddad had come home from Vietnam to take over the business. His dad hadn't run moonshine, but he had inherited enough money from his father to buy a ranch on Red Dirt Road out in East Texas. His last thought before the whole world swirled away into darkness was that this was a helluva way to die.

* * *

Bonnie drove so fast down the rutted lane that it sounded like the fenders were going to fly off her old truck and land somewhere out there in the wildflowers beside the road. The scene of the accident was only a few hundred yards up from the Malloy Ranch turnoff, and right away, Shiloh recognized the truck.

"My God!" she gasped. "That's Waylon's truck."

"What did you say?" the 911 operator asked.

"It's my neighbor's truck right on Highway 207 that crosses the Prairie Dog Fork of the Red River. Send an ambulance in a hurry," she said.

"I've got one coming out of Amarillo, but it'll be about thirty minutes before it can get there. I can patch you through to the EMT so he can give you some instructions," the lady said.

What little tread was on the tires of Bonnie's old truck took a big hit when she braked hard. When the vehicle had slowed down, she made a hard right-hand turn into the red dirt and brought the truck to a stop. Before she could turn off the engine, Shiloh had slung open the door, hiked up her dress, and was running toward Waylon's truck. She reached it in time to see Waylon fall out of the driver's side and wobble as he tried to stand up.

"He's alive," she yelled into the phone.

"Lay him out flat on the ground and don't let him move," the EMT said. "Is there something you can use to stabilize his neck? Is there anything like a blanket to keep him warm until we can get there?"

"I'll check," she said as she threw the phone at Bonnie. "Talk to them."

"Got to get home. Granddad has to make a run," Waylon muttered.

"What you are going to do is lay down flat and be still until the ambulance gets here." Shiloh removed her sweater and held it against the gash on his forehead.

"Anything for you, darlin'." He winced as he stretched out on the cold, hard ground. "Are you hurt?"

"Be still," she demanded. "You're losing a lot of blood, and you could have all kinds of injuries."

His eyes fluttered shut.

Her heart thumped in her chest, and her pulse raced. She'd never seen a man die, especially one who she knew so well, and had even flirted with on more than one occasion. Her hands shook as she pressed harder on the sweater, his warm blood seeping through the thin fabric and oozing up between her fingers.

God, don't let him die. She looked up at the stars. His breath rattled out of his chest and he coughed. Shiloh glanced at his mouth to see if there was blood there, and heaved a sigh of relief when his lips were clear.

"Don't you dare die, Waylon Stephens!" she yelled at him. "Open your eyes and stay with me."

"They say you're doing the right thing." Bonnie kept the phone to her ear. "Should I run back to the house and get a blanket?"

"Ask them how much longer until they get here," Shiloh said.

"They say fifteen minutes. They've got the sirens going, and they're taking the back roads to get here faster," Bonnie told her.

"It would take you longer to get there and back than it'll take them to get here," Shiloh told her.

"Then here..." Bonnie peeled out of her jacket and laid it over Waylon's upper body. "That might help a little."

"Thank you," Shiloh said. "You should get back in your truck and stay warm. There's nothing more you can do, and you'll get sick if you get a chill."

Seconds took hours to go by, and minutes were an eternity. Shiloh kept demanding that Waylon keep his eyes open and talk to her. Most of the time, he focused on her face, but he didn't say anything at all. She wondered what kind of work his granddad had done that he had to make a run, and why it was important for Waylon to get home to help him, but she didn't ask. The EMTs had said to keep him as quiet and as still as possible.

Finally, Shiloh and Bonnie heard the sirens and saw the flashing lights as the ambulance came around a curve in the highway. As soon as the vehicle stopped, the two EMTs seemed to be everywhere at once. They loaded Waylon onto a flat board, secured his neck with a brace, removed Shiloh's sweater and applied gauze to the gaping wound on his forehead.

"I'm going with him," she announced when they had him inside.

"Sorry, ma'am, it's not allowed," the older of the two men said.

"It is tonight," Shiloh told him as she hiked up her dress and got into the ambulance. Bonnie threw her phone toward her and said, "What should I do?"

The doors were closing when Shiloh caught the phone and yelled, "Bring me my purse and a change of clothes, and get Rusty to follow you in my SUV so I'll have a way to get him home."

She had to pull her knees to the side to give the EMT room to start an IV, take Waylon's vital signs, and check his eyes. "Okay, Derrick"—she read the embroidered name tag on his jacket—"tell me he's going to be all right."

"I hope so, but the doctors will have to check him out for brain damage, concussion, all kinds of things. He's got a nasty cut on his head that's going to probably need stitches," Derrick said above the high-pitched whine of the sirens.

"Hate needles," Waylon muttered, his first words in several minutes.

"So do I." Shiloh reached around Derrick and covered Waylon's hand with hers.

Driving on Texas roads was one thing. Driving in the Palo Duro Canyon was quite another with its curves, and hills, and valleys. Shiloh was glad when they finally came up out of the canyon just south of Claude, and the ambulance driver could go faster. She had flirted with Waylon at church and social gatherings, had even danced with him a couple of times at the Sugar Shack, the canyon's only honky-tonk. Now, she wished she'd stepped right up and asked him out. The opportunities had been there, and she wasn't shy, but she had a thing about rejection. Probably a deep-seated emotion brought on by her father not wanting her because she was a girl.

The driver made a hard left onto Interstate 40 and kicked up the speed even more. In just a few minutes, he was pulling up under the awning, and then he and Derrick were rolling Waylon into the emergency room.

"You can wait right here." Derrick motioned toward the seating area.

Shiloh gave him a dirty look and went right on through the double doors with him and the other guy. They did one of those one, two, three, counts and shifted Waylon onto a bed. He grimaced when they removed his cowboy boots.

"Foot hurts," he said.

"We'll get it seen about real soon," Shiloh told him.

A nurse with a no-nonsense expression pulled the curtain to the cubicle back and motioned for Shiloh to leave. "We've got to get him out of that suit so we can examine him. You need to leave."

Shiloh narrowed her eyes. "I'll step outside the curtain, but as soon as you have him changed, I'm coming back in."

"Are you related?" The nurse eased his black jacket off and was unbuckling his belt.

"No, I'm his girlfriend," Shiloh lied.

"Then I'll call you as soon as I'm finished," the nurse said.

* * *

Waylon chuckled, and Shiloh shot a look his way that said he had better not tattle as she slipped around the curtain. Things were a little foggy in his mind. He remembered something about a song about Red Dirt Road—no, that wasn't right. He lived on a road like that growing up over in—it took him a while to remember that had been over near Kiomatia, right on the Red River.

A doctor in a white coat pushed the curtain back, and said, "Well, son, what hurts?"

"My head and my ankle," Waylon answered.

"Let's get some tests run to see about both of those." He flashed a small penlight in Waylon's eyes, then gently felt his ankle. "I think you have a mild concussion and a sprained ankle, but the tests I'm ordering will let us know for certain. I want to be sure that you don't have any cracked or broken ribs from the seat belt. Good thing you were wearing one, or you might've been thrown through the windshield. While we're waiting, let's get that head wound taken care of. I think we can use some glue and Steri-Strips instead of stitches. The nurse will clean it up, and then I'll do my magic."

Waylon barely nodded.

"Keep the neck brace on until we get those pictures," the doctor told the nurse.

"Yes, sir," she said.

Shiloh pushed around the curtain and came back to stand beside him. She took his hand in hers as they took care of the gash on his forehead. He tried not to squeeze her hand, but dammit! It hurt like a bitch when the nurse cleaned the wound. He kept his eyes glued to Shiloh's face. Her beautiful dark hair had been pinned up for the wedding, but now it had fallen down over her shoulders. The red roses that had been scattered through the curls were wilted. Her pretty dress was stained and dirty, and her black rubber boots were muddy.

"Sorry," he said.

"For what?" she asked.

"Your dress," he muttered.

"Honey, this is just a dress. It can be cleaned or thrown in the trash. What matters is that you aren't dead." She squeezed his hand.

She had called him *honey*. He was sure of that, but he couldn't be her sweetheart. That much he was sure of. He was Waylon Stephens, of the moonshiners over in Red River County, Texas. Shiloh Malloy was way out of his league.

He closed his eyes, but she leaned down and said, "Don't you close your eyes. You can't sleep until the doctor gets done with you, and if you've got a concussion, I'll be waking you up every hour until twenty-four have passed, so get ready for it."

"Sleepy," he said.

"Me too, but we can sleep later," she told him.

Dawn was pushing night out of the way when the nurse finally came into the cubicle with a whole raft of papers in her hands. "Doc says his preliminary exam was right on the money. Sprained ankle and a slight concussion. He will need someone with him for about a week. No heavy lifting, no hard work, crutches for at least a week. I'm sending him home with a list of things he can't do, and those that he can."

"I'll stay with him, and see to it that he behaves," Shiloh said.

"I'm a big boy. I can take care of myself," Waylon protested.

"Yep, you can, in a week," Shiloh told him.

"You can have someone with you, or we can keep you here," the nurse said. "It's your choice, Mr. Stephens."

"I'll go home," he grumbled.

"And you'll be good?" the nurse asked.

"Yes, he will, because I give you my word," Shiloh told her.

"I've got cattle and chickens and—"

Shiloh put a finger on his lips. "I can take care of all that. It's only for a week, and if I need help, I'll call Rusty and Bonnie."

"How're we getting home?" He didn't want to tell either of them that the only thing he could picture in his mind was a little frame house set back in a grove of pecan trees. Back behind the house was acres and acres of corn that granddad used to make shine.

"Rusty and Bonnie brought my SUV up here. It's waiting in the parking lot, so let's go home and get the morning feeding chores done," she said.

Even the nod he gave made his head throb worse. "All right, but you don't have to..."

She patted him on the shoulder. "That's what friends and neighbors are for. I'll go bring the van up to the doors."

The nurse helped him get dressed and rolled him outside in a wheelchair in time to see a beautiful sunrise out there at the end of the horizon. His suit would never come clean again, but thank God, they didn't have to cut his boot off, since they were the ones that he saved for Sunday and special occasions.

When he stood up, the sunrise blurred, and he had to grab the door handle of the van to keep from dropping. The nurse told him to sit down in the passenger seat and then she pulled his bum leg up and put it inside.

"The doctor will see you on Friday. Your appointment and his address are in this file," she said.

"We'll be there," Shiloh assured her.

The nurse shook her finger at Waylon. "No driving until after he sees you."

"You got to be kiddin' me," he moaned.

"I'll see to it." Shiloh nodded.

Waylon waited until they were past Claude before he said, "All right, we escaped that place. You can drop me off at my ranch, and go on home. I'll get in touch with someone to tow my truck…"

"What we're going to do is go to your ranch, get a shower, and make breakfast. Then I'll let you sleep an hour while I take care of the morning chores. That's as much as you need to worry about right now. Your truck is already at the body shop. Rusty and Bonnie took care of that last night, and called the insurance company listed on the papers in your glove compartment."

"You don't have to do this." He used the lever on the side to lean the seat back a little.

"I'm not arguing with you anymore," she said.

Good God Almighty! It was going to be a long week.

Chapter Three

Shiloh felt like she'd just closed her eyes when the alarm went off right by her ear at three o'clock in the afternoon. She glanced over at the recliner where Waylon was sleeping, saw that he was awake, and reset the alarm.

"What's your name?" she asked.

"Waylon Stephens, and I live in Palo Duro Canyon on a ranch." He smiled.

"How old are you?" She covered a yawn with her hand.

"Thirty on my last birthday," he answered. "I'm fine. Go back to sleep."

She closed her eyes, but she couldn't sleep. Was he telling the truth about his age, or did he just make up something so that she'd leave him alone? She'd promised the doctor that for the first twenty-four hours she'd wake him every single hour and ask him something to be sure he was all right. Next time she'd have to remember to ask something she was absolutely sure about.

When her alarm went off the second time, she expected to see him in his recliner, but he wasn't there. She threw back the quilt that she'd used to cover herself and followed the sounds of his crutches on the wooden kitchen floor.

"Just exactly"—she popped her hands on her hips—"what do you think you're doin'?"

"I'm bored," he said. "So I'm making each of us an omelet for supper. We'll eat, and then we'll go do the evening chores."

"Not *we*." She crossed the floor and poked him in the chest with her forefinger. "I will do the chores. If you promise to be good, I might let you ride in the truck, but no driving."

"You're worse than my mother." One corner of his mouth turned up in a Harrison Ford grin.

"You're a horrible patient," she said.

"I hate being in the house," he told her. "Always have. That's why I went to work on a ranch right out of high school. The idea of sitting through four years of classes in college gave me the hives." He leaned his crutches against the cabinet and worked with his bad leg cocked back.

"You look like a flamingo standing like that," she told him. "Go sit down and let me finish the omelets."

"If I sit any longer, I will die of pure boredom. I can handle this. If I need help, I'll ask." He added ham, peppers, and cheese to the omelet and deftly flipped one side over to make a pocket.

That was more than she'd ever heard Waylon say at one time, so she decided to press her luck. "So just how bad was your mama? I'm askin' to see how much of that derogatory remark you made is true."

"Actually, my mama is a saint. She has had to live on the next farm over from my grandmother, who's always cankerous and always complains about everything. My folks and most of my family still live way back in the sticks next to the Red River on Red Dirt Road in East Texas," he said. "Is that enough to convince you that I don't have amnesia?"

"Maybe."

He scooted the first omelet off onto a plate and handed it to her, then added two pieces of toast and a small bowl of mixed fruit. "I poured the fruit from a bag of frozen so don't fuss at me for using a knife."

"And I suppose you just blinked and the peppers magically diced themselves too?"

"No, I keep bowls full in the fridge all ready to use for omelets or fajitas or whatever else I might need to use them for when I'm cooking on the fly," he informed her. "What about your mama? She would have been Ezra's second wife, right?"

"Her name is Polly," Shiloh answered. "And, yes, she was number two of the three wives. His dogs are named after his wives—there's Martha, Polly, and Vivien. Our mothers in that order. Never knew any of my grandparents. Didn't know Ezra or his kinfolk, and Mama's folks died before I was born." She carried the plate and small bowl to the table, and came back to stand beside him.

"Did I forget something?" he asked.

"Just that you can't carry a plate and work those crutches at the same time, and if you start hopping on one leg, there's a chance you'll fall," she reminded him. "So maybe you should quit bein' so macho and let me help."

"Yes, ma'am." There was that sexy little grin again.

Shiloh would have bet that anytime he went to the Sugar Shack, all he had to do was flash that shy smile, and all the women in the canyon would have trouble keeping their underbritches from sliding down around their ankles.

* * *

Waylon fought the chemistry between him and Shiloh with all his might and power, but the attraction did nothing but grow. Everyone in the canyon knew the terms of Ezra's will—his daughters had to live on the ranch together for one year. At the end of that time, whoever was still on the place would share the land.

Waylon's dad had always told him that if he dragged his feet, he might get left behind. He wanted to throw the crutches over in a corner, hold his leg up like one of those big-butted birds, and take Shiloh in his arms for a long, hot kiss, but that wouldn't be right. Why start something that he couldn't finish? Especially if it led to something more, and then she hated him for cheating her out of her half of a ranch that was twice or three times the size of his little spread.

He slipped his crutches under his arms and hobbled over to the table where she'd set his plate. When he had sat down, she gave him a long, quizzical look.

"What?" he asked. He couldn't have egg on his face or shirt, since he hadn't even taken the first bite.

"You sayin' grace over this food or am I?" she asked.

He bowed his head and said a simple prayer.

"You're not used to praying for your food, are you?" she asked.

She'd picked up on that in a hurry. His grandmother was super religious—one of those people who thought the earth would open up and the devil would drag a person right down to hell if they didn't say grace before they ate. But then she was so hateful and mean-spirited that no one really wanted to spend much time with her. It was a case of attitude versus actions. His granddad didn't always bless his sandwich at noontime when he and his crew were out in the field hauling hay in the summertime, but he had a heart of gold and never said a hateful word to anyone. Waylon had always wanted to be more like his granddad than his grandmother.

"Did I stutter all that bad?"

"No, but you were uncomfortable." She took her first bite of the omelet. "This is really good. Who taught you to cook?"

"My mother," he replied, glad that she'd changed the subject. "I have three sisters, all older than me, and two younger brothers. She said if the girls had to learn to drive tractors, haul hay, and build fences, then us boys had to learn to cook and clean. She was a wise woman. All of us can run a ranch, but we also know how to take care of a house."

"Your mama did good, but right now your ankle is sprained, and you have a concussion," she reminded him. "Everyone needs help at some time in their life."

"You got that right." He nodded.

"How in the devil are you running this place without hired hands or help of any kind?" she asked.

"I just bought it last fall and it was in pretty decent shape. I'm hoping to hire a couple of high school boys to help out in the summer. Kids around these parts are always looking for work," he told her.

Dammit!

He didn't want to feel comfortable talking to her. He wanted for things to be awkward between them, so the temptation to ask her out on a date wouldn't keep rising up to pester him.

"You got any half siblings back in Arkansas?" he asked.

"Nope, I'm an only child. All three of us—Abby Joy, Bonnie, and me—are only children. I guess our mothers all felt the same when Ezra threw them out because we weren't boys," she said. "Crappy way to treat a woman right after she's carried a baby for nine months and then went through delivery, isn't it?"

"It's a wonder one of those women didn't shoot him, but then—" He hesitated.

"But then," she butted in, "they'd have gone to prison, and left a child with no parent."

"Why do you even want something that belonged to him?" Waylon asked.

"My biggest dream has been to live on a ranch. Mama used to say it was in my blood. Now I have the chance, and I can always change the name to something other than Malloy Ranch."

"Ezra will always be buried there," Waylon reminded her.

"Yep, and he can see that I'm doing a fantastic job of running the place and be sorry that he shoved me and Mama out the door," she said.

* * *

Shiloh remembered well the first time she'd seen Waylon Stephens. She hadn't known his name back then, but he'd sure stood out at her father's funeral. With those steely-blue eyes set in a chiseled face, he'd been the sexiest cowboy at the graveside services. She had never met Ezra, so she couldn't bring herself to cry for him, and she hadn't paid much attention to what was being said. She had, however, snuck in a few long sideways looks at her two sisters and several at Waylon, who had stood off to one side.

Her sisters had teased her about him ever since they saw her staring at him in church that first Sunday, but looking was all she intended to do. Abby Joy had done more than look at Cooper, and it had cost her a third of a pretty nice-size ranch. Now it was down to Shiloh and Bonnie, and it was still nine months until the first of the year. Maybe Bonnie should be the one taking care of Waylon, since she'd caught the bouquet and the garter had landed on his cowboy hat.

That thought sent a streak of jealousy through Shiloh's heart. Bonnie could fall for someone else, preferably in the summertime, and that would give her time to get married long before the January first deadline. When it was all said and done, Shiloh intended to have her cake and eat it too. She'd own Malloy Ranch, and then she'd act on the strong vibes between her and Waylon.

"You got awful quiet all of a sudden," Waylon said, breaking the silence between them.

"Just thinkin'," she said. "How long have you lived in the canyon?"

"Little more than a year. I came over here with my cousin Travis, who's married to Nona, the daughter of the folks that own the biggest spread around these parts. My youngest brother, Cash, came with us, but he went back home after a few weeks. Got to missin' the girl he left behind," Waylon said.

"Did you leave a girl behind?" Shiloh asked.

He shook his head.

"Leave dozens behind?" Shiloh pressed.

"Maybe a few, but nothing serious. Had my mind set on buyin' my own place, so I had to work long hours. That didn't leave much time for gettin' any more serious than a few dances on Saturday night at the local honky-tonk," he answered. "How about you? You got a feller waiting to move in with you when you inherit Ezra's ranch?"

"Nope," she replied. "Any of the guys I dated wouldn't ever want to live in this place."

"It takes a special kind of person to appreciate the beauty of the canyon, don't it?" he asked as he reached for his crutches.

"Yes, it does, and I've got to admit that it took a while to grow on me. When I first drove down into the canyon, I thought I'd dropped off the edge of the world." She cleared the table and headed for the back door. "We'd best get the chores done before dark. You need help with your coat?"

"I reckon I can take care of that, but it would be nice if you'd hold the door for me," he said.

"See there. You asked for help, and it didn't kill you." She smiled over her shoulder at him.

"If I was home out in the eastern part of the state, my grandmother would tell me to suck it up and go to work," he said as he bent his leg at the knee and managed to get his coat on, then slipped the crutches under his arms.

The evening feeding chores didn't take long, and riding kept Waylon awake for a couple of hours, but Shiloh could tell that he was worn-out when they got back to the house.

"Hey, it's only six more hours until you don't have to wake up every single hour. At midnight you can go to sleep for a while," she told him.

"I'm going to take a shower and go to bed." He removed his coat and tossed it on the back of a kitchen chair. "Every bone and muscle in my body feels like they've been stomped on by a two-ton bull."

"Well, what do you expect?" Shiloh asked him. "You were in a wreck. When you hit that tree, it jarred everything. Doc says you can take the boot off for a shower, but you aren't to put weight on your foot. Probably the best thing you could do is take a kitchen chair into the shower with you and prop your knee on it."

"Reckon you could do that for me?" he asked.

"Sure." She nodded.

The chair took up a lot of room in the stall, but there was still room for Waylon, and it would give him stability.

"You ever do nursing work?" He followed her into the bathroom.

"Nope, but my aunt broke a couple of toes once, and mama came up with this idea so she could take showers," Shiloh replied as she backed out of the bathroom.

The house was small—living room and country kitchen taking up the right half of the place, a short hallway with two bedrooms and a bathroom on the other side. The doors to both bedrooms were open wide. One was empty except for a full bookcase on one wall and a leather recliner that looked like it had been around for years. The other was Waylon's bedroom—nightstands on either side of a king-size bed that was made up so tight that she could probably have bounced a quarter on it. A tall chest of drawers with a mirror above it was set against one wall and a dresser against the other.

She shouldn't go into his private space without an invitation, but she did anyway. She picked up a picture from the nightstand and stared at the six people in it. Waylon shared center stage with a tall woman who had to be one of his sisters. Two more girls were beside the lady, and two cowboys beside Waylon. They all wore jeans, western shirts, boots, and hats.

"This would make a great poster to hang in a western-wear store." She yawned.

The bed looked inviting after she'd caught only a few minutes of sleep between the times when she had to be sure Waylon was all right. It wouldn't hurt to stretch out on it while he was in the shower, would it? Just a thirty-minute power nap would absolutely give her the energy to make it to midnight, and then she could get some real sleep.

She eased down on the bed and bit back a groan. Waylon was obviously aching from the wreck, but her muscles were tense from worry and having no good rest for more than a day. She wiggled a little and closed her eyes—just for a minute. She'd be out of the bed and in the living room before he got through with his shower.

Chapter Four

A small night-light and what was left of a half moon lit up the room enough that Shiloh could see she'd slept more than a few minutes. She glanced over at the digital clock on the nightstand to see that it was eleven o'clock, and then she flipped over to find Waylon propped up on an elbow staring right at her. She was covered with a fluffy blanket that was warm and soft.

"What's your name? Are you lucid? Can you say the alphabet backward?" he asked.

"Oh, hush!" she said. "Some caretaker I am."

"I haven't been asleep yet, so there's no problem," he told her. "It's close enough to twenty-four hours that I believe we can both forget about that every-hour stuff. Good night, Shiloh."

"Good night." She slid off the bed.

"Where are you going?" he asked.

"To the sofa," she told him.

"Why? This bed is big enough for us both, and believe me, honey, I'm way too sore to make a move on you," he assured her.

The pesky voice in her head told her to get her butt to the sofa. Her body said that the bed was so much more comfortable and plenty big enough that she and Waylon would never even touch each other.

She stretched out again and pulled the throw up to her chin. "Thank you," she muttered as her eyes fluttered shut.

When she awoke again, Waylon was snuggled up to her, his chest against her back and one arm wrapped around her waist. They were wrapped up in the cover like they were in a cocoon. The sun was up and she could hear the cattle bellowing.

"Good morning." Waylon's warm breath on her neck sent shivers down her spine.

No, no, no! she scolded herself. She had her life planned out for the next nine months. She had never started anything that she didn't intend to finish. Even the two relationships she'd been in before she moved to the canyon—she'd fully well meant for each of those to last forever, and ever, amen. The men had been the ones to break things off. One had broken up with her because he'd slept with her best friend—she mourned the loss of her friend more than her boyfriend. The second one was in the air force and got sent to Germany. The long-distance relationship didn't survive after the first two months.

"I've made it through twenty-four hours. I'm a big boy. I can take a shower all by myself and cook, so you can go home," he said as he rolled over, got out of bed, and reached for his crutches.

She slid off the opposite side of the bed. "And who is going to drive for you? The doctor says you're not to get behind the wheel until he sees you next Friday. This is Monday. You think those cows out there are going to live without food all week. And there's the chickens and the hogs too. I suppose they can fast until the weekend."

"You sure are bossy," he muttered.

"Maybe so, but I'm not going home. I'm going to get a shower, make breakfast, and then we'll do the chores. After that, I expect you'll be ready to rest a spell," she said as she left the room.

"It's going to be a nice day. I thought I'd repair some fence." He raised his voice.

"Don't make me cranky this early in the morning." She went to the living room and rolled her suitcase down the hall.

"How about going out to the barn and cleaning the tack room?" His deep voice carried into the bathroom.

She cracked the door and said, "That might be doable but only if you don't try to do any heavy lifting. Doctor's orders, not mine."

She adjusted the water, stripped out of her clothing, and stepped into the shower stall. For a few minutes she just let the warm water beat out the tension from between her shoulders.

Why are you here? Why didn't you just call one of his brothers to come help out? She wished she could wash the thoughts from her head as easily as she rinsed the shampoo from her hair.

I want to know him better, and this is one good way to get to do that, she argued as she turned off the water.

You've met dozens of cowboys in the past three months. What makes Waylon so special? The pesky voice in her head wasn't ready to give up the fight.

Shiloh wrapped a towel around her body and one around

her head. She unzipped her suitcase and pulled out a pair of faded jeans, a T-shirt, and clean underwear. Six months ago Shiloh hadn't even known she had siblings, and now her baby sister knew her well enough to know what to pack for her.

That question about Waylon being special stuck in her mind as she towel-dried her hair and then pulled it up into a ponytail while it was still damp. She stared at her reflection in the mirror above the sink, and said, "I'm attracted to him because he's handsome and sexy and has a deep Texas drawl. But more than that, it's his brooding eyes that mesmerize me. To top it all off, he's kind and sweet and he listens to me when I talk. So there, are you satisfied?"

Her phone rang and startled her so badly that she dropped her hairbrush. She dug the phone from the pocket of her jeans that were on the floor and answered without even looking at the caller ID.

"Hey, how's things going over there?" Bonnie asked.

"The patient is restless," Shiloh told her.

"Has he said more than a dozen words?"

"Maybe a few more than that." Shiloh used her free hand to rearrange her suitcase as she talked. "It's going to be a tough job to keep him from working all week."

"Bring him over here one evening, and we'll have a game of poker," Bonnie suggested. "I'm not used to rattling around in this place without you and Abby Joy. I'll make finger foods, and—"

"How about tonight?" Shiloh butted in.

"Great!" Bonnie squealed. "Can you be here by six?"

"You bet we can. Get your nickels and dimes ready. I'm going to wipe you out tonight," Shiloh told her.

"Yeah, but in a few months I'm going to get a hundred bucks and a bottle of good Kentucky bourbon, so I'll get it all back," Bonnie joked.

"I didn't catch the bouquet. You did," Shiloh reminded her.

"But Waylon got the garter, so—" Bonnie started.

"I'm not going there," Shiloh butted in for the second time. "See you this evening. I'd say that I'd bring the beer, but Waylon can't drink until after the doctor releases him."

"Man, he's really got it tough. Can't drive or work. Can't drink, and worst thing of all is living with you," Bonnie said.

"I'm hanging up now," Shiloh heard Bonnie's giggles as she ended the call.

She rolled her suitcase out into the hallway and gathered up her towels as well as the ones that were in the hamper. She caught the first whiff of coffee as she headed toward the kitchen. When she got closer, she smelled bacon and was that cinnamon?

Waylon had dragged a kitchen chair over to the stove to prop his knee on and was humming as he made bacon and French toast for breakfast. When she passed by him on the way to the utility room to put the towels in the washing machine, he looked up and gave her one of his rare smiles.

"This chair idea works in lots of places," he said.

"If you had to be off it longer than a few days, they make a scooter just for that purpose." She started the washing machine and returned to the kitchen.

"If I had to live through more than a week of this, I'd be batshit crazy," he muttered.

"And here I thought we were getting along pretty good. I don't usually sleep with a man on the first date," she teased.

"We haven't been on a date, but when we do there won't be much sleeping." He winked at her.

"Pretty confident there, are you?" She knew she shouldn't flirt with him, but he started it with that wink.

"You'll have to wait and see." He put the bacon on a paper towel to drain.

"Does that mean you're going to ask me on a date?" She brought down two plates and set the table.

"Not in the kitchen with my leg propped on a chair. That's about as romantic as asking you out when you're hoisting twenty-five-pound bags of feed." He handed her a plate of cinnamon toast to take to the table and reached for his crutches.

Shiloh didn't know if he was bullshittin' her or if he was serious. She'd never dated a guy who thought that the mere act of asking her out required a romantic setting. She wasn't sure how to respond so she just changed the subject.

"Bonnie wants you and I to come over to our place tonight for a game of poker. You up for that?" she asked.

"Yep." He nodded as he maneuvered into a chair. "How high is the stakes?"

"Quarter," she answered. "Pennies, nickels, dimes, and quarters, no folding money."

"Sounds like a high-roller game," he chuckled.

"Hey, now, last time Abby Joy, Bonnie, and I played, I walked away with twenty bucks." She bowed her head.

He said a quick prayer and then put half a dozen pieces of toast on his plate. "That would buy us a drink at the Sugar Shack on Friday night."

"Maybe, but that's only if the doctor clears you to go," she told him. "For him to do that, you have to follow orders all week."

Waylon shot a sideways look toward her.

"Don't be givin' me that attitude. I didn't write the orders. The doctor did, but honey"—she drew out the word to four or five syllables—"I will enforce them."

"You're worse than a drill sergeant," he grumbled.

"I take it that you'd never ask a drill sergeant on a date?" She raised a dark eyebrow.

"That depends," he answered.

"On what?"

"On lots of things, but mainly if she had shown an interest in me." He took a sip of coffee.

"Oh, so you had a female drill sergeant?" She scraped half the bacon onto her plate.

"Didn't ever join the military. Went right into ranchin' after high school," he said. "When I asked that air force guy who came to our school about the drill sergeant, he couldn't guarantee that I'd get a female one, so I wouldn't join."

"And here all this time I thought you were shy, when in reality you're just a smart-ass." She pushed back her chair, went to the cabinet, and returned with the coffeepot. "I need a refill. You want a warm-up?"

"Thank you." He held up his cup. "If I was trying to pick you up in a bar, I'd have a comeback for what you just said."

"Oh, yeah." She poured for both of them and returned the pot. "What would that be?"

"Darlin', just looking at you warms me up."

Shiloh had just taken a sip of coffee and spewed it all over the table. "That is the worse pickup line I've ever heard."

"Now you've hurt my feelings." He narrowed his eyes at her, but they were twinkling. "And put coffee stains on my tablecloth, at the same time."

"I'll get the stains out, and surely you've got better lines that that," she told him.

"That one never did work," he admitted, "but I have a few that have netted me some good results in the past." He held up a palm. "Don't ask me to tell you. It's fun talking to you, Shiloh, but I know the rules over on Malloy Ranch. I'd never, ever ask you out, at least not until the year is over."

"You do realize that makes it sound like you're interested in doubling the size of your place," she said.

"Try tripling it, but, honey, I only want what I earn," he told her.

"Fair enough." She nodded. "I never figured I'd be having this kind of conversation with you."

"Me, either"—he finished off his breakfast—"and we've been acquainted since the first of the year. Guess we just never had an opportunity to be alone."

Everything about the whole situation should have felt awkward, but it didn't—at least not to Shiloh.

Chapter Five

Shiloh remembered that cold day of Ezra's funeral. After the last hymn was sung, she'd driven her van back to the house. Abby Joy had stepped out of her vehicle with an aura of confidence surrounding her. She'd slung a duffel bag over her back and started toward the porch. Bonnie had opened the door of her rusted-out old pickup truck like she owned the world and dared anyone to even try to cross her. She'd lined up plastic grocery bags on her arm and marched across the yard. Shiloh had felt like she was the only chicken at a coyote convention when she unloaded the monogrammed luggage her mother had given her when she graduated from high school all those years ago, but she vowed that she wouldn't let either of those women know that they intimidated her.

"Where are we? I don't recognize this place," Waylon whispered.

Her heart fell down into her cowboy boots. He'd been

doing so well, and he should know exactly where he was. He'd known Ezra well enough to come to the funeral. Surely he'd been at the Malloy Ranch at some time.

"You don't recognize this house? It's Ezra's place. It's where Bonnie and I live, where Abby Joy lived until day before yesterday. Look again," she said.

He shook his head. "Who is Ezra?"

"He's my biological father. Little short guy with blue eyes and gray hair. He died and we buried him on New Year's Day. Think hard"—she frowned—"you were at the funeral. You stood beside Cooper. You were wearing a black leather coat that came almost to your knees, and black cowboy boots. A cold wind was blowing, and each of us sisters put a daisy in the casket with Ezra. I never quite understood why, but Rusty told us to do it, so we did."

His brows drew down, as if he was trying to remember. "Ezra's not dead. I saw him last week at the feed store. He said that he and Rusty were ready for the spring grass to get high enough to put the cattle on it." He chuckled. "Ezra Malloy squeezes his pennies so tight that Lincoln squeals."

"Ezra has been dead for almost three months," she assured him. "It's not far back to the cemetery. Let's drive back there to his grave site. Maybe that will jar your memory."

He raised his palm and laughed out loud. "My name is Waylon Stephens. I just punked Shiloh Malloy."

"You rascal!" She slapped him on the arm.

He grabbed his arm and winced. "Ouch! You got me right on a big bruise from where the seat belt went across."

"I'm not sorry," she declared. "You deserved that and more. I was about to take you to the emergency room."

"Well, darlin', I'm not sorry I punked you, either. It was worth the pain just to see you get all worked up." He opened the van door. "Guess I proved to you that I've got a poker face and you'd best be careful with your bets tonight."

She pointed her finger at him as she got out of the vehicle. "For that mean stunt, I plan to take all your money."

He managed the crutches very well as they climbed the steps side by side. Her hand brushed against his, and the sparks didn't surprise her. She'd like to be mad at him for that crazy joke he'd just pulled on her, but she just couldn't. She would have never thought that Waylon would have a sense of humor, but that he did was a big plus in her books. He'd gotten to the top step when all three of Ezra's dogs came running up on the porch. Polly jumped up on Shiloh and sent her crashing against Waylon. One of his crutches flew to the left, the other one got tangled up in Shiloh's legs.

The fall felt like it was happening in slow motion, and yet there was nothing she could do to stop it. One second she was standing upright with Waylon beside her, the next she was flat out on the porch with him on top of her. Polly was licking her face. Bonnie and Rusty crammed through the door at the same time. Shiloh's chest hurt, not from Waylon's weight, but because the fall had knocked the breath right out of her.

Bonnie fell down beside her and slapped her face. "Breathe, sister! You're turning blue."

Waylon rolled off to one side, and let out a loud whoosh of air. "I didn't mean to make you so mad that you'd trip me," he said between deep breaths.

Shiloh tried to sit up. "I didn't trip you," she gasped as she kept trying to force more and more air into her lungs.

"What'd you do?" Rusty gathered up the crutches and helped Waylon to his feet.

"Must've been a pretty hard fall." Bonnie took both of Shiloh's hands and pulled her to her feet.

The porch did a couple of spins, but in a few seconds, Shiloh had her bearings. "Polly did it," she said.

"She pouted yesterday and has watched the lane all day today lookin' for you to come home," Bonnie said. "Y'all are all right, aren't you? Do we need to take Waylon to the hospital for a checkup?"

"I'm fine," Waylon said. "But we might need to have Shiloh seen about. I landed pretty hard right on top of her. She could have cracked ribs or even a concussion as hard as she hit the porch."

"You're just trying to get out of losing all your money," Shiloh said between even more deep breaths. "There's nothing wrong with me that a beer and some chips and dip won't cure." She squatted down and rubbed Polly's ears. "So you missed me, did you? Maybe you should come on over to Waylon's place and stay with us the rest of the week."

"Oh, no!" Rusty opened the door and held it for Waylon. "I'm not giving up my dogs. Ezra left them to me, and even if you and Bonnie stick around long enough to get the ranch, I'm taking Vivien, Polly, and Martha with me. Abby Joy didn't try to steal Martha from me, and y'all ain't gettin' Polly and Vivien."

Shiloh straightened up, and the world didn't do any spins. She was breathing normal now, for the most part, but thinking about Waylon on top of her put more than a little heat in her body. For just a split second there, she thought maybe he might kiss her, but then Bonnie was right there beside her.

"You slapped me." Shiloh tilted her head to the side and gave Bonnie the evil eye.

"You're welcome."

Shiloh's hand went to her face. "I'm not thanking you for hitting me."

"If I hadn't, you might've laid there and died, and then you'd never know what it would be like to really have that good-lookin' cowboy on top of you," Bonnie teased.

"You're certifiably goofy." Shiloh's cheeks burned with a bright red blush.

"Don't tell me that you weren't enjoying the feeling." Bonnie started inside the house. "And besides, I saw the way you looked at my grocery bag luggage when we first got here on the ranch, and I've wanted a good reason to slap the fire out of you ever since."

"I'll get even." Shiloh hadn't realized how much she'd missed the banter between her and her sisters until that moment. "It'll come at a time when you least expect it."

"Bring your lunch." Bonnie went into the house ahead of her. "It you hit me without good reason, I'll mop up the yard with your skinny butt."

"Hey, that's the pot calling the kettle black." Shiloh followed her. "My butt looks damn fine compared to yours."

Bonnie did a head wiggle that made her big loopy earrings dance. "In your dreams. Old Ezra saved the best until last."

Rusty and Waylon were already at the table with a bottle of beer in front of each one of them.

"And still couldn't get a boy," Rusty said.

Bonnie tucked a strand of blond hair into her ponytail, and air slapped Rusty on the arm. "That was his fault, not mine."

Tonight she was wearing her little diamond nose stud, her good luck charm when she went to the casinos or played cards. Rusty removed his wire-rimmed glasses and cleaned them with the tail of his T-shirt. He raked his fingers through his brown hair and then put his glasses back on. That was his good luck routine every time they played any kind of game. Shiloh watched Waylon to see if he had a gimmick, but he simply took a sip of beer and started shuffling the cards.

"Beer or a wine cooler?" Bonnie asked her sister.

"Wine cooler," Shiloh replied.

"That's her good luck charm, Waylon. Her tell is when she rolls her eyes at the ceiling and then takes a long drink from the bottle," Bonnie tattled.

"Bonnie's tell is when she fiddles with her nose ring." Shiloh ratted her sister out. "That means she's got a good hand."

"That's good to know in both cases." Waylon dealt the cards. "But I'm not banking on either of you telling us guys the truth."

"You shouldn't." Shiloh picked up her cards, fanned them out, and smiled. "After that stunt you pulled in the truck, you better be very careful."

"What was that?" Rusty asked.

Shiloh told them what had happened. "He deserved to fall after that. I need a card."

"You, sir, are one lucky cowboy. It's a wonder that she didn't push you down!" Bonnie said in her deep woodsy Kentucky drawl.

"Guess I am pretty lucky," Waylon said and threw a coin on the table. "I'm in for a quarter."

"Big spender right here at first, aren't you?" Bonnie threw one of her coins into the center of the table.

"Got to spend money to make money," Rusty said.

"That's what my mama says." Shiloh made a mental note to call her mother. She hadn't talked to her about the wedding, or all the things that had happened since then. Polly was going to have a million questions about Waylon. With that in mind, maybe she should drag her feet a little before she called her mama.

* * *

Waylon was two dollars richer when they got home that evening, but he was a million dollars poorer if they'd measured in tiredness rather than money. He'd been thrown from bulls and broncs and had been back on his feet and working within two days. Why did one little wreck affect him like this?

He crutched his way into the house, eased down on the sofa, and leaned his head back. "You can have the bed all to yourself. I'm not moving from right here tonight."

"Oh, no, you will not sleep on the sofa," Shiloh argued. "You'll wake up so sore in the morning that I'll have to carry you to the truck to do the chores." She dropped her purse on the end table and picked up his leg to remove his boot. Then she pointed down the hall. "I'm going to have a shower before I turn in."

"You can't sleep in here if I can't." He reached for his crutches. "After that fall, you're going to be sore right along with me tomorrow morning. The only way I'm sleeping in the bed is if you take the other half of it like you did last night."

"All right then." She nodded. "Don't wait up for me, though."

"Don't worry." He yawned as he stood up and headed down the hall. "I'll be asleep the minute my head hits the pillow."

When he reached his bedroom, he was surprised to see that the bed was made, and the clothes hamper was empty. He usually made his bed, but he'd been in a hurry that morning.

He was exhausted by the time he removed his jeans and got into a pair of pajama pants, but his eyes were wide open when he finally pulled the covers up around his chest. If he had any doubts at all about the chemistry between him and Shiloh, they had disappeared when he fell on top of her that evening. His lips were only inches from hers, and if Bonnie and Rusty hadn't rushed out when they did, he would have kissed her for sure. He laced his hands behind his head and stared out the window at the black clouds shifting over what was left of the moon. The weatherman had said that thunderstorms might be on the way the next day with the possibility of hail and high winds. He could be right this time. Waylon had been having his own personal tempest since his accident, and he was about to give in and forget all about the idea of not asking Shiloh out until the year's end. They could date now, figure out if they even liked each other for more than friends and neighbors, and not waste time wondering.

It took a blow to your head to make you come to your senses. The voice in his head sounded an awful lot like his granddad.

"I'm a little slow," he whispered.

"Were you talking to me?" Shiloh asked as she entered the room.

"No, just muttering to myself." He sat up in bed and pulled the covers back for her.

"Sweet Jesus!" she gasped. "Why didn't you tell me you had all those bruises on your body?"

He hadn't meant for her to see the black-and-blue marks, but he'd totally forgotten to put a T-shirt on that night. He was so tired that he'd almost crawled into bed in the nude, which is the way he usually slept.

"They'll heal," he said.

She ignored the covers and sat down on his side of the bed. She ran a finger over the worst of the bruises—the one where the doctor thought he possibly had a cracked rib, but the X-ray told a different tale. Her touch made his mouth go dry and his hands get clammy. She finally looked up at him and moistened her lips with the tip of her tongue.

He leaned forward, cupped her cheeks with his big hands, and looked deeply into her deep blue eyes. Their lips met in a sweet kiss that deepened into more and more until they were both panting. She finally pulled away from him and stood up.

"It might be best if I sleep on the sofa tonight after that," she told him.

"I'll put a pillow between us," he offered.

"I'm not sure there's one big enough. Remember what the doctor said about no strenuous activity. I reckon sex would be pretty vigorous," she said between long, deep breaths.

"I'll be good." He crossed his heart with his finger like a little boy. After that kiss it might not be easy, but he was a man of his word, no matter how tough it was.

Chapter Six

Shiloh awoke to the noise of something scratching on the door the next morning. At first she thought she was at home on Malloy Ranch and one of the three dogs wanted some-one to get up and feed them. Then she realized she was at Waylon's place. She hadn't seen a dog in the two days she'd been there, and hopefully, Polly hadn't followed them home the night before. If she had, Rusty would think Shiloh had stolen her.

She got out of bed carefully so she wouldn't wake Way-lon. The rising sun defined the trees, now with a few buds and minty green leaves, instead of only dry, brittle branches. The scratching continued and she was surer with every step that Polly had run away from home.

She opened the door and the ugliest dog she'd ever seen ran into the house. It had long yellow hair, short legs, and a wide jaw. Poor thing looked like its mama might have been a corgi and its papa a Labrador—and it had a rat in its jaws.

There were two things that Shiloh hated, and rats were both of them. She froze right there, door wide open, and a calico cat rushed in after the dog with another of those rat things in her mouth. The dog went to the living room, dropped the gray thing on the floor, and stretched out beside it. That's when Shiloh realized it wasn't a rat but a kitten.

The cat laid its little burden down, and Shiloh realized both of the critters were kittens. She started to close the door and the cat rushed out and brought in a third baby and took it to the living room. She flopped down so that the kittens were between her and the dog.

"What's goin' on?" Waylon asked as he crutched up the hallway. "Thunder woke me up. Is it raining?"

"Yep," she said. "It's raining cats and dogs."

He peeked out the door, and raised an eyebrow. "The wind is blowing, but I don't see any rain."

A loud clap of thunder caused the dog to whimper and wrap itself more securely around the mama cat and the kittens.

"Good Lord!" Waylon muttered when he saw the sight in his living room. "Where did those things come from?"

"The porch, I guess," Shiloh said. "I opened the door and both of them brought in the kittens and made themselves at home. Never seen anything like it. Thought they were car-ryin' in rats at first and then I thought it was puppies. Do we keep 'em?"

"Well, I was thinkin' about gettin' a dog, but one that would help round up cattle, not kittens." He crutched over to the sofa and sat down.

The dog's tail thumped against the hardwood floor, so Waylon reached a hand down. The mutt licked it and then nosed the cat toward him. The cat left the dog to babysit her three wiggling kittens and went over to wind around Shiloh's legs.

The rain came in like a huge sheet of water from the dark clouds. A powerful wind slammed it against the windowpanes so fiercely that Shiloh was sure it would break the glass. "We can't put them out."

"Guess you'd better scramble up extra eggs this mornin', and when the storm passes we'll ride into Claude and get them some food. We've got babies to raise. You going to stick around and help me with them after the week is over?" Waylon asked.

"I'll visit them on weekends and at least once through the week, but I can't leave Malloy Ranch permanently." She sat down on the floor, and the mama cat crawled up in her lap. "What's your name, pretty girl?"

"That'll be your job."

"They'll be your cat and kittens. You should name them," Shiloh said.

Waylon pulled his phone from the pocket of his pajama pants, surfed through it for a minute, and then laid it on the end table. Blake Shelton was singing "I'll Name the Dogs." The lyrics said that she could name the babies, and he'd name the dogs.

"Are we still talkin' about kittens?" she asked.

"Yep, we are, but that song came to mind," he told her. "This poor old boy is so ugly I'm not sure what to name him."

"Well, my cat and babies are so pretty, it won't be hard to name them once I find out if they're boys or girls," she told him. "But right now, I'd better get some breakfast started and hope this storm gets on past us so we can go get the feeding done and make that drive to town."

The mama cat followed her to the kitchen and purred its thanks as Shiloh made sausage gravy, biscuits, and scrambled eggs. Whoever tossed the poor creatures out, she thought, should be caught out in the rain without an umbrella—and then shot right between the eyes.

Her phone rang and she dug it out of the pocket of her pajama bottoms. "Hello, Bonnie! You're never going to believe—"

"Did you find the dog and cat?" Bonnie asked.

"How did you know about them?" Shiloh asked. "Did Waylon already call Rusty?"

"No, but I was hoping you'd find them before this damn rain started. I got soaking wet getting from my old truck to the house after I left them all on your porch," Bonnie told her.

"You rat! Why didn't you ask Waylon before you did that?"

"Because he might have said no, and you've talked about wanting a cat, and"—she stopped for a breath—"you remember Granny Denison, who comes to church?"

"The little old lady that sits behind us and sings off-key?" Shiloh asked.

"Yep, that's the one," Bonnie said. "She died yesterday, and Rusty found out her great-nephew inherited her house. The guy was going to put Granny Denison's dog and cat to sleep if someone didn't take them. Polly, Martha, and Vivien hate cats, so we couldn't have them."

"That's horrible." Shiloh couldn't imagine killing the dog, even if it wasn't the prettiest animal in the world, or that sweet cat and kittens.

"I thought so too, so when Rusty told me, I drove over there and got them. I didn't want either of you to say no before you saw them, so I kind of left them on the porch," Bonnie said.

"What's their names?" Shiloh asked.

"Callie is the cat. Blister is the dog. You can name the

kittens," Bonnie said. "And there's food, a litter pan, and their toys in your van. I didn't want to leave it all on the porch with the storm coming."

When something wasn't quite right—especially where either Bonnie or Abby Joy was concerned—Shiloh got the same antsy feeling that she had right then. "You are a sneaky one," she said when it finally hit her what Bonnie was doing, "but it won't work. I'm coming home as soon as the doctor clears Waylon."

"Are you accusing me of trying to get you to stay with Waylon so I'll get the ranch?" Bonnie laughed.

"Are you?"

"If I am, is it going to work?"

"Hell, no!" Shiloh said. "I'm hanging up, and you're still a rat!"

"Did you find their owners?" Waylon made his way into the kitchen.

"They belonged to Granny Denison, and she died. Her great-nephew was going to put them to sleep, so Bonnie brought them over here," she said. "The dog's name is Blister. The cat is Callie. So you don't get to name the dog. Do I still get to name the babies?"

"How about I name the boys, and you can name the girls." He smiled again.

Waylon had smiled twice in one day! She should've gone to the pound and brought in cats and dogs before now.

"Tell her thank you. It gets lonely around here," Waylon said.

Shiloh whipped around and stared at him without blinking. Surely she'd heard him wrong. Any other man would be cussin' and throwing things. "Are you serious?"

He dragged a chair over to the stove, which was no easy feat with crutches, and propped his leg on it. "Move over and I'll help out, and yes, I'm very serious. Besides, what were the chances that I could have a dog and cat both? Most of the time, they hate each other, and on the plus side, since you let them in, you have to come visit and babysit them from time to time. I'm sorry to hear about Granny Denison. When's the funeral? We should go."

"I'll ask Bonnie," Shiloh answered.

When he leaned over to get the butter, his arm touched hers. The chemistry was definitely still there. It hadn't died since the kiss from the night before. What would it hurt to see where a few dates might lead? A fling didn't necessarily mean wedding bells and a pretty white dress.

Chapter Seven

Shiloh could count the funerals she'd been to in her life-time on the fingers of one hand. The last one had been just a graveside service for Ezra, and she was expecting that for Granny Denison. She couldn't have been more wrong.

When she and Waylon entered the church that Friday morning, the place was already packed. If Bonnie and Rusty hadn't saved them a seat on the back row, they would have had to stand along the walls like so many other folks. A low buzz from whispered conversations made it sound like a beehive was nearby. Then Waylon reached over and took Shiloh's hand and suddenly the whole place went eerily quiet.

For a split second, Shiloh expected to see a picture of their hands with their names emblazoned across the bottom on the big screen that hung at the front of the church. She was re-lieved when she looked up and saw the preacher taking his place behind the podium. "I have specific written instructions from Granny Denison concerning this funeral. The first thing I'm to do is read the obituary. 'Mary Audrey Denison was born March seventeenth, 1921, right here in the Palo Duro Canyon to Henry and Wilma Denison. She was the oldest of ten children and the only girl in the family. She died March seventeenth, 2020, on her birthday, which is exactly what she hoped she would do. She said that when people die on their birthdays it completes the cycle of life. She was preceded in death by her parents and all her brothers. She leaves behind her dog, Blister, and cat, Callie.' I understand that Waylon Stephens has taken both of them in and plans to give them a good home. That's all I'm supposed to say, so now I'll turn the service over to our song leader."

The lady stood up from the front pew and made her way to the podium. "Granny Denison said that she couldn't carry a tune in a galvanized milk bucket but that she truly loved music, and that we were to sing her through the Pearly Gates today. Open your hymnals to page one seventy-nine and we will start with her first choice, 'Abide with Me.'"

Shiloh wasn't a bit surprised to hear Waylon's deep voice—after all, he'd probably been named for one of her favorite country singers, Mr. Waylon Jennings. Every stanza of the song ended with the words "abide with me." Shiloh should've been thinking about her spiritual life, but the lyrics made her think of where she'd been abiding the last week. Not only abiding, but sleeping in the same bed with Waylon—and getting into some pretty hot make-out sessions before they both went to sleep at night.

"And now turn to page four thirty-four, and we'll all sing 'Shall We Gather at the River,' which is the second song on Granny's list," the lady at the front of the church said, "and let's raise our voices so that if there's truly holes in the floor of heaven, Granny can hear us singing this morning."

If folks had been standing outside the building that morning, they might have seen the roof raising a little. Shiloh wondered when it came her time to gather where the angels' feet had trodden, like the song said, what her story would be. Would her obituary read like Granny's and say that she'd never married, that she'd only left behind a weird dog and cat? She thought about Blister and Callie and was reminded of that passage about the lion lying down with the lamb.

Or would the preacher say that she left behind several children, grandchildren, and great-grandchildren? As she sang, she pictured four or five little Waylons running around the yard with lassos trying to rope a calf.

"And now for Granny's last request," the lady said. "Let's turn to page two thirty-one and sing, 'O Love That Will Not Let Me Go,' and she said that we're supposed to pay attention to the words, because she is giving back the life that she owes."

Shiloh thought about those lyrics, all right, but not for spiritual reasons. Her thoughts went to Ezra. He'd given her life, and then thrown her away. She didn't owe him a damned thing, and yet here she was, fighting tooth, nail, hair, and eyeball for his ranch. She loved living in the canyon. She'd learned to love her sisters, but it would serve Ezra right if she and Bonnie both left the ranch before the year was up. It would go to Rusty then and maybe he'd change the name to something other than Malloy Ranch. Then all vestiges of Ezra would truly be gone, and the canyon—not to mention the whole world—would be a better place.

Not as long as you, Bonnie, and Abby Joy are alive. The pesky voice in her head decided to pop up just as the song ended.

Yes, but his ranch would probably have a new name,

Shiloh argued. *The three of us will have his DNA, and so will any children that we bear, but his precious ranch, the only thing that really mattered to him, would be forgotten. That seems like poetic justice to me.*

She was still struggling with those thoughts when they filed outside and headed toward the tiny cemetery just behind the church. When they arrived at the grave site, Waylon leaned one of his crutches against a tree and held on to Shiloh's hand. Several people, including Bonnie, gave her either strange smiles or go-to-hell looks when they noticed.

Granny's great-nephew and a few other relatives sat in the chairs facing the casket. A floral arrangement sat on a wire tripod at the end of the casket with a ribbon that said AUNT MARY on it. That alone seemed strange, since no one in the canyon had called her anything but Granny Denison—adults and children alike.

The preacher stood at one end of the casket and opened an envelope. "This is a letter from Granny, and when she made the arrangements for her funeral, this was to be read at the cemetery. Afterward, we're all to go to the fellowship hall for a potluck lunch. I was told not to break the seal on this until right now, so that's what I'm doing. Now I'll read it:

"'My dear friends who have gathered around to see me ushered out of this world and into the next. If you are hearing the preacher read this then I'm dead, and this is the end of the services. I have one bit of advice for you all. Live your life the way you want to live it, not the way someone else wants you to. Now, the preacher is going to play my last song, and then all y'all are going to go to the fellowship hall for a potluck dinner. My famous sweet potato casserole won't be there. One of you younger girls will be responsible for bringing it to the next funeral. It's just not a real church social without it. Goodbye, and I've loved living among y'all.'

"It's signed 'Granny Denison.'" The preacher folded the letter and nodded toward the funeral director. He pressed a button on a machine and Jamey Johnson's deep voice sang "Lead Me Home."

When the song ended, there wasn't a dry eye in the whole place. Even her relatives whom no one in the canyon even knew. Waylon pulled a clean white handkerchief from his pocket and handed it to Shiloh. She dried her eyes, but before she could hand it back, Bonnie reached for it.

The crowd began to head toward the church, the sound of their whispers like bees buzzing overhead. Shiloh wondered if they were remembering good times they'd had with Granny or if they were talking about the weather or food. Bonnie gave her back the hankie, and Shiloh tucked it inside Waylon's jacket pocket. He dropped her hand and resituated the crutches under his arms. Bonnie raised an eyebrow, and then whispered, "Looks like I might be winning the bet."

"Don't spend the money before you get it," Shiloh said out of the corner of her mouth. "I'll be home at bedtime if the doctor releases Waylon to drive."

"Did I hear my name?" Waylon asked.

"I was telling Bonnie that we have a two o'clock appointment in Amarillo so we'll have to leave right after we eat," Shiloh replied.

"And run back by the house on the way to let Blister outside for a little bit. Can't expect an old dog like him to stay in all day and not have an accident," Waylon told her.

Shiloh heard someone sobbing behind her and expected to see some of Granny Denison's relatives hanging back to pay last respects. She was surprised to see that it was Sally Mae, another elderly lady from the church, who usually sat on the same pew beside Granny—third one from the front, first two seats near the center aisle.

"Give me a minute," Shiloh said softly as she turned around and went back to the grave site. She sat down beside Sally Mae and draped an arm around her shoulders. They sat like that for several minutes before the silver-haired woman spoke.

"She's been my best friend since before either of us can remember. Without her, I'd never have lived through raisin' my three boys, grievin' when my husband passed away, or the hard times that came with just livin'. She's more like kin than my own sister. It's like losin' part of my heart." The elderly woman turned and sobbed into Shiloh's shoulder.

Shiloh hugged Sally Mae and patted her back. "Shhh..." She tried to soothe her. "Just remember the good times, and let that bring you peace." She looked over the top of Sally Mae's head to see Bonnie and Abby Joy walking toward the church, and a tear formed in the corner of her eye, then found its way down her cheek. Lord, she'd be a worse mess than Sally Mae if one of those two died suddenly. Then she glanced over to see Waylon waiting beside a tree, and another tear started down her cheek.

He could have died in that wreck if she and Bonnie hadn't been at the cemetery. The thought sent cold chills racing down her backbone.

Sally Mae finally took a step back, pulled a wad of tissues from her sweater pocket, and dried her eyes. "She would rather I rejoiced that she's in heaven, than weeping like this. It's selfish of me, but I can't help it."

"I understand." Shiloh wiped her own tears with the back of her hand.

"Ezra was an idiot for sending you girls away," Sally Mae said. "I told him so, but I didn't realize just how right I was until y'all came back to run the ranch. Now, I'm going to the dinner, and I'm going to try real hard not to cry anymore. Waylon is waiting for you. Y'all make a sweet little couple." She stiffened her backbone and walked away. "Just don't waste a bunch of time on things. Life, as we see today, is short."

"Yes, ma'am." Shiloh managed a weak smile.

* * *

"We'll see you in the fellowship hall," Rusty told Waylon as he and Bonnie walked past him.

Waylon nodded and sat down on a bench in front of a tombstone with Wesley and Sarah Banks's names on it. Pink, red, and yellow tulips bloomed in front of the gray granite stone. Wesley and Sarah had both died in 1922, almost a hundred years ago, but someone had seen fit to plant flowers for them. Waylon wondered where he'd be buried and whose name would be on the stone with his. A broad smile covered his face when he realized that the names Wesley and Sarah were an awful lot like Waylon and Shiloh. Could that be one of those omens that his sister, Emmylou, talked about all the time?

His phone rang, and he worked it up out of his hip pocket. "Hello, Mama, I was just thinking about Emmylou and her omens," he said.

"Why didn't you tell me about the car wreck?" she asked, bluntly.

"I didn't want you to worry. How'd you find out?"

"Cash called Jackson Bailey to congratulate him on his new baby girls, and Jackson told him all about it, and that you've got a woman living with you. Emmylou wants to know when the wedding is." His mother, Amanda's, voice went from serious to teasing.

"You tell Emmylou that she's older than me, and I wouldn't ever want to get ahead of her or any of my sisters, when it comes to matrimony," he answered.

"Hey, ain't a one of you can fuss too much about that. Patsy was only seven when I had Cash, and he was the sixth one. So tell me about this woman who's moved in with you," Amanda said.

Waylon rolled his eyes toward the dead branches of a nearby pecan tree. "She's my neighbor. Remember me talking about Ezra Malloy? She's the middle daughter, Shiloh, that I told you about." He went on to give his mother more details about the wreck, but he didn't tell her that he and Shiloh had been sleeping together all week. Amanda Stephens would never believe that they'd shared a bed without having sex.

"She's a good woman and a good neighbor to take care of you and your ranch like that, but I'm still pissed at you for not calling. Either of your brothers or any one of your sisters would have been glad to come help with things," Amanda told him. "Or for that matter, your dad and I could've left the bunch of them to take care of things here, and we would've come over there."

"No need, Mama," Waylon said. "I go to the doctor this afternoon. I'm sure he'll release me. Shiloh will go home, and I'll be back in my old routine."

"She might not be the one, but I'm gettin' tired of waiting on grandchildren." Amanda sighed. "You could start a rush to the altar for me."

"Talk to my sisters," he chuckled. "Tell them that you hear their biological clocks tickin' so loud that you can't sleep at night."

"They don't listen any better than you do," Amanda said. "Call me tonight with news about what the doctor says."

"Yes, ma'am, and I'll tell you all about Blister and Callie when I do," he said.

"Are you sure that wreck didn't rattle your brain? Who in the hell are Blister and Callie?" she asked.

"Blister is my new dog. Callie is my new cat. I'll send pictures of them, and then we'll talk," he told her as he ended the call and returned his focus to Shiloh.

Sally Mae stood up and, with the help of a cane, made her way across the grass toward the church. She didn't even glance toward Waylon when she passed him, but just kept her eyes on the ground. A minute or two after that, Shiloh stood up and made her way toward Waylon. She'd worn a little black dress that morning that skimmed her knees, a pair of black cowboy boots, and a black coat that was belted at the waist. Her dark hair flowed down over her shoulders in big curls, and even from a distance he could see the sadness in her blue eyes.

"Poor Sally Mae." She sat down beside him. "I can't even imagine how lost she's going to be without Granny Denison. I've only known Bonnie and Abby Joy a few months, and I'd be devastated if I lost either of them. She and Granny weren't related by blood, but they'd been best friends most of their lives."

"I figured you'd help her get back to the church." Waylon liked the way her body molded to his on the narrow concrete bench.

"I offered, but she didn't want me to." Shiloh leaned her head on his shoulder. "She said that she needed to go alone for closure. If that was Bonnie or Abby Joy, or even worse, my mama, I'd want someone beside me all the time."

"Each person grieves differently." Waylon remembered going into the woods behind the old farmhouse where he'd been raised after his granddad died. He'd screamed and shook his fist at the sky, but then he had been just a kid, and his grandfather was the first loved person he'd lost.

"I suppose they do." Shiloh nodded.

"Shall we go have some potluck dinner?" he asked.

"Yes." She got to her feet. "It almost seems wrong to be eating and visiting, doesn't it?"

"There's comfort in food and friends at times like this." He got his crutches tucked under his arms and walked beside her.

When they entered the room, Rusty and Bonnie were just inside the door with Loretta and Jackson Bailey on their right, and Abby Joy and Cooper on their left.

Abby Joy and Bonnie each had one of Loretta and Jackson's twin daughters in their arms. Both of the sisters took a few steps toward Shiloh. She held out her arms and Bonnie shared, but Abby Joy seemed to hold her bundle a little tighter. Waylon wouldn't be a bit surprised if she and Cooper didn't announce that they were having a baby before the year was out.

"Look at her, Waylon. She's only a week old and she's so alert." Shiloh held out the dark-haired baby girl for him to see.

"I thought the twins might have red hair," he said.

"This one does." Abby Joy took a step forward. "Martina looks like Jackson, and Jennifer is the image of Loretta."

"I like their names," Shiloh said.

"Had to keep it country." Loretta smiled.

If he and Shiloh ever had kids, Waylon wondered, would she want to keep the tradition of naming children after country music singers? His granddad had loved Patsy Cline, so his folks let him name their first daughter Patsy Ann. They'd planned on calling her Annie, but it hadn't worked out that way. Then the next one had come along, and another one, and they had just kept naming them all after singers, much like Loretta's family had done.

Whoa, cowboy! Jerk those reins up real tight! the voice in his head yelled at him. *You haven't even proposed and you're already naming babies?*

He turned his attention to Shiloh, who was handing the baby over to Jackson. She'd been so good to go back and comfort Sally Mae, and now she was planting a sweet kiss on little Martina's forehead. He remembered an old adage his granddad used to say.

"Your daddy knew that Amanda would be a good woman to ride the river with," Granddad said. "Your grandma never thought she was good enough for her precious son, but he was her only child, so probably no one would ever be good enough for him in her eyes."

"Ride the river?" Waylon had asked.

"The river is the journey of your life. You find a good woman to ride the river with, and the journey will be right nice. Just be real sure that you're listenin' to your heart and not your head when you make your choice. Sometimes you might get them confused," Granddad had said.

Shiloh laid a hand on his arm and jerked him out of the past and back to the present. "Ready to get in line for food."

"I sure am," he said. "You looked pretty good holding that baby."

"I love babies and kids. I just hope I don't have to pay for my raisin' when my kids get to be teenagers," she told him.

"Ain't that the truth?" he agreed.

"Excuse me." A man wearing creased jeans and a western shirt stepped through the crowd. "I'm Dillon McRay, Miz Denison's lawyer. I'd like to meet with you for just a few minutes in the sanctuary. I promise it will only take a few minutes, and then y'all can come on back in here and have some dinner. The line will probably be pretty well done by then."

"Y'all as in . . . ?" Waylon asked.

"You and Shiloh Malloy," he said.

"Yes, sir," Waylon said, "but may I ask what is the nature of this?"

"I understand that one or both of you have adopted Miz Denison's dog and cats. Is that right?" Dillon asked.

Waylon nodded. "That's right. We've got Blister and Callie and the kittens. It didn't take us long to get attached to them."

"Then I need to see y'all. Her nephew and his family are already in the sanctuary, so if you'll follow me." He led the way across the fellowship hall, through a door that led straight into the sanctuary and up to the front pew.

Waylon laid his crutches out on the pew and sat down beside Shiloh.

Dillon chose to sit on the altar, where his black leather briefcase waited. He opened it and removed several papers. "This is very short and won't take long. I won't take time to read Miz Denison's will, but I have a copy for Waylon and one for Carl. This is what it says. Carl, you and your family inherit the house and everything in it, but you cannot sell it. If you don't want to possess it and the ten acres that goes with it, then you can take whatever you want from it, but again, you can't sell it, and when you are dead whoever inherits it can't sell it either. I'm supposed to ask you what you plan to do with the dog and cats at this point."

"I figured she'd do something like this," Carl, a tall, lanky man with thick glasses, said. "She was a cantankerous old girl and never forgave any of her brothers for moving away from the canyon. I don't want the house or anything in it if I can't sell it."

His wife held up a hand. "And we damn sure don't want those animals, so I guess we drove all the way up here from Sweetwater for nothing."

"I guess maybe you did," Dillon said. "Since you've stated your desires"—he held up a minirecorder—"and I have it right here, then you are free to go."

"Let's just go back to her house, get our things, and leave," Carl's wife said. "I never have liked potluck dinners. We can stop at that little café in Silverton. They made a pretty good chicken fried steak last time we ate there."

"One more time," Dillon asked. "You don't want the house, the land, or anything of hers from the house?"

"You got that right." Carl nodded. "We'll be out of this godforsaken canyon in an hour and probably never come back."

"Okay, then, but would you please sign these papers for me stating that is your decision before you go," Dillon asked.

Carl whipped a pen from his pocket and put his signature on all the places where the lawyer had stuck fancy little blue tabs. "I wish I'd known before we came that this was the way it was going to be. I wouldn't have wasted my time."

Shiloh took a deep breath and started to get up from the pew, but Waylon put a hand on her knee. "Some people are born assholes," he whispered.

"And just get bigger with age," she said out of the side of her mouth.

When the papers were signed, Carl and his wife didn't go back through the fellowship hall at all but left through the front door. Dillon took a deep breath and said, "Okay, now to what I have to say to you, Waylon. I need you to sign this paper saying that you bought your ranch from Oliver Watson and there were no other owners besides you and

Mr. Watson. I know all this already, since I live on up toward Claude and do the legal business for a lot of folks in the canyon, but we have to keep everything documented and legal."

Waylon scanned through the single sheet of paper and signed it. "I don't understand what I've got to do with all this, but there it is."

"I've got something to read to you now," Dillon said.

"'If Dillon is reading this then I'm dead. I like you, Waylon Stephens. You're a good man. I'm glad that you bought the ranch next to my place. Even though our paths only cross at church since I don't keep goats or a steer or two anymore, I feel good knowing you are next door. This ten acres was at one time a part of the Watson Ranch. My dad bought it from his cousin, but you aren't interested in all that history. Here's the deal, if my nephew, who is my oldest living relative, declines to take possession of my house and land, then it should go back and become a part of the original property so it's now yours...'" Dillon stopped and looked up.

Waylon could hardly believe what he'd just heard. "Are you saying that I just inherited her house and property?"

"Exactly," Dillon answered and continued reading: "'To whoever takes in my precious pets, Dillon has orders to hand over my entire bank accounts. He will take care of all the particulars concerning the transfer, but this is my desire. So if you are in this room, and Blister and Callie are at your house, then Dillon will explain the rest to you.'"

Waylon shook his head slowly. "What does all that mean?"

"It means that her savings and checking accounts and her portfolio of investments now are totally yours. All you have to do is sign a document saying that you will take care of the animals, love them, and give them a good home until they die." Dillon shuffled through more papers and handed them to Waylon to sign.

"Why did you need me?" Shiloh asked.

"If Waylon is living with someone or married, then they have to agree to help take care of the dog and cat," Dillon told them.

"I'll be moving out tonight," Shiloh said.

"Then I only need Waylon's signature," he said.

"I don't need to be paid to give those animals a good home," Waylon said as he signed the papers.

"You're a good man," Dillon said. "But this is the way she wanted things done. I have the past year's bank statements and her portfolio right here. She paid me enough to retain me for the rest of this year, so if you need anything call me. That pretty much concludes our business, so if you have no more questions, I'm going to make myself a plate of food. I sure like potluck dinners."

Waylon glanced down at the figures on the top paper, blinked a dozen times, and still couldn't believe what he was seeing. "I don't think I've ever seen so many zeroes in my life. I'd never have guessed that Granny Denison was so rich!"

"Well, I for one do not intend to tell Bonnie about this. She was the one who rescued the animals to begin with and brought them to us." Shiloh smiled.

Waylon's mind went around in circles so fast that he had trouble catching a single thought, so he finally said, "Let's take all this out to the van and then have some dinner. Then we better go home and take good care of Blister and Callie. You think maybe I should buy them gold-plated feeding and water dishes?"

"No, but I think maybe you should turn her house into

a bunkhouse and hire some full-time help," she suggested. "Or maybe even buy the Dunlap Ranch that borders you on the south. It's been for sale ever since I got here."

"I wanted that piece of property, but it's twice as big as the Watson Ranch, and I couldn't afford it," he admitted.

"Well, darlin', now you can." She stood up and handed him his crutches. "A bit of advice though. I'd only tell about inheriting the property and house but not the money. If you do, you should at least wait until your foot is fully healed."

"Why's that?" he asked.

She picked up the stack of papers. "Because you're going to need to outrun every single girl in the canyon when they find out how much you're worth."

Waylon hoped that Shiloh was way out in front, leading the pack, should that ever become the case.

Chapter Eight

The doctor cleared Waylon to do anything that he felt like doing, including driving and lifting, so long as he took it easy on the ankle for another week. As soon as they left his office, Waylon asked Shiloh to drive him to the body shop to see about his truck.

Suddenly, Shiloh's heart felt like someone had laid a rock on top of it. She thought she'd be relieved to go back to her routine on Malloy Ranch. Her mother used to tell her that she couldn't have her Popsicle and eat it too. That rang more true right then than it ever had before. She wanted to go home so she and Bonnie could get used to not having Abby Joy around all the time, but she wanted to stay with Waylon too.

"Man, it feels good to get off those crutches," Waylon said on the way out to her van. "It's still a little tender, but I've had a worse sore ankle after being thrown from a bull."

She just nodded, then got into the van and drove back

toward Claude, where the body shop was located. From there he'd drive himself down into the base of the canyon and home.

"What're you goin' to name the kittens?" she asked.

"That's your job, remember?" He turned on the radio. "You're supposed to name the babies like Blake sings about."

"But the dog came with a name and so did the mama cat," she argued.

"I checked when we went by the house. We've got two girls and one boy kitten. I reckon if we're going to keep four cats in the house, we'd better be gettin' in touch with a vet before too long." He kept time for a few seconds with his thumb on the console, and then he began to sing with Willie Nelson doing "Help Me Make It Through the Night."

Shiloh sang harmony with him, and agreed with the lyrics, which said he didn't care what was right or wrong, and that the devil could take tomorrow because he didn't want to be alone and needed help to make it through the night. That's the way she felt too—just one more night with him beside her in that big king-size bed, and this time they'd do more than sleep.

The body shop had his truck ready, so he drove it back to his ranch, and parked in front of the house. He got out and sat on the porch steps and waited for her to get the van parked. She got the papers the lawyer had given him from the backseat and handed them off to him on her way inside.

"My suitcase is packed. I just need to get it, unless you want me to stick around to help with chores tonight," she said.

"I think I've got it covered." He stood to his feet. "Shiloh, thank you for everything. If I can ever return the favor, just give me a call. I programmed my number into your phone."

"I surely will." She walked past him into the house.

She wanted to say that he could ask her to stay, but why would he? With what he'd inherited that day, he could have any woman in the state of Texas. He might even have to get himself one of those number machines like they had in the fancy coffee shops just to give them all a turn.

She rolled her suitcase out onto the porch and started to carry it out to her van.

"I'll take that for you." He picked it up and followed her to her vehicle. "You will come back on weekends to visit the animals, won't you?"

"Of course." She smiled as she settled behind the wheel. "We still have to name the kittens. I'll be thinkin' about the two girls' names?"

He tilted his hat back and leaned into the van, cupped her cheeks in his calloused hands, and kissed her with so much passion that the whole world disappeared. For the length of one long, hot kiss, she forgot about everything but being close to Waylon. When it ended, she leaned her head on his shoulder.

"I'll miss you, Shiloh," he whispered. "Don't be a stranger. You're welcome anytime."

"I'll remember that, and the same goes for you. Come on across the highway anytime you want a little company," she told him.

"Thank you." He took a step back and closed the door for her.

He limped back to the porch and waved until she couldn't see him in the rearview mirror anymore. The house was empty when she got home that evening, so she rolled her suitcase into her bedroom and fell backward onto the end of the bed. With her feet dangling off the end, she stared at the ceiling. How in the hell had she fallen in love with a man in only a week's time?

"You're home!" Bonnie dragged herself into the room and sat down beside her. She removed her own well-worn cowboy boots and tossed them to the side and then leaned back so that she was in the same position as her sister—legs hanging off the end of the bed. "I missed you, and I'm tired of doing all the chores around here, so welcome home."

"So you don't want to own the ranch all by yourself?" Shiloh asked.

"Yep, I do, but if there's a chance you ain't never comin' back, I'll hire some help. I guess since you're here that the doctor released Waylon, right?"

"He did," Shiloh answered.

"And then Waylon released you," Bonnie giggled. "So what did that lawyer want with y'all?"

"Seems that if Granny Denison's relatives didn't want her property with the stipulation that since it was family land, they couldn't sell it, then she was giving it to Waylon. So he gained ten acres and her house today," Shiloh answered. "You ever been in that house?"

"One time," Bonnie said. "Remember when one of Waylon's cows got out and came across the road? You'd gone to Claude to buy groceries, so me and Abby Joy herded the old heifer back over to Waylon's place. Only it wasn't his cow. We walked her over to Granny Denison's, only to find out that it wasn't hers either."

Shiloh nodded. "I remember you telling me that story." "Whose cow was it?"

"Belonged to the Dunlaps on the other side of Waylon's place. Granny called them and they brought a cattle trailer down to get her," Bonnie answered. "Anyway, Granny invited us in for a glass of lemonade. It's a pretty good-size house. Maybe four or five bedrooms. She said that her folks raised a bunch of kids there."

"Should make a fine bunkhouse then," Shiloh said.

"Oh, yeah, but he might want to do some paintin'. Every room I saw was either painted pink or pale blue. I can't see cowboys appreciating that kind of livin' quarters." Bonnie slapped her on the arm. "Enough lazin' around. We've got supper to cook. Rusty will be in here in a few minutes, and he'll be hungry as I am."

Shiloh sat up. "You ever think that maybe we should both follow in Abby Joy's footsteps and leave this place to Rusty? I don't think Ezra wanted us to get along when he made his will. He wanted us to fight and be hateful to one another, and then leave the canyon so that a boy would still get the place."

"I'm here to prove him wrong," Bonnie said. "You havin' second thoughts?"

"Let's just say that I'm lookin' at things from a different perspective," Shiloh told her sister.

"Why's that?" Bonnie asked.

"It all started at Granny Denison's funeral. Sally Mae was crying, so I went back to comfort her. I realized that Ezra isn't worth the grudge I've held against him, or the energy I've put into tryin' to prove that I can run his ranch." Just saying the words out loud made her feel like a load had been lifted from her shoulders.

"It'll cost you a hundred dollars and a bottle of good whiskey." Bonnie headed out into the hallway.

"It could be the best money I'd ever spend," Shiloh muttered as she stood up and stretched her arms over her head.

Chapter Nine

Blister ran out of the house as soon as Waylon opened the door that Friday evening after he'd taken care of the evening chores. The short-legged mutt ran to the nearest bush, took care of business, and was already yipping to be let back in by the time Waylon removed his coat and hung it on a hook.

"And here I was afraid you'd run off and try to find your way back to Granny's house," Waylon told the dog when he opened the door. "You know something, Blister? I wish that Shiloh would find her way back home to this ranch, but that's not likely to happen. She's got her heart set on owning the Malloy place, and besides, after the way Ezra tossed her to the side, I don't know that she'll ever trust a guy."

Blister sat down, and his tail thumped against the kitchen floor.

"So you agree with me?" Waylon opened the refrigerator and pulled out everything he needed to make himself a couple of hot dogs. "I already miss her, and she's only been gone a couple of hours. Should I call her after supper?"

This time Blister swished his tail back and forth across the floor.

"I thought so," Waylon said. "I should let her know that you and Callie miss her, and she should come over to Sunday dinner, right?"

Blister yipped in agreement.

"You and I are going to be buddies." Waylon tossed the mutt the end off a hot dog. "We understand each other, don't we?"

Waylon's phone rang, ending the conversation he was having with Blister. He saw that it was his brother Cash and put it on speaker while he finished fixing his supper.

"Hey, I was goin' to call y'all after supper, and tell you that the doctor released me, so I'm back on full ranchin' duty," Waylon said.

"That's great, brother." Cash's tone indicated something was wrong.

Waylon's blood ran cold until Cash sighed and started talking again. "Me and Rachel broke up, for good this time. She's been cheating on me with Mitch, and they're going to get married."

Waylon hated to hear that, but he was so glad that it wasn't even worse news—like his dad had been hurt in a ranch accident or his mother had dropped with a heart attack. He opened his mouth to say something, but then he remembered Granny Denison's house. "You need to get the hell out of East Texas?" he asked. "I kinda came into a little bit of property today. I was thinkin' of turnin' the house into a bunkhouse. If you need—"

"Yes," Cash butted in. "Can I bring Emmylou with me? She needs to get away too."

"What's goin' on with her?" Waylon asked.

"Mama is stomping on her and Patsy's last nerve about

grandbabies," Cash told him. "They both need a vacation, but Patsy has a boyfriend, and things aren't quite as bad for her."

"And June? What's goin' on with her?" Waylon asked.

"She's the only one that can stand Grandma. She spends a lot of time over there helping her out, but me and Emmylou could sure stand a change of scenery. We can be there by suppertime tomorrow night if that's all right," Cash said.

"I'll have a pot of chili waiting and enough work to keep you both busy for a year." Waylon grinned. Tomorrow he was going over to the Dunlap Ranch and make an offer on it. If they accepted, that would triple the size of his ranch, but he didn't tell Cash that bit of news right then.

"Work might keep me from shooting Rachel and Mitch," Cash said. "Thanks so much. I'm going to tell Emmylou to pack her bags. See you tomorrow."

Waylon finished making his hot dogs and sat down to the kitchen table with them. He looked to his right, where Shiloh had always sat, bowed his head, and said a silent grace. When he opened his eyes, she still wasn't there, but he sure wished that she was. He wanted to tell her how overwhelmed he was with what all had happened in the last twenty-four hours.

He ate his supper, washed the dishes, and then went to the living room, where he surfed through the channels on the television. There was nothing that he wanted to watch, but the house seemed so empty without Shiloh there. He picked up a ranching magazine, flipped through it, and tossed it on the far end of the sofa.

He heard a vehicle outside, and was on his way across the floor, when someone rapped on the door. He slung it open to find Shiloh. The expression on her face said that she was anxious about something.

"You told me not to be a stranger, and I wanted..." she

stammered. "You told me I could name two of the kittens and it didn't seem right to do something that important over the phone."

He butted in, "I was just thinking about callin' you." He slung open the screen door and motioned her inside.

Callie came out from her basket to greet Shiloh the moment the cat heard her voice. She dropped down on her knees in the living room to pet the mama cat. "I knew you'd miss me."

Old folks, babies, and pets all adored her, Waylon thought. Granddad just might say that she'd do to ride the river with.

"Want a beer or a glass of sweet tea?" Waylon asked.

"Love a beer," she replied.

He went to the kitchen, brought back two bottles, and handed one to her before he sat down on the floor beside her. "I just got off the phone with my brother Cash. He and my sister Emmylou will be here tomorrow evening. They'll be stayin' over at Granny Denison's house, so I guess the idea of turning it into a bunkhouse has happened quicker than we thought."

Shiloh laughed out loud. "Have you been in that place?"

He shook his head. "I sat on the porch with her a few times and had cookies and sweet tea, but I was never invited inside. Why did you ask?"

She told him what Bonnie had said about the place being totally feminine. "I just hope Cash don't mind."

"I guess the first money of what I inherited will be spent for paint," he chuckled. "Emmylou hates pink. Mama always dressed the three girls alike from the pictures I've seen, and most of the time it was pink."

He didn't want to talk about paint or bunkhouses, but he'd gladly listen to her read the dictionary if she'd just stick around a while.

"I've been doing a lot of thinking this evening," Shiloh said.

"About what?" Waylon hoped that she'd say she'd been thinking about the past week and those heated good night kisses they'd shared.

She inhaled deeply and let it out ever so slowly. "I'm wondering what Ezra's true motive was in putting us all on that ranch together. He was a sly old son of a bitch, and he probably wanted us to fight, get mad, and leave. Abby Joy wouldn't say how much one-third of the money he left behind was, but she did say that if she'd known about it before, she might have never stayed on the ranch as long as she did. So"—Shiloh stood up and took a seat on the sofa—"knowing the way he felt about girls, I figure he wanted Rusty to have the place, and he left us money to ease his conscience for the way he treated us. After all, Rusty is a guy, and he wanted an heir to leave his land to, not an heiress."

"I'm not sure Ezra had a conscience." Waylon joined her on the sofa. "If he did, it was buried pretty deep. What are you going to do?"

"It would be just what he deserves if me and Bonnie stuck it out and kept the ranch, but then even if we changed the name, it would take a hundred years before everyone quit calling it the Malloy Ranch. Rusty liked him, so I figure he'd keep the name. Hell, he might have even had a deal with Ezra to keep the name and maybe even change his name to Malloy to make it legal. Who knows what that old codger had up his sleeve?" Shiloh took a long drink of her beer.

"Well, if you decide to move out, there's a spare room here, and from what you've told me about my new bunkhouse there's lots of room over there. You can have your choice of any of them," Waylon told her.

"That's so sweet. Are you going to give me a job, too?" she asked.

"Honey, you know what I just inherited." He moved closer to her and put an arm around her shoulders. "I'll give you half of it to move across the highway and work with me."

* * *

Shiloh noticed that he'd said *with* me, not *for* me. She met his eyes and didn't blink, "Don't joke with me."

"Honey, I've never been more serious in my life. I wanted to ask you out the first time I saw you," he said as he leaned in for a long, lingering kiss.

"And that was when?" Her heart pounded in her chest when the kiss ended.

"At Ezra's funeral," he admitted. "And then at the church the next week, and every time I saw you after that."

"Why didn't you?" She shifted her weight so that she was sitting in his lap with her arms around his neck.

"After the way Ezra treated you girls, one of you deserves to have that ranch, no matter what the damned place is named." He planted another kiss on her forehead.

"But I'm not sure I want it. I'm struggling with living there since this past week. I've been thinkin' about what I really want, and I'm not so sure it's his ranch," she whispered.

"Like I said, you've got a job and a place here if you want to move." He kissed her on the tip of her nose.

"Moving over here to take care of you is…was…" she stammered.

"Spit it out," Waylon said.

She moved away from his lap and began to pace the floor. "I've been attracted to you ever since Ezra's funeral too, but there was something about going to Granny Denison's services today"—she hesitated—"that made me wonder about letting opportunities pass. At Abby Joy's wedding, it seemed like a sign for me to get to spend more time with you. Then the wreck happened and gave me the opportunity to do just that. But living with you this week made me restless at home."

"Are you uneasy here?" he asked.

"No, this is where I'm at peace," she told him.

He stood up slowly, took her by the hand, and led her to his bedroom. Callie and Blister followed behind them, but Waylon closed the door before they could get through. He sat down on the edge of the bed and pulled her down beside him.

"I'm only at peace when you're with me," he said.

"Fate sure had a crazy way to bring us together." She pulled at the top snap on his western shirt and unfastened them all with one quick tug.

* * *

Sometime after midnight Shiloh woke to find Waylon staring at her, much like he had that first night they'd shared the bed—only that night they'd slept and last night there had been so much more than sex. Two soul mates had met and fallen in love. She wasn't sure if it happened right when she made the decision to leave Ezra's place, or when she turned onto the Wildflower Ranch property. As she stared at the sexy cowboy beside her, she realized that maybe she'd been in love with him longer than she even realized.

Callie jumped onto the bed and curled up between Waylon and Shiloh.

"Kittens!" Shiloh popped herself on the head. "I came over here to name the kittens, and I forgot. You make me forget everything, Waylon."

"Honey, you do the same thing to me," he said as he traced her lip line with his forefinger, and then leaned over the cat for a good-morning kiss.

Callie cold nosed his chin and broke up the make-out session. They both laughed as they moved away from each other a few inches.

"Evidently she thinks it's time to give her babies their names," Waylon said.

"Well, since I thought they were mice, my girls' names are Minnie and Perla," Shiloh told him.

"I understand Minnie, but where'd you get Perla?" he asked.

"From *Cinderella*," she told him. "There were three little girl mice and three boys."

"Never watched that one." He grinned. "But our boy will be Mickey."

"Sounds good to me." She yawned. "Now we just have to raise them and hope that we live through their teenage years."

He chuckled. "I believe that's Callie's job."

"I should go home." She pushed back the covers on the bed.

"This is home. We just have to give it enough time to work out the details." He began to massage her back.

"How much time?" she whispered as she moved the cat to the foot of the bed.

"As much or as little as you want." He gathered her into his arms and held her close, their naked bodies pressed against each other. "Just don't forget where home really is, Miz Shiloh Malloy."

"I won't," she said. "You've got my word on that."

He buried his face in her hair. "I've always thought that love at first sight was a crock of bull crap, but now I believe in it. I love you, Shiloh."

"I love you, Waylon." She didn't even mind that what was going to happen would cost her a hundred dollars and a bottle of whiskey.

Chapter Ten

There wasn't a cloud in the sky the last Saturday in May. The sun was just setting over the western bank of the canyon, and wildflowers were in full bloom everywhere. It all made for a perfect setting for the wedding reception that was about to take place on the Wildflower Ranch—the brand-new registered brand for Waylon and Shiloh's property. She'd spent the night before at the bunkhouse with her sisters, Bonnie and Abby Joy, and Waylon's sisters, Patsy, Emmylou, and June.

Shiloh was barely awake when Bonnie and Abby Joy bounced into her room and jumped onto her bed. "Wake up, sleepyhead," Abby Joy said. "You're getting married in three hours and you look like hell."

Shiloh kicked off the covers, sat up, and looked at her reflection in the mirror above the dresser. Abby Joy was right. Her dark hair was a fright. She was sunburned from helping bring in the first cutting of hay the day before, and her eyes were puffy from staying up too late with all the ladies the night before.

"You've got your work cut out for you," she moaned.

"Not to worry," Bonnie said. "We'll get you beautified and to the church on time."

Shiloh's mother, Polly, poked her head in the door. "Breakfast is on the bar. Amanda and I made pancakes and bacon. You don't want anything too heavy on your stomach for the wedding." She came on into the room and sat down on the end of the bed. "As much as you were going to prove Ezra wrong and inherit your part of that ranch, I'm surprised that you're giving it all up."

"I figured out that some things are more important than revenge." Shiloh leaned over and gave her mother a hug. "I love Waylon, Mama."

"He's a good man," Polly said. "And I can tell by the way he looks at you that he loves you. I couldn't be happier for you than I am this day."

"How does it feel for you to be back here? Does it bring back painful memories?" Shiloh asked.

"Honey, I put Ezra out of my heart years ago. Some folks just aren't worth stealing your peace. I'm glad that you found that out for yourself," Polly said.

Shiloh scooted closer to her mother. "I'm glad you let me do it on my own, and that you didn't lecture me, but just let me do what I had to do. If I hadn't I would have never met Waylon." She kissed her mother on the cheek. "And he's my soul mate."

Bonnie slung an arm around Shiloh. "You lost a bet. I'll expect you to pony up on it."

"Wouldn't dream of forgetting that." Shiloh stood up and handed her younger sister a bottle of whiskey with a hundred-dollar bill held tightly around it with a rubber band.

"Here it is. Now you can celebrate me being gone. Break it open, and we'll celebrate together."

"I can't drink with y'all." Abby Joy shook her head. "I teased Cooper about getting pregnant on our honeymoon, and the test I took yesterday said that it happened, so Bonnie gets that whole bottle of whiskey all to herself."

"That's fantastic!" Shiloh hugged her older sister.

Bonnie jumped off the bed and did a happy dance. "I'm going to be an aunt, and the baby is going to love me more than Shiloh," she singsonged as she pulled Abby Joy out of the room and toward the kitchen.

"We'll just see about that," Shiloh yelled.

"I can only pray the same thing happens to you, my child." Polly held up a hand toward heaven.

"Whoa!" Shiloh grabbed her mother's hand and put it down. "One thing at a time."

Polly patted her on the back. "Well, darlin', the first thing is breakfast. Today, you're marryin' Waylon. He's everything I ever hoped that you'd find in a husband, and honey, I'm glad you left Malloy Ranch. You would have never been happy there."

"But, Mama, I was happy there with my sisters," she said.

Polly smiled. "The key words are 'with your sisters.' Without them, you would have been lonely, and besides, you belong with Waylon."

"You're so right, but I sure hope Bonnie sticks around, because I rather like having sisters." Shiloh looped her arm in her mothers and together they left the room.

"Even Waylon's sisters?" Polly whispered.

"Emmylou is outspoken, but I like her. Jury is still out on the other two. They only got here a couple of days ago, and things have been crazy, with trying to get hay baled and attending to wedding stuff," Shiloh said in a soft voice.

* * *

Waylon sat down to breakfast with his two brothers and his father that morning. If he'd followed Shiloh's advice and gone to the courthouse, got married, and then told his family and her mother and aunt, he could be plowing a field or hauling in that sixty acres of small bales of hay that was ready. But he was the first one of the six Stephens siblings to get married, and he knew his mother would be disappointed if they didn't at least have a small wedding. So having to get dressed up, go to the church, and say his vows was no one's fault but his own that day.

"Got what you're goin' to say to Shiloh all memorized?" his father, Jimmy, asked.

"Pretty much goin' to wing it," Waylon answered.

"Just say what's in your heart," Buddy advised. "Even if you stutter a little, it's better than a rehearsed thing that has no feelin'."

"Great advice, Dad." Waylon pulled out his phone and stepped to the other side of the room.

He typed in a text to Shiloh: *I wish we would have eloped.*

One came right back: *Me too!*

He was typing another text when his phone rang. When he saw that it was Shiloh, he almost dropped it, trying to answer on the first ring.

"I'll be so glad when—" she started.

"I know—" he said.

"I am looking forward to the reception and dancing with you out in our new gazebo, and Waylon, you're never going to believe what my one-third of the money is. I almost fainted when I saw all those zeroes," she said. "The lawyer brought me the check last night, and I signed the papers saying I was giving up my rights to the Malloy Ranch."

"That's your money, darlin'," he told her.

"No, it's ours, and I'm thinkin' we might make an offer for the land to the north of us. We've got plenty of room in the bunkhouse to house the hired help," she said. "I'm not interested in anything but building a life with you."

"I love you," he said.

"Me too. See you at the church at eleven o'clock. I'll be the one in the white dress."

"I'll be the one that has eyes for only you," he whispered as he made his way out to the porch. "I'm the luckiest cowboy in this whole canyon."

"You're almost as lucky as I am," she said.

* * *

The church was packed that morning at eleven o'clock when Shiloh arrived. Her sisters, her mother, and her aunt waited with her in the nursery until Loretta Jackson came to tell them that it was time to start the ceremony. "Jackson is going to seat your aunt Audrey, then Bonnie and Abby Joy will make their way up the aisle, and when you hear the first of the song you've chosen to walk in to, then your mom will take you down to where Waylon will be waiting."

"Got it." Shiloh gave her the thumbs-up sign.

The next couple of minutes went by in a blur. Then the first chords of "Mama He's Crazy" started, and she took her mother's arm.

"Not exactly wedding music," Polly whispered.

"Waylon and I aren't exactly traditional folks," she said as she took her first step down the aisle.

When the lyrics said that he was heaven sent, Waylon

gave her one of his special smiles, and the whole world disappeared. To Shiloh, they were the only two people in the church, and nothing mattered but the vows they were about to say.

It wasn't planned, but he left his place in the front of the church and met her halfway down the aisle. Polly gave him a kiss on the cheek and then put Shiloh's hand in his. She waited until the two of them finished the walk together and then went forward to sit on the front pew.

"Well, I usually start with 'dearly beloved,'" the preacher chuckled, "but after that song, I think we'll just let these two say their vows."

Shiloh handed her bouquet to Abby Joy and raised her dress to show off the pair of brown cowboy boots that she wore to work on the ranch. "See these boots. I come to you today in my pretty white dress, but under it is a ranchin' woman who wants to spend her life with you. I love you, Waylon Stephens, and I give you my promise that I will love you longer than forever, and right into eternity."

Waylon took her hands in his. "My granddad told me once that life is like a river, and I should find the right woman to ride the river with. I didn't find the right woman. I found the perfect one. I love you, Shiloh, and I give you my promise that my love for you will last through eternity."

Shiloh heard a couple of sniffles from the front pew. She was glad that she'd had a few moments in the nursery after her mother left. That had given her time to switch out the pretty white satin shoes for her old cowboy boots that she'd snuck into the church in a duffel bag.

They exchanged plain gold wedding bands, and then the preacher pronounced them man and wife, and told Waylon he could kiss the bride. The new husband bent his bride backward in a true Hollywood kiss, then stood her up to the applause of everyone in the church. "And now it's my turn," he whispered.

"What?" she asked.

The music started and Blake Shelton's voice came out loud and clear with "You Name the Babies, I'll Name the Dogs."

She giggled. "It's fitting after the one I walked down the aisle to."

He took her in his arms and two-stepped all the way out of the church with her. He scooped her up at the door and carried her to his truck. When he'd settled her into the passenger seat, he leaned in and kissed her one more time. "Love the boots."

"I'm excited that I get to ride the river with you. Let's go enjoy our reception," she said.

"Yes, ma'am." He whistled all the way around the truck.

*   *   *

Want to read Abby Joy's story? Look for Daisies in the Canyon *wherever books are sold.*

About the Author

Carolyn Brown is a *New York Times*, *USA Today*, *Wall Street Journal*, *Publishers Weekly*, and #1 *Washington Post* bestselling author, and a RITA finalist. She has sold more than seven million copies of her books. They have been translated into 19 foreign languages. *Cowboy Courage* is her 101st published book.

She presently writes both women's fiction and cowboy romance. She has also written historical and contemporary romance, both stand-alone titles and series.

She lives in southern Oklahoma with her husband, a former English teacher, who is not allowed to read her books until they are published. They have three children and enough grandchildren to keep them young. For a complete listing of her books (in series order) and to sign up for her newsletter, check out her website at CarolynBrownBooks.com or catch her on Facebook/CarolynBrownBooks.

Looking for more hot cowboys?
Forever has you covered!

COWBOY COURAGE
by Carolyn Brown

Heading back to Texas to hold down the fort at her aunt's bed-and-breakfast will give Rose O'Malley just the break she needs from the military. But while she may speak seven languages, she can't repair a leaky sink to save her life. When Hudson Baker strides in like a hero and effortlessly figures out the fix, Rose can't help wondering if the boy she once crushed on as a kid could now be her saving grace. Includes a bonus novella!

Discover bonus content and more on read-forever.com.

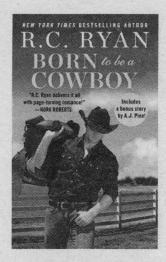

BORN TO BE A COWBOY
by R.C. Ryan

After running wild in his youth, Finn Monroe is now on the other side of the law as the local attorney. Between his practice and the family ranch, his days aren't as exciting as they used to be—until Jessica Blair steps into his office. Gorgeous and determined, Jessie has a hunch her aunt is in trouble, and Finn is her last hope. When she and Finn start poking around, it becomes clear someone wants to keep them from the truth. But as danger grows, so does their attraction. Includes a bonus novella by A.J. Pine!

ROCKY MOUNTAIN HEAT
by Lori Wilde

Attorney Jillian Samuels doesn't believe in true love. But when a betrayal leaves her heartbroken and jobless, an inherited cottage in Salvation, Colorado, offers a fresh start—until she finds a gorgeous and infuriating man living there! Tuck Manning has been hiding in Salvation since his wife died and isn't leaving the cottage without a fight. They resolve to live as roommates until they untangle who owns the cottage. As their days—and nights—heat up, they realize more than property is at stake...

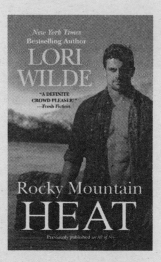

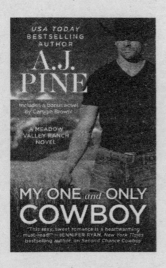

MY ONE AND ONLY COWBOY by A.J. Pine

Sam Callahan is too busy trying to keep his new guest ranch afloat to spend any time on serious relationships—at least that's what he tells himself. But when a gorgeous blonde shows up insisting she owns half his property, Sam quickly realizes he's got bigger problems than Delaney's claim on the land: She could also claim his heart. Includes a bonus novel by Carolyn Brown!

UNFORGIVEN by Jay Crownover

Hill Gamble is a model lawman: cool and collected, with a confident swagger to boot. Too bad all that Texas charm hasn't gotten him anywhere in his personal life, especially since the only girl he ever loved has always been off-limits. But then Hill is assigned to investigate her father's mysterious death, and he's forced back to the town—and the woman—he left behind. Includes a bonus novella by A.J. Pine!

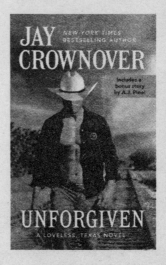

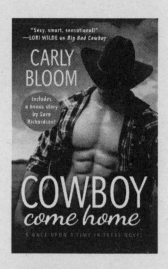
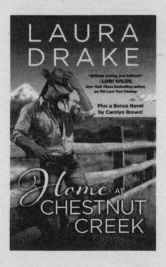